Sparks is dedicated to all of you who supported me with your love, your time, your encouragement, and your advice. You know who you are. Thank you very much.

Greed, in the end, fails even the greedy.

—Joshua San Chapelle, Sparks

PROLOGUE

Before the Fall

May...

Expected, yet dreaded, it arrived. The invitation to Stephen's wedding. Thanks to his constant Facebook updates, Gabrielle Winston was acutely aware of his experiences in Chicago: the new job, the new friends, the new love, the whirlwind courtship, and finally the impending wedding.

Absentmindedly, yet appropriately, she placed the invitation on the table next to the chaise she and Stephen had always shared. A symbolic end of their life together; a reminder that she was the one still scarred. Last New Year's Day, Stephen had been so sure that she would give up her career after accepting his marriage proposal; Gabrielle hadn't understood how he could expect her to. Their five-year romance ended, mortally wounded by their inability to reconcile their different visions of the future.

One month later, just before his move to Chicago, Stephen's private message on Facebook scraped across her raw, tormented heart. "Any man who is a high achiever will feel the same way I do, Gabs," he had written. "I wish you could have understood that for me. But since you can't, maybe you'll be able to for someone else."

Hunger pangs brought Gabrielle back to the present as aromas from the forgotten Toshi's warming bag captured her attention. Though her kitchen was stocked with the accoutrements of gourmet cooking, she hadn't used any of it since last New Year's Eve. Her refrigerator contained only water and juice; her pantry barely held more than cobwebs. Toshi's had been tonight's stop on the way home to Loft IV from the Loft I gym.

At the bar, which separated her large rectangular great room from the kitchen, Gabrielle removed the noodle bowl and chopsticks from the bag. Sliding onto a stool, she swiveled toward her eastern wall of windows, and while she ate, gazed absently at Lofts III and V across The Green; the fifty acre park surrounded by the thirty-story Lofts and the train station. In spite of the visual distraction, her thoughts returned to Stephen.

I refuse to fantasize about doing something stupid.

This wasn't a romantic comedy where she could rush off to create havoc at his wedding. Her head knew that it was over. Her heart, however, still throbbed painfully with every mention of him; every Facebook sighting of him. She had a full life; grieving for what had been lost was unhealthy. It had to end.

Though she'd just resolved to stop mourning, Gabrielle lost herself in memories of their last night together: A few of their guests, engaged in conversation, lounged on the adjacent semicircles of the outrageously large sectional. More gathered at the window walls admiring her twenty-fourth floor view of the lighted trees dotting The Green, the festively lit Lofts to the east and north of it; and to the south, the station, the eastern edge of Crescent City, and the suburbs beyond. Watching the large, wreathed clock atop the station, they all counted down to the New Year; the others erupting into cheers as, at the stroke of midnight, Stephen dropped to one knee and proposed. Gabrielle accepted, but her joy was short-lived; perishing the next day with Stephen's edict to leave her career.

Infuriated when she refused, he left her instead.

Visualizing him sprawled in his usual position on the chaise—jacket unbuttoned, tie undone—should not have been so easy. Unless...it was the condo itself. Understanding dawned while Gabrielle inspected her living space. The great room was exactly as it had been New

Year's Eve. Though she'd removed their portrait and other pictures of the two of them together, five months later she still lived in a capsule of memories.

Leaving her meal at the bar, Gabrielle walked out into the great room and took stock. If she separated and rearranged the sectional semicircles, the room might feel like a new space.

No time like the present.

She turned the semicircle on the north end toward the fireplace for cozier seating, and the one on the south end toward her office nook so that she could talk to guests—usually only Julie and Sarah these days—as she worked. She left the largest semicircle facing the eastern windows, but exchanged Stephen's chaise for one of the recliners in the new fireplace grouping. The pictures of their favorite places, keeping memories of him within easy reach, had to go...

Twenty minutes later, Gabrielle stood near the center sectional grouping and surveyed her changes. The room did feel different, and as a bonus, navigating it was much easier. The only thing missing was new wall candy, but finding the right pieces would take time. She lifted the lid of the long storage ottoman in front of her and took out her yoga mat. For the first time, she unrolled it onto the floor between the ottoman and the windows without having to avoid Stephen's chaise.

The chaise, she corrected herself. It was time to stop thinking of it as his. Beginning her yoga practice in Shavasana, she concentrated on breathing herself into serenity.

~*~~~**~~~*~

June...

Jarin Cole San Chapelle attracted attention. He knew it, he accepted it, but it was a pain in the ass all the same—the inescapable result of the life he had been born into and of the way he chose to live.

Even had he not belonged to Skye Pointe's most prominent family, he would still have caused heads to turn. At six-foot-four, he had the lean, broad shouldered build of a yachtsman. Strands of his unruly waves of jet-black hair were lightened to various shades of blonde by years of exposure to salt water and sun. His grey eyes ranged from translucent smoke to cold, forbidding steel depending on his mood. In short, he was an eyeful.

Tonight, accompanied by Anna-Claire Martin, he attended the June Solstice Soiree at the Skye Pointe Yacht Club. The opening event of the Skye Pointe summer season, it encouraged guests and visiting former residents to mingle with the locals, striking up new friendships and rekindling old ones.

In black tie and tails, hair tamed and trimmed, freshly shaven without even the hint of a shadow, Jarin was impossible to ignore—except by the children. Their screams of delight rose above the distant staccato bursts of sound, answering each multi-colored eruption into the darkening mid-evening sky.

Seeing Anna-Claire concerned about ruining her gown, Jarin graciously shielded her; guiding her carefully around the dancing, ecstatic children. The little ones were too captivated by the first fireworks of the summer to pay attention to the adults who occasionally zigzagged among them. Jarin relished their youthful abandon, reliving, just for a few moments, his favorite childhood experiences of this event.

Too soon, the couple rounded the Marina Cove side of the club, leaving the ooohs, ahhhs, and laughter behind them. Though outwardly attentive to Anna-Claire, Jarin was preoccupied with other thoughts. He glanced down into the marina toward his cruiser yacht, *Island Rose*, knowing the odds were high that he would be sleeping there alone tonight. Anna-Claire was dressed for an ultimatum and Jarin suspected that his refusal of her terms would end their romance. There would be no second summer together.

Rousing sounds from the orchestra greeted the couple as they stepped through the open double doors into the party. Dancers and swaying, toe-tapping listeners surrounded the brightly lit bandstand at the center of the dance floor. More guests mingled in small groups near the floor-to-ceiling windows on the western, southern, and eastern sides of the room, delighting in the views of the Atlantic Ocean and the nearby coves. Others occupied the long and short rectangular tables that surrounded the dance floor, and a few more sat at several of the petite, round couples tables tucked into secluded areas beyond the larger tables, buffered from the noise of the festivities.

Anna-Claire led the way toward the cluster of San Chapelle family tables near the middle of the western wall of windows. Jarin followed, returning the greetings of friends and acquaintances along the way. The tables were unoccupied except for Jarin's father, Joshua, and his close friend and third cousin, Nathan Gibson—both seated at the center table, deep in discussion. The two of them had grown San Chapelle Industries, or SCI, from a modest holding company of ship-building related businesses into an extremely profitable global conglomerate. Joshua, and Jarin's mother, Candace, were soon leaving for an extended visit with the European side of the family and Nathan was leaving his seat as board advisor to become acting chairman of the board during Josh's absence. To Jarin, it appeared that Josh and Nate were taking advantage of the solitude afforded them by the attraction of the fireworks and the music to hash out a few last-minute details.

Grey eyes met grey eyes when Josh looked up as Anna-Claire and Jarin approached. Though Jarin gave an imperceptible shake of his head that both Joshua and Nathan understood, they warmly greeted Anna-Claire. After a quick exchange of small talk, Jarin steered her toward one of the couples tables in the as yet unoccupied northern area of the room. There they passed the evening, *tête à tête*, oblivious to glances constantly flickering in their direction. Tonight especially, such attention was of no consequence. Tonight, Jarin readied himself for the ultimatum that appeared imminent.

~*~~~**~~~*~

Not every look toward Jarin and Anna-Claire was an admiring one. Brett Crawford, seated with his wife, Roxanne, at their table on the eastern side of the room, threw glances filled with disdain. The animus he felt for the San Chapelles had been passed down through his family dating back to the early twentieth century, when Josh San Chapelle's grandfather and the other members of the Skye Pointe governing board refused to lift the fifty-year ban on construction for just one more estate.

Brett's great-grandfather built in Hampton Cape instead, using part of his fortune to foster the small seaside settlement into a thriving tourist destination. A bribe here, a greased palm there, and the new coastal highway from Crescent City to Port Hudson passed through Hampton Cape on its way past Skye Pointe. Vacationers driving north along the highway rarely drove any further. Brett savored that Hampton Cape cost Skye Pointe tens of millions of tourist dollars each season. It amused him to continue his family's membership in the Skye Pointe Yacht Club, confident that his presence reminded the current generation of irretrievably lost revenues.

Other members of the San Chapelle family slowly trickling back to their tables drew Brett's attention.

The little JCs. A ridiculous nickname—especially now that they're all adults.

Josh apparently had to put his stamp on everything. All five of his children were named using his and his wife's first initials—and Jarin, spelled with 'J' but said with 'Y' was the most ridiculous of them all.

He does nothing but run, sail, and paint.

The Crawford children were all earning their way up through the various companies of Avanti Holdings, even though Brett was the major shareholder and Chairman of the Board. Josh had *given* pretty boy Jarin Cole control of SCI's technology sector, though Brett was sure that he lacked the management acumen to provide the guidance that such companies required. He intended to go after SCI, making use of Josh's blunder.

But, first things first.

Brett was just a few months away from gaining control of Nathan Gibson's National Economic Institute, or NEI, and he looked forward to his victory. At least one senior partner was unhappy with Nathan's leadership and Brett now owned him. He had already milked the partner of the inside information necessary for putting together a lucrative, unsolicited merger proposal; and once submitted, he expected it to cause mutiny among the senior partners.

At his behest, the disgruntled partner had also modified the NEI analysis application to throw business to Avanti companies. In return, Brett promised him the reward of managing partner, Nathan's current position, and he would keep his promise—as long as the partner did what he was told. Once Brett took over NEI, business etiquette demanded that he offer Nathan a position on the Avanti Board. But knowing how Brett ran his board, Nathan would most likely decline.

Checkmate. NEI would belong solely to Brett, and his first directive to the new Managing Partner would be to drop SCI from the client list. Well-deserved payback for the both of them—Josh *and* Nathan. They had contributed to the generational feud by blocking Brett's father from buying companies he had targeted, each having preferred the "safe haven" alternative of SCI.

What a crock...

~*~~~**~~~*~

Jarin stood and held Anna-Claire's chair as she rose to go to the powder room. After reseating himself, he passed the time watching the guests who had been dancing or mingling return to their seats for dinner. Many of them watched him as well. Skipping over the looks of open admiration, and carefully avoiding the stares of blatant invitation, he took note of those whose gazes held—sometimes veiled—malevolence. Finding no surprises, he turned his attention to his family's now occupied tables.

The atmosphere in the ballroom subtly shifted; a new undercurrent of conversation started to build. Jarin easily spotted the cause. Sultry and curvaceous, her hair a fiery halo under the lights, Anna-Claire approached their table from the far side of the room. For the first time, the other guests had a clear view of the shimmering sapphire she wore.

That is one hell of a dress.

Keeping his smile carefully in place, he stood and held her chair as she sat. As soon as he joined her, Anna-

Claire snuggled close to him, the fragrance wafting from her skin rousing his senses.

Hadn't noticed it before. Smells good. Too good.

Moving even closer, Anna-Claire smiled up at Jarin. He returned her smile, his gaze slipping downward as she turned to sip her champagne. Jarin took another swallow from his snifter and waited.

She's got to know the view I have from here. It's tonight all right.

"I've been thinking," said Anna-Claire, "I'm thinking that it's time we moved beyond sex and fun."

Jarin swore silently as he lowered his snifter to the table. She knew the rules, she agreed to the rules, they hadn't changed. Taking her hand between both of his, he attempted to lessen the pain he knew he was about to inflict. "Anna-Claire," he said, his deep, rich voice caressing her name, "we've talked about this. You know I don't want more than that right now."

As he expected, the evening—and their relationship—deteriorated from that point, rapidly and with finality.

~*~~~**~~~*~

Bright, pulsating light beating against his eyelids awoke Jarin. For a tense moment, he wondered if Anna-Claire had spitefully sent law enforcement after him. But very quickly, he realized his stupidity. The lights were not a threat. It was unlikely that a threat could even get to him on *Island Rose*. Still sprawled along his workroom sofa where he'd crashed last night after the soiree—and several more snifters of cognac—Jarin peered around the arm he had raised to block the light and saw that he had forgotten to shutter the porthole. Muttering expletives, he lurched unsteadily to his feet and staggered toward it. Maybe someone was having a little fun at his expense? Torn between amusement and aggravation, Jarin adjusted his path to the wall beside the porthole and slid his face warily toward it until one squinted eye saw the source of the light.

Ho-ly shit. It's the sunrise.

The storefront windows of the newly renovated Marina Cove facade reflected the day's first rays of sunlight. The scene gripped him with its energy and vibrant, dynamic hues. Saturated with pulsating rays of color, the sleepy coastal town became a stunning, sensuous vision. The sun continued to rise; the colored lights faded and then disappeared. Jarin knew that he had just witnessed the phenomenon that residents and visitors had been so excited about, but that he had not yet been on *Island Rose*—awake—to see. Energized, his fatigue and foul mood forgotten, Jarin picked out a large canvas for stretching and priming, impatient for the work he would begin the next day.

~*~~~**~~~*~

August...

It had taken far longer than expected. Leaning away from the easel, Jarin studied the painting through narrowed, critical eyes. Oblivious to everything else, he shifted his gaze repeatedly, checking the painting against every angle of the view through the porthole. Working that way was awkward, but he had resigned himself to it. The one day he'd tried to work from the deck, he'd learned that although the scene was breathtaking; diffraction of the reflected sun rays through the workroom porthole heightened their brilliant colors. Capturing the added vibrancy made him reach deep inside himself; pushed him to the brink of his ability.

Racing the sunrise, he dabbed more red into the yellow for a vivid, electrifying orange. He touched up the highlights on the buildings; then, still glancing through the porthole for reference, he deftly adjusted the reflections in the big storefront windows. A few more dabs of color; a few more highlights lightly brushed onto the canvas.

It's done.

Abruptly—and for the last time—Jarin pushed off of his stool and stepped away from the easel. Outside, the sun continued to rise, and Marina Cove lost its mystical glow.

Empty snifter in hand, Jarin left the workroom for the bar in the upstairs salon. He poured himself a light finger of cognac and tossed it down, savoring the spicy burn. Not only had this painting taken the longest time yet, it had also drained him more than any other. Even having declared it done, the desire to apply just one more brush stroke tugged at him, but he suppressed the urge to return to the easel.

As he had passed his stateroom, Estelle's delicately arched foot peeking from beneath the covers of his bed had drawn his attention, tapping...tapping...lightly against the side of the mattress; letting him know she was awake while leaving the choice to him.

He now considered joining her, but decided against it. Even after distancing himself, *Vibrancy* was still his mistress.

So that's her name...

He disrobed, leaving his clothes in the salon. Noiselessly he climbed the stairs to the deck and ran quickly aft. Vaulting onto the railing, he balanced briefly on the balls of his feet, and then dove into the cold, clear waters of Marina Cove.

~*~~~**~~~*~

Now...

The vibration of his cell against the mahogany desk was an unwelcome intrusion. Relieved to see that the caller was his sister, Jarin answered. "Hey Jules, what's up?"

"Hope you're not busy. I need to bug you for some advice."

"On what?"

"You know my friends—Sarah and Gabrielle," Julie began.

"You've told me all about them," answered Jarin, resisting the urge to hurry her.

Her hesitation ended with a sigh. "I'd like to tell them who I really am—that I'm not just Julie Carleton."

Immediately, Jarin understood. This was a big step. Julie had been painfully disappointed the last time she'd told friends she was a San Chapelle. He pushed away from his laptop.

"So why don't you?"

""Last time didn't go so well."

"Jules, if they're truly your friends, things won't be any different than they are now—you know that."

"How did you tell Carson? Julie countered. "He's your best friend other than Landry—and Landry doesn't count."

Jarin laughed. "He doesn't count? I'll tell him you said so."

Chagrined, Julie said, "You know what I mean."

"Only teasing," Jarin assured her. "But as for Carson, that's different. We were about to go into business together and he's ex-Covert Ops. He was sure to have found out anyway, so I told him." It occurred to him that Julie may want their sister's point of view. "Why don't you see what Janine has to say?"

"That's no good," said Julie dismissively. "Whatever I ask her, she just pats my head and gives me a cookie."

"That's because she's the oldest. She treats us all the same way."

"And don't ask about James and Joseph. I can rarely get James' attention and Joseph just says 'Go with your gut.' That's his answer for everything."

Jarin laughed again. "Maybe so—but it's true. Even if it doesn't turn out the way you want, you rarely go wrong by going with your gut. So...have you decided?"

"I guess I'll talk to them," Julie said.

"Them who? The rest of us or your friends?"

Julie clicked her tongue in amused annoyance. "My friends, silly."

"Well let me add my two cents," Jarin said. "There's a reason it's occurred to you to tell them. Don't be surprised that they find out another way if you delay too long."

It was Julie's turn to laugh. "You're saying it's déjà vu?"

"Hardly. I'm just saying that sometimes things happen, and right now you've got a chance to tell them before they unexpectedly find out another way."

"I'll tell them this week, then. Do you mind if I invite them up to the house?"

"Why should I? We'll be sailing, but there's plenty of room for all of us." Taking advantage of having her attention, Jarin quickly changed the subject. "Since we're talking..."

"Uh-oh..."

"...thought I'd ask if you changed your mind about competing for a sector of SCI."

"Jarin, you know I'm not ready for managing a sector," Julie objected. "I haven't started a business or anything."

"I can help you if you want," he offered. "In fact with what you've done since you've been at Charleston Eddy's—"

"You know I have to do this on my own," Julie reminded him. "I thought you wouldn't push."

"I'm not. Just sayin'."

"I like it in your sector—and I've got no place left to go if you start leaning on me."

"You know if you get uncomfortable," Jarin teased, "you can always go back to one of the other..."

"Yeah, right," Julie interrupted testily, "Janine's people treated me like a two-year old; James' people smothered me; and Joseph's sector is full of attention-seeking piranhas."

"He knows he has to fix that. It's his penchant for individual recognition."

"I like your way of recognizing teams better," Julie said. "Still competitive, but at least someone's got your back when someone else is trying to cut your throat."

"That, my dear baby sister, is the best description of business competition I've heard in a while."

Predictably insulted, Julie said, "Time to go. You called me baby sister."

"Sorry, love, that just slipped out. Well, looking forward to meeting your friends."

"Speaking of which... You won't go after one of them, will you? I'd hate to lose a friend when you break it off."

"*When* I break it off? So you call me up to get my advice—then you insult me?"

"You know I didn't mean...I just meant..."

"Forget it. I've got seven years on you—your friends are a little young for me, Jules."

"Now you're mad. It's just that..."

"I'm not mad. It's true, my relationships don't last long. And I'm the one who breaks it off all the time. So now, that's what you expect from me. Guess Janine is right—I'm destined to be a permanent bachelor."

"Maybe you're just stuck in a rut. All your girlfriends seem to be the same type."

"Good night, Jules."

"Just sayin'. Think about it."

"G'night, Jules. I'm hanging up." And he did. The SCI Technology Sector reports on his laptop summoned, but thoughts of Julie's attempt to protect her friends kept interfering. The imminent breakup with Estelle—and it was only September—heightened his exasperation. The breakups were always for the same reason. *She* wanted the relationship to go further; obstinately, *he* wanted more than just sex and time served. Maybe he just hadn't yet found his soul mate; or, maybe it was time to face the fact that at thirty-eight, he wasn't likely to.

~*~~~**~~~*~

NEI had a policy against it, but analyzing clients' funding alternatives had become routine for Gabrielle, who, along with other exceptional NEI analysts, ignored the policies that hindered their work. As was typical in the analytics industry, NEI looked the other way and would continue to—unless someone got caught.

Gabrielle never reported the results of the funding analyses, but used them to tailor her business improvement recommendations more closely to clients' cash flow. This time, the client wanted to fund with cash, but as a contingency would use returns on their mortgage bond investments. Gabrielle's review of their projected cash flow showed that they would need to use that contingency.

As always, she was exasperated by the tedium of having to prepare the analysis using a manual checklist. Again, she promised herself that automating it would be the first update she would make to Sparks once she could again modify it. Her attorney, Quentin Sands, had advised her against making any changes until they had told NEI about Sparks and negotiated an agreement that protected her rights to it. So for now, she had to suffer.

The next item on the annoying checklist was to identify the input data. For the most accurate results, Gabrielle needed data for each of the individual mortgages in each bond. Surprisingly, every data service to which she subscribed had only bond level data. Using that alone was akin to describing her laptop as a rectangular object—not nearly enough detail. She considered abandoning her quest for accuracy; then yielded to her desire to perform the full analysis. It took more than two hours to find a service that had the mortage data she needed—and the subscription price was exorbitant.

This had better be worth it.

Gabrielle subscribed to the service and configured Sparks to read from it—and from one with bond level data. With both, Sparks would match the earnings of the individual mortgages with those of the bonds in which they were packaged. She checked her work again, and finally, as she had many times before, clicked "Submit."

She had only meant to start Sparks, but this time, she unleashed much, much more...

CHAPTER ONE

Busted

"Sarah!" exclaimed Gabrielle. "Why did you say that?"

"Well, what do y'all think I should have said?"

"Oh I don't know," said Gabrielle. "You could've just tossed the drink in his face."

"That's real subtle," laughed Julie.

"He brought me the darn drink and before he even introduced himself, he asked me to his condo on "a semi-private island" in the Caribbean. I felt like booty for hire."

"But, Sarah." objected Gabrielle, "saying you already had plans to 'fly on a friend's private jet to his chateau in Saint Trop' surely made him think that's exactly what you are."

"I know that," Sarah said. "But you know how competitive men are. Now he has to swallow that my booty's out of his league."

"Geez." In one Skype frame, Julie looked as befuddled as Gabrielle felt, but in the other, Sarah looked smugly confident that she had handled the situation. Certain that their silence was short-lived, Gabrielle seized the opportunity to get them back on track. "So can we quit talking about Sarah's booty and get back to our investments?"

"Oh, right," said Julie, her voice still lightened with humor.

"You've already shown us the earnings," said Sarah. "What's there left to talk about?"

"Just wanted to mention that parts of our portfolio are still trending downward," Gabrielle replied. "The investments don't seem to be related, so maybe we're at the start of a bear market."

"Is that bad?" asked Sarah.

"No, just a normal part of the cycle," said Gabrielle. "But we may want to sell the ones most likely to keep going down so we can buy them back at lower prices."

"That's smart," said Julie. "Is that what you suggest?"

"Not yet," Gabrielle cautioned. "I want to investigate the markets a little more. Getting a chance at the mortgage bonds tonight—running an investment analysis on

Sparks for one of our clients. Maybe the results will show me what we should do."

"What if the results don't show you anything?" asked Sarah.

"Then we'll watch and wait for the next quarter or two," Gabrielle answered, flipping through the investment applications on her desktop.

"Sounds okay to me," said Sarah. "By the way, when are you going to tell us why you call it 'Sparks'?"

"Yeah," Julie chimed in. "We've been asking for ages."

Caught off-guard, Gabrielle admitted, "Just a silly joke. It's because... well, sparks will fly if NEI ever finds out about it."

Sarah's lips started to twitch. She ducked out of camera range, but Gabrielle could hear her laughing.

Julie smiled. "Oh, Sarah. It wasn't that funny. Unless...what are you thinking?"

Sarah came back into the Skype frame, her face twisting as she tried to maintain her composure. "It's a good thing Gabs didn't name it after what would hit the fan."

When their laughter finally subsided, Julie said, "Gabs, I hope you're still following Quentin's advice."

"Absolutely."

"Good," said Julie as she glanced down. "Look at what time it is! We'd better go—so maybe you'll get some sleep?"

"Of course I will," said Gabrielle.

"Sure—like we believe you," said Sarah.

"I *will*," replied Gabrielle. "See ya on the 7:40." Waving to them both, Gabrielle ended the session.

It's not insomnia. It's just that I still haven't gotten Stephen out of my head.

Instead of leaving her desk, she stared out at the lighted Lofts, listening to the whirring of the terabyte disk drives on her server; the only sign that Sparks was running an analysis. At last soothed enough to attempt sleep, she reached to switch off the twin monitors. Just as she did, the Facebook icon on the left monitor lit. Thinking it was Sarah or Julie, she clicked it. Instantly, she wished she hadn't.

After months of no contact—except a sweetly penned thank-you note from his new wife, Stacey, for her thoughtful gift—and forcing herself through day after gut-wrenching day of living without him, Stephen just sent her a private message. Memories quickly overwhelmed her: entire lazy days spent on a chaise in his condo or hers, exhilarating hiking and biking through the foothills west of Crescent City, their laughter, sharing their innermost thoughts and dreams. But it was the visions of their intense nights together—so real that Gabrielle could almost see him...feel him...taste him—that ignited her frustration.

How dare he?

She clicked the message. He wanted to know why she hadn't commented on his *wedding album!??!* Angered beyond words, Gabrielle opened the Edit Friends page and unfriended him. Almost immediately her cell vibrated, ringing jarringly over the quiet hum of the server's drives. It was Stephen.

Seizing the opportunity to vent, Gabrielle answered it. "Is that what *does* it for you now?" she spat. "You *get off* on trying to inflict pain?"

Using the placating tone he always used when he knew he couldn't win the argument, Stephen said, "I deserve that. I..."

"You sure in hell do. What do you *want*, Stephen?"

"Please, I didn't mean...Gabs, please don't unfriend me. It was a stupid thing to do. I just wanted...I need..."

"This *isn't* healthy for me."

"I know. I won't call or write again—I swear. Just *please* let me see how you're doing."

She shouldn't. She wouldn't. She would hang up. *Now.* But, in spite of her internal admonitions, Gabrielle friended him again. It disturbed her to not only hear, but to *feel* his relief through the phone.

"*Thank* you."

"*Good-bye,* Stephen."

"Goodn—"

Gabrielle snapped off the phone and shut down her monitors. The baseboard lights of her office nook and great room immediately illuminated the darkness; the soft muted light a welcome relief after the past few hours of brightly lit intensity and Stephen's unwelcome call. But Gabrielle was still dejected. It was unhealthy, but she wanted to be with him—just once more. It was wrong, but when she slept, she relived their long, hot nights together in her dreams.

Nevertheless, he had made his decision; he was supposed to be happy with it. Stacey certainly was. Gabrielle left her desk, retrieved her yoga mat from the ottoman, and unrolled it onto the floor. Working through her practice, she achieved a level of relaxation. But when she finally bathed and went to bed, sleep eluded her.

~*~~~**~~~*~

This is insane.

Gabrielle could not believe what Sparks had found:

For years, investment brokerages removed defaulting mortgages from their residential mortgage bonds and replaced them with mortgages in good standing. Then suddenly last spring, the replacement stopped. Defaulting mortgages now remain in the bonds. Not only that, but even the "good" mortgages in the bonds are moving into default. Almost half a million individuals and families are now unable to reliably continue making their payments and are heading

> *toward foreclosure. Even worse, their number is growing—rapidly.*

She had only wanted to forecast the return on the client's mortgage bonds. Instead, having stumbled upon hundreds of thousands of catastrophes in the making, Gabrielle turned to Sparks' prediction models to find out how bad it would get if the defaults kept growing:

> *The worsening economy is further depressing the housing market, slowing home sales. It is also forcing more people out of work. Both factors are feeding the increasing default rate, and most low-rated bonds are already showing losses. In a couple of months, a quarter, or maybe even two, the number of defaults will be pushed to almost a million—enough that even the highest-rated bonds will have an extreme loss of value. The residential mortgage market sector, already under strain, will not be able to handle losses of that magnitude and will collapse.*

Every month, before she Skyped with Julie and Sarah, Gabrielle reviewed the market as well as their investments.

How could I have missed this?

Then it hit her: the data for the individual mortgages. Had she not taken the time to find it and use it, the mortgage defaults and their impact would have been invisible to Sparks.

Are they invisible to analysis applications used by other investors?

Hastily, she checked the trading histories of the major stock exchanges. She found no large selloffs of the bonds.

Unbelievable. It looks like nobody knows...but is there bleed-over from the bond market into the stock market?

Opening Sparks' menu, Gabrielle selected the three-dimensional graph that showed risk, value, and time for both the bond and stock markets. It appeared, escalating her alarm into horror. The graph resembled the type of roller coaster that, while speeding downward, continuously rolled its cars upside down. But instead of accelerating into an even more dizzying upward roll as did the real roller coaster, those on the graph accelerated downward in a nearly vertical tailspin, crashed—and then flat-lined.

The meaning was clear: once the residential mortgage bond market sector started to spiral downward, there was no way to avoid being stuck on the roller coasters. Too many publicly traded companies were also investors in the bonds. Secondly, there was no sign of when—or even if—the overall market would recover.

Transfixed, she could only stare at the graph and its superimposed plummeting roller coasters. The defaulting mortgages formed the inside one; the bonds that contained them were the next outer one; the companies investing in the bonds were next, and so on. Corporations, individual investors, and potentially, stock exchanges, caught in the death spiral of the crashing bond market and pulled into an assuredly horrific crash.

Madness.

Or...Sparks' analysis contained an insanely large error. Breaking free of her paralysis, Gabrielle quickly powered down her laptop and reached for her cell. It was already after seven. Sure that she would never make the 7:40, she tweeted Sarah and Julie to go on without her. With the extra fifteen minutes she had a prayer of making the 7:55: the last train before the heart of the morning rush. Barely hearing their answering tweets, Gabrielle undocked her laptop and stuffed it and the client materials into her backpack.

As the reality of her predicament dawned, she lost herself in a brief fit of hysterical laughter. "I am *so* busted." As always, she had ignored an NEI policy and analyzed a client's funding alternatives. This time though, she'd have to tell them.

What's done is done. I can't sit on this. NEI's holdings are large enough that they may be able to intervene before the worst can happen.

Gabrielle dropped her backpack on the sectional near her desk as she raced from the office nook up the hall and into her bedroom. She quickly tossed aside her pajamas and threw on the linen suit and silk blouse she had laid out the night before.

Considering her alternatives, she realized that taking her findings to Garrett Stratford, the senior partner in charge of the Analysis Group, would waste valuable time. It was his policy that she had so flagrantly flouted. He would want to exact retribution before he even listened to what she had to say.

In the next instant, she saw that she had a reprieve. Garrett had been acting as head of their team since Matthew Burke took the promotion to senior partner of Information Technology, or IT. But just last week, Garrett had finally chosen Landry Wyatt as the junior partner replacement for Matthew—and his first day was today. Though she had never worked closely with him, Landry had been outstanding on Matthew's team, and she respected his work. Hopefully, she could depend on him for direction. If not, she would just have to figure out her next move on the fly. Even if luck was with her and she avoided a direct confrontation with Garrett, he was sure to retaliate. She would just have to be ready to fight back.

At the bathroom mirror, dragging dampened fingers through her hair, Gabrielle froze, seeing her harried face for the first time since the discovery. Her expression looked normal, but her eyes were wide and frantic—as though trapped in the middle of a scream. Turning away from her disturbing reflection, she rushed through her bedroom to the great room; grabbing her stockings, pumps, socks, and cross-trainers along the way. At the sectional, she stuffed her stockings and pumps into their pocket in her backpack, hoisted it onto her back, and nearly sprinted the few steps to the eastern window wall. Balancing precariously while pulling on her ankle socks and cross-trainers, she searched The Green for signs of rush-hour foot traffic and mapped out a path that would keep her ahead of most of it. Briefly interrupting her dash for the door, she took a quick detour to the office nook credenza to grab one more item. Sunglasses.

Have to hide my crazy looking eyes...

~*~~~**~~~*~

On a stretch of beach just up the coast from Hampton Cape, Brett Crawford paced the damp, packed sand, cooling down from the first half of his run. He had stopped at the midpoint because he expected a call.

After the months of infiltrating and compromising NEI, the victory he had been anticipating since the June Solstice Soiree was at hand, and better yet, he was in position to deal Nathan Gibson an even greater blow.

When Brett had seen the analysis that NEI had performed for Blackhawk, an Avanti subsidiary, he had been impressed—and alarmed. Impressed by the thoroughness with which business inefficiencies were discovered and analyzed; alarmed because implementing the recommendations would ruin Avanti. The extraordinary slackness with which Blackhawk was managed allowed several shadow organizations to operate within it, one of which ran the arms smuggling operation that had been hidden at the company for over sixty years.

Furious that Blackhawk's new president had commissioned the analysis without his approval; Brett snatched him out of the presidency and "rewarded" him with a seat on the Avanti Board, which he rigidly controlled. Neal, who knew how to do *only* what he was told, was now president. One satisfying outcome of the debacle, other than Blackhawk's secret remaining undetected, was that Brett had a firsthand look at NEI's capabilities. An analysis company of that caliber would be a stellar addition to his portfolio and he expected to score a win against the San Chapelles by taking it away from Nathan—at little or no cost.

Finally—the call...

Walking away from the crashing surf, he answered his vibrating cell. "What's the news?"

"The processing is done outside of NEI. Only one analyst has access. She sets up the parameters in the office and when she comes back the next day, the analysis is completed."

"I need the app that runs the analysis," said Brett.

"Working on it."

"That's *not* good enough," Brett replied. "I want that app—and I want it by the end of the week." He disconnected the call, and to finish his run, turned toward the western slope that ran up from the beach.

Though surprised to learn that a distant cousin was an analyst at NEI, Brett had wasted no time in recruiting him. The cousin was hesitant at first, but the chance to move his side of the family out of poverty was a great motivator, and finally, he bit. When he had been unable to duplicate the Blackhawk results with the NEI analysis application, Brett got suspicious and had him infect the NEI network with a surveillance virus.

The virus exposed sensitive information about NEI and its clients, but it was the recent, unexpected discovery of another software application, hidden away from the NEI premises in a secure location, that captured Brett's interest. It appeared to be the one used to perform the analysis of Blackhawk, and from what he had seen of its capabilities, it was a killer app. The kind that comes along very seldom; giving whomever controls it mastery over an entire industry.

Brett's thoughts dwelled on the app he now wanted so badly. The information his cousin had just given him indicated that it may not even belong to NEI. If they were fronting for another company, he may not even need them—but he did admire the sneaky move by Nathan, having one app out front visible to everyone and keeping the killer app known only to a few.

Touted as one of their best analysts, Brett's cousin should have been in on it—but he wasn't. The senior partner Brett had compromised also had not mentioned the other app—even though he'd had a chance to when they had discussed throwing business to Avanti.

Is it possible he doesn't know—or are his loyalties still with Nathan? That's why you always need more than one infiltraitor.

Barking a laugh at his unintended pun, Brett pumped his legs even faster, mastering the last—and steepest—hundred yards. Though forty-four, he was breathing fairly easily. A few more minutes of climbing the slope and he reached the forty-acre plateau on which the Crawford family estate sat. Halfway to the main house, Brett slowed to a walk. Whoever controlled the app also controlled what business partners it recommended to clients. It was merely a matter of modifying the right module, as had been done on the other NEI app.

Brett's cell vibrated. After checking the number, he answered. "This is unscheduled—it had better be good."

"I've just gone through the latest data from the surveillance worm—thought you'd want to know. SCI submitted an unsolicited merger proposal to NEI. I've put it in the usual spot."

What the fuck. "Thanks."

He quickly disconnected the call, accessed the Internet, and navigated out to the appropriate Blackhawk server. Then he opened the proposal and began to read.

~*~~~**~~~*~

Reaching the platform just after the train pulled in, Gabrielle quickly boarded behind the few commuters who had arrived ahead of her. Removing her backpack, she walked quickly through the train to a car toward the front, where she slid into a window seat. After a seemingly endless wait, the train left the station. On other days, she loved watching the artistry of the approaching Crescent City skyline until the train hurtled underground on its way downtown. But today, sitting tensely, Gabrielle saw nothing. Silently, she urged the train, already flying, to pick up the pace.

Hurry up! I could still be wrong. I hope I'm wrong. Maybe I pushed Sparks too far.

But it was too late for doubt. She'd already performed the analysis; she was on her way to tell Landry about it. If Sparks had been in error, she'd find out soon enough.

Finally, the train pulled in to Calhoun Street Station, the closest stop to Twelfth Street Tower, where the NEI offices occupied the topmost two commercial floors. Hurriedly sliding from her seat, Gabrielle nearly ran from the train and headed toward the street-bound escalator, zigzagging among the groups of commuters before they could meld into a crowd. In her haste, as she stepped onto the escalator, she stubbed her foot. For the second time that morning, a short, slightly hysterical laugh escaped her lips.

Just my luck to stumble, hit my head, and get amnesia.

When the escalator reached the street, Gabrielle hopped off, barely in time to catch the crossing light at the corner. Another block up, around the corner and Twelfth Street Tower was dead ahead. Usually she sat on one of the lawn benches to exchange her cross-trainers for the pumps in her backpack. Today when she reached the tower, she rushed up the walkway, extracting her badge from her backpack as she went. Flashing it at the security guard in the lobby, she blew by him into a waiting elevator. A few more nervous minutes and she stepped out onto the main NEI floor.

Staring through the tall, gilded double doors emblazoned with the words "National Economic Institute" and the company logo, Gabrielle saw Sheila Ruiz, the far too effective NEI gatekeeper, at her post. Without a good enough poker face to bluff her way past, and too wired to make something up, Gabrielle quickly pivoted away from the doors before Sheila looked up. Instead, she headed down the left corridor toward the employee-only entrance at Partners' Row. Landry's office was only three doors down; she had a good chance of making it there without interruption. She badged herself in and took a quick look around.

As was his habit, Cleve Harper, the other Junior Partner on Garrett's staff, was at the administrative assistants' coffee bar. Gabrielle had forgotten that he preferred going there for coffee rather than having it in his office as did all the other partners.

"Hey, Gabs, sneaking in today?" He laughed. "Guess that's why you're wearing sneakers."

The joke was stupid enough, and it further annoyed Gabrielle that he continued to call her "Gabs" when she had expressly asked him to use her formal name.

Idiot. "Just a change of scenery for once," she replied, brushing quickly past him. "Sorry, can't stop to talk—late for my meeting with Landry." *Just a little further...*

Squeezing in through the partially open door, Gabrielle realized too late that she should have knocked. Landry sat at his desk, totally absorbed in whatever he was reading. The clock on the credenza behind him read just after 8:30. Gabrielle pushed her sunglasses up into her wildly tousled hair and knocked on the door she had just come through. Landry looked up.

"I know I didn't reserve time on your calendar," she began. Her voice trailed off as she tried to interpret his rapidly changing expressions.

Unexpectedly, Landry bolted out from behind his desk and strode toward her. "What's wrong?" he demanded.

Surprised by his intensity, Gabrielle backed away, bumping against the door.

"You look..." Stopping just in front of her, he dissected her appearance. "Your color's a bit off, your eyes..." He inspected her even more critically as he reached behind her and closed the door. "Come on—sit down. What's happened?"

Gabrielle followed him past his desk to the conference table and perched tentatively on the edge of the nearest chair. "I was trying to look normal," she started.

"I'd say you've missed that boat." He sat in one of the other chairs and turned toward her. "Now, what's up?"

"Last night, I was working on a client business analysis," she said as she unpacked her laptop. "Their contingency for financing our recommendations is to borrow against their residential mortgage bonds." She hit the laptop power button, her shaking hand betraying her agitation.

"Is that a problem?" asked Landry, watching her hand.

"Not in itself," replied Gabrielle. "Look, I know I wasn't supposed to analyze the stability of the client's investments—Garrett said absolutely no analyses of that type. But all my recommendations require that they borrow against those bonds…so I did one."

Obviously relieved, Landry smiled. "Is that all? The way you look, I thought you were going to tell me somebody died." When Gabrielle didn't smile in return, his quickly faded. "Tell me the rest of it."

Wanting his objective opinion, Gabrielle took care to reveal very little. "Let me bring up the analysis and show you." She logged in and opened the analysis and the graphs. Balancing the laptop on her hands, she moved to a chair closer to Landry, turned it toward him, and placed it on the table. "Could you please take a look? I need to know if you see the same thing I see."

Landry held her gaze for a long moment. "You really look like hell, you know," he said sternly. He then focused on the laptop.

Disregarding Landry's comment, Gabrielle studied him, looking for any reaction as he reviewed her findings. There was nothing. Giving in to her restlessness, she stood and wandered from the conference table to stare absently through the windows that formed the back wall of his office. Though an interior wall, the windows framed a lush garden. Gabrielle wasn't familiar with the types of plants she saw, but the varied shades of green, sparsely dotted with brilliantly hued blooms, soothed her anxiety and occupied her attention while she waited.

Time crawled by. She paced in front of the garden, frequently glancing in Landry's direction. Still no sign of his thoughts. At last she heard his chair move and turned to see him push away from the computer.

"Hmph," was all he said as he ran both hands through his cropped, sandy hair.

She hurried toward him. "Well? What do you see?"

Comprehension and apprehension in his hazel eyes, he responded. "I sincerely hope you made a mistake somewhere."

Relieved to finally be able to discuss the analysis, Gabrielle again sat down beside him. "I want there to be a mistake," she said, her fingers drumming on the table. "It's too bizarre. If it's true, we have to do something."

Landry covered her hand with his, silencing the increasing tempo. "Whoa...slow it down a little." Briefly rubbing the back of her hand before withdrawing his, he assured her, "We have time—and we have to use it to be *absolutely sure* of your findings."

"But—"

"Gabrielle, we have to be sure," he said. "The market is not going to crash today, tomorrow, or next week—is it?"

"Not according to the analysis," she admitted.

"And if it were, we're already screwed. Any divestiture policy we come up with would not be quick enough. NEI's holdings are too large. Since that's the case, we take the time—*right now while we still have it*—to be sure of your results."

Gabrielle finally acquiesced. "You're right. It's just that I think we need to already be doing something."

"We *are* doing something—verifying your findings." Landry stood. "Now—the first thing is for you to walk me through your process and procedures. Let's do it at my computer."

Gabrielle froze. She had been so focused on the crisis, and secondarily, facing Garrett, that she hadn't considered that she was also putting herself in the situation where NEI could lay claim to Sparks. "I didn't use Retro…I mean the NEI application."

"I know what you mean by Retro. What did you use?"

"There's something I haven't yet shared with NEI." Gabrielle admitted. "I wrote an application in graduate school using my algorithms—the same ones I tried to update Retro with."

"But you did update Retro with the algorithms from your thesis," said Landry.

"Not all of them. Retro's architecture is too primitive to run the predictive algorithms."

"Ah yes, I remember that," he responded, amused. "That's when it got its nickname."

"Well, those are the algorithms that are used in investment analyses."

His intense gaze focused on her again. "So, you've done this more than once?"

Though prepared to accept the consequences, Gabrielle found herself wanting him to understand. "Yes but only to improve my recommendations."

"I see," Landry was noncommittal. "Well, we'll run it on your laptop then."

His lack of disparagement unsettled her, and it didn't help that she had to tell him "no" again. "It's not on my laptop. It's on my server at home. I can't access it from here without having IT open a port."

Landry paced in front of Gabrielle, his silence increasing her uneasiness. Just when she was about to interrupt, he said, "I'm glad you confided in me, Gabrielle. It was the right thing to do." Crossing to his desk, he pulled out his chair for her. "We have to rerun the investment analysis on your app, but first, as a crosscheck, let's make sure we get the same results on Retro for the business analysis."

Gabrielle moved to Landry's desk bringing her laptop with her. She set up the business analysis on his laptop, using hers for reference. "It's going to run for a while."

"How long?" Landry asked.

"Sparks ran the business analysis in about a half hour." Gabrielle did a quick calculation in her head. "It'll take around two hours."

"Sparks?" he asked.

"My software application."

"I see." he said, pensively. Then he added, "The partners' meeting is at 4:30. It's 9:15 now. Our goal is to have both the business and investment analyses completely understood and—if we confirm your findings—our presentation of it flawless by then."

His detachment mystified Gabrielle as she started the analysis. *I've just told him the sky is falling and he isn't even fazed.* To ensure that Retro had started correctly, she brought up the logs and opened them. Queasiness quickly overtook her.

No, no, no. This can't be right. I modified Retro with algorithms I borrowed from Sparks. She closed her eyes, urging herself to calm. "Something's changed," she said tightly. "The results are going to be different."

"How can that be? Aren't the algorithms the same?" Landry asked, his voice coming from above Gabrielle's right ear, catching her by surprise. She had been so consumed with this newest problem that she hadn't heard him approach.

"Yes and I don't know," she said desperately. *Check the source—that's the first rule.* Gabrielle navigated out to the shared drive and examined Retro's files. Immediately, the modification date stood out. "Oh, they've been changed." she laughed, almost giddy with relief. "I know I last updated the files from the repository on the twenty-first because that's Sarah's birthday. A few of these are dated the twenty-third."

"Sarah?" asked Landry, confused.

"Yes—my friend Sarah," Gabrielle explained, still on a high from finding the root cause so quickly. "I remember specifically because it was her birthday. All I have to do is replace these with the files from the repository..." she rambled on. "But wait, I'll copy them off first just so I can see what got changed. Someone was probably trying a new scenario and overwrote them by mistake." After copying the changed files to a folder on Landry's laptop, she refreshed Retro with the latest version from the repository.

As soon as she restarted the analysis, Landry whipped her chair around to face him. Too fast—it made her head spin. Unprepared for his overreaction, Gabrielle tried to lean away from him. But trapped in the squared U formed by his desk and the credenza, there was nowhere to go.

"You've got to be straight with me," he said harshly, accentuating each word with a shake of the chair. "You're the only person authorized to change Retro. How could the files be different? I'm about to put my ass on the line for you—I want answers—and I want them *now*."

CHAPTER TWO

Stepping Up

"IT doesn't have deployment security in place." Gabrielle sputtered. Then she added firmly, "Anyone can *change* the files. It's just that I'm the only one whose changes are kept in the repository. That's how I was able to copy down the right set so quickly."

Landry straightened up and stared down at her, his expression unchanged. "That's true about security," he allowed. "That's one of the reasons Matthew has a challenge on his hands." He turned away and resumed pacing. Gabrielle grabbed her laptop from his desk and went to the conference table where she retrieved her backpack from the chair and threw it onto the table. Then she placed the laptop carefully beside it.

His voice a touch softer, Landry said, "Gabrielle— listen to me. This is extremely important—if there's anything else, tell me now. I'm trusting you—you have to trust me."

Already on edge and further angered by the extremes in his behavior, Gabrielle snapped, "Whatever it is you think I've done, you had *no right* to get in my face."

Inexplicably, he was surprised by her reaction. "I, well...yes, you're right." Approaching her slowly, he stopped on the far side of the chair that had held her backpack. "I apologize. I must have seemed over the top."

"You *were* over the top."

"But I'm still asking," he pressed. "Is that all of it?"

"That's all of it, Landry—the findings, Sparks—there isn't any more."

"Then, it's time for you to show me Sparks. That is, if you're still willing?"

"Sure," Gabrielle replied curtly. With the demo of Sparks behind them, Landry could move on to the next step and she could get back to her unfinished analyses—if she still had a job.

"We'll take a car," said Landry. He pulled his cell from his pocket and hit a single button. Meandering toward the garden wall, he held a brief conversation before turning to Gabrielle. "Where d'you live?" he asked.

"2450 Loft IV on The Green." replied Gabrielle.

After Landry relayed that information, he said, "One second," then turned to Gabrielle once more, his brow contracted, his expression clearly disapproving. "By the way, when did you last eat?"

~*~~~**~~~*~

Flipping his cell out of its holster, Landry answered it, listened for a few moments, and then said, "We'll be right down. Yeah, from now on, this phone only. Thanks for the reminder." Replacing his cell, he turned to Gabrielle, who looked up from packing her laptop. "The car's here. Listen to me carefully—we need to be as inconspicuous as possible."

"Why are you being so cautious?"

"The fewer people that see us, the less we'll have to explain," he replied. "Do you know where the Partners' Row elevator is?"

"No, I've never used it."

"It's in the alcove just past the copiers and the Executive Conference Room. If you pass Garrett's office, you've gone too far."

"Got it," Gabrielle replied. She finished packing her laptop and then, remembering that she wanted a copy of Retro's modified files, pulled a thumb drive out of the backpack's front pocket.

"I'll go first," Landry said. Give me about thirty seconds, then you follow—and close my door behind you."

"I'm sorry, but is all this really necessary?" asked Gabrielle.

Landry's expression was somber. "Yes," was all he said. Then he left.

That's not good enough. I need an explanation. At Landry's desk, she copied the files from his laptop onto her thumb drive and then carefully zipped the drive into the backpack front pocket. Keeping her eye on his credenza clock for the time, she slung her backpack over her shoulder and paced back and forth by the door.

This is starting to feel like a bad spy movie. After the last five seconds elapsed, she quietly slipped through the door, closing it softly behind her. *...and I feel like Bond, Jane Bond.*

Keeping a casual pace, she walked past the copier area, and then ducked into the first accessible area on her left. There was a closed door in the right wall of the alcove, and two elevators in the opposite wall. She peeked into the one that was open. Landry waved her in. When the door closed, he pressed the button for level EG.

She said, "EG? That's not in the outside elevators."

"Executive garage," replied Landry. "It's the third level garage. Elevator access is restricted, but everyone can reach it using the stairs."

"I didn't even know there was an executive garage."

"Not many people do," he said. "Did you see anyone?"

"No," she replied, "There were conversations, but I didn't check to see if anyone was paying attention to me."

Landry simply nodded and leaned against the back wall of the elevator, hands in his pockets, eyes closed. Though seemingly relaxed, there was a tension about him—as though he was very tightly wound, and merely a touch would release the spring. It was only when the elevator door opened that he moved, striding quickly into the garage. Displeased by his expectation that she would simply follow, Gabrielle walked after him to the car waiting in the passenger pickup area. Backpack in hand, she climbed into the open door behind the driver. Landry closed it behind her, and then got in on the opposite side. Touching a button on the console between them, he said, "We're ready, Carson." The car pulled away.

~*~~~**~~~*~

"I don't know how inconspicuous we'll be using a car and driver," Gabrielle said.

"It's off the books."

Fed up with his too short answers, she pursued, "Isn't this an NEI car?"

"It's a personal car," he replied with a note of finality.

"But what about the security cameras in the garage?" *Okay M, got you there.*

"They're managed automatically," said Landry. "It's building policy that the tapes are retrieved only in the event of a subpoena. Otherwise, they're recycled every two weeks. Protects executives' privacy." After a short pause, he asked, "Anything else?"

"No, I guess that's it for now," she answered.

"Good," Landry said, busying himself with the console between their oversized seats. "You haven't eaten, so we'll have a snack on the way." Cold air wafted out of the refrigerated compartment while Landry pulled out two containers of finger sandwiches and raw vegetables, one of which he handed to Gabrielle. Then he pulled out a bottle of Chardonnay and a couple of bottles of Evian, sat them on the seat beside him, and closed the compartment. Seeing that she was balancing the container on her lap he said, "Here, let me help you pull out your tray." He lifted it from the outer pocket of the console and laid it flat over her lap.

"Thanks," said Gabrielle, placing the container on the tray. The sight of food made her suddenly ravenous. She tore the off the wrapper, picked up a turkey and cheese sandwich and bit into it. It was delicious. She quickly wolfed it down. Embarrassed by the haste with which she'd consumed it, she sneaked a peek in Landry's direction and was relieved to see him preoccupied with the bottles of wine and water.

"You can't have any wine." he said, moving the bottle of wine to the holder in his tray and handing her the two bottles of Evian. "You're probably very close to being dehydrated." He retrieved a corkscrew and goblet from the front of the console, laid the goblet carefully on his lap, and extracted the cork from the Chardonnay. As he poured the wine, he glanced at her with a frown. "What were you thinking—skipping breakfast?" he scolded. "You should be faint."

"I should be *faint*? I bring you what appears to be a monumental market crisis and you've hardly said a word—except when you *lost* it about the files. And now you're worried about my eating habits?"

"I'm really very sorry about that, Gabrielle. I can never apologize enough," he said. "It's just that there are...things...going on at NEI that make that file change very suspicious."

"What things?"

Shaking his head, he said, "Sorry. Now that I know you aren't involved, I'm going to try to keep it that way. Besides, the problem you've discovered dwarfs any other we have." He looked at her tray, which had only the one sandwich missing. "Now will you please eat? This is going to be a very long and stressful day."

"And you?" she questioned. "You haven't even unwrapped your tray, yet you're halfway done with your wine."

His unrestrained laugh rang through the cabin. "I had sausages, a two-egg omelet and roasted potatoes for breakfast this morning. And you had...?"

Acknowledging defeat, Gabrielle said, "You win. But you still haven't said anything about my findings."

"I need to be analytical and detached so I can see any fallacies. Also, I need to make sure I don't color the results by imposing my views on your explanations. It needs to be clear that the process you used was completely objective...because if you're right, you're forecasting what may be the worst market crash since the Great Depression."

"Because publicly traded companies are also investors in the bonds?" she asked.

"That's what you've shown," Landry replied. "You aren't aware of the risks that were taken by big players in the mortgage bond market. But your analysis says those risks are now coming to light and are exposing how interconnected the stock and bond markets really are."

"Shouldn't I be aware?" asked Gabrielle. She subscribed to major market reports, and hadn't seen anything that came close to the disaster she had uncovered.

"As an analyst with any of the brokerages, you would get industry reports that aren't disseminated to individual investors," he replied. "But even those reports only indicate a downturn in the residential mortgage bond market. In no way do they suggest there may be an impact on the broader market."

"How do you get the industry reports?"

"Let's just say I know someone who knows someone," Landry stopped short. His continued evasion and maddening pause fueled Gabrielle's curiosity. Unexpectedly, he followed the pause with a flood of words. "Last month, NEI senior partners decided to investigate branching into investment analysis. Brokerages and investment funds have created a variety of instruments that are difficult to understand. Our largest clients have expressed wariness—but interest—because they don't want to miss out on potential profits. The economy is slowing, so conversely, their need is becoming more immediate." His flow of words slowed. "The biggest drawback is that we aren't sure we know how to do it or can develop the expertise to do it quickly enough to meet the current need. Then you show up with your analysis." His expression became grave. "Under any other circumstances, I would be thrilled that your app could be a starting point for what we are trying to do. But the accompanying news is so cataclysmic that we will undoubtedly drop everything else while we address this."

Gabrielle's focus turned inward, her mind wrestling with the problem. "But what can we do about it?"

"First, we need to be awfully damn sure," he said. "Then we at least figure out what we need to do to protect our interests and the interests of our clients."

Just minutes earlier, Gabrielle had believed that alerting NEI was the endgame for her. Instead, it was only the opening move. Down time was *not* going to be an option. "Do you think anyone else has seen this coming?"

"That's a very good question," Landry replied, the tightness around his eyes softening. "This is not something that would make the evening news—the resulting panic alone would devastate the markets. The answer is that we don't know whether anyone else has seen this coming. And we won't know unless," He paused, then corrected himself, "until we figure out how to read the signs." He flashed a quick glance in her direction. "Now eat. And make sure you drink both bottles of water. Can't have you dropping of exhaustion in the middle of reporting to the partners this afternoon."

"*I'm* going to do it?" asked Gabrielle. "But I'm not prepared."

"You found it, you report it." Then he added, "But don't respond to Garrett's comments or questions. Leave him to me."

Gabrielle chose a broccoli floret and chewed it absently. Personal car...Insider market knowledge..."Leave Garrett to me." Landry sounded more like a senior partner than a junior partner not even four hours into his first day on the job. *What's his story?*

~*~~~**~~~*~

Estelle. Again.

Jarin hesitated, his attention still focused on the quarterly report for SCI's technology sector. He'd have to remind her—again—that he actually worked during business hours. He answered the call. "Estelle."

Her ecstatic reply shattered his concentration. "Oh, Jarin, it's the most exquisite thing I've ever seen!"

Ah, a thank you call. Should be short. "So you like your bracelet?" After searching for weeks for something that suited her taste, he had given up and had the bracelet made. An appropriate good-bye present—if that's where they were heading. He suspected the ultimatum was coming tonight, or if she wanted a perfect birthday, Thursday after the showing.

"Of course I do! Can't you tell? It's perfect. I'm going out now to get something to wear with it on Thursday."

Another call came in. Jarin glanced at the number. It was Carson. "Estelle, sorry to cut it short, but I've got to take this call."

"I know you're busy. You'll just have to make it up to me tonight. After all, it is my birthday! See you at eight."

"Absolutely," he replied and quickly switched to Carson's call. "On your way?"

Over the low background hum of an engine, Carson said, "Nah, it'll be Devon instead of me...for a while. Landry called."

"I see." Jarin pushed away from the laptop on his desk and propped up his legs beside it. The enormous clock on Twelfth Street Tower, ten blocks east of his forty-eighth floor office in the SCI Building, read almost ten. "What happened?"

"He didn't say much, just that it's still breaking. But he wanted me to relay messages to you and Nathan. I'm driving them to her condo now."

"What's at her condo?"

"Beats me. All I know is Landry looked awfully tight. I've had her building looked over. Nothing stands out. Security detail's in place for both of them."

"Okay, then. So we wait."

"Yeah, except for the message. He wants Joseph to make discreet inquiries about residential mortgage bonds. Heavy emphasis on discreet. Says there 'may' be a problem in the market."

"Wonder what kind of a problem. Did he mention timeframe?"

"Just that the message for Nathan is that he may want to pre-empt his partners meeting."

Abruptly, Jarin lowered his legs from the desk and stood. "Today, then. Joseph should be in his office prepping for our quarterly review meeting. On my way over now. Keep us posted."

"Will do."

~*~~~**~~~*~

Just minutes away from The Lofts, they rode in silence, Gabrielle preoccupied with managing the stress exerted by the dual threats she faced. The one brewing in the market could cause widespread financial devastation; the consequences of the other were ruinous only to her. Soon she would demo Sparks for Landry and would have to face those consequences. At the first opportunity, she would have to call Quentin, admit that she'd talked to NEI without him, and beg him to still advise her even though she'd likely given up any chance of legal protection. *But what other option was there?*

A smaller, yet substantial worry was that she had to face the fallout from crossing Garrett. Despite Landry's assurances, she didn't see a way to dodge that particular bullet. It seemed unavoidable that she would lose Sparks, get fired, or both. But whatever NEI's plans, she would insist that they keep her on until they were protected against the market crash. They owed her that.

The car pulled into the Loft IV garage and, to Gabrielle's surprise, drove past the public elevator bank, and stopped in the loading zone near the four partially hidden elevators exclusively for residents. These elevators had no "Up" button; only a slot for inserting a condo door key. "How did Carson know to stop here?" she asked. "Most people stop at the mall elevators."

"You remembered the driver's name?"

"Shouldn't I have?"

"I'm just surprised because you'd only heard it once," Landry said. "I guess he's very thorough when he looks up addresses." A green light lit on the console between them. Landry pushed the button beside it and said, "Let's go."

Leaving the car, they boarded one of the elevators and rode it silently up to the twenty-fourth floor. Once inside her condo, Gabrielle led the way to the office nook. Allowing her backpack to slide off of her shoulder onto the desk, she turned to the wall between the nook and her bedroom, opened the control panel, and changed the setting for the great room windows from clear to mild translucence. The setting gave them privacy, but did not eliminate the view. She also turned on the recessed ceiling lights and wall sconces. A glance toward Landry, who stood near the sectional, reminded her that like Stephen, he wouldn't fit in one of the guest chairs for the desk. Passing him on her way to the bar, she said, "How about I get you a stool? It'll probably be more comfortable."

Noticing the guest chairs for the first time, Landry laughed. "I guess everything here is your size."

"How tall are you, anyway?" asked Gabrielle, trying to hide her embarrassment as she half-carried, half-dragged the stool from the bar. The nook was the only place, including her bedroom, which held furniture compatible with her height. Everything else had been chosen with Stephen's comfort in mind. Landry seemed taller.

"Six-four," he said, going to help her.

So, three inches taller than Stephen.

Looking down at her as he took the stool, he added, "I'd say you're about five-four."

"Five-four and a half." she corrected, walking back to the desk.

Following her and carrying the stool in one hand, Landry said drily, "Let's not forget those half inches." He positioned it to the left of and slightly behind her desk chair, and then sat. Watching Gabrielle unpack her laptop, he asked, "Now, what is it that you're going to show me?"

Gabrielle snapped her laptop into its docking station and powered it on. "The laptop connects to the server that Sparks is running on—it's under my desk," she said, pointing it out to Landry. "And to the full-size keyboard and the two monitors." She sat in the desk chair and entered her user name and password for the laptop. She then looked over her shoulder at him to make sure he could see both monitors.

He smiled slightly. "I'm looking over your head."

"Very funny." Gabrielle turned back to the laptop and typed the user name and password for her server. Once logged in, she opened the development environment, loaded Sparks into it, and configured it in such a way to show Landry how it worked. "Landry, this is Sparks," she said, gesturing toward the right monitor.

"So, this is it," Landry said, looking past Gabrielle to focus on the screen.

"Yes," she replied, "I'm running it in the IDE so you can see how it works."

His eyes never leaving the monitor, Landry asked, "IDE?"

"Oh—sorry. It means integrated development environment."

"I see," he said, glancing from one monitor to the other. "Which one do I watch?"

"The IDE is on the right monitor and the results and reports will come up on the left," she said. "I do as much of the setup as I can at NEI, and then I bring it home on my laptop and run it on Sparks." Gabrielle paused, expecting at least an admonition from Landry. She'd just admitted to removing client data from NEI—another serious protocol violation. But he gave no frown, no look of displeasure, not even surprise. She went on, "Sparks runs about four times faster, and has far more options and algorithm choices than Retro. I'm sorry, but many of the algorithms were not transferrable to Retro because of its architecture."

"No need to apologize," Landry said, his voice as noncommittal as his expression.

Gabrielle started Sparks, and step by step, showed Landry how it had performed the client business process analysis and the investment analysis. Then she explained Sparks' predictive models and how she had used them for forecasting the behavior of the mortgages, the bonds in which they were packaged, and the effect on the market.

"Let me get this straight," he finally said. "You used business process algorithms and models for the client's investment analysis?"

"Yes," Gabrielle replied. "And I also analyzed a number of publically traded companies which invest in the same types of bonds. Then I used the models to forecast the effect of the mortgages and the bonds on those companies, their major investors, the major investors in those investors—and well, you know the rest." Anxious for his reaction, she asked, "What happens now?"

Ignoring her question, Landry left the stool and walked slowly toward the windows where he stood looking out toward the lofts across the park. After several minutes, he said, "You've been using Sparks since you came to work for us?"

"Yes," admitted Gabrielle. "I have personal subscriptions to all of the same data sources, and I'm using my own laptop."

"And I suppose you haven't modified it or used it from our offices or used anything from our offices to run it."

"True."

Landry turned toward her. "Who is your attorney?"

"Quentin Sands."

"I know Quentin," Landry said, eyeing Gabrielle speculatively. "Sands, Jensen, Palmer & Associates also takes care of...my family's affairs. He's not going to like that we've had this conversation."

"I know," said Gabrielle. "I've done exactly what he told me not to do—but what choice did I have? These are extraordinary circumstances."

"Ahh, so they are," Landry observed, turning back to the windows.

Her need to know escalating, Gabrielle ventured again, "What happens next?"

Drawn by her concern, he returned to the bar stool, and gently lifted her hands, covering them with his.

"This isn't just your problem anymore. You brought it to me, and we will do what we can to protect as many as we can."

His compassion was unexpected; his words a lifeline. Gabrielle held on to them, her anxiety receding. "Thank you."

Releasing her hands, Landry folded his arms across his chest and leaned against the back of the stool. "Now that I've seen what you did and how you did it, it's highly unlikely that you could have made a mistake."

"I don't think I can be happy about that."

Instead of replying to her statement, Landry said, "You must know that you are one of NEI's most valuable assets."

"I've never really thought about it."

"Well, accept that you are. It's in our best interest to protect you—and Sparks," Landry said. "There's nothing to fear. Once this immediate situation is handled, you and Quentin will meet with our attorneys to make appropriate arrangements."

Landry is just a junior partner and today is only his first day. How can he make these promises? "What about Garrett and the other partners?" she asked tentatively.

"The other partners can't fail to see the value you've brought the company. Regarding Garrett—as I've said, leave him to me." His expression became more calculating as he checked his watch. "It's one o'clock now. I'm moving up our timetable and changing the game plan."

Her intuition flickering a warning, Gabrielle eyed him warily. "I knew it. You're just as worried as I am."

"About what, specifically?"

Given an outlet, Gabrielle's apprehension explosively resurfaced. "About the market, about the partners, about what we should do, about how we can protect..."

"Hold on. Take a breath. That's a lot to be worried about," interrupted Landry.

"But those are real concerns," Gabrielle insisted.

"Yes, they are. We *do* have to do something," Landry agreed. "Quickly and efficiently, but not 'in a hurry'. We take the time to make a plan, and then we execute that plan. For instance, what are you going to do about the market?" He paused, giving her time to think about it. "What are you going to do about the partners?" After a longer pause, he asked, "You see the difference between planning and worrying?"

Landry's skill at mentoring made Gabrielle feel as though she was back in class. "Yes," she answered.

"Worry is a paralyzing emotion," he added. "It leaves you unable to act."

"You're right. I know..."

"You have to let it go—here and now. I'm asking you to step up to the next level. You have to plan, and then you have to execute."

"Why does this feel like the pep talk before we face the lions?"

Landry's laughter relieved the tension. "Because it is—in a way," he said. "But everything I've said is true. Are you ready?"

Lions or no lions, I can't stop now. "I suppose," Gabrielle answered.

"Love that confidence," Landry said wryly. "We'll pull together a few slides—quickly—and then we're going back to NEI for an immediate meeting with Garrett and Nathan."

Ah hell—we are marching into the lion's den. Gabrielle was sure that Garrett would want her head. It wasn't clear how Nathan would react, but as managing partner he wouldn't be easy to convince. "You think it'll be *easier* with just the two of them?"

"Absolutely not," said Landry shooting her an amused glance. "But as you pointed out, we don't have much time. Our plan is to make Nathan aware of this situation as quickly as possible so that as head of NEI, he can direct us as we protect ourselves from this. And we don't want to muddy the waters by going over Garrett's head."

"I see—that would be bad."

"*Very*," emphasized Landry.

"What about the analysis we left running in your office?"

"We don't need it. We'll use the results from Sparks. Trust me, Lo...Gabrielle. Now that we've verified your results, moving quickly and decisively is the best way."

He almost called me Lois. But she's Nathan's admin. Maybe he's more stressed than he's letting on. In another attempt to manage her own stress, she closed her eyes, drew a deep breath, and slowly let it out.

"You all right over there?" Landry asked warily.

"Just trying to sharpen my focus. Keep my head in the game."

"Don't try to force it," he advised. "You'll stress yourself out. Your head will be in the game when you need it to be." He gestured toward the monitors, "We should get started." As Gabrielle turned toward them, he added, "We need the slide deck to be short and sharp."

"Do we mention the client?"

"Of course. We tell the whole story...just a highly abridged version."

Gabrielle pulled the relevant diagrams from the analysis package, crafted the first two slides, and quickly walked Landry through them.

"Good. Move on," he said, again checking his watch.

She then crafted the next two slides. "Where do we explain the process? Won't they want to know that?"

"Remember—you have both the business analysis and the investment analysis for reference," he said. "All we want to do with this deck is to get their attention. Your roller coaster graph certainly does that. Run through the whole thing again. Remember, keep it brief and let the graph speak for itself."

After having gone through several dry run iterations, updating the slides where necessary, Gabrielle said, "I've got the talking points, and I know when to refer them to the analyses."

"We're—or you're—there," said Landry, checking his watch one last time. "Time to go." Removing himself from the stool, he took it back to the bar. At the sound of her backpack zipper, he asked, "Ready?"

"I'm all packed," said Gabrielle. *Not so sure I'm ready.*

On the way to the elevator, Landry said. "Remember, Gabby, let me field any antagonistic, aggressive responses."

Disregarding that he hadn't used her formal name, Gabrielle went for his apparent lack of trust in her ability to manage adversity. "You don't think I can handle it."

"That's not the point. You report to me, I protect my people. It's my job to secure your work environment. That includes removing anything—or anyone—that is an obstacle."

Landry was quiet again on the ride down to the garage—eyes closed; his posture just as it had been in the elevator at NEI. Surreptitiously watching him, Gabrielle was sure he was analyzing the situation, measuring the probabilities of potential outcomes. Planning instead of worrying.

~*~~*~~*~

Elevators had become a significant part of Gabrielle's recent living scape. She and Landry were taking this one from the Twelfth Street Tower executive garage back up to NEI. *Plan and execute, plan and execute.* Over and again, she practiced her new mantra. Landry was in his usual posture. In a muted voice, Gabrielle said, "You're still planning...using every available moment."

He looked down at her, his hazel eyes now closer to green than brown. "Not this time. I'm reminding myself to be calm, to focus my energies on my goals."

"What are your goals?" she asked. His expression tightened. "I'm sorry. My questions are bothering you."

"It's not that," Landry was quick to say. "I have...several...goals, some more immediate than others." His eyes darkened as he leaned slightly toward her. Abruptly, he straightened up and faced the doors. "I'm trying to maintain focus on my two immediate goals—namely getting NEI to act and preventing Garrett from interfering."

"Why would he?" Gabrielle asked. "He may be unhappy with us—me—but interfering is counterproductive. Against what's best for the company." Bristling at

Landry's slight smile, Gabrielle expected him to be condescending. Instead, she got another lesson.

"You still think logically and objectively," he said. "You haven't had enough exposure to executive management to be aware of undercurrents of self-interest that can be at odds with what's best for the firm. It's possible your findings may affect someone's agenda and sometimes people refuse to see past their own agenda to what's best for all." His expression changed to one of resignation. "You'll soon be exposed though—today's events have probably accelerated that timeline."

So one of the consequences of her findings was involvement in the intrigues and hidden agendas of Partners' Row. Reading the message underlying Landry's words, she'd just put herself in the game. *As what though, a pawn? Or is there a more important role for me to play?*

The elevator opened. Landry said. "Let's go see Nathan." Hard pressed to keep up with his long strides, Gabrielle followed him along Partners' Row. They had barely passed the door of the executive conference room when it opened. Taking a quick glance behind her, she caught a glimpse of the person coming through the door. Her anxiety intensified into alarm. It was Garrett. His angry, demanding voice boomed throughout Partners' Row as he started after them. "Where the *hell* have you been?"

CHAPTER THREE

Partners' Row

Gabrielle pressed against the wall as Landry passed by, putting himself between her and Garrett. Though he spoke calmly, it was clear that he took "protecting his people" very seriously. "I beg your pardon?"

"I asked where the hell you've been," Garrett responded coldly, his mouth twisted in distaste. "I've been looking for you and here you are coming back from some sort of tryst."

Gabrielle was stung by his words. *He thinks we...*

Striding past Garrett through the still open conference room door, Landry said, "We're taking this inside—*now*. Gabrielle, wait for us in Nathan's suite."

"The hell she will," said Garrett. "Gabrielle—inside."

As she edged past Garrett into the conference room, Landry motioned for her to go toward the far end of the table. Once there, she sat her backpack down and faced the two men.

Garrett closed the door and leaned against it, glaring at Landry. "This had better be good."

"There's a crisis developing in the market that NEI needs to be made aware of." Landry said, propping himself against the edge of the table. "Gabrielle discovered it while working on the Chandler project and I've verified her findings. We're on our way to report out to you and Nathan."

"I'm here now—let's have it." Garrett looked past Landry, directly into Gabrielle's eyes. "You seem to have your materials, Ms. Winston."

With extreme difficulty, Gabrielle met his frosty green gaze. "Yes, I do."

"In the interest of time, it would be prudent to report out to you together," Landry said. "You would then be able to prepare for the partners' meeting if it were warranted."

"You presume," Garrett said, "to have found something that impacts NEI at the executive level—without any corroboration?"

Landry pushed away from the table and stood. "It's not presumption—it's fact."

Stunned, Gabrielle was sure he'd crossed the line.

Garrett's even frostier expression mirrored Gabrielle's thoughts. "Okay, then. Your funeral. Get some time on his calendar—but if this is a false alarm, don't look to me for support."

Without looking away from Garrett, Landry said, "Gabrielle, please let Nathan know we'd like some time on his calendar as close to now as possible."

"Sure thing." Gabrielle snatched up her backpack and left the room, closing the door behind her. *Landry's out of his mind taking on Garrett. His first day may well be his last.* Fearing that the animosity between the two men might lead them to blows, Gabrielle hurried past the senior partner office suites toward Nathan's office. He had to be briefed. She would go it alone if she had to.

~*~~~**~~~*~

Lois looked up from the open folder on her desk as Gabrielle rushed into Nathan's corner suite. "Hey Gabs," she said with a smile. "These aren't your usual haunts." Her expression became alarmed as Gabrielle drew closer. She rose from her chair. "What's happened?"

Too late, Gabrielle worked to conceal her anxiety. "I just left Garrett and Landry in the conference room." She held herself to the minimum explanation. "They sent me ahead to get some time for us on Nathan's calendar—as close to now as possible."

Lois's expression smoothed. "They were going at it again, weren't they?"

"Again? But I thought today's Landry's first day."

"Officially, yes," confided Lois. "But for the past few weeks, they've been discussing the terms under which Landry would accept the position." She beckoned Gabrielle around her desk and whispered, "Nathan calls it 'close quarters negotiation'. But to me, it's as if they're always on the verge of ripping each other to shreds." Lois gave Gabrielle's shoulders a quick squeeze and then headed toward the inner office. "I'll see if Nathan can carve out some time. Don't let them get to you, hon."

Relieved that she hadn't had to give up any critical information, Gabrielle said gratefully, "Thanks, Lois."

"Don't mention it," Lois replied. Giving a knock at the door, she went in. Within seconds, she reappeared, leaving the door open behind her. "Nathan says he has ten minutes—starting now. Go on in. I'll send Garret and Landry in when they get here."

In response to Lois's encouraging gestures, she approached Nathan's door. He sat at his desk staring expectantly in her direction. "Ah, Ms. Winston," he said. "I thought there would be three of you."

Noting that he looked very relaxed, Gabrielle could only think how badly they were about to disrupt his morning. "Landry and Garrett are on their way," she replied, stepping just inside his door.

To her surprise, he laughed. "So you're the placeholder."

"Placeholder?" Seeing that he was having fun with her, she hoped to keep it light.

"You're supposed to keep me occupied until the others show up," Nathan said, waving slightly toward the guest chairs in front of his desk. "Come in, have a seat."

"I didn't know I was supposed to do that so I expect I'll fail miserably," Gabrielle said. She entered his office and sat in one of the chairs he indicated.

"You're doing fine—the only way to fail is to make inane conversation," he said. "You have no idea how much that irritates me."

Gabrielle sighed. "Maybe I'll just be quiet then."

Nathan laughed again. "When in doubt, silence is always the best plan."

They heard Lois's voice, "Go on in."

Nathan winked at Gabrielle. "No matter now—you're saved."

Gabrielle turned toward the door in time to see Garrett enter the office, his mood seemingly even more contentious than before. Landry followed at a leisurely pace and closed the door behind him. Their faces were set with similar harsh expressions. Gabrielle peeked at Nathan. *He must see their animosity.*

"More space at the conference table," said Nathan, leading the way toward it.

As Gabrielle approached the table and pulled out a side chair, she was struck by an absurd desire to laugh.

Nathan's furnishings complemented his height, and when she sat down, she found that her feet barely touched the floor. *I'm a shrub among redwoods. Any shorter and they'd have to get me a high chair.* Unobtrusively, she shifted forward in the chair, planted her feet solidly on the floor, and crossed her arms on the table.

"I've been assured that a crisis is brewing," Garrett said to Nathan in a biting tone. "That is the *only* reason I've concurred with this injudicious imposition on your time."

"As I've tried to explain, Garrett, the situation seems dire enough that we need to be as expeditious as possible," said Landry.

"By all means then, continue," said Nathan, ending their exchange.

Glancing at Garrett, who continued to glower, Gabrielle began, "It started with the Chandler analysis. I saw that, as a contingency, they expected to fund their expansion with the returns on their mortgage bonds."

"What has that to do with us? It's their business if they want to use their investment earnings." Garrett broke in scathingly. "We do not perform investment analyses."

Gabrielle started to respond, but Landry answered for her. "That is an Analysis Group policy," he agreed, his glance toward Gabrielle warning her to silence. "In this particular case, since our recommendations necessitated that they use their contingency, we chose to perform the analysis." Nathan waited patiently. Garrett continued to glare. "Nathan, do you have time for four slides?"

"Why?"

"We found that the client's return on those bonds will be negative over the expansion time period," said Landry. "What's more, we found that the residential mortgage bond market sector, in general, will decline rapidly—with a negative impact on the full market."

Nathan left the table for his desk and buzzed Lois. When she answered, he said, "Cancel my appointments for the rest of the afternoon—except for the partners' meeting."

"Yes, Nathan."

He released the button and turned to Landry, his expression grim. "I have time."

"Thank you," said Landry. "Gabrielle will walk us through her findings."

Gabrielle unpacked and powered up her laptop, connected it to Nathan's projector, and ran through the four slides as she had rehearsed with Landry. When she got to the roller coaster graph, Nathan and Garrett stared at it in grim silence. Still glowering as he turned away from the graph, Garrett focused his ire on Gabrielle. "I'm very familiar with Retro's capabilities, Ms. Winston. Even augmented with your algorithms, it could not have performed this analysis. So tell us, how did you achieve the findings?"

Landry cut in, "Our first priority should be coming up with an action plan."

Undeterred, Garrett brushed Landry's statement aside. "I was speaking to Ms. Winston."

Accepting that her words would give NEI leverage to claim Sparks, Gabrielle answered. "I used the application I wrote in graduate school. It uses the predictive algorithms that Retro can't run." Nathan reached for her laptop, claiming her attention. She slid it over to him saying, "I've also pulled up both analyses." He studied each of them, lingering on the graphed results. His expression, reminiscent of Landry's during his review of the analyses, got progressively tighter.

Addressing Nathan, Garrett said, "I think we may find that Ms. Winston has been performing her duties with her application more than just this once. We should investigate with our attorneys what rights NEI may have in reference to it."

"That may very well be true, Garrett," Nathan agreed, still studying the reports. "But our first responsibility is to protect ourselves and our clients from what she has found. Determining what to do about the application can wait."

"She has trodden over several NEI directives. You propose to ignore that?"

"We have just been apprised of an approaching financial crisis of phenomenal proportions," Nathan reminded Garrett, looking up from the reports. "You are suggesting that the matter of the app rivals that?" He held up his hand as Garrett prepared to answer him. "I'll make some inquiries; I don't know how long it will take for responses, but we're going to proceed with the expectation that they will be affirmative. Our immediate actions will be to address the NEI investment portfolio and the interests of our clients. We also have two merger offers on the table that we have to address. Quite honestly, this will severely impact the one from the Avanti Consortium unless they can find another funding source." He said sternly to Gabrielle, "You did not hear that. If I hear it out on the floor, I'll know where it came from."

"I understand."

Checking his watch, Nathan said, "Two-ten now—we'll move up the partners' meeting and preempt the agenda." He nodded appreciatively toward Gabrielle and Landry. "This is extremely thorough work. Garrett, you've got a good team. You should be proud."

"Thank you, Nathan," Garrett replied. "But as soon as this crisis is handled, I insist we address Ms. Winston's transgressions."

Sliding the laptop back toward her, Nathan said courteously, "Please excuse us, Gabrielle. I expect you back in twenty minutes."

Aware of the growing impatience in the room, Gabrielle put her laptop in sleep mode rather than wait for it to power down. *They are about to deliberate my future. I should be here to speak for myself.*

Putting an end to those thoughts, Landry said, "Gabrielle, my office."

Not only were they were throwing her out, she couldn't even go to her cubicle. She zipped her backpack, slung it over her shoulder, and headed toward the door. The conversation resumed as she opened it and stepped through; the rising voices cut off as soon as she closed it.

Lois looked up. "Sounds like things are heating up in there."

"Close quarters negotiation," Gabrielle replied with a dejected grin. "Is every room on Partners' Row soundproofed?"

Lois laughed. "No—just the executive conference room and Nathan's office." As Gabrielle passed her desk she asked, "Where can I find you if they ask?"

"I'm being banished to Landry's office," Gabrielle answered.

"Just as well that you're staying clear of the other analysts," said Lois. "Don't take it personally, but your face is very expressive. If I can see something is wrong, so can everyone else." Then she winked. "Don't worry, hon, unless you've committed murder, Nathan's in your corner. It'll be all right."

"Thanks, Lois." Gabrielle resisted the temptation to explain that even in the face of financial Armageddon, Garrett was out to make sure she paid—dearly—for using Sparks and for ignoring his rules. Despite Lois's words, she didn't see how Nathan could get around the fact that she had broken them. She left the suite for Landry's office.

Barred from going to her cube, Gabrielle had twenty minutes with nothing to do but think about catastrophe—the broader financial one and her personally devastating one. Thankfully, an idea struck when she was midway down Partners' Row.

As did all the partners' offices, Landry's had network connections wired through the conference table. She could at least set up a test environment to investigate the changed files she had found earlier; far better than watching the minutes tick toward disclosure of her fate. Thinking through how she might perform the investigation, she quickened her pace, concerned that what was left of the twenty minutes might not be enough. By the time she got to Landry's door, her plan was well formed, and she had only to execute.

Closing the door behind her, Gabrielle hurried to the conference table where she set up her laptop and connected it to the NEI network. After logging in, she emailed IT to let them know that she was using two of the test environments.

First, she loaded both environments with the current version of Retro. Next she modified one of them with the files that she had earlier copied from Landry's laptop to her thumb drive. Then she started both versions of Retro and made sure that they were running correctly.

Choosing twenty business analyses that Sparks had already completed, she converted the setup files to the format that Retro understood and submitted them to both versions of the app. Tomorrow morning she would make two sets of comparisons: Sparks versus the Retro versions to determine which one was correct, and then one Retro version versus the other to expose the effect of the modified files. She watched the apps until they both began the first analysis and then took her laptop off the network, returned it to sleep mode, and repacked it.

Again with nothing to do, Gabrielle was grateful that there was little time left until she was expected back in Nathan's office. She found sitting at the table impossible in her current state of agitation, so she wandered the office, wishing there were paintings or pictures on which she could focus. The window garden couldn't hold her attention forever. With no other distractions, her thoughts returned to Lois's assurances. Still, she couldn't allow herself to think that Nathan could fix her problems. He was managing partner, but NEI had rules. Employees, including Gabrielle, signed contracts pledging to obey them. She and other analysts routinely violated the contract terms, but now, she was caught. In her case, NEI could no longer look the other way.

~*~~~**~~~*~

Even in his best mood, Garrett's natural gait projected menace. So now, it was unlikely that anyone would detect his rising anger. Nathan had summarily waved aside his concerns about Gabrielle's app and sent him off to apprise the other partners of the earlier, urgent meeting as if he were an errand boy. It took all of his control to maintain a calm facade until he reached his office suite. For what was surely not the last time, Garrett applauded himself for opting to forego glass walls and curtains for the front of his inner office. He urgently needed the absolute privacy afforded him by the solid walls he had chosen instead. It was also fortunate that Elaine wasn't at her desk in his outer office. In his current state of mind, he could not have simply walked past her.

As soon as he quietly closed the inner office door, his tightly restrained anger erupted. Landry had played him for a fool—had circumvented his authority by arranging the meeting with Nathan. Certainly, fifteen more minutes in the conference room would *not* have made a difference. Had they briefed him, he could have taken the information to Nathan and into the partners' meeting without them. Instead, Landry used the crisis to put himself in contention for the senior partner position that would be open when Garrett took over as managing partner. Landry hadn't been a junior partner for a whole day, but Cleve's ineptitude combined with Landry's handling of this situation could easily eliminate Cleve from consideration. The ferocity of Garrett's thoughts escalated, and he slammed his fist down on his desk as he passed it. The harsh sound disrupted his rage, bringing a few instants of clarity. He was extremely close to achieving his objective—stupid to put it in jeopardy because he was too incensed to think strategically. After several more minutes of intense concentration, Garrett reined in his anger and conformed to his usual pacing pattern.

NEI acceptance of either merger proposal would put him in the driver's seat as managing partner. In the case of the Avanti proposal, Nathan would be completely out of the picture; but even if Brett didn't find another funding source, and SCI bought NEI, Nathan would—without question—accept the SCI Board Member seat. From there he could provide guidance, but without demonstrable cause, he could not interfere in daily operations. Garrett would still be able to maneuver as long as Cleve got his senior partner spot. His immediate objective was to make sure that Landry *didn't* get it. He paced between the garden wall and his desk, struggling to keep his thoughts on strategy. A situational weakness—that's what he needed.

Gabrielle defied me and ran an investment analysis. I know what Landry said—but I'm betting she did it on her own and went running to him when it hit the fan. Garrett uttered a series of expletives. Nothing he could do about it…yet. Taking it to Landry was the right move—no refuting that. But Landry should have brought it to him as soon as he confirmed her findings. He didn't. Garrett stopped mid-step. *When and how did he confirm those findings? What's more, Gabrielle seemed very well rehearsed. When did they have time to do that?* That was the crux of it—he needed to know where they were before the meeting in Nathan's office.

Armed with a starting point, Garrett allowed his thoughts to change gears. He had gotten ahead of himself—hadn't protected his own interests. He needed to apprise Brett of the crisis and the SCI proposal. Garrett leaned against his credenza and pulled his cell from its holster. After retrieving his recorder from his pocket and plugging it in, he hit a speed dial number.

Brett picked up. "Yeah?"

"Your ears only. There's a market issue with residential mortgage bonds," Garrett said urgently and quietly. "Strong probability they're about to tank and affect the entire stock market within the next quarter or two. I'm giving you a head's up so you can rework the proposal."

"Tank? How could you know that?" Brett asked sharply.

"Our recommendations would've forced a client to go to their bonds for financing. We followed up—found the issue." Garrett summarized the situation for him.

"I thought NEI didn't perform investment analyses."

"We don't usually," Garrett replied. "But as I said, our recommendations prompted their necessity to go to their bonds. So we investigated."

"Very thorough analyst team. Can't wait to get them onboard." Brett mused. "Damn...within the next two quarters. The probability—how high have you heard?"

"About ninety percent," replied Garrett, throwing out a number. He needed Brett to act—and from Gabrielle's analysis, it looked like a sure thing.

"I was counting on using those bonds for the merger," said Brett.

"A high percentage of the publicly traded corporations in the domestic and international market segments are invested in them as well," Garrett told him. "All of them could be affected."

"Son of a...wow...how did you..."

"Yeah, it's scary as hell," agreed Garrett. "Another thing—we got an unsolicited merger proposal from SCI. They're the front-runner now because their offer is unaffected. They're financing mainly in cash. If you want NEI, you've not only got to beat our counter, you've also got to beat the SCI proposal."

"What? Oh, yeah. We'll rework the proposal and address the counter. Damn Jarin. Why'd he submit a proposal out of the blue?"

"Said he heard 'rumors' on the street. You must have a leaky ship over there."

"Not us. Only a few people know about it. It must be NEI."

"Doubtful, but you're right, somebody leaked it. I'll keep an eye out," Garrett agreed, simply to appease him. *No need to bite the hand that forks over that extra cash.*

"We'll position ourselves to start our sell-off of the bonds as soon as we get your bulletin—that is—you are sending one out?"

"Haven't made the decision yet, but there will be some sort of notification. Protecting our clients is high on Nathan's list."

"Good. In the meantime, I'll put people on the proposal update. When do you suggest we submit it?"

"Wait for Nathan to officially notify you. Should be within the next few days."

"You're sure he'll call?"

"Positive. Nathan's old school—feels compelled to follow proper business etiquette. He's honor bound to give you another chance."

"One more thing—does this situation affect our other endeavor?"

"Not at all," said Garrett.

"Perfect." said Brett. "We've seen an increase in business in the affected subsidiaries and I don't want to lose that."

"You won't—the change hasn't been detected."

"I'll be in touch," Brett said.

"Good," said Garrett and hung up. He returned the recorder to his pocket. *Always have an insurance policy.* He speed dialed another number.

"Hello, Mr. Stratford," his broker warmly greeted him.

"Mark, I'm considering an investment," Garrett said. "I need you to liquidate my real estate holdings over the next two months."

"Sure," Mark replied. "What do you want me to buy with the proceeds?"

"Just park it in Treasury notes for now," said Garrett.

"That's thirty percent of your account—must be a pretty big deal," Mark hinted.

"It is," Garrett replied. "If it gets any more solid I'll give you a call." *Leech. Hope you go down with the ship. But that's a rat, isn't it?*

"Good deal," said Mark. "You'll see confirmation in your inbox. Anything else?"

"That's it. Thanks," said Garrett. He holstered his phone and resumed pacing. Now that he'd conquered his anger and looked after his own interests, it was clear what had to be next.

Seeing that the attendant light on his desk phone was lit, he buzzed Elaine.

"Yes, Garrett?" she asked.

No matter how many times he heard it, the silky, melodic quality of her voice sometimes caught him unprepared, distracted him, and turned his attention toward more pleasant diversions. "Find Cleve and send him in—after the partners' meeting."

"Yes, Garrett."

Giving in to his strong urge for those diversions, Garrett said, "By the way, I'm working late tonight." Liz was consumed with her B&B and wouldn't miss him.

"I can stay if you need anything," Elaine answered, her way of saying that she would be free.

"And one more thing—check the logs and let me know what cars went out today."

"Yes, Garrett."

Calling Cleve in wouldn't seem odd, but would indicate his anxiousness to get things moving and would also obscure his true goal of finding out what Landry and the wunderkind had been up to. Little Gabby was too smart for her own damn good. She had single-handedly disrupted the endeavor to unseat Nathan that he and Brett had been working on for months.

I can't touch her yet—Nathan hovers behind her like a doting father. They aren't related though—I checked. There's also nothing going on between them—I checked that, too. He would just have to be patient until Nathan was out of NEI. He already had the advantage of intimidation. Though Gabrielle tried valiantly to hide it, she cringed every time she had to talk to him. As for Landry, Garrett expected little difficulty in maneuvering him out of the way.

Anticipation of his future brought a disturbingly ugly cast to Garrett's chiseled features. Whatever happened, he would be managing partner when Nathan moved on—the most powerful position in the analytics industry. Among other things, he looked forward to the pleasures he would enjoy. He already had Elaine, but was not averse to a little variety. Gabrielle would not be in a position to refuse him. *I want her. I'll have her...no matter what she wants. I'll ruin her if she refuses me—a whisper here and there, and she's done. It will be my pleasure to put Gabrielle in her place.*

~*~~~**~~~*~

The turning doorknob drew Gabrielle's attention and arrested her pacing. As Landry walked through and closed it quietly behind him, the tormenting question came quickly to her lips. "What's the verdict?"

"You haven't spent this entire time worried about Garrett's remarks have you?"

"Of course I did—you heard what he said."

"Yes, I did," Landry replied. "But what Garrett failed to remember, until Nathan reminded him, is that his rules are not NEI directives unless voted as such by all the senior partners. Many of those rules, including the one about 'no investment analysis', have never been subjected to a vote."

Gabrielle's relief was profound. "You mean..."

"That's right. Technically, there has been no violation." Landry smiled as he walked toward her.

"But what about Sparks?"

"Nathan shelved that discussion for now," he replied.

"Until when?"

"Trust me, Gabrielle; no harm will come to you or Sparks."

Despite her lack of conviction, she had no choice but to wait. "All right," she hesitantly replied.

Throwing her a sharp glance, Landry changed the subject. "Now, I know you're feeling sequestered, but we needed you to stay away from the rest of the staff. You don't look normal."

"My hair must be all...and we have to go back..." Frantically, she combed her fingers through her tousled curls as she looked around Landry's office. *Men don't have mirrors in their offices?*

Laughing, Landry caught her hands and pulled them together to his chest. Holding them in both of his, he looked down into her eyes. "I'm sorry—don't take it that way. Nothing's wrong with the way you look—physically. Besides, Nathan's given us a little more time. He and Garrett were still talking when I left."

Unexpected visions of being cradled in his embrace, her head pressed tightly to his chest, disturbed Gabrielle. She began to pull away. *Not here. Not now. Especially with what Garrett already thinks.*

Landry quickly released her hands. "You look fine. Same as always."

"Then what do you mean?" she asked, turning away to hide her struggle for composure. But she couldn't pretend that she hadn't heard his words, which had implications that she was determined not to acknowledge.

"You're clearly pumped up about something," he explained. "It'll draw questions and we haven't yet formulated any answers."

Having strengthened her resolve, Gabrielle faced him again. "I'm sorry," she said. "I don't know what to do about that."

"Not your fault—just don't ever play poker," replied Landry, his expression becoming even less guarded. "By the way—if you're looking for a mirror, it's over there." He nodded toward the armoire in the corner by his desk.

"Thanks." Relieved to put distance between them, she moved her backpack from the conference table to the small reading table in the corner near the armoire and took out her comb. Opening the armoire, she saw a fully functional sink, and shelves filled with shaving stuff.

"The mirror pulls out," said Landry.

A shaving mirror. Dad had one of these. The customary short, sharp pain pierced Gabrielle's heart, just as it always did when thoughts of her father came up unexpectedly. She pulled out the mirror and looked. It could have been worse. She wet the comb, shook out the excess, and looking into the mirror, dragged it a few times through her hair. There was no time to really tame the chaos.

"I don't know why you're doing that," Landry said.

Surprised, she turned in the direction of his voice. He was now lounging in one of the chairs at the table behind her, watching with a puzzled expression. Gabrielle turned back to the mirror and sighed dejectedly. "I know—it's a lost cause."

"Again, not what I meant." Through the mirror, she saw that his eyes were dancing with humor. Again, Gabrielle held herself from warming to him. "I sometimes overhear some of our lady staffers wondering how you get your hair to look like that." His expression was now appraising.

Gabrielle turned back to the mirror, looking for what he apparently saw. "You must be kidding. I can't do a thing with it."

"Well, it seems to work for you." He checked his watch and then stood. "It's just about time. We're going to the conference room—not Nathan's office. You ready?"

"I have to be," she said as she turned toward the table, almost bumping into Landry who now stood very close behind her. He lifted his hand to her head; she felt it gently running through her curls. *I cannot allow this to happen.* Hesitantly, she looked up to his face. Landry held her gaze.

"You probably didn't mean to wear this as a hair ornament," he said and handed Gabrielle the comb he had taken out of her hair.

Relieved to have misunderstood his intent, she said. "I have lost my mind."

He laughed again—loudly. "Believe me, Gabs, you're not the only one."

~*~~~**~~~*~

The senior partners—Garrett, Russell, Fiona, Larry, Matthew, and August—were already in their places when Gabrielle and Landry entered the executive conference room. As they seated themselves, Gabrielle smiled at Matthew. Though he looked puzzled, his return smile was a reassuring one.

"Garrett's letting you crash the party?" Russell asked Landry.

Before he could answer, Nathan entered the conference room and shut the door behind him. He also activated the controls that transformed the clear glass walls back to opaque, giving them privacy. "Our agenda for today is preempted and as you can see, we have guests," he said as he walked to his chair at the head of the table and sat down. "Gabrielle, please walk us through your findings."

Having spent the day presenting her findings in various ways—and even under Garrett's icy scrutiny—Gabrielle should have been comfortable with doing it by now. And she was, except for the subject. The menace was barely visible in the distance, but every day would bring it closer. She connected her laptop and gave the other senior partners the same presentation she had given in Nathan's office. Glancing around the table as she went through the slides, she wasn't surprised to see that the partners wore various expressions of disbelief—except for Garrett, who looked impatient for the end. Putting up the roller coaster graph, she said, "As you can see, the analysis forecasts a steep decline that feeds on itself. There is no data with which to predict an upturn."

Chaotic discussion erupted around the table. Gabrielle returned to her chair and listened. Nathan did not intervene. After several minutes, the give and take died down, each partner seemingly lost in thought.

Breaking the silence, Russell challenged, "Have you checked the analysis? Any chance of a mistake?"

"Look at their faces. Nathan preempted our normal agenda and moved the meeting up by over an hour," answered Fiona. Russell glared. "The question is how do we make damn sure we're not on one of those roller coasters?"

"Our own staff has verified it to the best of our ability," Nathan said. "But I've made a few external inquiries and there is very little substantiation. Other executives have noticed odd behavior in the bonds market, but they haven't yet put the pieces together. We may be among the fortunate few to have performed an investigative analysis."

"Then how do we know it's right?" asked Matthew.

"Lois is arranging meetings for me on Wall Street tomorrow. I'm flying up in the morning to speak directly with executives at the investment houses managing our holdings. I'll get their take on it—face to face. In any event, I think our best move is to plan for the worst."

Amidst the groans and muttered expletives, there were nods of consent.

"Any chance of it going public?" asked Fiona.

"Not for a while," Nathan answered after a few moments of thought. "I can imagine that like us, anyone else who knows doesn't want a panic in the market. The first public indication will likely be the next GFSR."

"The what?" Gabrielle whispered to Landry.

Nathan overheard. "Sorry—Global Financial Stability Report. It's a periodic report by the International Monetary Fund, or IMF. The latest one was just released, so there'll be an update around January. Let's assume we have until then to execute whatever actions we've decided upon. So, despite the extremely strong evidence that a disaster is upon us, we are still in position to take preemptive action."

Speaking for the first time, Garrett said, "As we discussed earlier, our first act should be to protect ourselves."

"True," agreed Nathan. "Our immediate exposure is in the investments we've made for research and employee benefits funding. Larry, no need to wait for a plan. It's clear that we need to divest any mortgage-backed bonds we own and shift our holdings away from real estate, and those companies that are heavily invested in real estate."

"Agreed. It's also clear that we should avoid companies in the financial sector. Many of them have been less than candid about their real estate exposure and now Gabrielle has shown us why," Larry answered. "I'd like to work with SCI on this if it's ok with you—pool our resources."

"Good idea," approved Nathan.

"Don't you think such a large selloff would tip everybody off?" asked August. "Our holdings are substantial."

"True." Larry acknowledged, "But we aren't divesting everything. Because of our current—" he eyed Landry and Gabrielle, "situation, I can imply that we're considering acquisitions and ask for a moderate—rather than aggressive—schedule. It'll also support my request to keep a sizeable amount in cash."

"Moderate schedule, aggressive schedule—what does that mean?" Nathan asked.

"That divestiture will occur over the next six months rather than three. We'll take a hit if the nosedive starts before we're totally out."

"We'll miss January by two months." Nathan mused. "But on the other hand, if we're too aggressive, we could help trigger the problem." The silence lengthened while he weighed the alternatives. "Considering what would happen if we inadvertently tip off the market, it's a good risk to use your approach."

"Sure thing," answered Larry.

"Great job Garrett," said Russell. "Your guys may have just saved our ass."

Garrett gave a curt nod in reply.

"What about the merger offers? Are either of those affected?" asked Fiona.

"Fiona, you shouldn't have raised that in front of the guests," reprimanded August. Larry nodded his agreement.

"Nathan hadn't asked them to leave," retorted Fiona.

"Next thing—" Russell began.

Nathan cut him off. "They brought us the information. They may be able to contribute to the strategy, and they will certainly be part of its execution." Though Russell still looked displeased, he made no further interruptions. "The SCI proposal is financed mostly by cash and their privately held stock. The incentives—specifically the partner incentives—in the Avanti Consortium proposal are financed by returns on their investments. If I remember correctly, a very high percentage of those investments were residential mortgage bonds and their derivatives. The exposure may be higher depending on what other market segments they've invested in. We need to revisit our analysis of their offer and see what changes they'll have to make."

"What about our clients?" asked Matthew.

"That's our second priority," answered Nathan. "How do we protect—or a better word is forewarn—our clients?"

Garrett responded, "Our alert bulletin. They automatically go out to subscribers of our services. The question is what do we say?"

"Can we release the results of the investment analysis without mentioning the company?" Landry asked.

Gabrielle stiffened as Garrett's icy gaze swept past her toward Landry, who remained unperturbed. Then she understood. Hostility was inherent to Garrett's nature; attack mode was his normal state of being. Seeing Garrett for what he was didn't make him any less dangerous, but it did make her more confident about interacting with him. *Must be hell to live with.* She tuned back in to Nathan's answer.

"...bulletin containing a specific example of borrowing against the expected return on mortgage bonds," Nathan was saying. "We can state it in such a way that our clients may be compelled to launch their own investigations."

August asked, "What if, instead, they call us for clarification?"

"We draft standard verbal and written responses intended to encourage them to act—the closest we can legally get to 'the sky is falling' without actually saying it." After another short pause, Nathan continued, "I'm sure there's more we can do, but this serves as our initial plan—our initial point of execution."

Gabrielle easily recognized the subtly different phrasing in Nathan's message. She had been hearing it all day.

There was a sudden change in the atmosphere as Nathan left the table and walked pensively toward the garden wall. There he stood, studying the plants much as Gabrielle had done in Landry's office. "We're discussing divesting ourselves into the market—but the only way we can do that is if others in the market invest. We're basically passing the problem along."

The same dilemma had been nagging at Gabrielle since her discovery. Saving themselves meant relying on others who were willing to take the risk, or, far worse, who were unaware. Some group of investors would be left holding the—empty—bag.

"That's the way the market works," said Matthew. "Unfortunately, some group of people—and corporations—will be holding the bad investments when the downturn accelerates."

"True, but we are still left with our consciences," said Nathan. I'm sure we all want to protect as many as we can. So, I am going to impose some rules of comportment. This most likely goes without saying, but there will be no spoken or written statements in any public medium or arena. We must be aware that even though we face an apparent statistical certainty, we can't expect official corroboration until the GFSR comes out—mid-January at the earliest." He returned to the table. "However, your conscience may compel you to speak quietly with people close to you on an individual basis, alerting them of the situation. I find that to be...acceptable. If you do so, please use discretion and craft your delivery to be consistent with the message to our clients."

Abruptly, he changed the subject. "Now—back to our plan. Fiona, you and yours focus on the delivery medium. Russell, get your team focused on the delivery method. Garrett, focus your team on who we'll deliver the message to and its content."

"Who?" asked Garrett. "I thought it would be obvious from the subscriber list."

"The list is certainly a start," answered Nathan. "I also want an investigation of the analyses we have done this year to see which clients we need to specifically—maybe personally—target with our message."

"Got it," Garrett responded.

"I want the first draft of the plan to review when I get back tomorrow. Lois will set up the meeting. It will be late afternoon, I'm afraid." He concluded, "Do what you must to get it ready. Consider all resources to be available. Meeting adjourned."

~*~~~**~~~*~

Gabrielle had spent more time on Partners' Row in this one afternoon than in the five previous years. It was beginning to feel familiar. Seated with Landry at his conference table, she was anxious to learn what her contribution to the plan would be.

"I need you to go home and get a good night's sleep," he said. Gabrielle started to disagree. "Wait a moment—hear me out," he interrupted. "The action is going to ramp up extremely fast tomorrow and you need to be alert and ready to handle it. You'll lead the team. I'm your backup, but I'll be spending most of my time supporting Garrett. The remaining analysts will work with Cleve to finish the analyses that are on deadline for Friday." He paused, giving Gabrielle time to absorb the news. "So I'm sending you home with Carson—and your favorite mango smoothie—but it isn't intended to replace dinner."

"I'll have dinner," she promised, "and I'll see you in the morning." *But a good night's sleep? Impossible.*

The market crash was real, Sparks was exposed, and Garrett was determined to make her pay.

CHAPTER FOUR

Strategies

Garrett's desk phone buzzed. He pressed the answer button. "Yes?"

"Cleve's on his way in," said Elaine, "and I didn't get a chance to tell you before—the only car that went out this morning was the one that Nathan took to SCI around eleven."

"Thanks." Garrett released the button just as a knock sounded at his door. "Come in." Seated at his desk, Garrett watched pensively as Cleve entered the office and closed the door. His normally heavy tread lightened by enthusiasm, Cleve walked over and dropped into one of the chairs by the desk, eyeing Garrett with anticipation. He expected perks when they spoke privately, and it was obvious he relished this opportunity for more. Garrett turned away and stared through the garden window, making Cleve wait. Silence from authority figures rattled him and loosened his tongue.

"How much do you know about what's been going on today?" Garrett finally asked.

"I knew there was something!" Cleve exclaimed, his face animated with expectation. "Gabrielle came in this morning looking like...I don't know. Really stressed out I guess."

"What time?" Garrett asked, slowly turning to face him.

"Around 8:30. She tried to play it off, but you know Gabs. Her face is an open book."

"Then?"

"She slipped into Landry's office—said she was late for their meeting."

"How long was she there?" Cleve faltered. Garrett waited, knowing that Cleve hated not having the answer. He was so damn anxious to please that sometimes he made things up.

This time, Cleve appeared to opt for honesty. "I'm not sure. I passed by a little before nine and could hear them talking. But around twelve-thirty they weren't there anymore. I know because I needed Landry's status for your weekly report. I knocked—but no answer. What's up with those two?" Cleve asked with excessive interest.

Suppressing his exasperation, Garrett said, "They're on a special project. It will be up to you and the analysts assigned to you to complete the analyses that are on deadline for Friday."

"Why do *they* get the special project?"

"It has to do with something Gabrielle found. Naturally, she took it to Landry," Garrett responded, using the opening Cleve had presented him. "You had the chance to have her on your staff when Matthew took Horace's place—you didn't want her. So," he shrugged, "this is the price you pay."

"Who knew?" Cleve defended himself. "She's just a *girl.*"

"I respected your opinion—against my better judgment," said Garrett. In truth, Landry had made keeping Matthew's staff together—especially Gabrielle—the major condition under which he would take the junior partner position, forcing Garrett to manipulate Cleve's opinion. It had been easy because Cleve didn't see that she had a computer for a brain. He expected smart women to be like Fiona—chip on her shoulder, nothing attractive about her. *But Gabrielle...* Garrett quickly brushed aside his burgeoning thoughts. "In addition to making sure that we keep abreast of new business, I need you to keep an eye on Gabrielle and Landry. I don't want them slacking off."

"I'll be happy to," Cleve said. "Can you clue me in further?"

Right on cue, the quid pro quo. Garrett leaned over his desk closer to Cleve and lowered his voice even more. "What do you know about the merger talks?"

"There are merger talks?"

"Yes," replied Garret. "Your ears only, so if I hear any talk on the floor, I'll know where it came from."

"You know I can keep my mouth shut," said Cleve.

Because of Cleve's tendency to let information slip while trying to paint himself as 'in the know', Garrett rarely trusted him with the whole truth. This time he used a blatant lie, intended to spur Cleve into action. "The party tendering the merger is very interested in the results of the analysis that Landry and Gabrielle are performing. Their failure to produce may cause the party to withdraw. We need to make sure they keep their heads down and get the job done—this is no time for half-ass mistakes."

"I'll do everything I can," Cleve vowed. "You can count on me."

"Thanks, Cleve. I really appreciate your support and discretion." Cleve performed best when rewarded, so Garrett tossed him a perk. "By the way, how about taking my reservations at Celeste's this Friday as a 'thank you'? Liz and I won't be able to make it. Shame to let them go to waste." *Liz'll be disappointed, but she'll get over it.*

Garrett stood and offered his hand, which Cleve fervently shook as he also rose. "Thanks, Garrett. I appreciate it."

After Cleve's departure, Garrett closed the door and resumed his pacing. Gabrielle and Landry were gone by twelve-thirty—but didn't take a car. Landry's condo was upstairs on one of the residential floors. It couldn't have taken that long to rehearse four slides. *What did they do, screw?* He hated when there was missing information. But, at least he could watch them from now on. Returning to his desk, he picked up his cell and hit another speed dial key. "This is customer 5487553," he said. "I need some surveillance work."

~*~~~**~~~*~

A few steps outside Garrett's suite, Cleve realized he had forgotten to mention that the files had to be copied out to Retro again. Looking back, he saw that the door to Garrett's inner suite was closed. He considered leaving a message with Elaine and then decided against it in case she wasn't aware of what they were doing. Congratulating himself on making a good decision, Cleve filed the incident away to mention later. With the other stuff going on, it probably wasn't that big of a deal.

~*~~~**~~~*~

Several hours had passed since Brett had talked to Garrett. The drumming fingers on the arm of his chair were the only outward sign of his displeasure. NEI knew about the bonds going bad. But they didn't know that he knew.

Avanti had ridden the wave until too many marginal mortgages went into default. Brett had expected that it was only a matter of time before those mortgages drove the bond market into recession, but according to Garrett it was heading into a tailspin...perhaps taking some of the stock market with it. If that happened, Avanti would not be in trouble; he had already sold off all their bonds—except the ones he was using for the buyouts. Brett congratulated himself for keeping the proceeds in Treasury notes. When the market bottomed out, Avanti would make a far greater killing than he had earlier anticipated.

Though he hadn't admitted it to Garrett, his merger gambit was finished. He hadn't intended to spend *real* money to buy NEI. He had merely wanted to sucker them into going for the deteriorating bonds; getting NEI for nothing—leaving Nathan empty-handed. At least he was still in play with the other corporations he had targeted—except those who were NEI clients. He would enlist his cousin to find out which ones were so that he could pressure them to accept the proposals before the bulletin came out. In the meantime, he would alert the Merger and Acquisitions division to accelerate their efforts across the board. When he got the client list, he would narrow their focus to just NEI clients. Brett picked up his desk phone and dialed. It was a short, terse call.

Instead of wasting time being disappointed about the failure of the merger maneuver, Brett concentrated on his new tactic of going after the hidden NEI app. It was obvious that Garrett didn't know about it. Evidently, he wasn't as trusted by Nathan as he thought. *That's his problem—I'm moving on.* Xalan Software's architecture team had already been primed. They couldn't wait to tear the app apart and figure out how it worked. If it was as good as it appeared, he wouldn't need NEI at all and would still have dealt them a crippling blow. *But what if I can't get it?* Brett left his chair and, from the stand beside his desk, retrieved his putter and a few balls. He randomly tossed out the balls, and then toed the ball returner from under his credenza to the middle of the floor. There was no sound in the office except that of the ball returner spitting out the ball after each putt.

Getting the app was too important to leave to a cousin he barely knew *and* who had proven that he could be bought. Brett did have a number he could call in the event he needed a 'clean-up crew'. It had been passed down to him by his father, who had gotten it from his father. Until now, he had only called once a year on a pre-arranged day and time to verify that it was still in operation. *Is the app important enough to use that number?* NEI dominated the analytics industry; its position assured by that app—the killer app. Brett decided. He had to have it. At any cost.

~*~~~**~~~*~

With Gabrielle comfortably settled into one of its sumptuous seats, the car eased out of Twelfth Street Tower garage and into the early evening rush hour traffic. The privacy glass separating her from Carson gave the illusion of solitude, but the silence in the passenger cabin did not lull her into restfulness. Instead, her mind raced through the events of the day. That morning, she had hoped to be wrong. Now, the only question was how bad the crash was going to be—something that would not be known for certain until afterwards. Gabrielle chafed at her inability to prevent more investors from being hurt. But no matter how certain her findings appeared, they were still only a forecast. As hard as it was to accept, Nathan was right about whom they could protect and how they should go about it.

Resigned, Gabrielle turned her thoughts toward her immediate next steps. Clearly, her first priority was convincing Sarah and Julie to liquidate their investments.

She also had to liquidate her mom's account. No need to ask; she fully trusted Gabrielle's judgment. Though they were not heavily invested in real estate, both accounts were small enough that a crash of the magnitude she had projected could wipe them out. In the single figure millions, they would also not cause even the tiniest ripple in the market as they sold off. To avoid being caught in the selloff action that they expected would result from the publication of the January Global Financial Stability Report, she decided to time the exit strategy to finish no later than the end of the year, giving them a little over three months to divest.

A cold spasm of realization heralded Gabrielle's second priority. She had to call Quentin, confess how badly she had erred, and beg him to advise her while she faced the consequences. Any chance of fair negotiations with NEI regarding Sparks might now be ruined. Landry had assured her that she had nothing to worry about, but it was hard to ignore Garrett's insistence that NEI assert its rights. Nathan's position on Sparks was a question mark—she had only Landry's word. It was folly to put her fate in the hands of a junior partner with only one day of experience, no matter how certain he seemed. She considered that calling Quentin should be her first priority; then decided against it. *That* situation was a done deal—whether she called now or later wouldn't affect the outcome.

Not a priority, but just because she hated starting something and then leaving it unfinished, Gabrielle decided to get the analysis of the changed files behind her before the real work started tomorrow. Left in Retro's main environment during business hours as these had been, the files could have affected a few analyses that got delivered to clients. She hadn't mentioned the changed files to Matthew—the issue was insignificant compared with the far more urgent cleanup he had ahead of him as IT senior partner. New technology and practices had overwhelmed Horace during his last few years in that position. He retired; but the word was that Nathan forced him out after the results of the independent IT readiness review. Good thing Matthew loved a challenge.

Satisfied that her immediate priorities were lined up, Gabrielle retrieved her phone from her backpack. Wondering if she could prevent Carson from listening in, she inspected the buttons on the console. They were unlabeled. *If he hears...he hears.* She called Julie, who was more likely to be home.

There wasn't a ring, but Julie picked up. "Where are you?" she demanded.

"On my way home from work," Gabrielle answered. "Something's come up—we need to talk about our investments. I want to move our money."

"Why?"

Gabrielle hesitated, searching for the words to frame her answer so that it would be truthful, but not alarming.

Julie didn't wait. "We can come over."

"Perfect," said Gabrielle. "I should be home in about twenty minutes. If you're hungry, I can call for takeout. There's nothing in the fridge."

"Don't worry about it. We'll pick something up on the way. You okay, Gabs? You didn't answer our calls—or tweet us back. You've never ig'ed us before."

"I'm so sorry. My phone's been in my backpack on vibe. When I called just now, I didn't think to look at my messages or voice mail. I just picked it up and dialed."

"Now you want to move our money...sounds scary."

"You have *no* idea," said Gabrielle. "I'll explain when I get there. See you in a few."

~*~~*~~**~~~*~

The car turned in to the Loft IV parking garage, pulling to a stop in the passenger loading zone for the residential elevators. Just as Gabrielle grabbed her backpack, Carson opened the door. "Oh., I didn't hear you get out."

Carson held out his hand to help her from the car. "My instructions are to make sure you get safely home, Ms. Winston," he said pleasantly.

"That's not necessary, Carson," replied Gabrielle. "Besides, you might get ticketed."

"I insist," he said, his voice courteous, but firm. "Don't worry about the car. I've made special arrangements."

Deciding not to argue, Gabrielle took the hand he offered and allowed him to help her out of the car. They approached the elevator, Carson keeping her positioned between himself and the wall; his intense blue eyes constantly flickering around the garage. Stepping into the elevator while he held the door, she again tried to excuse him. "Thank you, Carson."

"You are most welcome, Ms. Winston—but you aren't yet safely home." After one last visual sweep of the garage, Carson stepped into the elevator and pressed the button for her floor.

"You don't have to babysit me."

Carson smiled briefly, "Just following orders, ma'am."

Nice way of saying my orders don't matter. Wait a sec...ma'am? Maybe he's ex-military.

"I was also instructed to give you this." Gabrielle studied the card he placed in her hand. It wasn't a business card—there was no company name. "It's my name and phone number. You are to call whenever you need a driver. Mr. Wyatt hopes that you will use my services throughout this situation."

His words and demeanor were disturbingly out of place. Gabrielle reviewed the 'situation', and could not discern the event that led to his presence. She finally had to ask. "Why?"

Again he flashed a brief, barely-there smile. "That is a question for Mr. Wyatt."

The elevator stopped at the twelfth floor. A couple got on and Carson adroitly maneuvered himself between them and Gabrielle as everyone spoke polite hellos. Gabrielle expected Carson's uniform to attract more of their attention, but they were totally absorbed in each other. They left at the fourteenth floor. Making a point of repositioning herself toward the center of the elevator, she said, "Carson, I suspect you're not the average chauffeur." He merely winked. Gabrielle continued to mull over the puzzle of his presence, even after they stepped off the elevator at her floor.

At the condo door, he tensed and leaned his ear in closer, his hand on the knob. In an instant, his piercing eyes were trained on her. "I thought you lived alone."

Surprised by the intensity of his reaction, Gabrielle listened, but didn't hear anything. Then she put her ear to the door. She smiled in recognition. *At least that means he didn't hear our conversation.* "That's just Julie and Sarah."

"People have *keys* to your condo?" he asked, in what Gabrielle read as disapproval.

"Only Julie and Sarah," she answered. "We all have keys to each other's condos."

"Hmph," he said as she opened the door.

"Well, thanks," said Gabrielle.

"Not quite yet," said Carson, reaching past her to open the door wider. His gaze was resolute. "After you," he said, waving her in. Mainly to get it over with, Gabrielle turned and walked through the door.

"Hey girl," said Sarah as Gabrielle emerged from the foyer into the great room. Seated on the sectional just outside her office nook, she and Julie watched Gabrielle with expectant concern. "We brought...whoa...look what *you* brought!"

Caught off-guard by Sarah's shamelessly flirtatious reaction, Gabrielle had to remind herself that everything was still normal for her and Julie. Now standing beside Gabrielle, Carson had removed his hat and was tucking it under his arm. His white blonde hair, in a close buzz cut, was in stark contrast to his tanned complexion, intensifying the blue of his eyes. Reluctantly tearing her eyes away from his face to look at his card, Gabrielle said, "Carson...Hawthorne, this is Julie Carleton and this is Sarah Richard." Sarah still looked as though she had just found a new treat, but Julie was uncharacteristically silent. If anything, she looked more concerned. *Probably wondering what could be so bad that I need a bodyguard.*

Looking at each of them as if memorizing their faces, Carson said pleasantly, "Good evening, ladies." After their murmured replies, he turned to Gabrielle. "Please lock the door behind me." Leaving her backpack on the sectional, she followed him to the door. After he pulled the door closed behind him, Gabrielle pressed the lock, certain that he was listening for it.

"You are *so* going to spill." Sarah threatened as Gabrielle returned. "Who *was* that?"

"I'll fill you in on everything," Gabrielle promised as she retrieved her laptop from her backpack and snapped it in to the docking station. "But first things first..."

"Oh right—the reason we're here," said Sarah. "I forgot all about it when you walked in with 'tall, uniformed, and handsome.' Is he some sort of bodyguard? What did you do, Gabs—figure out how to get rid of the national debt?"

"I wish." Gabrielle said as the laptop booted up. "If NEI is right about what I've found, everybody's debt will be *far* worse." She beckoned them over to the desk. When they joined her, she cautioned them, "It's all strictly your ears only."

"Our lips are zipped," promised Sarah.

Julie only said, "Of course."

"Well, you know I missed the train this morning." Gabrielle filled them in on her day while pulling up the presentation on one of the monitors. She opened the roller coaster graph. "This is what it all means."

"What the hell is that?" asked Sarah as she leaned in closer.

"It shows that mortgage bonds are going to pull down companies invested in them; and those companies are going to pull even more companies and investors down and so on."

"*Un-believable,*" said Julie from just over Gabrielle's head. "It looks like crashing roller coasters."

"Exactly," replied Gabrielle.

"We're *screwed*," said Julie. "Do they think it will affect global markets?"

"Maybe," answered Gabrielle.

"Wow—just...geez," said Julie.

Sarah voiced her confusion. "Why would you keep it a secret? Wouldn't you want to tell as many people as possible so that they can protect themselves?"

"Because even though *we* are taking it very seriously, it's still just a forecast. It would be irresponsible to publicize it and start a panic. We could get sued—or worse, we could be wrong." Gabrielle paraphrased Nathan's directive. "But, as individuals, we can speak to other individuals and alert them. That's what I'm doing now with you. Then if you want to speak to someone else, please do, but not as a recommendation from NEI."

Julie asked, "Isn't that like insider trading?"

"No—we're not publically traded, and even if we were, this isn't information about NEI stock," explained Gabrielle.

"So you're wanting to act on what is basically a really good guess?" Julie persisted.

"That's about right," admitted Gabrielle. "I can always reinvest later if we're wrong."

"Which you doubt," added Julie.

"Which everybody I've talked to so far doubts," confirmed Gabrielle.

Sarah asked, "How later is 'later'?"

"There's a public financial report due out in January," she answered. "We need to wait and see what happens afterwards—I'd say about three months to be safe."

"What are we looking for?" asked Sarah.

"We're looking for the market to either stay the same or go up. As long as it trends downward, we stay out," replied Gabrielle.

"You're the investment manager, Gabs—so get us out," Julie acquiesced. "Honestly, I'm going to have nightmares about that graph. All those families..."

"Tell me about it. I see the damn thing every time I close my eyes. Sarah?"

"How can I disagree?" asked Sarah. "It scares the hell out of me, too. Your reasoning is sound, so the worst that can happen is we lose some profit."

"Okay then," Gabrielle said as she turned back to the monitors and accessed their online trading service. "I'm setting up a rule that will transfer us into Treasury notes two percent per day for the next fifty trading days. I'm pulling my Mom's money out, too."

"How *is* your Mom?" asked Sarah.

"Better now," said Gabrielle. "But you know she visited Dad's grave every day for months and cussed him out for leaving her. *So* glad it's finally behind her. She's vacationing with her sisters in Scotland for the next few weeks. I don't have to warn them—they're so distrustful of the market, they're only in CDs and Treasury notes."

"I'm glad your mom is moving past her grief," said Julie. "I know you were worried."

"Yeah, I was," Gabrielle said. "It's insane to yell at a grave." She completed the changes to the two accounts. "That's done. By the way, why haven't you two had dinner?" she asked, following Julie and Sarah back to the sectional. "It's late."

Sarah and Julie exchanged guilty glances. "We were at Julie's debating whether or not to call nine-one-one," Sarah answered. "We didn't really notice the time go by. We were so worried. Now we know why you went missing."

"How many times did you try to get me? I'm *so* sorry. I should wear my phone instead of carrying it in my backpack."

"We understand—really. It's not like it was a normal day," Julie assured her. "So what d'you think NEI's going to do about Sparks?"

"That's exactly what I was just wondering about," Gabrielle said. "Do you mind if I call Quentin? It shouldn't take too long—he's just going to yell at me and hang up."

"He's not going to do that," consoled Julie. "Call him. You know you have to."

"Yeah, Gabs," Sarah chimed in. "Man up."

Gabrielle made a face at Sarah as she fished her cell out of her backpack and dialed Quentin's private number. He picked up. "Hi Quentin, it's Gabrielle Winston. I know it's late, but have you got a moment?"

"I'm still at the office, so no worries," he responded. "What's up?"

"I messed up today..." She went on to explain the crisis.

"Sounds like you had a hell of a day. I won't comment on the situation you think is brewing, because that's not why you called," he said. "As your attorney, I'm obligated to say you should have called me first. However, it's obvious why you did what you did. Don't worry. I know Nathan and Landry well. Landry made promises about how NEI proposes to address the existence of Sparks, so I'm going with the premise that we can work something out."

Gabrielle let out a relieved sigh. "Thanks for not being mad at me."

Quentin laughed. "I'm your attorney—not your father." Another involuntary twinge of sadness stabbed at Gabrielle. "I don't get mad at my clients—bad for business," he continued. "Since you've given me a head's up, I can plan. You just need to make sure you go back to our policy. Don't make the mistake of thinking that since the cat's out of the bag, everything goes."

"Okay, I will—I mean I won't—well you know what I mean."

Quentin chuckled. "Just another few words of advice—stay calm and get your bearings. For the next few months, sounds like you'll have to be more alert than you've ever had to be."

"Thanks so much, Quentin. I really appreciate it," said Gabrielle. She saw a sudden swirl of movement in her peripheral vision. "Just a sec, I think Jules wants to talk to you."

"All right," he said. Wondering why he sounded displeased, Gabrielle handed Julie the phone.

Julie rose from the sectional and wandered along the windows toward the fireplace. "Hi Quentin, I wanted to see if you had time..." Gabrielle tuned out and dropped down beside Sarah.

"Want some Chardonnay?" she asked, holding up the half empty bottle.

"Better not—not now anyway," said Gabrielle. "Save me a glass though. I've got some work left to do tonight. Odd—having it while I work doesn't bother me, but having it before usually means that I don't."

"I don't envy you—working tonight. I want to get that graph out of my head so I can sleep," said Sarah, taking another sip.

"Good luck with that."

Julie returned to her spot and handed Gabrielle the phone. "Thanks." Gabrielle clipped it into the holster at her belt.

"Now can we move on to Mr. Carson Hawthorne?" Sarah asked. "I've been dying to ask—what's he to do with you?"

CHAPTER FIVE

Confessions

Julie answered. "He's a personal protection agent from ISS."

Astounded, Gabrielle asked, "A what? From where?"

"What's ISS?" Sarah wanted to know.

"International Security Services," Julie replied, leaving the sectional and pacing in front of them. "It's a personal security agency."

"And you know that...how?" Gabrielle asked.

"Because...," Julie's voice trailed off as she nervously toyed with her hands. "I should have told you..."

Reassuring her, Gabrielle said, "Jules, we'll understand."

Sarah took a direct tack. "Just spit it out."

"My name isn't just Julie Carleton," she said hesitantly, her extreme agitation far different from the cool composure to which Gabrielle was accustomed. "It's Julie Carleton San Chapelle." Fear tugged at Julie's expression as she waited for their response.

"So that's it," said Sarah. "I knew there was something."

"There was obviously more than you let on," said Gabrielle.

"What do you mean?" asked Julie.

""I didn't know exactly *what* it was, but you're a buyer for Charleston Eddy's." said Sarah. "I'm sure it pays well, but twenty-eighth floor, three-bedroom suite, penthouse condo well?"

"Even sharing your employee discount, we can't afford to buy the things that you buy," Gabrielle added.

"And who gets art for gifts? My family sends me things I need—not paintings and sculptures, added Sarah, "and—"

"Okay, okay I get it." Julie gave a hesitant smile. "Then you're not mad?"

"Don't be silly," said Sarah. "Actually I'm relieved—I thought you were about to tell us you were on the lam and Carson was on your trail."

Gabrielle asked. "How do you know Carson?"

Blushing from embarrassment, Julie said, "He's on the same yachting team as two of my brothers."

"Yachting team?" interrupted Sarah. "People *race* those big boats?"

"A different kind of yacht, Sarah. Quentin, Landry, and Drew Kreft make up the six."

"Landry Wyatt?" Gabrielle asked incredulously. *I guess that's why Landry, Quentin, and Carson are all so beautifully tanned.*

"Yes, but I didn't know you two worked together until today. You only ever talked about Matthew and Garrett," Julie explained.

"I just started working for Landry today," Gabrielle said. Within the space of a few minutes, her two separate worlds had linked themselves together. "This is bizarre."

"Nuh-uh," contradicted Sarah, beaming at Julie. "It's better than the soaps. What else is there?"

"Don't tease, Sarah," Julie pleaded, tucking her blonde hair behind her ears. "I love you two and I don't want to lose your friendship...but I have to let the others tell their own stories."

"We'll just go with it, Jules," Gabrielle assured her. "It's not like—"

Sarah cut in laughing, "Don't worry. We'll just blackmail you for higher discounts at Charley's." Her laughter abruptly cut off as she eyed Julie appraisingly. "Wow—a real live San Chapelle. I wonder what the kidnap rate is for one of you?"

"Oh, stop it," said Julie, smiling in spite of herself. Then her expression sobered and she asked hesitantly, "Would you mind coming up to Skye Pointe with me on

Saturday? I've wanted to ask you for a long time. Some of the others will be there—they're sailing."

Gabrielle could not hide her surprise. *Mind? We're not idiots.*

"Hmm, let me check my calendar." Sarah held up an imaginary planner, turning the pages. "Sorry Jules—I seem to be booked that day." The last words were almost incoherent as she struggled to keep a straight face. She lost the battle, her laughter infecting Julie and Gabrielle.

"Hope you're wired," Gabrielle said. "I may have to work a little. Where on Skye Pointe?"

"Coral Cove. We've got you covered—public facing structured wiring with local wireless," assured Julie.

What the hell? I didn't know she speaks geek. At that moment, her stomach growled—loudly. Embarrassed, she glanced at Sarah and Julie. "Sorry, what'd you get to eat? I'm starved."

"We can tell," said Sarah. "How about noodle bowls from Toshi's? It's set up on the bar. We forgot about it when you walked in with Carson."

"Perfect," replied Gabrielle, nearly running to the bar.

"By the way," said Julie as she and Sarah joined Gabrielle at a more leisurely pace, "Carson's not just a body guard." She paused, waiting for their comments, but Gabrielle and Sarah just stared. "A personal protection agent is more than that."

"You have *got* to be kidding." Sarah straddled a bar stool, looking at Julie expectantly.

"Now we're a few degrees past bizarre," Gabrielle sighed. "You mean there're different types of bodyguards? What's a personal protection agent?"

"I don't know all of the right terms, but I know by his uniform that he's licensed to carry concealed weapons and run his own surveillance. His car is probably tricked out with his preferred security gadgets and other stuff. He's like a personal security manager."

"You mean," said Gabrielle as Julie climbed onto a stool. "The car Carson's driving doesn't belong to Landry?"

"Most likely not," said Julie. "And it's at least armored, got encrypted Wi-Fi and GPS tracking."

"Ah, hell. This *is* a bad spy movie," Gabrielle said. "Why could Landry possibly think I need all that protection? The market isn't going to rise up and come after me."

"Gabs, you know the market. There's always a few who gain on widespread loss," said Julie.

"That's true," Gabrielle allowed. "So what?"

"Maybe some big player who's making tons of money off the mortgage situation just might get upset at being found out."

"They're *investors*," said Gabrielle. "Not organized crime."

"Something's at stake," insisted Julie. "Carson's not just a babysitter."

"Could be another reason Landry's being really careful with you," Sarah mused. "You think it's business only?"

"Oh, Sarah. Of course," said Gabrielle. "He's about ten years older, and today he was mentoring me like I was a student trainee."

"Seven," interrupted Julie.

"So now we're throwing out random numbers?"

"He's only *seven* years older. The same as my brother," Julie explained.

"Still, why would an executive hotshot with his own James Bond be interested in me? Besides, I'm a whole foot shorter than he is. You should have seen him trying to fit into my office nook today. Looked like the Jolly Green Giant visiting Lilliput."

Julie looked exasperated. "You should know that doesn't matter."

Gabrielle said quietly, "But he's even *taller* than Stephen."

"Ancient history," said Sarah, waving off Gabrielle's statement and throwing Julie a disapproving glance. "As far as Landry's concerned, you're still cute, and he can cuddle you on his lap. I don't see the problem."

"I'm insulted." Gabrielle laughed. "What the hell am I—a stuffed toy? I don't think he's into cute and cuddly."

Sarah was not deterred. "You've got boobs. That's a different kind of cuddly."

Glaring at Sarah, Gabrielle just shook her head. Julie was trying very hard not to laugh. "Go ahead and let it out, Jules, before you give yourself an aneurism."

Julie laughed—loudly.

"What's so funny?" asked Sarah.

Recovering, Julie said, "Gabby's just told us that crashing financial roller coasters are about to pulverize us all and you're talking about boobs."

"I get that a disaster is coming—and that we're lucky to be able to protect ourselves from it. What *you* don't get that is that it's no time to be alone—as we all are." Sarah corrected smugly. "So no—I'm not talking about boobs. I'm talking about Landry's interest in Gabs."

Torn between amusement and frustration, Gabrielle insisted, "There isn't any!"

"Say you," Sarah calmly replied.

"So where are we going tomorrow?" asked Gabrielle, abruptly changing the subject.

"Good one, Gabs. I'll allow myself to be distracted." Sarah's face lit up. "I wanted it to be a surprise, and it still will be. I'm just telling you tonight instead of tomorrow night. We're going to the Vennergy reunion tour launch party!"

"No way!" exclaimed Julie loudly. "They're doing a reunion tour?"

"Wow!" Gabrielle said. "You landed *them?*"

Sarah jumped down off the stool and launched into a happy dance. "It's going to be so much fun! I'm not going to tell you any more—I don't want to ruin it for you."

"No way you can ruin it—no matter how much you tell us," said Julie. She glanced at her watch. "*Darn it!* Gabs, it's almost ten. How much work do you have to do tonight?"

"How did you know I have work to do?" asked Gabrielle, wincing at the reminder. *I know I told Sarah, but I hadn't mentioned it to Julie.*

"You always do," replied Julie.

"Guess I don't have a life," sighed Gabrielle. "Hopefully just a couple hours worth. You can see how excited I am to get started."

"We'd better leave then," said Sarah. "Not going to blame us if you don't get it done."

"I could probably find a way," mused Gabrielle.

"Behave, you two," admonished Julie. "Gabs, if you can figure out what you want to wear tomorrow night, I'll take it with me. You might not make it up to my condo before we take the train in the morning."

"I didn't think of that. Thanks," said Gabrielle. They followed Gabrielle into her bedroom and flopped onto the bed. Gabrielle opened her closet and looked through the racks, ripping the dry cleaner bags off as she went. "Is it dressy, casual, or what?" she asked.

"It's Vennergy," said Sarah, laughing. "There *is* no attire—everything goes."

"Well, what are you wearing then?"

"Don't go by me—I'll be working," Sarah answered.

"Anything goes...anything goes..." Gabrielle searched through the hangers before she finally chose green leggings and an oversized, multi-colored, shimmery silk top. "What about this?"

"That works," said Sarah. "What shoes?"

"I usually want to wear flats," said Gabrielle. "But, what about these?" She held up a pair of dark purple, stack-heeled pumps.

"Perfect," said Julie. She took the hangers and shoes from Gabrielle. "We'll see you tomorrow. Please try to get a good night's sleep," she said, concern breaking into her voice. "You look like you've had a helluva day."

"Yeah, you do look raw," agreed Sarah. "You know we worry about you. You work too hard. And that Garrett person—"

Gabrielle walked them to the door and stared wistfully after them as they walked down the hall, waving as they got onto an elevator. Then mindful of Carson's last words, she closed and carefully locked the door.

~*~~~**~~~*~

It had been a helluva day. Landry welcomed the respite. Relaxing in the oversized wing chair by the fireplace with his legs propped on its ottoman, he took a draught from his snifter of single malt. The outlook was not good for Nathan's trip up to Wall Street. Though most had hedged when he called, NEI's sizable holdings carried weight, and in the end, each executive he contacted had elected to see him. While he attended his full slate of meetings, NEI partners faced a frenzied day readying a plan for his return. There would surely be more frenzied days ahead during execution of the plan that won his approval.

Landry's thoughts of tomorrow sparked memories of his day with Gabrielle. A ghost of a smile lightened his expression as he imagined her beside him. *I'm kidding myself. She wouldn't be beside me. I would have her in my arms. Holding her, kissing her, loving her...*

He again raised the snifter to his lips, this time to ease his frustration. Those were thoughts he couldn't indulge, especially after today. She looked so broken this morning. His first impulse had been to blame Garrett, sure he had harmed her somehow. *Stupid. If he had, why would she come to me? She doesn't know what I feel for her. I can't let her know.* "Not yet."

Every time even a hint of worry crossed her face, he had felt driven to tangle his hands into her curls and pull her to his chest. Then there was that damn comb.

Touching her had been a mistake. It had taken *all* of his control to keep himself in check. They would be working closely together to address this crisis. He had to keep their relationship a purely professional one. It wouldn't do for the new junior partner to be caught screwing his star analyst. *That's not the way it would be for me—for us—but that's how it would look. That's why Garrett jumped to the wrong conclusion this morning.*

Taking another swallow of whiskey, he watched the city lights flicker on in the growing darkness. If only the problem Gabrielle had brought to him was as simple to solve as an issue with Garrett. Instead, it was potentially so disastrous it could stress or even crack the foundations of the financial system. There was a mad—yet clandestine—scramble among NEI executive management to protect themselves, their families, friends, and as many more as would heed their subtle urgings. The protection of NEI employees rested on the moves Larry was making to preserve the portfolio. Maybe the official bulletins might reach an even broader audience than just their clients. He and Nathan were liquidating their vulnerable investments and reinvesting the returns in more shares of SCI. It was a private safety net; however Nathan and Josh were working to develop a more inclusive solution. No matter the extent of their efforts, there would be far more harmed than protected or forewarned. His melancholy thought was punctuated by the ringing of his cell phone. Reluctantly, Landry left his comfortable position to retrieve it from the fireplace mantle. It was Jarin.

"Yeah man, what's up?"

"Nathan said you could fill me in on Sparks."

"Ah." Landry spent the next few minutes briefly outlining the events of the day; then highlighting what he understood of Sparks. "It has adaptive and predictive algorithms, which Gabrielle used for investment analysis."

"Predictive and adaptive?" Jarin asked. "Sounds like it can be used across multiple industries, not just different scenarios within a single industry."

"Exactly. But it doesn't eliminate the need for highly educated personnel. It just broadens their effectiveness. Otherwise, it's like any other app, garbage in—garbage out."

"True," agreed Jarin. "You have *no* idea how many assholes come through my office trying to pitch 'infallible' apps."

"Hope you take it easy on them," chuckled Landry.

"Why should I? Some days, toying with them is the only fun I get to have."

"Toying?" Landry laughed outright. "If that's what you want to call it."

"It's deserved," Jarin insisted. "First, for wasting my time; second, for presuming their brilliance is beyond my comprehension."

"I've seen a few after you're done with them—not a nice way to treat your toys."

It was Jarin's turn to laugh. "I only need to play with them once. But, back to Sparks—what do you think of Nathan's plan for Gabrielle to sell it to SCI?"

"Is that what he's thinking? I hadn't talked to him about details," Landry said. "It makes sense now that you mention it. Sparks never belonged to NEI."

"That was his reasoning. He wants to make the transfer of it a separate agreement, not contingent on the merger."

"Gabrielle would have to go too. At least on loan for a while."

"Just want to be sure it's okay with you. I know she's on your staff."

"Actually," said Landry, "I think it would be best for her to stay at SCI—she'll get to use her skills across multiple industries."

"Glad you see it that way. Sounds like a plan."

"It's settled, then," agreed Landry. "By the way, any exposures on your end?"

"Only in Joseph's sector and just in the bonds themselves. He never trusted the more exotic types of instruments," answered Jarin. "Good thing Ms. Winston found it."

"Damn good thing. Still, we'll be up to our asses in alligators for the next few months. Maybe even years."

"We're taking the position that, worse case, it could be years," said Jarin. "Gotta run—it's Estelle's birthday. You coming up for the weekend?"

"Aren't we sailing?"

"If the weather holds."

"See ya Saturday then." Landry's mood lightened as he disconnected the call. The disaster still loomed, but if Gabrielle agreed to Nathan's plan, he would be free to declare himself. Neither of them would have to face the crisis alone.

~*~~*~~~*~

Using the Virtual Private Network—or VPN—connection to the NEI network, Gabrielle checked the progress of the analyses she had earlier started in the two Retro test environments. Only the first few had completed. A quick review of the two sets of results showed that they were wildly different. That in itself came as no surprise. It was typical for 'what-if' scenarios; the point of which was to inject change into a copy of the original system and then analyze how the results of the copy differed from the results of the original. She was, however, still worried that the changed files had been found in the main environment. There was nothing to tell the analysts that Retro was running on the wrong files.

Gabrielle preferred not to trust Cleve's team to investigate the issue, and it would be irresponsible to leave it for later. But there wasn't time for the two sets of comparisons that she had earlier decided on. Retro was too slow. The fastest way to determine whether reports had been compromised was to pull some of Retro's completed ones from the NEI archive and rerun them on Sparks, utilizing its speed advantage. The results would surely be available by morning, but she would be violating a long-standing, partner-approved NEI directive against removing confidential documents from the premises. *Not like Garrett's edict. What do I do? It's too late to call anyone.*

Gabrielle pushed away from the desk and leaned back in her chair. Facing the southern window wall, she had an unobstructed view of the starry late-night sky. The lighted monitors below her line of sight enhanced the illusion of being in a cockpit. *Except for the glass of Chardonnay in my hand. At least, I hope pilots don't drink while they're flying.*

As she weighed the options, her cell vibrated. A quick glance down at the desktop clock confirmed that it was eleven-thirty, the time that Stephen had always called. She unsnapped her phone and checked the display. *I won't answer. But the crisis... I have to let him know.* Reluctantly, she connected the call.

"I was afraid you wouldn't answer."

"I didn't answer for personal reasons, Stephen," interrupted Gabrielle, keeping her tone formal. "There's a situation I need to make you aware of..." She explained the crisis.

"You can't be serious," he said.

"It's your choice to believe me or not."

"Can you share any evidence?"

"Afraid I can't," she replied. "Guess I wasted my time sharing this with you."

"No—I'm glad you did," he said. "But, I'd rather take it to my management with proof."

"Your firm is an NEI subscriber, so they'll be getting a subtle hint in a bulletin that's due out in a couple of days. That'll be all the proof NEI can provide."

"But Gabby, for old time's sake..."

"I answered your call for old time's sake, Stephen."

"Well I...thank you," he said.

"You're welcome."

"Gabby, if this is true you shouldn't have to face it alone. Let me h—"

"No Stephen. You closed that door," Gabrielle reminded him. "I'm keeping it closed." She ended the call. Having lost her line of reasoning and now running out of time, she abandoned the effort to weigh the risks versus the benefits of her actions and pulled twenty of Retro's completed reports from the archive onto her laptop. She then converted the setup files to Sparks' format, submitted the analyses to Sparks, and verified that the first one was running properly. After that, she quickly showered and went to bed. But irrepressible thoughts of the mortgage defaults, the changed files, and Stephen made sleep impossible. Still, she had to get some rest. Landry was counting on her.

The bottle of prescription-strength pain medication in her medicine cabinet was left from last year when she'd sprained her ankle biking with Stephen. *Everything is about Stephen. Maybe I also need to get rid of this damn bed.* Throwing off the covers, she went into the bathroom for a couple of the capsules. Back in her room, she chased them down with the remains of the Chardonnay from the goblet that was still on her nightstand. Then she clambered back into bed, closed her eyes, and hoped for dreamless sleep.

~*~~~**~~~*~

Wide awake, Landry followed his usual remedy of walking the NEI analysts' floor. The twenty-four-hour staff were rarely on this floor and he had it to himself. Only the occasional, soothing whirr of a disk drive interrupted the silence. Along with the whiskey, the solitude helped to quiet his other thirsts. His pace slowed as he relaxed. Finding himself at his closed office door, he turned and leaned against it, staring out across the open floor at the eastern city skyline. He swallowed *the last of the whiskey.*

Garrett is going to attack—that much is clear. Gabrielle has to be protected; she's not prepared for that level of engagement. Got to keep her and Sparks beyond his reach, especially if he becomes managing partner. He's not the right person to lead NEI. Got to take him down—for all our sakes. And I wonder why she calls it Sparks...

~*~~~**~~~*~

Sudden loud music jolted Gabrielle upright, searching frantically for its source. *What the hell?* It was the alarm clock: five am. She leaned over and silenced it, the slight movement unexpectedly making her light-headed. She lurched toward the bathroom, dizziness and the urge to retch threatening to overtake her. Shoving open the door to the toilet, she bent over it just as spasms of dry heaves hit. She sank to her knees in front of the bowl and held on until the convulsions subsided.

I'm an idiot. Last time, waking up wasn't nearly this bad. But I was seven years younger then, in grad school trying to finish Sparks. She had sworn never again to mix pain relievers with alcohol. But she had badly needed the sleep. Gabrielle leaned back against the open door. *Can't stay here. Gotta get up.* Using the doorjamb for support, she pulled herself unsteadily to her feet. Still reeling, she staggered to the counter top and reluctantly raised her eyes to the mirror. They were crusty with heavy sleep; her cheeks were stained with the tracks of too-salty tears. *Scary.* And she felt worse than she looked. Her eyes began to sting, but no tears fell. She couldn't afford to be dehydrated.

Stumbling her way from the bathroom, Gabrielle made it through the bedroom and the great room to the kitchen. She grabbed a glass from the drying rack and filled it with cold water from the refrigerator door. She downed it greedily, followed by two more. Her stomach started to heave again and she quickly bent over the sink. Gradually, the urge subsided. More weakened than before, she laid out across the counter. *Mmmm, feels good.* She turned her head over to feel the cool granite against her other cheek. *Can't stay here—got to move.* Forcing herself up, she filled her glass again with water. This time, she drank more slowly as she weaved her way back to the bathroom.

Landry expected her to lead the team today. *Looks like I'm off to a good start. Follow the zombie leader.* And before she left, she needed to review the results of the analyses she'd been running. Gabrielle started the shower, steeled herself, and stepped in. Needing to feel the sting of the cold water on her skin, she peeled off her sleep shirt and tossed it over the wall into the tub, making herself dizzy again. Gasping and shuddering, she held herself under the cold spray as long as she could take it. Then she shut off the shower and got out, wrapping herself in a towel from the towel warmer. In front of the mirror, shivering, she examined her reflection again. At least she now looked human. Her eyes were still red, but she could clear them up with eye drops.

Desperately in need of a sounding board, she had no one. Her father had gone beyond her reach. *So has Stephen.* Tears started to well up again, but she held them back. The last thing she needed was to make her eyes more bloodshot.

~*~~~**~~~*~

The second trip to the kitchen was worth it. Gabrielle had made cold compresses for her eyes and found food. She placed the compresses on the credenza and then, leaning against it, quickly shoveled in the last few forkfuls of the leftover noodle bowl. The change was immediate and dramatic. Tentatively, she moved her head from side to side, relieved to find the queasiness waning. It was already past 5:30 and she had made 6:30

her deadline. Leaving the bowl on the credenza, Gabrielle sat in front of her monitors and clicked them on.

The fastest way to highlight where to focus her attention was to expose the differences between each set of Retro and Sparks analysis files. She pulled up the first Sparks analysis on the left monitor, side-by-side with its Retro counterpart. Then she ran a difference utility, directing the output to the right monitor. If the analyses were identical, the output of the difference utility would be empty. *It's not.* At least one bad analysis had gone out. Reviewing the differences, Gabrielle saw that Sparks had recommended a local vendor for ergonomics expertise and Retro had recommended a company named Carruthers. That recommendation resulted in a twenty-six percent inflation in cost.

She examined the next set. The Retro version in that set also had erroneous results, this time recommending Blackhawk instead of a local company for a long-haul transportation partner. *I analyzed Blackhawk. No way it should be recommended. There are no checks and balances and they didn't want to change.* Working with them would cost the client an additional twenty-nine percent. Hurriedly, she created a spreadsheet and filled it with the results she had so far. Her anxiety ratcheted up as she worked. In each analysis, Sparks had recommended local partners; Retro recommended the same local partners in only two of its analyses. The other eighteen recommended Blackhawk when a company needed long-haul transportation; Xalan, when they needed a software development partner; and Carruthers when they needed ergonomics expertise. Recommendations of those companies as partners increased a client's partnering costs by as much as thirty-five percent. *Time to study the changes in the Retro files.*

Gabrielle's eyes began to burn. Frustrated, she grabbed the cold compresses and slapped them on. Using one hand to apply the compresses to her eyes, and the other one to type, she engaged VPN, downloaded the application files from both test environments to her laptop, and ran them through the difference utility. To her relief, only the partner specification file was different. Laying both compresses aside, she opened up the file and immediately saw the problem. Someone had changed the logic to specify those three companies when their area of expertise was required.

Why didn't my test catch this? She looked further. Within seconds, the reason was clear. This wasn't a 'what if' scenario put in the wrong environment by mistake. Whoever did it *meant* to throw business to those companies. *He or she gamed my test.* Landry's reaction of yesterday now didn't seem so out of place. She had just found what he had apparently suspected was there. *I've done it again.* Just like yesterday, she had unexpectedly found a serious problem while ignoring NEI rules.

There was no way to dodge the bullet this time. She had gone against a written NEI directive, on Page 2 of the New Employee manual as well as in her contract. But twenty reports, when NEI typically released twenty-five per month, was a very small sample.

We need more data. My situation can't get any worse. May as well go the distance. Gabrielle retrieved thirty more reports from the NEI archive, converted the set up files to Sparks' format, and started Sparks. The analyses would finish in the afternoon and she would have more data points to give them before they kicked her out.

The burn in her eyes prompted her to again reach for the compresses. Alternating hands, she made sure that Sparks was running correctly and that she had all the materials she needed on her laptop. Then she powered it down. *Almost 6:30.* Another day that she wouldn't be riding into the city with Julie and Sarah.

The only person I should see right now is Landry. She smiled wryly as she thought of Carson. *And my personal protection agent.* First she tweeted Julie and Sarah, "Go on without me again." Then, she TM'ed Landry, "I'm coming in around seven—problem with Retro." Lastly, she called Carson's number.

He picked up. "Yes, Ms. Winston?"

"I'm sorry to wake you," she said.

"I wasn't asleep—and besides, that's what I'm here for."

"I'm going in to the office in half an hour," said Gabrielle. "I could take the train, but would you drive me?"

"Of course," he said. "I'll be at your door in half an hour."

"I'll come down," she said. "I need to stop in at the drugstore for some eye drops."

"Do not come down," Carson instructed, "I'll be at your door in half an hour—with eye drops. You did the right thing by calling me."

Sure I did. You'll probably be the one Landry tells to toss my ass out onto the street.

~*~~~**~~~*~

Carson was prompt. The doorbell chimed exactly thirty minutes later. "What the *hell* did you do?" he demanded as soon as she opened the door.

"I had a bad night."

"That is an understatement," he said scathingly, closing the door behind him. "There's more to it than that." Gabrielle held her silence. "I can wait," he said, leaning back against the closed door, his gaze unwavering.

Gabrielle met his gaze for a few moments longer, but then had to look away. "I've found something wrong at NEI."

"That's a start. What's the rest of it?" Refusing to be bullied, Gabrielle tightened her lips. After several minutes, Carson relented. He held out his hand and opened it. "Here's the eye drops," he said. "They're stronger than anything you can get in a drugstore. Only one drop in each eye."

"Thank you," she said gratefully, taking the bottle from his hand.

After she had turned toward the guest bathroom, he said, "Perfect for covering up an episode of over-medication." Gabrielle glanced quickly at him, giving herself away.

Acknowledging her gaffe, he said, "It's obvious for anyone who can read the signs."

"I couldn't sleep."

"That's no excuse," he said sharply. Then more softly, "You have enough problems without making more for yourself. Go on, fix yourself up."

Gabrielle closed the bathroom door behind her and stared at her reflection. *I feel like such an ass. He probably thinks I'm about to crack. Am I?*

~*~~~**~~~*~

The car pulled out of the Loft IV garage. The cityscape sped by as Carson maneuvered it through the wakening streets. Certain that she was taking her last ride in the employ of NEI, Gabrielle wanted desperately to discover how the file got changed, but she knew she wasn't likely to get the chance. The failure of her test had caused NEI to send inferior, costly recommendations to clients.

There was nothing left to plan. *All that remains now is the execution—probably mine.* She relaxed into the cushions and closed her eyes, grateful to have even the shortest amount of time to rest them. Gradually, as the drops took effect, the itchiness and tightness subsided.

Too soon, Carson pulled into the Twelfth Street Tower parking garage and cut the engine. Gabrielle got out of the car, parked as before in a loading zone; this time adjacent to a small square building. The odd, windowless building, barely larger than NEI's executive conference room, sparked Gabrielle's curiosity. "Why is there a building without windows in a dark garage?"

"It's a guard shack," Carson replied. "No windows because there are monitors inside for real-time viewing of the security camera feeds. Too bad the monitors aren't manned. Twelfth Street Tower occupants aren't willing to give up their privacy."

"I remember, Landry told me about the cameras," said Gabrielle. "By the way, this isn't the way to the elevators we used yesterday."

"We're going to one of the executive suites private elevators. You key in and it'll take you to up to the office suite that matches the key," said Carson as they reached the octagonal elevator bank. He inserted a key in the console and turned it. "We're going to Nathan's office."

Nathan's office? So this is the end. Carson obviously isn't going to let me make a run for it. Carson positioned Gabrielle between himself and the wall, and his eyes roamed the garage.

"Interesting," he said, very softly.

"What?" asked Gabrielle, squinting to see what had caught his attention.

He didn't respond, but continued to scrutinize the garage as they entered the elevator. Once the door closed, he focused on Gabrielle. "Whatever you've found, Ms. Winston, you cannot—*must not*—try to handle it alone."

Disconcerted by his intensity, Gabrielle said, "Why? What do you care?"

"Just listen to me—tell them *everything*. Do you understand?"

If he's here to help me, someone thinks I'm important enough to protect. But if he's here to make sure I don't run for it...I'm toast. She decided to trust her instincts. "I understand."

His expression smoothed and he flashed his barely-there smile. "Good." The elevator stopped in Nathan's suite and the door opened. Carson checked his watch as Gabrielle got out. "Seven-forty. I'll be back toward the end," he said as the door closed.

The end of what? He never answers my questions, just gives me more. Gabrielle turned away from the elevator and saw that the usually clear windows of Nathan's outer office were opaque, as were those of the inner one. Not a good sign. The last time she'd seen them that way was just before Horace announced his resignation. She knocked at the closed door of Nathan's inner office. *Time to pay the piper.*

CHAPTER SIX

It Gets Personal

"Come in," said Nathan. Wondering who Carson had meant by "them", Gabrielle apprehensively opened the door and went in, closing it behind her. Only Nathan and Landry were here, seated at the conference table, talking quietly. Though apparently discussing a matter from different viewpoints, their interchange resembled a debate more than an argument.

Uneasily, Gabrielle approached them. Landry, whom she had never seen less than completely in control, looked ragged. Nathan's expression revealed nothing, but the atmosphere felt strained. Stopping behind one of the chairs, she set her backpack on the table and said, "Good morning." It felt like a ridiculously trivial thing to say.

"Good morning," Nathan answered. "I understand you have something to tell us?"

Profoundly relieved that Garrett was not joining them, Gabrielle forged ahead. "Yes. May I set up my laptop? It will be easier to show you."

"By all means," Nathan said.

While powering up the laptop, Gabrielle said, "We're to start working on your plan for avoiding the crash today, but yesterday we found a problem with Retro when I was running through the client analysis with Landry."

"What kind of problem?" Nathan asked.

"The results didn't match what I had gotten with Sparks," she said. Despite his haggard appearance, Landry had become attentive and focused. "I ran a comparison test in Retro's test environment yesterday; and another on Sparks last night."

Abruptly, Landry challenged her. "How could you? The files are on my laptop."

Feeling a further flush of anxiety, Gabrielle explained, "I also copied them onto my thumb drive."

Landry relaxed. "Of course you did."

"Please, continue," said Nathan.

"I compared the results of the Retro versus Sparks' tests this morning, and they were very different," she said.

"You got analyses from the archive to run on Sparks?" asked Landry.

"Yes," she admitted. "I know that I shouldn't have accessed them, but I needed analyses that Retro had already run so that I could have results by this morning."

Again Nathan said, "Continue."

Landry's responses bordered on hostility, but Nathan's lack of emotion rattled Gabrielle more. She returned to the story. "Eighteen of the twenty reports I ran on Sparks showed that Retro had made erroneous conclusions, with the same three recommended companies when the area of expertise matched theirs. Only two had good conclusions."

"How can that have happened?" Landry demanded.

"The partner selection file was modified to override the selection logic for their area of expertise," she hastily explained. "The erroneous analyses have already been submitted to clients, partnering them with inferior vendors and increasing their implementation costs. I'm very sorry, Nathan. This is my fault. The analyses went out because my test was not robust enough. The file had also been modified to fool it."

"Your fault?" asked Nathan, his voice still neutral. "Did you change the file?"

"No, but—"

"Gabrielle, your sense of responsibility is admirable." Nathan said as he leaned back and crossed his legs. "I can see that you violated a rule or two during your investigation—something that would not normally have been brought to my attention. So, those infractions are a matter between you and Landry. That said; please don't get into the habit of blaming yourself for someone else's actions. I'm not looking for a martyr. I need answers."

For the second time, Gabrielle felt profound relief. But what she felt was at odds with the grave expression Nathan now wore. Something was still disturbingly awry. To alleviate the tension, she sought to give him some preliminary answers. "I do have some initial findings."

"Oh?" Landry moved to the chair next to Gabrielle's laptop. "What did you find?"

Gabrielle sat at the laptop and opened the comparison spreadsheet as Nathan came to look over her other shoulder. "It's simply a list of the results from Retro compared with those from Sparks. Retro only recommended Blackhawk, Carruthers, and Xalan when clients were looking for their type of expertise. In most cases, Sparks recommended a local firm. I've also started thirty more analyses running on Sparks. They'll be done sometime this afternoon. I'll have a sample of fifty, which is almost two month's worth."

As Gabrielle turned toward Landry, he looked up at Nathan; his face the embodiment of fury. Shaken, she thought back to her explanation, for the source of this latest hostile reaction. Abruptly leaving the chair, Landry approached the window garden, where he stood, hands in his pockets, head bowed. Hearing Nathan moving behind her, Gabrielle turned to see him pacing between the table and his desk. *What the hell?*

As if he had heard her, Landry said, "Gabrielle, please understand—my anger is not directed at you. It's what your findings confirm." His eyes found Nathan.

"We must tell Gabrielle everything regarding this situation," Nathan said. "Ignorance makes her vulnerable. We shall *not* allow her to become a casualty of this conflict."

"You make it sound like we're at war," Gabrielle said.

Scowling, Nathan confirmed, "A war within a war." Landry turned back to the garden. "We are in the same situation as everyone else as far as the market crash is concerned, except that forewarned, we're all most likely scrambling to save ourselves, our families, and as many others as we can. Unlike the world at large, we're also faced with losing our company to a hostile takeover—facilitated from within. The situation is localized to just NEI, but from our perspective, it is potentially just as financially devastating."

"Great," Gabrielle murmured. "If the great white sharks don't get us, the piranhas will."

"Not quite the way I would put it, but appropriate." Nathan sat beside Gabrielle in the chair that Landry had vacated. Landry returned to stand behind him as he spoke. "Unfortunately my dear, you stand in the eye of the two concentric storms."

Gabrielle tried to keep up with the rapidly changing metaphors. "What does that mean?"

Landry answered, "It means that you are every bit as much a target as Nathan and I."

"*You?* Why are you a target?"

"NEI was founded fifty-five years ago by Nathan's father—my grandfather. Nathan is my uncle."

~*~~~**~~~*~

At the desk in his study, Brett reviewed the "Honey Do" list Roxanne had brought in with his breakfast. Though not quite October, she was ramping up for their annual Christmas Party. It was a tradition that they had taken over from his parents years ago, when his oldest was just a toddler. Roxanne's list held token things she always asked of him for the party; enough that he felt involved, but not enough to get in his way. She knew him well, took care of him, and had given him four children who filled him with pride. He was fiercely protective of her, of the children, and of the life they had built. Scoring this win against NEI would insure that Avanti was that much closer to taking over the premier spot that SCI now held. The course adjustment he had made was now in play. NEI was in the dark.

Feeling the phone vibrate in his pocket, Brett left his desk to close the door. This was a call that none of his family should overhear. "Yeah," he said, walking slowly away from the door toward the fireplace.

"One moment," said the man on the phone. "All clear. It's Winston."

"What's the word?" Brett asked.

"You didn't tell us she was protected," Winston accused.

"Protected? Why would she be protected?"

"Whatever the reason, she's being driven and personally escorted by an ISS agent."

Thrown by Winston's revelation, Brett searched for the game changer. "What could warrant that level of protection? Maybe it's *her* app, not NEI's," he mused. "I know they're unaware of what I'm doing. I wonder if someone else is trying to take it."

"There was an amateur in the Twelfth Street Tower garage. The ISS man spotted him easily," answered Winston. "But our operative is sure that she wasn't made."

"Wonder who the amateur belongs to?" Brett hated it when new players turned up out of the blue. "Still, any security agency would do. Why escalate up to ISS?"

"What's so important about that app?"

"NEI used it to find all the inefficiencies at Blackhawk," said Brett, going for the simple explanation. "Implementing its recommendations would have exposed our endeavor."

"What do you want with it?" asked Winston. "Why not just destroy it?"

"Impossible." said Brett. "Who knows how many copies exist? The best thing is to get our own copy—level the playing field. Obviously, I won't use it to change Blackhawk."

After a few moments of silence, Winston said, "We would be amenable to granting our participation in the recovery of the app in exchange for your helping us to leverage it."

Brett didn't hesitate. "Deal."

"The cleanest way is to use someone she knows on the inside who can separate her from her security."

"Already in place," said Brett, returning to his desk and sitting on its edge. "Just concerned that he won't pull it off or he'll want too much when does."

"That's where we come in. Looks like she carries a laptop all the time. All he needs to do is get her and her laptop to an isolated location and we'll take it from there," said Winston. "You need to understand—there will be casualties."

"That's not acceptable," Brett objected. "We only want a copy of the app."

"Can your insider be trusted not to break under the pressure of questioning?"

"I doubt it," Brett answered. "But that has nothing to do with the girl."

"She's a witness."

"Can't you just take him and leave her? She won't know about our involvement."

"We can't be sure—he may have said something. She'll just have to be collateral damage," said Winston. "If you don't have the stomach for this, tell me now. We'll call it done and I'll hang up."

As far as his cousin was concerned, Winston's was a clean solution. It would prevent him from infecting the life that Brett had built for his family. But the girl's only crime was possession of the app. Now that he knew it existed, Brett had to have it; had to give Avanti a concrete advantage for the next Crawford generation. Sacrifices had to be made. "Do it."

~*~~~**~~~*~

The three of them had been banished from the conference table as Lois and the delivery waiter from one of the building lobby restaurants, Cafe Eiffel, laid out their breakfast buffet. Across the desk from Gabrielle, Nathan moved impatiently in his chair, often checking his watch. In the guest chair beside her, Landry leaned on the desk, restlessly drumming his fingers. Gabrielle found that keeping her eyes averted from the pair of them was nearly impossible. Were it not for the enticing aromas that occasionally wafted their way, her progressively longer looks would have verged on staring. Nathan's cap of tight, jet black curls, his dark brown eyes, and warm brown skin were so very different from Landry's reddish blonde cropped waves, hazel eyes, and ruddy tan; but they were still very much alike. Their faces were shaped differently; but their eyes were shaped the same—as were their noses. The way they both moved—so alike—but not as though Landry copied Nathan's mannerisms; it was more that he was imprinted. The similarities were genetic. Gabrielle wondered why she hadn't before seen the resemblance.

"It's all ready for you," Lois said, leading the waiter past Nathan's desk. She gave Gabrielle a cheery wave before closing the door behind them.

One of the men cleared his throat. Gabrielle saw that they had already moved to the buffet. Nathan was filling a glass with orange juice. Landry stood near the table, staring at her, clearly exasperated. Then he pulled out a chair. "You need breakfast—something more substantial than biscotti and espresso to get through *this* day." Gabrielle went to the table and took the plate that he held for her. "Did you have anything at all this morning?" he asked.

Feeling guilt steal over her face, she said, "I'll plead the fifth." Both men chuckled—again so much alike. She surveyed the buffet. Sausage, fresh fruit, muffins, two-egg omelets, strawberry crepes, and more. She filled her plate and accepted the steaming mug that Landry handed her. "Latte?" she asked, setting it down by the chair Landry had earlier indicated. He nodded, drinking from his mug.

Gabrielle gave in to her curiosity. "Does Lois know you're related?"

"It's not a secret. We just don't make a big deal of it in the office," said Landry, sitting in the seat next to Gabrielle's latte. "Not many people know, but Lois *does*. We don't want the assumption to be that I'm guaranteed to inherit NEI. If I get it, it will be only because I've earned it. All of the partners and junior partners have the same chance that I do. Nathan made sure I understood that before he hired me."

"But when those who don't know find out, won't they assume you hid your relationship because you have the advantage?" Gabrielle asked as she sat beside Landry.

Nathan answered as he sat in the chair at the head of the table. "No one in the family is guaranteed anything by birth, Gabby. When Josh and I expanded SCI, we wrote provisions into the bylaws that prevent unqualified assumption of executive duties. Not long after, NEI partners approved similar rules."

There hadn't been any indication that Nathan was involved with SCI, yet he was—and closely enough that

Joshua San Chapelle was 'Josh'. It took all of her control not to ask questions about that part of the story. It was a tangent—she needed to stay focused on the main thread.

"It's a little before eight right now," Nathan said. "I've got to leave by eight-thirty to make it to The Street in time for my first meeting, so we're going to have to talk through breakfast. There's much you need to know, Gabrielle, and we have little time." He picked up his apple-cinnamon muffin. "First of all, we're operating outside of company lines on this. We're working it as a family matter because the future of NEI is at risk, and we don't know who we can trust."

"How do you know you can trust me?" Gabrielle asked.

"Because of what you did with what you'd found," Nathan answered, "You didn't act to curry favor, you acted because it was the right thing to do."

"Thank you for your trust," she said. "It isn't misplaced."

"I thank you as well," replied Nathan. "You didn't have to tell us about Sparks—yet you did, despite accurate legal advice. I assure you, it won't be forgotten."

"And as for what company rules you may have broken," Landry added, looking less haggard now that he was having breakfast, "you'll see that it doesn't matter much in comparison with what we're facing."

"What you are about to hear shall go no further than this room. Feel free to ask questions as you need to," said Nathan. "About two months ago, we received an unsolicited buyout—or merger—proposal from the Avanti Consortium, a holding company of other businesses. It was surprising because we've had contentious dealings with them in the past."

"Contentious?" asked Gabrielle.

"Very," Nathan allowed. "Josh and I have prevented their hostile takeover of various companies over the years."

"Does this have anything to do with what you said before about expanding SCI?"

"Not directly," said Nathan. "But the way we restructured SCI made it a safe haven for takeover-targeted companies."

"Sorry, but what's the difference between a buyout and a merger?"

"Avanti called it a merger, but only two of our staff got positions of any permanence in the new NEI. Myself, as a board member at Avanti, and whoever became managing partner," said Nathan. "The other partners got significant compensation, but with no guarantee to continue. In my mind, that constitutes a hostile buyout." He paused for a last forkful of omelet. "They also seemed to know a lot about our internal structure. The distribution of payment they suggested really caught my interest."

Gabrielle was astonished, surmising that it must have been a whole lot of money to get Nathan's attention.

"The distribution itself isn't important," he continued. "It's just that it seemed crafted with internal help, specifically designed to cause us to argue among ourselves." Finished with his breakfast, he left the table to pace between it and the desk. "Russell was the most vocal proponent, so when we confirmed that there was an insider; he was high on our list."

"How could you tell there was an insider?" asked Gabrielle.

"We asked for some technical revisions and got a second version of the proposal from Avanti. Not only did it contain responses to our requests, it also contained several subtle changes that addressed concerns raised in our partners' meetings."

"Is it possible that staffers other than the senior partners could have known what went on in the meetings?" she asked.

"Possible. The admin staff sometimes stick their heads in," replied Nathan. "But not to the extent that they could have reported back our conversations. Have you heard any comments regarding a buyout on the floor?"

Gabrielle shook her head. "I haven't."

She looked to Landry, who shook his head. Nothing," he said.

"That's good. It supports that only the senior partners are aware. The next step I took was to ask our attorney to dissect the revised proposal. Like you," Nathan directed a smile at Gabrielle, "he wasn't satisfied with the initial findings, so he dug. At around the same time, I began hearing concerns from other executives that some of NEI's work appeared to be biased. Just whisperings—nothing verifiable, but still enough to be unsettling. I suspected Retro because it is the common denominator in our analyses. Landry pulled a copy and we sent it to Princeton for independent analysis." He glanced at Gabrielle. "Your old advisor, Professor Donner, gave it to a team of doctoral students, and they had high praise for the algorithms—words like 'exciting' and 'innovative'. They found no problems, so I filed the concerns away and kept listening for something definitive. If Landry had pulled it on a different day, we may have caught this sooner."

"If it had been pulled with the bad file, wouldn't you have assumed Retro was in error?" Gabrielle asked.

"Absolutely," Nathan replied. "But Landry would have come to you with the results, and we would have gotten answers long before this morning. By the way, Professor Donner remembered your algorithms. I think he knew it was your work before we asked about you."

"You *asked* about me?"

"Of course," Nathan replied evenly. "Being in business is a high-stakes undertaking, Gabrielle. Our families, our employees, and their families are dependent on the decisions we make. You have to understand that we will investigate everything. Don't take it personally."

It was maddening that they had investigated her; impossible not to be offended. "Are you still investigating me?"

"No, no." Nathan was quick to say. "We've never investigated *you*. We merely verified information you voluntarily shared with us—that's all—and quite sufficient. It's imperative that you understand why. Do you?"

Relieved that they weren't indiscriminately prying, Gabrielle gave some thought to Nathan's question. She asked, "Because you need to know who you can trust?"

"Good guess, but not exactly," replied Nathan. "Think of our view of this situation as a gigantic jigsaw puzzle, comprised of only accurate pieces of information. The more we fill in, the clearer the picture, and the less of a target we'll be. Remember what I said about ignorance making you a target? That applies to us as well." Eyeing his watch, Nathan continued, "Gabby, you've provided us with significant puzzle pieces over the past couple of days. Yesterday, the revelation of the impending residential mortgage bond disaster blew the Avanti proposal out of the water. I don't know that they have the cash to continue with it. However, I'm honor-bound to give them the opportunity, even though I've already decided to go with the SCI proposal."

"The SCI proposal?" asked Gabrielle. It was becoming clear that Partners' Row was extremely good at keeping its secrets.

"Yes, I've not yet mentioned that. Josh and I always intended that NEI would eventually join the SCI family of companies." He added pensively, "Though I admit I didn't think it would be during my tenure. But, it looks like I'll be the one to bring it home."

Gabrielle had to ask this time. "Home?"

"Yes," answered Nathan. "Back to the family. Josh and I are cousins."

So that was it. In one sentence, Gabrielle found herself embroiled in the intrigues of one of the most powerful families in the region; and in the line of sight of their enemies. *"...I have to let the others tell their own stories." So that's what Julie meant.* "I see," she said, her thoughts spinning too fast to attempt anything more.

"I don't have time for our family saga; perhaps another day," Nathan said. "But to continue with *this* tale, SCI submitted an 'unsolicited' proposal to NEI. In reality, it had been prepared some time ago, with annually updated financials, for just such a situation. Even without this year's rewrite, it surpassed the Avanti proposal, with the additional safeguards of cash financing, and

NEI remaining, for the most part, autonomous." Nathan reseated himself in the chair at the head of the table. "The information you brought to us this morning confirms two things. First, there is at least one insider working with Avanti, and second, Retro is being used to throw business to several Avanti corporations. All the companies in the reports you showed us are Avanti's."

Nathan's and Landry's earlier words abruptly resurfaced in Gabrielle's thoughts. *Target. War within a war.* The modified file, which she had thought just a simple matter, was now revealed to be the tip of something far greater.

"Too much?" asked Landry.

Not trusting her voice, Gabrielle merely shook her head.

Both men carefully watching her, Nathan resumed his story. "What you showed me this morning gives more weight to our attorney's supposition – after he reviewed your analyses – that the Avanti proposal was made with their full knowledge of the developing market crisis. A significant share of the payments are percentages based on their residential mortgage bond returns. Had we signed that proposal, we would have basically given NEI away. No returns, no payment."

Unaware of the situation or the consequences, Gabrielle had ruined the carefully orchestrated takedown of NEI. Rather than being, as Nathan had earlier said, in the 'eye of two concentric storms', she felt more in the crosshairs of a high-powered rifle. But despite her growing anxiety, her need to understand was greater. "Why would they do that? There would be ill will toward them from NEI employees. What benefit would that be?"

"Very good questions. To understand the answers, you must first understand Avanti," responded Nathan. "There are, and always have been, rumors that Avanti doesn't conform to the letter of the law. I must admit to first-hand knowledge of the way they operate because of the dealings I mentioned earlier." He paused, gazing reflectively at Gabrielle. "There are also rumors that they use any opportunity to rid themselves of competitors and other companies that stand in their way."

"By buying them up?" asked Gabrielle.

"Not only that," answered Nathan. "But as you have demonstrated in this case, buying them up with worthless paper, leaving their executives powerless with little or no income from the buyout. They have no choice but to stay and tow the party line or get out."

"Why would they want to hinder their ability to run the company?"

"To either put the company out of business or use it for their own ends. If it went out of business, they could liquidate its assets or write it off against profits from other Avanti companies," Nathan explained.

The pieces finally fell into place: Avanti was a predator corporation, owing no allegiance to anything except their bottom line. "Why do they want us?" she asked.

"Ah," said Nathan, his expression suddenly guarded. "We are a special case. The enmity between Avanti and those of us at SCI and here at NEI is generational."

Thrown by the implications of his statement, Gabrielle took refuge in her ability to analyze. The truth of it then became clear. If corporate owners were families, or if there were long corporate memories, generational enmity could certainly result if one corporation had harmed another. *Next he'll be talking about vendettas.*

Nathan continued, "Not only that—but now, our analyses are steering companies away from their subsidiaries, losing them customers. Landry, how bad is it?"

"It's getting worse. Last month's quarterly survey of clients whose analyses recommended new partners showed that twenty-two percent of those who acted on the recommendations severed ties with what we know to be an Avanti subsidiary."

Gabrielle stated the obvious. "I guess that means Avanti is severely pissed off."

"That's an understatement," said Landry. "Remember that loss of clients translates directly into loss of revenue. Whoever it is, either here or at Avanti is likely to retaliate. Last quarter's numbers indicate a significant loss of income for them."

"But two of their companies are our clients," Gabrielle pointed out. "We told them what to change in the processes at Xalan and at Blackhawk—especially Blackhawk. They're terribly inefficient. We could have examined others of their companies as well."

"It appears that they only became clients so they could find out how we work, and to meet and turn whomever has become the insider." Gabrielle found herself under Nathan's increasingly intense scrutiny as he spoke. "To understand their perspective, you have to realize that business is personal, and from what I know of them, it appears they took it as a personal affront that NEI found so many inefficiencies in their businesses. They've chosen not to act on our recommendations. Instead, they're reacting the old-fashioned way: take NEI out by any means necessary. Retribution. Retaliation."

Faced with the certainty that a vendetta truly did exist, Gabrielle asked. "Isn't that rather extreme?"

"From your perspective, yes," answered Nathan. "From the point of view of the owners and managers of Avanti—a ninety-five year old consortium—no. They stand to lose their livelihood. They've not changed much from the strong-arm days. That's what's worked for them in the past, so that's what they continue to do. This isn't the first time we've crossed paths."

"Will it work in our case?" asked Gabrielle.

"We got lucky," Nathan said. "*You've* made sure that we're forewarned, so the merger won't work. We called in a world-renowned—in certain circles—security agency, which protects us from personal retaliation. We've taken all the proactive measures that we can. Now, we look for their next move."

"Retaliation. Retribution. Those are words I would never have associated with conducting business," said Gabrielle.

Catching her gaze, Landry said softly, "Avanti is not the only business that operates that way. It's more prevalent than you think."

"How big is the internal threat? Do you think the insider knew the true goal?" she asked. "By the way, do you have an idea who the insider might be?" It was unfair to think of Garrett as the insider—just because she didn't like him. Still, she couldn't shake the feeling that he was somehow involved.

Landry and Nathan exchanged glances. "You're asking very astute questions, and I don't have definitive answers. I can guess, but guesses aren't good enough," Nathan replied with deep, yet controlled anger. "In any event, I want that person, or possibly, those people, exposed and out of NEI. Gabrielle, if you choose to stay, you need to be involved in developing our strategy because steps we take may paint targets on all of us."

"What do you mean 'if I choose to stay'?" It was true that she felt fear, but it came from the knowledge that she was a part of the solution and had to see it through; not from a desire to recuse herself.

Nathan's voice softened yet again as he looked at her. "This is a potentially dangerous situation. We don't know what the insider or Avanti has at stake; or what lengths they'll go to—either to get what they're after or to avoid detection. Their reaction could be extreme, or it may be nothing. It would be criminal to accept your involvement in this without your full knowledge and consent." He continued musingly, "Even then, my preference is to keep you out of it. You know what? Now that we've talked this through, that's the way to go." The tension in the room faded noticeably.

"I agree," said Landry, suddenly more animated than he had been all morning. "We can say Gabby has a family emergency."

Nathan went to his desk and hit a speed dial button on his desk phone. Carson's voice responded, "On my way up."

Gabrielle refused to allow Landry and Nathan to decide her future. "I have to stay. What if you need me or Sparks? Won't the insider get suspicious if I disappear?"

Frowning, Landry answered, "You can work remotely."

"It makes sense that someone on the analyst staff is an insider. You need a non-management analyst to help expose that person," said Gabrielle. "We have a better chance of doing that if I stay."

"We don't know that for sure," Landry responded.

"You need me to stay," Gabrielle repeated as Carson walked through the door.

"We've decided," Landry said with finality.

"So have I," said Gabrielle. "I'm staying."

"*No*," Landry said emphatically. "This is *not* your fight."

"If I may interject," interjected Carson politely. "We are fully capable of insuring Ms. Winston's safety. You need not allow that concern to shape your strategy."

It wouldn't help her case, but Gabrielle could not refrain from asking, "Who is watching out for Landry now that you're watching out for me?"

"You're worried about who is watching out for *me*?"

"Wasn't Carson your, um, driver?" She glanced apologetically at Carson as she asked.

"I *did* give you that impression," said Landry. "I have a driver—or personal protection. But he isn't Carson."

Though Gabrielle looked to Carson for an explanation, it was Nathan who provided it. "We were candid about our situation with SCI. They proposed that we use their security firm and deploy agents as needed for our protection. Landry called for Carson yesterday while you both were in his office—to protect you."

~*~~~**~~~*~

I'm already stressed enough—Landry is not helping. His predatory pacing had started while Carson was setting up a conference call for Nathan, Lois, and Nathan's security manager. He was still at it. The near silence made him impossible for Gabrielle to ignore. Amazingly, she seemed to be the only one affected by the ugliness of his mood. In stark contrast, Carson leaned comfortably against the wall next to the white board, showing no signs of worry. Still at his desk phone having only glanced at Landry once or twice, Nathan spoke quickly and quietly as he and Lois tried to wring more time out of his schedule without breaching his security.

Gabrielle's disquiet grew as she surreptitiously watched Landry. It was probably best that he ignored her. A wrong word could ignite their unspoken disagreement. Gabrielle searched for a way to get him to understand that it was right for her to stay. Nathan had said that the situation existed because of her, and she knew she had to be a part of the solution. Surely, Landry knew that he didn't have a position from which to argue. Besides, he was the one who had encouraged her to 'step up to the next level'. Surely he hadn't forgotten. She approached him, determined to win him over with reason.

In one of his momentary pauses, looking toward the window garden, Landry scowled as Gabrielle drew near. "I'm not happy about this, Gabrielle," he bit through his teeth.

"It's my choice," she reminded him, hesitantly reaching out to touch his arm. "I need to be a part of fixing this; if it weren't for me, we wouldn't even be in this situation." Stiffening at her words, Landry turned to look down at Gabrielle, who was forced to look away from his intense anger. For good measure, she removed her hand.

Touching her chin, Landry gently raised her head so that she had to meet his gaze. His anger-ridden eyes softened as he looked into hers. "Yes, we would most certainly still be in this situation, just without the level of awareness you have given us. Gabby, you *have* to leave—you have no idea how nasty this could get."

"That's why I'm grateful that you called Carson. Thank you," she said, reminding him of her protection. "I'll be safe with him."

"Carson being with you is all that makes your involvement even feasible," said Landry reluctantly. "But I still don't agree."

"No," Gabrielle sighed, turning to walk away. "I can't make you agree."

Landry caught her hand, turning her toward him again. "No you can't," he said to the top of her head. Hesitantly Gabrielle looked up. She was relieved to see his anger fading. "But I can't deny that strategically, it's the right move for you to stay." His hand tightened around hers. "I'll just have to adjust." The sound of Nathan hanging up his phone caused them both to look his way. He was now approaching the conference table. Landry squeezed her hand once more, then let go. "Let's get on with it."

As they seated themselves, Nathan said, "Lois was able to find another twenty minutes in my schedule. I'll be taking the helo to the airport instead of the car. Let's get started."

Carson spoke first. "I'd like to share some thoughts about flushing out moles."

Astonished, Gabrielle stared at him. *Did he really just say that?*

"The most successful approach is to layer your strategy on top of normal ops."

Nathan's expression smoothed as he understood. "Took me a moment—your 'normal ops' is my 'business as usual'."

"Yes," said Carson.

Landry asked, "Does that include our personal lives as well?"

"It does," Carson replied.

"Then Gabrielle goes back to riding the train," Landry said. "How will she be protected?"

"It's the same as with your personal agent," Carson replied. "I'm the coordinator for her security team and I'll call in resources when I need them."

Stunned that she had a security team, Gabrielle's anxiety momentarily burst through its restraints. She quickly reined it in.

Carson continued, "I've already increased the team—something I want to discuss here. Gabrielle's being followed, or someone is attempting to follow her. We haven't allowed him to get close."

"Followed?" *This isn't a bad spy movie; it's the real deal.*

"Damn," muttered Landry. Gabrielle winced at the fierceness in his tone.

Carson glanced at Landry and then said to Gabrielle, "Since you're going back to your normal routine, I'll teach you how to live within a security pocket so that you don't expose your protection."

Gabrielle's anxiety escalated again. Determined, she regained composure. "Security pocket? Expose my protection? What does that mean?"

CHAPTER SEVEN

The Game is On

"It means you'll be very well taken care of," Nathan assured Gabrielle. "Carson, after our discussion, use my office and educate Gabrielle regarding your security measures." Carson gave a single nod. "Since we're going with the business as usual model, I'd like to do three things. Gabrielle where's your... you've packed it up. Use mine then. First, I'd like to watch Retro's files and see if any are changed again. Check them now, please."

"Sure." Gabrielle left the table, relieved to be in action. She offered a way to improve on Nathan's request. "I can set an event on it to email me when it changes."

"Not a good idea," objected Carson. "Have you ever set an event on a Retro file?" Gabrielle shook her head as she sat at Nathan's desk. "Then it could be noticed and the email could be intercepted. Stick with low tech."

Undeterred, Gabrielle added Carson's reasoning to her knowledge base. Until she understood the environment of covert operations, she had to accept that her assumptions would mostly be wrong. The only way to improve was to keep trying. "Okay then. How often should I check?"

"Twice a day should be sufficient," replied Nathan. While Gabrielle logged into his laptop and accessed the main Retro environment, he said, "Secondly, I'd like to float the supposition to the senior partners that Avanti could have known about the mortgage bond situation. I want to see if we can elicit a response from the insider. Thoughts?"

"What type of response?" asked Landry.

"That's certainly a good question. I don't know."

Nathan's reply disturbed Gabrielle. *That's like poking a stick into a hornets' nest.*

"With your mandate, there will be a lot of activity, so it will help to know what to watch for," said Landry. "*Can* we know what to look for?"

After navigating to the files, Gabrielle saw that again, she was to be the bearer of bad news. "Excuse me," she called, interrupting their conversation. They all looked in her direction. "The file has already been modified again, yesterday at about one-thirty."

Landry's earlier anger was mild compared with what Gabrielle now saw—on all three faces. It was obvious that someone was going to pay, and she was fervently relieved not to be that person. Whoever it was had no idea what they had unleashed. But according to Nathan, Avanti and its insiders were worse. Uneasiness stole over Gabrielle in the lengthening silence.

At last, once more composed, Nathan voiced his decision. "Given what Gabrielle has found, given that we don't know what to look for, and given that our general activity level will be intensified, I say not only do we float the market supposition to the partners, we also float that we're onto the changing file. Then we watch for something to happen. Since we don't know what to look for, we must be vigilant for anything out of the ordinary."

"Can IT tell us who accessed the shared drive yesterday at that time?" Gabrielle asked.

"I'll ask Matthew," said Landry.

"For the last thing," Nathan said to Gabrielle, "run all the Retro analyses recommending an Avanti company through Sparks and complete the spreadsheet you showed us this morning. I need to know how badly we've been compromised."

"Got it," Gabrielle acknowledged, returning to the table.

"Gabby's supposed to lead the team looking for clients who will be most affected by the crash," Landry said. "I'll get Raphael or Mary Alice to cover it. They're both less experienced so I'll have to be more hands-on."

"The team will think you've bypassed me and there will be questions," objected Gabrielle. "I can do both."

"How's that possible?" asked Landry.

"I'll make sure I get the analyses for the light months. It won't be too hard. We're very competitive and they'll all want the toughest assignment. Then I just need to be available for questions."

In spite of his resistance, Landry's lips curved into a slight smile. "I can see when I'm beaten. By the way, you'll give the team the work plan."

Pleased to have at last won his approval, Gabrielle said. "Thanks. How do I frame it?"

"We're *not* going to say anything about the crash," mused Landry, "Let's have each analyst review their own analyses plus those from an analyst on Cleve's team, looking for clients who need to finance and from what source. Garrett and I can then use those findings to identify the clients who expect to finance from real estate holdings. We'll also be able to see if additional analysis is required, though I doubt it will be."

Nathan nodded slowly. "It conceals the real intent."

Thoughts of the team unexpectedly brought to mind the new addition to Steve's family, Cristin's new condo, Raphael's burden of paying for his sister's education.

And they didn't know about the crash. "I wish we could tell them," Gabrielle murmured.

"It would be irresponsible to increase those of us at NEI who know, beyond the partners and those in this room," said Nathan. "But remember, we are taking the necessary steps to protect the staff and their families. I know you think we should do more, but when it comes to disclosure, we are treading a *very* fine line—between protecting ourselves, and causing the very problem we are all trying avoid. The trick of it is to do the most we can possibly do without causing a panic."

"We get to see the alert bulletins when they go out," Gabrielle reminded him. "Some of them might figure it out."

"It's possible," acknowledged Nathan. "But remember—the bulletin won't specifically mention the crash. It will merely caution against certain types of investments. Those who see it are free to act if they 'get' and choose to heed the message. I have no legal grounds to stop them."

Though it was a better answer than she expected, Gabrielle still wished they could do more. But it would be devastating to cause a rumor-induced panic, maybe worse than the real thing. She had to accept that Nathan was right. But there was still the certainty of questions from the team. "What if someone asks why we're performing the analysis?"

"Simply say that we want to know, by the end of the quarter, how many clients require financing to carry out our recommendations," Nathan answered. "We'd like to see if we can add value by making financing recommendations as well; and want to use the last quarter of this year for assessment and, if warranted, implementation. That's a true statement by the way. The partners have been discussing whether or not to get into the business of financial instrument analysis. This is a good first step."

As Gabrielle moved past her misgivings, another thought formed. It wasn't "normal ops," but it would make her job easier. "Can we open a VPN port to Sparks from here?" she asked. "That way, I can work on both projects while I'm in the office."

Carson spoke. "If I may,"

Gabrielle suppressed a grin. *As if someone would say no.*

"If you're opening a port, I suggest you put a trace on it. Does anyone else need to access Sparks?"

"I don't think so." Gabrielle looked to Landry for confirmation.

"Absolutely not," said Landry.

"Then Gabrielle's laptop will be the only approved accessor," said Carson. "But we'll allow other attempts for tracing, disabling, and/or reverse infection."

Nathan nodded. "Work with Landry and Matthew to assign someone to our IT staff."

"Will do," Carson replied. "It may be that someone from IT is part of the problem. With your permission, we'll *covertly* assign someone, maybe as an intern. Only Matthew need know the real reason for his or her presence."

"You have it," Nathan said, checking his watch. "That's it then. I'll bring up the Avanti supposition and the changed file in our strategy meeting this afternoon. I won't link them; I'll simply say it's curious that the file was changed, and that it's being looked into. Let's see if I get questions or if someone feels the need to act." Leaving the table, he added, "This is just our first step. Carson, what do you suggest for keeping us on the same page and adjusting strategy as events transpire?"

"We can use the secure ISS conference lines. TM me and I'll connect us all."

"Good deal," said Nathan on the way back to his desk. Packing his portfolio case, he glanced back toward the table. "I hear you're one of the ISS founders, Carson. How many times have you been through something like this?"

"Quite a few, sir."

Gabrielle clenched her jaw to keep from gaping. *Founder? Why has he assigned himself the job of protecting me? It can't be just because he and Landry are sailing buddies.*

"I'm glad you're here now," said Nathan. "I really appreciate your help."

"Thank you, Nathan," said Carson. Then he added as he glanced at each of them, "And when we talk—use your cell phones. We've proven them to be clean."

"Good reminder," Nathan concurred. "Use the office as long as you like. I won't be back until late this afternoon." Grabbing his packed portfolio, he left for the elevator.

Landry turned to Carson. "Mind if I stay?" he asked.

"Not at all. You need to see how well she'll be protected," replied Carson. "Gabrielle, I need your cell." He reached into his inside coat pocket and pulled out a folded sheet of paper.

Gabrielle retrieved her cell from the front pocket of her backpack, feeling as though she were handing it over for spy gadget installation. Hesitantly, she gave it to Carson as she took a seat closer to him and Landry.

Unfolding the sheet of paper and smoothing it out on the table, Carson said, "I'm making you some new contacts." He began loading them onto her phone. "They are all camouflaged as phone service contacts, and I'm setting them up with a two-digit speed dial." He glanced at Gabrielle and asked, "You do know how to use two-digit speed dial?"

"Of course," she said, insulted.

"I didn't," offered Landry, looking somewhat embarrassed.

Oops, guess I'm being too touchy.

"Many people don't," said Carson. "Before I explain how to use your new contacts, I need to explain a little about your security team. There will be four agents forming a perimeter around you at all times when you're in public."

"Isn't that kind of obvious?" asked Gabrielle, immediately feeling ridiculous for questioning a professional.

Carson smiled slightly. "They won't be that close to you. They merely have to keep you in sight—not even eavesdropping distance most of the time." His smile widened, "Although they do carry directional mikes."

"Sweet. Big Brother times four," said Gabrielle, thinking of all the times she had checked her teeth for lettuce, or had found an empty corner to discreetly adjust her underwear. Those days were over.

Landry's question interrupted her silent rant. "Why does Gabby need four agents? Nathan and I have three."

"Two reasons. First, because your security coordinator is your driver. Gabrielle's normal means of transportation is the train, so I won't be with her as much." He then said to Gabrielle, "A distant second is your height."

"Height?" she demanded.

"Don't take it personally, but we can't see you above the crowd," Carson said. "We need keep to all of you in view at all times, so to be less conspicuous, the three of us who are security coordinators for you, Nathan, and Landry share a rotating team of twenty agents. You can help us out by remembering to keep a reasonable pace; no unexpected changes of direction."

"Because you can't keep me in sight?" asked Gabrielle.

"Almost," answered Carson. "It's really that if we have to scramble to keep up with you, we're exposed." Now finished updating her phone, Carson folded the paper and returned it to his pocket. "I know you need to get to work, so let's wrap this up."

Waiting anxiously, Gabrielle expected Carson to give her something spy-like—another device to carry or a long list of codes to remember.

Instead, he said, "Here's the speed dials for your new contacts. The first, ninety-nine, is the emergency number. You can talk to whoever answers, but the most important thing is that calling this number activates the GPS transmitter on your phone, and keeps it active as long as the call is active. The second one, forty-four, alerts us that you are changing your routine. For example, if you usually get off the train at Calhoun Street to come to NEI, and you want to get off somewhere else. It will allow us to adapt more covertly. The last speed dial is thirty-three. Use it if you see something disturbing. For example, a person you've seen more than expected, a car that may be following you, that sort of thing. You can also use it to explicitly tell us you're changing your routine. This is the only number where you'll need to talk to the person who answers. The agents will hear your conversation on their earpieces. Got it?"

Gabrielle's anxiety ebbed. No sudden movements and three numbers. That's all there was to it. "No code words? Don't I get a lipstick gun?"

"That would be some of our equipment. Not all of us are male," said Carson, with a slight twitch of his lips. He handed Gabrielle her phone. "I've programmed and tested your numbers. Now all you do is go about your life as usual and let us handle anything that may come up. By the way, I've given you an extra number in case you want to talk directly to me. It's seventy-seven."

"Thank you, Carson," she said. She walked over to her backpack and opened the front pocket. Being able to call him made it seem like he was always near.

"Gabrielle," Carson's voice interrupted her thoughts. "Wear your cell *all the time.*"

"Of course," Gabrielle replied, chagrined. She clipped the holster to her belt. Suddenly, she remembered an earlier statement he had made. "What about the person who's following me?"

Carson glanced her way and then turned to address his comments to Landry as well. "There are actually two. I'm going to take out the amateur. I want the pro to think that we haven't made her. See if we can follow her and find out who she's working for."

"What does that mean for Gabrielle?" asked Landry.

"She won't be affected. The amateur's not a threat, and we won't let the pro get close."

Landry seemed about to disagree. "I don't know about this."

"I want to know why she's following me," said Gabrielle, without hesitation. "Besides, won't she figure out that you've made her if you don't let her get close?"

"Eventually," said Carson.

"Then I vote for your plan," said Gabrielle.

Landry said, "If there's any sign of danger to Gabrielle..."

Nodding in agreement, Carson said, "We'll take care of it."

~*~~~**~~~*~

Preserving the secrecy of their early morning meeting, Carson and Gabrielle left Landry in Nathan's office and rode the suite elevator down to the executive garage. He then escorted her into an empty public elevator. "We're always near," he said quietly. She smiled her thanks as the door closed.

On the ride up, Gabrielle leaned against the back wall, her eyes nearly closed, barely paying attention as people got on and off at various floors. Instead of her thoughts being on the role she was about to play, they were on Landry—maybe because she was mimicking his behavior. Mostly she thought of him as a mentor. *But sometimes...* Their relationship was a puzzle that begged to be solved. As much as she wanted to figure it out, now was not the time. Her focus had to remain on managing the crisis.

Gabrielle suddenly remembered that she had to get past Sheila, who usually managed the reception desk because she turned solicitors away so subtly that they didn't realize they had no chance of being called back for an appointment. She called it "the soft no." But it was her role as the nexus of NEI gossip that worried Gabrielle. There wasn't much that went on that she hadn't heard something about; and she was always happy to share her "knowledge" with everyone else. Gabrielle wished she had mentioned Sheila to Carson so that they could have rehearsed her approach. Now she just had to wing it.

The elevator door slid open on the NEI main floor and Gabrielle stepped off. The clock above the long reception desk beyond the glass double doors read nine forty-five. Sheila seemed to be using "the soft no" with a man trying to see one of the partners. The elevator she had just exited stayed open, thanks to Sheila's strategic use of her elevator call button. The solicitor would find it conveniently waiting for him when he was politely dismissed from the lobby. "Morning, Sheila," Gabrielle called as she entered the lobby and walked quickly past the desk.

"Hey, Gabs," Sheila responded. "Wait a minute, honey—not so fast."

Already leaving the lobby when Gabrielle turned warily toward Sheila, the man shot a curious glance at her over his shoulder. Watching him just as curiously, Gabrielle wondered if he could be the man following her. If he was, she pitied him. Carson was on his trail. At the reception desk, Gabrielle waited until the elevator door closed behind him, and then asked Sheila, "So what's happening today?"

Giving Gabrielle the once over, Sheila beckoned her closer, and then whispered quietly, "Something's up with Garrett and Landry today, so watch yourself. You're already looking a little overworked—I think something else is coming."

Relieved that Sheila had drawn her own conclusions, Gabrielle laughed her noisy, infectious laugh.

"Shhh!!!" admonished Sheila, smiling in spite of herself.

"I'm sorry," whispered Gabrielle. "But that's not exactly news. There's always something up with Garrett and somebody—and there's always something new for us to work on." She winked. "Job security."

"That's true about Garrett," admitted Sheila, still whispering. "But Rachel said that he and Landry disagreed about something in his office just now—something that has to do with you and some new work that came in yesterday."

"Yesterday?" asked Gabrielle, amazed at how fast news traveled. Taking advantage of the graceful exit that Sheila had given her, Gabrielle said, "Guess I'd better go find out what's up."

"By the way, where were you yesterday?" asked Sheila. "I didn't see you *at all*."

Thinking fast, Gabrielle replied, "Working from home." *It was almost true.*

The phone began to ring. Before Sheila turned to answer it, she wagged a finger at Gabrielle. "Remember, watch yourself today."

~*~~~**~~~*~

In the shaded alcove formed by the rear of an elevator bank and a stairwell, Carson waited for the "all clear" vibration pattern on his cell. One of Gabrielle's security team was posing as a cold-calling salesman in the NEI lobby and would notify him and the rest of the team of her safe arrival. Once the call was received, the team would execute their operation against the amateur. The professional operative had apparently decided that her location was too vulnerable, and in Carson's absence, had moved from her car to an extremely good vantage point in one of the stairwells. Unfortunately for her, it was the one behind Carson. He had chosen this position as the center of the operation partly to add to her discomfort, but mainly to keep her in place until after the team dispersed. A secondary benefit of his choice was that she would assume she hadn't been made. Though a professional, she lacked the training and background of ISS operatives and had, in their eyes, made several mistakes. The crucial one was that she hadn't investigated building security. She was unaware that Twelfth Street Tower belonged to SCI and that ISS, as the SCI security services company, had installed the garage security cameras. She may not have even been aware that she was watching ISS agents.

Though the cameras recorded only to tape, Carson's car had the ability to enable audio, and to intercept and decrypt the encrypted wireless signal streams. The signal capture would be in place for the duration of the operation—and until the professional had left the garage. Using the cameras wasn't illegal for ISS. Building tenants were fully aware that the security services company reserved the right to periodically test the live system. ISS would analyze the video and audio of their "test" capture of the pro and her car to start their investigation of her.

Carson's cell vibrated, indicating that Gabrielle had arrived safely. The team was now free to move against the amateur. Simultaneously with the "all clear" call, and from different locations, two other members of the team began weaving their way toward a car a few rows away from Carson. A man sat in the car, ostensibly reading a newspaper; unaware that he was giving himself away with the outdated tactic. Within seconds, the cold-calling salesman stepped off the elevator and headed slowly toward the car as well. Carson watched the well-orchestrated intercept. It wouldn't matter if anyone entered the garage. The team was well practiced and would stall until the garage was empty again. It amused him that the pro was in an uncomfortable position. Having been in a similar spot many times, he knew that she barely dared to breathe. Before another minute had elapsed, the team surrounded the car. One of them opened the locked door and quickly pulled out the protesting man. After whispered instructions, they surrounded the amateur and walked him to Carson's position; looking very much as though they were a group of carpoolers on their way to the elevator. A simple intercept, expertly executed. No weapons, no violence; merely intimidation.

More for dramatic effect than for anything else, Carson emerged slowly from the shadows and maneuvered the man into the corner he had just vacated. "Good morning," he said. "And who might you be?"

Predictably, under Carson's polite questioning, the man told all that he knew: the company he worked for, the targets, that there was another operative for the other target; that his job was to follow Gabrielle Winston and build a dossier.

"That's going to be difficult," mused Carson. "How do you plan to get past us?"

Clearly at a loss, the amateur stuttered, "I'll have to get in touch with m-my firm."

"You do that," said Carson, stepping out of the man's way and watching as he ran back to his car, jumped in, pulled out of the parking space, and peeled out of the garage. The entire operation took less than ten minutes. *One down, one to go.*

~*~~~**~~~*~

Falling in step with Gabrielle as she walked to her cube, Mary Alice said impatiently, "Something's up and Landry said you would tell us. What's going on?"

"Get the team together," replied Gabrielle. "Then I'll explain to everybody."

"Where?" asked Mary Alice, not quite concealing her exasperation.

"West conference room. We may be joined by some of Cleve's team."

"*That* explains it," Mary Alice cut in.

"Explains what?"

"Stan. Cleve said he's sending him over to help us," said Mary Alice. In perfect imitation of Cleve's curt tone, her feelings obviously injured by his disparagement, she added, "'Because you obviously need the help'."

"I guess Cleve doesn't get the meaning of cross-organizational teams. Both our teams are supposed to contribute to the project. But better for us. I'd rather have all our own team anyway." said Gabrielle. "See you in the conference room."

Mollified by Gabrielle's clarification, Mary Alice hurried off to bully, cajole, or nag the rest of Landry's team away from their monitors.

In her cubicle, Gabrielle dumped her backpack into the desk chair, unpacked her laptop and docked it; leaving it to power up during their meeting. On her way to the conference room she caught a glimpse of Raphael at the refrigerator as she passed the break room again. "Morning," she called. "We're meeting in the west conference room."

"Mary Alice told me," he said. "I'll stop by Cristin's on the way. She usually has her headphones on."

Standing guard at the conference room door, Mary Alice announced, "We're all here except for you and Raphael."

"He's on his way," Gabrielle replied, walking past her into the room. "He thought Cristin might be under her headphones."

Cristin looked up and smiled. "I was, but you know Mary Alice."

Everyone laughed except Mary Alice, who wore an expression of righteous annoyance. "I *told* you I'd get everyone."

Commiserating with Mary Alice for her lack of poker face, Gabrielle leaned against the credenza at the head of the table. "We've got a special project." All heads snapped up and looked her way. "But first, we have a member of Cleve's team helping out. Stan, I think it is?" He nodded. "Please introduce yourself."

His face flushed with embarrassment, Stan said, "I'm Stan Thornton and I've been an analyst on Cleve's team for the past four months. Before that, I finished my master's degree in process analytics at the University of Tennessee."

Harry immediately chided, "Oh no, a rookie."

"Lighten up," Cristin replied. "He's probably the best that Cleve's got."

Laughter sounded around the table, turning Stan's face an even deeper shade of red. Hearing a deep chuckle behind her, Gabrielle turned to see Raphael at the door, leaning on the doorjamb.

"Grab a seat," Gabrielle said.

"Here's fine."

"Sorry, but we need to close the door."

"Oh, sure." Raphael closed the door behind him and slid into the chair at the head of the table. Swiveling to face her, he made a big show of moving his legs to the side so that his feet would not be resting on hers.

At first irritated by Raphael's insistence on playing unnecessary workplace head games, Gabrielle realized that he was unaware of the conflicts in which they were all now immersed. In fact, none of them were aware—unless, of course, one or more were insiders. Though she had to keep an open mind, Gabrielle detested thinking that it could be any one of them. Much more than that, she hated that Avanti had targeted them all for harm. Glancing at Raphael, and then looking past him to the rest of the team, she gave the brief as they had discussed in Nathan's office; relieved to see only open, friendly faces. She concluded, "Our purpose is to generate a graphical report—spreadsheet, charts—for Garrett, the other senior partners, and Nathan."

"What brought this on?" demanded Raphael.

"The partners are evaluating whether it makes sense for NEI to expand into investment analysis and this project performs the logical first step," explained Gabrielle.

"If there aren't that many clients who require financing, the investigation dies. If there are a significant number, further assessment will be assigned. Each of us is to review our own analyses for the past year, and those of one of the analyst's on Cleve's team. Stan, take your own and overflow from any of our other team members. I'll take Dan's since he's the lead. They need our results by tomorrow morning, nine a.m. at the latest." There were answering groans and exclamations.

"Why's the timeframe so tight?" asked Harry.

"The partners want to complete the investigation this week, giving us a quarter before the first of the year for assessment and possible implementation. The deadline leaves time for a second round of review, the results of which will be due tomorrow afternoon. Cleve's team is to help us out by finishing up all of our work on deadline for tomorrow." There were more groans around the table.

"Maybe we should try to finish the project and all our scheduled analysis by tomorrow morning, so we don't have to go back and clean up their mess," said Steve. After the laughter died away, he added, "No offense, Stan."

Taking the pressure off Stan, who looked as though he felt like a ridiculed outsider, Gabrielle said, "Stan is on our team for this project. Raphael, Cristin, how about you bring him up to speed on our procedures, processes, and tools?"

"Sure," said Cristin. Raphael nodded in agreement.

"I wasn't kidding, by the way," reiterated Steve. "I can finish the analysis I'm on deadline for as well." There were nods and sounds of agreement around the table.

"If you can, by all means go ahead," said Gabrielle. "But this project is your highest priority. Anyone who is handing work off to Cleve's team needs to give it to Mary Alice within the next half hour. She's the project coordinator this time. Please provide her your results and CC me." Watching the exchanged glances and murmured conversations around the table, she guessed that no one would be handing over analyses for Cleve's team to complete. Frankly, she expected that most of the team had already completed their scheduled work. "Unless there're any questions, that's it," she said. There were none. "Then I'll let Landry know we're on task." She turned and left the conference room, leaving the door open behind her. When she reached her cube, she was surprised to see that Cristin, Stan, and Raphael had followed her.

Raphael's face was all lit up. "We have an idea to run by you," he said.

"What's up?" Gabrielle asked as she turned and sat on her horizontal file cabinet, making room for them all to fit into the tight space.

Cristin replied, "The teams are even in number, so Stan is unlikely to get any reports except his own. He hasn't been here long, so he only has a few."

Raphael cut in, "If we work as a team, we could take on the work of three analysts from Cleve's team."

Not the way I expected, but I'll take it. "So, you want Dan's reports?" asked Gabrielle.

Cristin smiled, "Yes, what do you think?"

"Great idea," replied Gabrielle.

"Thanks," said Raphael.

Cristin and Stan didn't seem to think it was all his idea. Raphael knew all the tricks for keeping himself in the forefront. "Thanks for freeing me up to manage workload more," said Gabrielle. "I'll email the team and let them know of the change and that I'm free for overflow." Gabrielle looked from Cristin to Stan and lingered on Raphael. "Don't try to be heroes. We need accuracy and the deadline is our highest priority. If you find that you're overloaded, give a shout out for some help. Got it?"

"Got it," Cristin agreed.

"No prob," said Raphael. "Bet we're done before you are."

"You're on," laughed Gabrielle. "Loser buys lunch?"

"Too tame," said Raphael. "How about loser springs for a night at Cafe Spore?"

"Awesome!" agreed Stan.

"Cafe Spore? The online game cafe you go to?" Gabrielle asked.

"Yep. We keep asking you to come—now you'll have to." said Cristin. "Big fun on Friday nights. They've got over a hundred stations in there."

Probably all with food left rotting in the keyboards. "Okay, I'll take your word for it." Then Gabrielle spotted a way to avoid going. "But it's not a fair split. If I lose, I pay for three."

"Not a problem," said Raphael. "You win, you get three nights, one on each of us. You lose; you chip in a third for each of us, one night."

Seeing the excitement in their faces, Gabrielle decided, for the sake of morale, to take the bet. *Maybe I should also let them win.* "That's more than fair," she acknowledged. "You're on."

"Sweet," said Raphael. He turned to leave with the others, then hesitated and turned back to Gabrielle. "Anything else you want us to take off your hands?"

Always the cowboy. She replied, "I'm good, why?"

"You look a little overworked."

~*~~~**~~~*~

Using the archive search application, Gabrielle made quick work of Nathan's request; finding that the first recommendation of an Avanti company happened during the past March. She had configured the search app to sort the retrieved list by team, then by analyst so that she could add those columns to the spreadsheet and look for tendencies. The rest of the morning she analyzed the spreadsheet, working to the soothing background staccato of fingers tapping keys. Drawing on brainpower and computer power, making bits fly, disks spin. Time passed unnoticed.

Landry's voice startled Gabrielle. He seemed to be walking among the cubes, saying something encouraging to each analyst. When he reached her cube, he said, "Looks like the team is all set up. Good work." Then he winked and slipped his hand briefly through the opening for her to take a note. Opening it, she saw that it was the login information for the VPN port IT had opened for Sparks. She looked up to thank him, but he was already gone, speaking briefly to the others down her row. Whether or not he had only walked through as a cover for giving her the note, Gabrielle was happy that he had. It wasn't often they got visits praising their efforts.

Using the information in the note, Gabrielle set up VPN and accessed the server in her condo. Many of the analyses she had submitted earlier to Sparks were completed. She downloaded them to her laptop. She then used her new list to copy the Retro reports and their setup files from the archive. After converting the setup files to Sparks' format, she copied them to its input folder on her server. Now all she had to do was periodically check the output folder for finished analyses.

Next, Gabrielle reviewed the ones she had just downloaded from Sparks, and entered the data into the spreadsheet. So far, all of the analyses completed on Retro resulting in recommendations of an Avanti company were in error, and represented seventeen percent of the analyses NEI had completed since March. Affected clients had been led to work with a sub-optimal partnering corporation at higher costs. NEI would have to alert them and offer remuneration of some type; costly, but far less so than losing trust and future business. It stood out that Cleve's team was responsible for almost ninety percent of the bad analyses.

Although this appeared suspicious, Gabrielle knew that they routinely got the simpler projects where increased efficiency resolved to changes in external relationships. Apparently Cleve chose projects that his team could turn around faster. A side effect of his approach was that it caused a noticeable, often ridiculed, imbalance in expertise between the two teams.

Able to go no further until Sparks finished more analyses, Gabrielle pushed away from her desk. The desktop clock read four-thirty. Badly in need of something to divert her thoughts from the roller coaster graph and the repercussions of the changed file, she looked forward to her night out with Julie and Sarah.

Sparks was sure to be finished with more of the analyses by the time they got back to Julie's. She would update the spreadsheet then finish in the morning if she had to. For the first time, Gabrielle tapped the thirty-three speed dial into her cell.

"Yes, Ms. Winston?" asked a pleasant female voice.

"Thursdays are different for me," Gabrielle said. "I'll be going to Loft V, then going out with two of my friends. We're coming back to Loft V, and will be leaving from there for work together on the train tomorrow morning."

"Thank you, Ms. Winston," replied the voice. "Will that be all?"

"That's it," replied Gabrielle. She hoped her crew could keep up.

~*~~~**~~~*~

Too tense to sit, Garrett leaned against his desk looking toward the window garden. The simulated sunset filled the interior garden with intricate patterns of shade and color, but the view failed to soothe him. He had spent an aggravating day working with Landry, sanitizing the client report for the alert bulletin. Though something he could have delegated, he didn't dare, given the severity of the market situation and Landry's newfound propensity to shine. Some of his annoyance stemmed from his hatred of feeling cornered, and he had felt that way all day. His expectation had been that the successful acceptance of the partners' mitigation plan in Nathan's meeting would free him to return to business as usual. It did not.

Sending a shockwave around the table, Nathan had suggested that Avanti knew about the bond situation. Showing that the payouts to the partners would have dwindled to zero, his supposition was enough to sway the others toward the SCI proposal. Garrett's current edginess stemmed from his inability to shake the thought that there was another reason for Nathan's revelation. His office suddenly too small, he moved through the outer office onto the Partners' Row floor. Since it was after hours, he had it to himself. Looking out through the exterior windows as darkness crept over the city, he sifted through his thoughts.

All of the senior partners were aware of the Avanti proposal, so it was no surprise that Nathan shared his thoughts. But it was his seemingly unrelated mention of a changed Retro file that now had Garrett wondering whether he suspected that there was an insider. If so, he could have voiced the revelations in an attempt to goad that person into action. *Very smooth on Nathan's part. Well orchestrated.* He didn't link the two situations, but Garrett bet that Nathan hoped the insider might link them, and be panicked enough to do something to expose himself. Thinking it through, Garrett relaxed slightly. *Nathan's fishing.* The changed file indicated that at least one analyst was involved, but there was no proof tying that person directly to him. Experienced enough not to be reactionary, Garrett knew that he didn't have to act just because Nathan was suspicious. He had time to develop a strategy. Nathan didn't know anything for certain. All he had to do was stay on top of the situation; key his strategy off situational aspects as they developed, put his pieces in place, and make the right plays.

Now certain of his position, Garrett lingered; allowing himself to be soothed by the spectacle of the city donning its nighttime finery, light by brilliantly sparkling light. He then headed back to his inner office and closed the door behind him.

Whatever the direction of events, the first piece to put in place was a scapegoat. Garrett thought scathingly of Cleve, and his plentiful instances of incompetence. After his firing, Garrett would only have to plant evidence from time to time as indication of his complicity. Cleve had been useful, but it was time to cut him loose. More with an eye toward the future than any hint of guilt, Garrett decided not leave him completely out in the cold. Instead, he'd set him up with a job where he could later be used, making it look as though he had really stuck his neck out for him. An added benefit was that he could then elevate Gabrielle to junior partner;

maybe get what he wanted sooner than expected. But he would have to get rid of Landry first.

The vibration of his cell interrupted Garrett's thoughts. He unholstered it, looked at the number, and then quickly picked up. "Garrett."

"Sir, this is Alan calling with your daily status," answered a crisp, businesslike voice.

"Continue."

"We've been unable to get close to either target. They have protection agents in place."

Garrett could not hide his shock. "Bodyguards?"

"Yes, sir," replied Alan. "We can't get through their security teams with basic surveillance. The agents are too highly skilled. If you require, we can escalate our procedures."

If the agents were that skilled, they were probably already tipped off. No need to give them any further clues. "No. I'll cancel the request. Thanks."

"As you wish," Alan replied. "We'll call in our agents."

Garrett stood immobilized, his thoughts racing. Nathan didn't just suspect—he knew *everything*...except whom. *But, Nathan does suspect me. If not, I would be central to his plan.* Gabrielle must have found out about the file and they somehow linked it to Avanti's proposal. One had nothing to do with the other, but it was a logical link to make.

The situation was now clear. Knowing that Avanti had the reputation of fighting dirty, Nathan wasn't taking any chances. He was going after them and the insider; Landry and Gabrielle were being protected against possible retaliation. What still eluded Garrett was how they had linked the merger to the failing bonds. Maybe it was a ruse to get the insider to expose himself. At the wet bar, he grabbed a mug and filled it with coffee, glancing at the inset clock. It was a little after six. Reflecting on his position, Garrett realized that it may be time to sever ties with Brett. *Last time we talked, he was surprised when I told him about the crash—but his surprise could easily have been because we found out.* He railed at himself for having made the rookie mistake of taking Brett at his word. Following a money trail was tedious, but still, researching the proposal was the first thing he should have done. He had to verify for himself that Brett knew—and he had to do it tonight.

CHAPTER EIGHT

Diversions

"What happened?" asked Gabrielle.

"Vennergy cancelled their reunion tour at the last minute," Sarah answered, sitting motionless on Julie's sectional, her head in her hands. "Lee Ann thinks I should have seen it coming. We've lost money because of all the late cancellations we had to make and it's my fault."

"That is *so* unfair," Gabrielle's anger kindled, her disappointment over the cancelled evening quickly forgotten. "It can't *possibly* be your fault. They're rock stars for crissake! They change their minds all the time."

"Part of my job is to babysit. Work very closely with the client," Sarah interrupted. "I was doing that and I *still* didn't see this coming. How could I not have? Lee Ann is right; I should have known. I don't know how I didn't."

"Don't they have to pay a penalty if they cancel?" Gabrielle asked.

"Sure, but it's hardly ever enough to cover everything," said Sarah. "Even worse is that the guests will remember that we had to cancel such a huge event."

Julie asked, "When did they decide to cancel?"

"I don't know," moaned Sarah. "Everything was fine just yesterday. When I talked to James, he seemed excited about the launch party."

"Who's James?" asked Gabrielle.

"Their publicist," Sarah said, falling backward onto the sectional cushion and staring despondently at the ceiling. "I've got a failure on my record now. Five years, and this is the first one. Things are slow lately, and events are going to the agents with the best track record. Just like that, I've taken myself off the A-list."

"You're saying they aren't going to give you events?" Julie asked.

Gabrielle shot a quick glance at Julie. It appeared they were thinking along the same lines. Something was missing in Sarah's story. She was one of Prentice and Associates best agents, and then out of nowhere, this happens, taking her out of contention. "Sarah, did you ask James why they cancelled?"

"I haven't talked to him. He left a message with Yvette," Sarah said.

"Who's Yvette?" asked Gabrielle.

"She's an agent-in-training. Right now she's my assistant," replied Sarah.

Some assistant. Gabrielle and Julie again exchanged glances.

"You need to talk to him yourself," Julie advised. "What have you got to lose?"

"I'll get second-tier events," Sarah said sadly to the ceiling. "I'll have to work my way back up to first tier. Competition's so fierce, I'm wondering if it's worth it. I haven't had a second-tier event in three years."

"Did you hear Julie?" Getting Sarah to listen was almost impossible at the best of times.

"I heard," sighed Sarah. "I'll call him. Whatever he says, I still should have known."

"If things are going to get that bad, what about changing agencies or going out on your own?" Gabrielle asked.

"Actually, I was thinking about freelancing." Sarah smiled ruefully, as she sat up. "Who knows, I could end up as a wedding planner. Not a bad life."

"Why *don't* you give freelancing a serious look?" asked Gabrielle. "You may be surprised at how well it turns out."

"I'll go in tomorrow and see how bad it is," Sarah replied. "Today was pretty brutal. Let's still go out though. I don't want to bring y'all down." She asked hopefully, "Any ideas?"

"What about a gallery showing? There's a card here on your end table, Jules." Gabrielle picked it up and handed it to her. "At the Shearing Fine Arts Gallery. It caught my eye because I've been curious about his work and I need some new wall candy."

"Who *needs* wall candy?" Sarah wanted to know.

"I do," said Gabrielle firmly.

"Oh, right," said Sarah. "Your walls *are* bare now."

Julie barely looked at the card in her hand. "I really hadn't thought about going."

Taking the card from Julie, Sarah read it and said, "Cool! It opens tonight and it's featuring his newest painting. I've wanted to see his work, too."

"We can go to dinner and then to the gallery," Gabrielle suggested.

"I don't know," Julie said.

"We don't have to go to the show," said Sarah, clearly trying to placate her. "Anyone have a better idea?"

"Come on, Jules," encouraged Gabrielle. "It'll be fun."

"Okay," said Julie petulantly. "I'll have to rummage around for different accessories." Though trying to hold it in, Sarah and Gabrielle burst into peals of laughter.

Sarah teased, "Not everybody has a vault full of accessories they have to dig through. Must be tough." They laughed harder.

"Very funny," scowled Julie, heading reluctantly toward her bedroom. "Everybody's a comedian tonight."

"You're the funny one," Sarah said, still laughing. "Thanks, hon. I really needed that."

A thought bloomed in Gabrielle's mind. "I know, we can open a Charleston Eddy's accessories store in one of the Loft Malls so Jules won't have to walk so far." Their laughter broke out again. Julie glanced back over her shoulder, surprised.

Sarah glanced at Gabrielle and winked, "We'll call it Sparks at the Lofts."

Whipping around to face them, her hands on her hips, Julie broke in, "That's actually a good idea." Their laughter faded, replaced with looks of skepticism. "Think about it. Sparks at the Lofts, by Charleston Eddy."

The idea slowly sinking in, Gabrielle said, "I think we're on to something, Jules."

"It does have a nice ring to it," agreed Sarah. "An accessories-only store from Charleston Eddy here at The Lofts. I'd shop there."

"Especially with what looks like bad times ahead," agreed Gabrielle. "Updating accessories costs far less than updating a wardrobe."

"If it works here, they can put it in other residential towers," Julie said, her excitement growing. "There could be Sparks at the Presidio, Sparks at the Crest, blah, blah, blah." She turned back to Sarah and Gabrielle. "Do you mind if I pitch it?"

"To Charleston Eddy?" asked Sarah, her voice higher than usual.

"Of course," said Julie, in exasperation. "Who else?"

"Go ahead," said Gabrielle.

"Yay!" Sarah exclaimed. "Something to celebrate after all."

~*~~~**~~~*~

Wearing only his boxer briefs, Jarin stood at the bathroom mirror, his face buried in a steaming towel. The day had been too hectic for his usual trip to the barber, and he was giving himself a much-needed shave. He also needed a trim, his hair a tad too long to be coerced into behaving. But out of time, he'd just have to put up with it. As he dropped the towel onto the counter to pick up the shaving mug and brush, his cell buzzed. Using his discarded towel, he cleared the steam from the waterproof Bluetooth caller-id display and saw that it was Nathan. Hurrying from the bathroom, he crossed the stateroom in three long strides, and grabbed the cell on the last buzz before it transferred to voicemail. "Jarin."

"It's Nathan. Have you talked to your dad?"

"About an hour ago. He conferenced us all in," Jarin replied. "Sounds like you had a helluva day."

"To say the least." Nathan's voice betrayed his fatigue. "Every manager tried to bluff, but Gabrielle's report caused them all to blink big time."

"At least they're forewarned, but Dad said you didn't think it would make a difference."

"Not soon enough. They've got their own analysts, apparently telling them something different. They haven't dug deep enough to find what Gabrielle found, but will they? We can't afford to wait."

"Can't believe they've got blinders on."

"That's exactly what it felt like," Nathan said wearily.

"I hope something pulls them back from the brink," Jarin said. "By the way, Dad mentioned...what's his name?"

"William. Larson. That alone made the trip worthwhile. Met in the elevator for crissake. I'll have to thank Joseph—and ISS I understand. Got him vetted in record time. Now we've just got to put the money together for his hedge fund, which is why I called."

"No problem at all. Dad asked about it too."

"You sure?"

"Absolutely. I'd want to do the same thing. They're clients or own companies in my sector—all our sectors—but they're also your friends and classmates. One of you needs to speak to them personally, beyond business protocol."

"Glad you see it that way. Thanks."

"No problem. Personal relationships trump the org chart." Curious about the hedge fund, Jarin changed the subject. "Think you'll be able to pull together the two and a half bil?"

Nathan laughed. "The hard part will be keeping it to that size. That's the most Will can handle. Everyone'll want to hedge more. Joseph's verifying Will's assumptions, but they're both figuring fifteen percent will cover. We just have to convince everyone else of the same."

"Wow, you're serious?"

"I know it's hard to believe. We're conservatively allowing twenty percent, with a cap at two hundred mil each. The main goal of Will's fund is to take the opposite position of the Wall Street houses."

"That means—"

"Yep, Will's betting that they're on the wrong end of a sucker bet. He was relieved by what he read in Gabrielle's report. He said it was far more thorough than their internal analysis. It verified for him that they're on the right track."

"Which brings me to the reason I'm glad you called. About Sparks—Joseph is hot to get his hands on it."

"Dovetails nicely with my strategy," said Nathan. "Already brought Josh up to date on our problems at NEI, by the way. We need to get Gabrielle and Sparks out of harm's way while we clear up our insider situation. How about I commit to a partner vote by Monday, which will have Gabrielle and Sparks transferred to SCI by say, Wednesday?"

"Sooner than I'd hoped. Thanks, Nathan. We need to get some of Joseph's financial analysts working with her ASAP. Being able to leverage Sparks should take some of the pressure off; help them get to the better alternatives faster."

"Agreed. Joseph's got a big job ahead of him."

"We all do," said Jarin. "It's going to be all hands on deck for the foreseeable future."

"Yeah," said Nathan. "We all have to do everything we can to survive this thing."

"Amen to that."

~*~~~**~~~*~

Going to The Corner Bistro had been a good idea. From there, it was only a four-block walk to the gallery. Gabrielle congratulated herself for remembering to forty-four her crew. Enjoying the short stroll under the city lights, she said. "It's a great night to be out."

"Don't know that I could've walked it if we'd had wine with dinner," said Sarah.

"You're already five-seven. Why do you need four-inch stilettos?" asked Gabrielle.

"So I can be as tall as Jules. Besides, I like them," answered Sarah, executing a perfect dancer's pirouette. Then she added mischievously looking down at Gabrielle, "Shorty."

Julie tried to stay composed, but a smile broke through followed by a short, loud laugh. "Sorry, Gabs, but that was funny."

"Ha ha," replied Gabrielle, trying hard to scowl. "Not my fault my genes are cutoffs. Pick on someone your own size."

Their laughter hadn't yet subsided when they reached the gallery door. Infected by their gaiety, the attendant grinned broadly. Taking their invitation from Julie, he waved them in. In the foyer, after they had all signed the guestbook, another attendant pointed them toward the exhibit entrance. "Right this way."

They turned the corner and were bombarded with color. Multihued, vibrant layers of it, radiating from all of the canvases. The outrageously rich visual tones astounded Gabrielle's senses. It was as if the very air was color. Julie and Sarah forgotten, she immersed herself in the vivid renderings, wandering among the stark white pillars where the smaller paintings hung.

At last able to look away from the canvases, she saw that colors worn by the guests reacted with colors in the paintings—both those on the pillars and on the walls—creating transient visual illusions. Even the greens and purples of her silk smock top participated in the dance. Unexpectedly, her eyes locked onto a spot empty of color. She blinked, trying to make sense of the void, and then realized that it was a consultant. They all wore black tonight. Everywhere, colors on the walls and pillars, in dazzling consort with colors in motion on the floor, disappearing into the occasional black hole. Enthralled with the visual effects, Gabrielle had not yet noticed the *scenes* in the paintings—landscapes, seascapes, cityscapes. Wandering slowly around the room for the second time, she again lost herself in Jarin Cole's work.

~*~~~**~~~*~

"Here to unveil his latest painting, *Vibrancy*, the artist, Jarin Cole!" The consultant stepped away from the open double doors, allowing Jarin and Estelle to enter the reception room. Guests greeted them with applause. Gesturing his thanks, Jarin left Estelle at the front of the half-circle forming around the painting and approached the four-by-three-foot canvas resting on its sturdy easel.

Turning back toward the sea of faces, he recognized many who had been with him from his very first show in Erin Shearing's Marina Cove gallery. Now, she also owned this exclusive Crescent City gallery, and he was about to reveal the painting that was sure to validate all of his previous work—and that yet to come. Whether or not those familiar people had bought any of his paintings, their wholehearted support and well wishes sustained him. He spoke especially to them when he said with humble sincerity, "Thank you very much for your support over the years. It has meant the world to me."

Another smattering of applause sounded as he reached for the edge of the drop-cloth and threw it off the painting. A momentary hush fell, followed by a few gasps, and then deafening applause accompanied by shouts of approval. Guests rushed forward, everyone anxious to congratulate Jarin on the new painting. He thought he recognized several of his security team among the guests. They hated evenings like this.

Within moments, Estelle appeared at his side, tucking herself in close to him as she lifted her face to his ear. "It's beautiful, Jarin. I had no idea how beautiful until now." As he turned toward her to whisper his thanks, she gently swept back an errant lock of hair from his forehead, brushed his lips with hers and disappeared into the crowd. Though surprised by her departure, he was grateful to be free to converse with the guests. Always deeply interested in others' perception of his work, he savored the opportunity to see it through their eyes. They, in turn, were delighted with his openness and willingness to engage.

Between conversations, Jarin noticed Estelle mingling throughout the room, her ruby and sapphire birthday bracelet flashing and sparkling against the black silk sheath she wore. She had only approached him once since the unveiling, bringing a light finger of cognac. His attempt to thank her was again silenced with a swift brush of her lips—and she was gone.

Having another quiet moment, Jarin now focused on Estelle. He noticed something decidedly different about her tonight. Abruptly, she turned toward the open doors, where Julie had appeared with another young lady he didn't recognize. *Gabrielle Winston perhaps?* Giving Julie a big hug, Estelle gestured toward Jarin and moved on to other guests. Though startled by the overt friendliness of someone she barely knew, Julie quickly recovered and met Jarin's gaze; her eyebrows raised. He gave her a subtle shake of his head. In response, Julie turned to her friend, said a few words, and dragged her back into the main gallery.

Understanding dawned regarding Estelle's behavior. There would be no ultimatum. Apparently, he had done something to cause Estelle to think that their relationship had risen to the next level, but he hadn't a clue what it was. It couldn't have been the bracelet. It was no more extravagant than the weekends on the Cape, or her personal Charleston Eddy's credit card. With her change in behavior, tonight was very pleasant. It would be easy to slide into the relationship she wanted. Almost effortless. *Except*, he reminded himself, *it isn't what I want.* As much as he enjoyed spending time with her, he needed to get away for increasingly longer periods of time. He could not accept that he would need the separation if she was the one. It would cause her pain to end their liaison, but it would be far crueler to continue it; allowing her to believe that there was potential for it to grow into more. He had no choice but to end it. *Tonight.*

~*~~~**~~~*~

Gabrielle came to the last painting in the main gallery...again. Peeking through the open double doors beside it, she saw a number of guests milling around a large canvas. As she approached the painting, those who had been blocking her view stepped aside to join other conversations.

Hit by the full force of the scene, Gabrielle was overpowered by its energy and beauty. Wild with vibrant, electrifying, unrestrained color, it was far more vivid than the others. The reflected rays of sunlight depicted on the canvas seemed to pulse gently in rhythm with her heartbeat. It was impossible to tear herself away.

"What do you think?"

Startled by the deep voice above her left shoulder, Gabrielle turned and focused on the man standing behind her.

"I'm sorry to startle you," said the consultant.

Released from the pull of the painting, Gabrielle formed a coherent question. "Is this of a real place?"

"Marina Cove at Skye Pointe, from the perspective of the center pier."

"How much is it?" Gabrielle asked tentatively.

"Vibrancy has sparked a bidding war," he confided. "It's in the high five figures now."

Turning back to the canvas, Gabrielle sighed, "It's worth any price."

"It certainly is," he agreed, wandering away to speak with other guests.

Better enjoy it now. I certainly can't afford to buy it. Gabrielle again lost herself in the painting.

"Gabby!" Sarah called from behind her. "Oh, my," she said, stopping mid-step.

Julie just stared. "Wow. I hadn't seen it yet."

"We're looking for you so we can meet Jarin Cole," Sarah finally said. "But here you are. You've probably met him already."

Gabrielle turned back to the painting. "No, I haven't met him."

"He wasn't here when you came in?" asked Julie anxiously.

Embarrassed, Gabrielle said, "He could have been, but I saw the painting and..."

"When will we ever have another chance to meet him?" asked Sarah. "I'll go find out if he's still here."

"Wait." Julie peeked around at the others in the room. Then she whispered, "You can meet him Saturday."

Sarah was enthusiastic. "You can introduce us?"

"Yes," Julie replied warily. "He's Jarin Cole San Chapelle—my brother."

Sarah and Gabrielle stared at Julie for several full heartbeats. She finally couldn't take it anymore. "Well, say something!"

Exaggerating a sigh, Gabrielle lifted Julie's lantern sleeve and pretended to peek under it.

"What?" asked Julie apprehensively.

"Just checking to see what else is up there. I already know about Landry and Nathan."

"What about them?" asked Sarah.

"They're my cousins," Julie replied. "Please understand. I had to respect their privacy."

"Believe me, Jules, I understand," Gabrielle assured her.

"Well I don't," admonished Sarah, crossing her arms. "Come on. Spill. What else is there?" The smirk she couldn't hold back ruined the effect.

Julie chuckled in relief. "That's the last of it, I think."

"No opera stars?" Sarah couldn't resist. "Maybe a president or two?"

"Well," started Julie, "there's a cousin on my mother's side," she said to Gabrielle and Sarah's disbelieving stares, "who everyone claims is the devil himself." Grinning mischievously, she added, "He can get us in."

"Just what I need," said Gabrielle through her laughter, "free tickets to hell. Maybe I can give them to Garrett."

"Bad Gabby," Sarah said, wagging her finger. "Bad, bad, bad."

"I'll behave." Gabrielle said, feigning chagrin as she turned back to *Vibrancy*. "Your brother must have a truly beautiful soul."

~*~~~**~~~*~

Estelle let them into her condo and reached for Jarin's jacket as she closed the door. "Let me hang that up for you," she said. He relinquished it as they walked past the formal living and dining rooms into the great room. "Something to drink?" she asked.

"I'll get it," he said. "Can I get one for you?"

"Just something light," she called over her shoulder, disappearing down the hallway to her bedroom suite.

At the bar, Jarin decided against something for himself. He expected a difficult conversation and wanted a clear head. For Estelle, he poured a half glass of the Zinfandel he found in the cooler. Leaving her glass on the bar, he wandered toward the great room window wall. Though blocks away, the dominant feature of the view was the SCI building. Estelle had bought herself this condo as a reward for finishing her dissertation. Jarin couldn't help but think she would hate the view after tonight.

Bare arms encircling his waist announced Estelle's return. It was time. "Estelle, we need to talk," Jarin said as he turned to her. She had stepped away and now stood facing him, nude. Her lusciously full lips and perfectly rounded heart-shaped hips beckoned, arousing him as they had never failed to do. Tonight, even knowing that he must end it, was no different.

"Tomorrow, darling," she said holding out her hand to him. "I've got something else in mind for tonight."

Taking her hand and squeezing it, Jarin said, "No, Estelle. This can't wait."

"Oh?" she challenged, stepping closer to him. Though he needed no further invitation, she again encircled him with her arms, pressing herself tightly to him.

Jarin looked down into her eyes, remembering their times together. Here. The Cape. *Island Rose.* She was right. It was fitting that they have one last time together. Having lost all restraint, he knew it would be a night for them both to remember. "Tomorrow then," he conceded, gathering her into her arms and leaning down for the first of their last kisses.

~*~~~**~~~*~

Seated comfortably in the rear-facing seat of the car speeding them back to The Lofts, Gabrielle sipped the Merlot that Julie had just poured for her. "I did it," she said. "And I'm really happy about it. Guess that means I've lost my mind."

"You wanted it, you bought it." Sarah shrugged. "What's the big deal?"

"But five thousand dollars? That's not wall candy. That's wall bling!" Gabrielle said. "I'll be paying for it for the next few months."

"Bling or candy, it's going to a good home," said Julie.

"Do *you* have any of his?" asked Gabrielle.

"Of course I do."

"I didn't see them," Sarah said, scrunching up her face as she tried to remember.

"They're in the bungalow I use on Coral Cove," said Julie. "Now that you mention it, maybe I'll bring some to my condo."

"You really should Jules," said Gabrielle. "I don't see how you could have them and not want them where you can see them every day." *M'Lady the Sea.* She even loved the name. "I can't wait to see it hung. Too bad it won't be delivered until Tuesday. I wonder, is *M'Lady* the ship, or the sea?"

"Who cares?" asked Sarah. "Either way, it's a beautiful painting."

"Wish I could have bought *Vibrancy*," Gabrielle mused. "I wonder how much it finally went for."

Sarah laughed. "You'd have to sell your condo."

"I finally got one of the consultants to tell me," Julie said, "Bidding was well into the mid six figures when we left."

"Geez," said Sarah. "I take it back, Gabs—you'd have to rob a bank."

After their laughter subsided, Julie said, "I feel sorry for the museum, though. Mr. Kirks, the curator, told me they really wanted it, but they'd been outbid and couldn't go any higher."

"That's too bad," Sarah replied. "By the way, why did you ask the consultant instead of your brother?"

"He never keeps track during a showing. Besides, he'd already left by then."

Alerted by the guardedness in her tone, Gabrielle and Sarah eyed her questioningly. "Look," started Julie, before either of them could ask. "I love Jarin. Very much. I'm the only one of us younger than he is and he looks out for me—always has. Sometimes he's so protective, he gets on my nerves. So I bark at him and he backs off, mostly. But as much as I love him, he's not someone for either of you to get involved with."

"No, you don't. You can't just stop there," said Sarah. "Explain."

Fishing for the right words, Julie finally said, "Jarin loves women—I mean he really *loves* women. But he's never loved any one of them enough to give up all the others."

Gabrielle and Sarah both replied with "Oh..."

"So I'm going to ask the nosy question. Tonight was he with someone?" Sarah asked.

"Yeah, and I could see a problem brewing," said Julie. "Better to leave them to it and talk to him later."

"Oh," said Sarah again, her voice full of understanding. "No wonder you pulled me out of the reception room tonight. Was he with the lady at the door?"

"Uh-huh," confirmed Julie. "We only met once before."

"Seriously? It looked like you were long-lost friends."

"I know. And Jarin didn't like it."

"Were we at the same show?" asked Gabrielle, amazed at what she had missed. "When did all this happen? Did you even get to *see* any of the other paintings?"

Julie laughed. "Yes we were. While you were looking at the paintings, and sure we did– while we were looking for you."

Trying to lighten the mood, Gabrielle said faking a swoon, "I'm in love," Julie and Sarah glanced at her sharply. "With his paintings." They all laughed, but Julie still looked a little worried. "Jules, you know I'm teasing, right?" Gabrielle asked.

Though Julie nodded, her expression was pensive. Then shaking off the mood, she held up the half full wine bottle and said, "Let's finish this off before we get home. Sarah, I want to see you make it upstairs in those stilettos."

"You're on," Sarah accepted the challenge and held out her glass for more.

~*~~~**~~~*~

Propped against the headboard, watching the sun as it rose above the eastern skyscrapers, Jarin waited patiently for Estelle to acknowledge that she was awake. The sun cleared the tip of Steeple Tower, setting Estelle's bedroom awash with sunlight. Unable to feign sleep any longer, she finally raised her head and met his gaze. Instantly, Jarin knew that he had not unwittingly given her misleading signals. She wore the same expression he had seen countless times on the faces of executives who had given their best pitch, yet had been forced to accept that the presentation of their software had fallen short. Now aware that last night had been her play all along, it was a little easier to do what he knew he must do.

Estelle turned away. "Can we at least have breakfast first?"

"It won't matter, Estelle," Jarin said gently. "Before breakfast, after breakfast—what I have to say will be the same."

"I don't want to hear it," she said, throwing herself out of bed.

"I'm sorry, Estelle, truly I am," he said, preparing for the onslaught. "But it's time to say good-bye."

Snatching her robe from the chaise, she covered herself. "It's *true* what they say about you," she said harshly, each word poisoned; each an attempt to inflict him with her pain. "I thought we had something different. But *you*. You are incapable of loving anyone!"

Jarin suffered the wounds from her words in silence. Though she would never know it, they cut to the heart of what he feared about himself.

"I'm having a bath." Estelle headed toward the bathroom door. Without looking back, she said, "I want you gone before I come out." She went in and closed the door behind her.

Focusing strictly on action, Jarin left Estelle's bed for the last time. Crossing the room to the chaise, he retrieved his phone from the pocket of his pants and speed dialed thirty-three. "Devon, I want the Spyder. Fifteen minutes." Within five he was dressed—without his jacket. He didn't know where Estelle had put it and refused to open the door to more pain—hers or his—by asking. On his way out of the bedroom, he noticed the bracelet and credit card prominently displayed on her chiffonier, as if for him to take. In a couple of weeks, he'd send an attorney to negotiate a settlement for the closure of her account. The bracelet was hers to keep.

Stepping off the elevator in the garage, he was relieved to see that the Spyder was already there. However, it wasn't Devon who stood by its door. "Give me the damn keys, Carson," Jarin said. "Aren't you supposed to be somewhere else?"

"Took a slight detour." Carson scrutinized him. "Wanted to make sure you didn't have a death wish."

"You're *insane*," said Jarin, his voice still abrasive with anger. He took the keys. "Just want to get the hell on the road."

"Don't let me stop you," Carson said, stepping away from the door.

Jarin stepped over the door and slid into the driver's seat. "Don't intend to." Starting the car, he gave Carson one last look of exasperation and peeled out of the garage.

His thoughts rigidly constrained, Jarin concentrated on driving. Weaving in and out of the light morning traffic until Crescent City was behind him, tearing north up the coastal highway to a barely visible westward juncture, he channeled his frustration into tight control of the car. Slowing the car to eighty miles per hour, Jarin turned the wheel just enough to direct the car in roughly the right direction onto the westward road, oversteering at the last moment to keep the wheels on the pavement. He negotiated the narrow, winding two-lane road, accelerating and braking in perfect synchronicity with its obscured hairpin curves. Bypassing the downhill turnoff to Marina Cove, he banked into yet another curve on the westward climb up to the lookout on Coral Point, some twelve hundred feet above the coves. *If only love were like driving. I'd be an ace.* After miles of intense concentration, he abruptly broke into the clearing atop Coral Point. He braked one last time, bringing the Spyder to a stop across three of the seven parking places.

Jarin climbed out of the car and walked to the lookout point. The panoramic view of the five Skye Pointe coves and the southern tip of Port Hudson relaxed him enough to release the flood of thoughts he had imprisoned since Estelle pronounced her edict.

Xavier San Chapelle had been the driving force behind all that Jarin saw below. Despite the hardships Xavier had faced and the improbable tasks he had set himself, he still managed to find the love of his life—not once, but twice. Here Jarin stood, his three-times great-grandson, with comparatively trivial relationship problems to which he had no solution. And he was facing dangerous days; in their way, as dangerous as the days when Xavier built the family fortune. Jarin refused to jeopardize the future of the family because he was preoccupied with failed relationships. "I can't do this anymore."

There was nothing left but to go the route of contracted companionship. The terms and conditions all spelled out; the two parties affirming their understanding by affixing their signatures to the page. No room for unrealistic expectations; absolutely no chance of a misunderstanding. Or at least if there were one, the agreement was there to remind them of the Ts and Cs. Such liaisons were inherent to the cultures of some of his European cousins, where the separation of physical need from matters of the heart was clearly understood. For Carson, still consumed by the adrenaline rush of running field operations, it was the only thing that made sense. Landry saw it as the logical choice. He expected to find love one day, but wasn't going out of his way to search for it. *For me though, it has become the last resort. I've run out of time.*

From this point forward, steering SCI through the impending storm had to be the only thing that claimed his attention. It would take all of his concentration. But first, he needed to clear his head. As it was Friday, there was nothing on his calendar that was pressing or needed his direct input. His supremely competent office staff always relished the opportunity to keep things going in his absence. They would get a chance today. On the way back to the car, Jarin pulled out his cell and called his office.

Though barely seven o'clock, Lia picked up. "Good morning, Jarin."

"I'll be on cell and laptop today Lia," he said, clambering over the side of the car into the seat. "Postpone my face-to-face meetings, and ring me only for the other managers, Dad, Nathan, Landry, or Carson."

"Will do," she replied.

He started the engine and navigated slowly back down the road, in desperate search of a new scene to paint and the solace painting would bring him.

CHAPTER NINE

Exposed

It was 7:25 a.m. Garrett sat at his desk, bleary-eyed, and in an extremely foul mood. Instead of going home, or even to Elaine's, he had sacked out on the sofa in his outer office at around four a.m. and was now wearing his spare suit and a bad shave. It was doubtful that Nathan was as aware of the details of the Avanti money trail as he now was. *I feel like hell, but it was worth it.*

Absently flipping through the analysis, Garrett reflected on the hours he had spent researching; mining bits and scraps of information from the data services to which he personally subscribed. In his hands were the details of how Avanti had sold off most of their real estate bonds six months ago and had transferred the rest, including the ones being used to finance the NEI merger, into the subsidiaries of one of their holding companies, Great Creek Holdings.

It further illustrated that Avanti had used those bonds to tender offers to various companies that were either competitors or could enhance their position. Additionally, it showed that all of the subsidiaries of the holding company were on the negative side of the balance sheet, although Great Creek Holdings itself was not. That Avanti had hidden the bonds in Great Creek, and shared only its overall performance, intimated that they knew the bonds would deteriorate and were taking advantage of it; sending targeted competitors and "trouble makers" spiraling downward, and also buying valuable companies on the cheap. Though it would be difficult to prove in court, it was obvious to anyone who could read a balance sheet that Brett had to have been aware.

In spite of his anger and as much as he hated to admit it, Garrett felt a grudging admiration for Avanti's creativity. Then a blaze of resentment intensified his wrath. He would have gotten nothing for his efforts; would have been dependent on Brett for both his income and to keep his involvement secret. Expecting that NEI would be his once they had forced Nathan out, Garrett had put his position, and his future, on the line. The evidence he now held proved that he had done it all for naught. Contemptuously, he tossed the analysis aside. It was not in his nature to merely be relieved that he had discovered Brett's ruse before it caused him irreparable harm. He needed to exact retribution. Garrett's cell buzzed. It was Brett. He hastily retrieved the recorder from his attaché case, attached it to his phone, and picked up the call.

"It's Brett. Wanted to see if there was any more news."

Brett's casual expectation that he was still in the dark escalated Garrett's anger into full burn. "As a matter of fact there is," he replied coldly. "I'm ending our association." As soon as the words were out, he realized that he had made the wrong move. He'd let his temper do the talking, telegraphing his punch before he was ready to take the full swing. His only choice now was to follow through. Still, he savored dealing Brett a blow he hadn't seen coming.

"I beg your pardon?"

"You heard me," Garrett said. "I'm ending our association—the merger, throwing business to your companies, all of it."

"You don't want to do that." Brett said.

"Hell yes I do. I followed the money trail, Brett. You were setting me up."

"What d'you mean?"

"You know damn well what I mean," Garrett said. He summarized his findings. "Don't try to deny it."

"It's not what it appears to be."

"What is it then? And when were you going to tell me?"

"Let's sit down and hash this out. You're overreacting."

"There's nothing to hash out," Garrett said harshly. "My decision is final."

"You'll regret this, Garrett."

"The only thing I regret is trusting you. You should have played it straight up, Brett. I'm *nobody's* patsy."

He ended the call, turned off the recorder, and placed it with his analysis into his attaché case. As he did so, the analysis Gabrielle had performed for Blackhawk entered his thoughts. After becoming aware of it, Brett had elevated the Blackhawk president to his board; a ceremonial position with no real authority. *Fishy.* If Garrett could prove that Blackhawk inefficiencies were hiding something underhanded, he could take the offensive. But he had to act quickly now that Brett was forewarned. Abruptly, he left his inner office. Elaine had just arrived and was powering up her computer.

"Brew up some coffee—and get me some breakfast will you?" he said as he strode through the outer office. He would wake himself up with a brisk walk before working out the details of his strategy.

~*~~~**~~~*~

Leaning against the golf cart, Brett watched the others of his foursome approach the green. His composure belied the fierce anger that he concealed; all of it focused on Garrett. *He followed the money trail. Damn good piece of work. Too bad it won't do him any fuckin' good.* The golfer furthest away took a mighty swing and the ball dribbled forward a few yards. Brett cussed in annoyance.

Garrett hated being used. Odds were that NEI was using him, too. The idiot apparently didn't realize that he had no career path with Nathan at the helm. He wasn't connected; he was just there until someone in the right family showed up to replace him. *I would have rewarded him as long as he toed the line. I would have allowed him to run NEI—like Neal is running Blackhawk.* Incensed that Garrett had thrown his generosity back in his face, Brett had no intention of turning the other cheek. Heedlessly, he unholstered his cell and hit speed dial.

Winston answered, "Is there a problem?"

"There's a situation I need taken care of," Brett said, stalling. He should have thought through a plausible scenario before he called. It needed to be significant enough that Winston would act, and also had to be connected to the current operation. "The message needs to be clear, but nonfatal."

"What's the situation?" asked Winston.

Having come up with a good cover, Brett replied, "He's getting too close to what's happening at Blackhawk, It's not an NEI investigation. He's doing it on his own."

"We'll take care of it. Just give me the name."

"Garrett Stratford."

As soon as Winston hung up, another voice filled Brett's head—that of his father. "I'll tell you what my father told me. If you ever have to use this number, you may find yourself sliding down a slippery slope. Once you consider them as a legitimate part of your operations, you've gone too far." Even without that reminder, Brett knew he had crossed the line. Before considering anything else, he had just picked up the phone and dialed. What's more, he had lied to get their cooperation. His father was right. Pronouncing punishment was becoming too easy. There was no such thing as a rescinded order. Winston had already told him that. Brett now had to live with the knowledge that he had sentenced three people. Garrett deserved it; his cousin maybe less, but the girl... *No more—for my own sake.* Brett pulled up the contact on his phone and erased it. Having the number in his safe was all he needed; difficult enough to get to so that he would use it only as a last resort.

But the analysis... Garrett was likely to share it with Nathan. Brett considered the possible outcomes. He had already conceded that the NEI merger ploy was dead. Having that app would counterbalance anything Nathan tried to do. *Even if all I ever use it for is leverage. No need to act.* The sound of club hitting ball drew his attention. The golfer had managed to loft the ball onto the green. As though he hadn't seen the earlier one, Brett called out, "Nice shot Leland." *Hate wasting my time with these assholes. But they're inking the merger deal as soon as we're done. One down, six to go.*

~*~~~**~~~*~

Breakfast and the train ride into the city with Julie and Sarah, a short walk to NEI, and Gabrielle had not seen anyone that could have been in her security crew. *I guess that's the point.* Completing the semblance of a normal Friday was yet another dire warning from Sheila that Garrett was in the worst possible mood. Feeling deep sympathy for Elaine, Gabrielle was again relieved that dealing with his behavior was something that she seldom had to do.

Once through the doors beyond Sheila's desk, the facade of normalcy fell away. No one conversed in the corridors or aisles, the various coffee and water stations were empty of visitors; even the break room lacked its typical Friday morning crowd. The sound of feverish typing dominated, a sign that all of NEI was honed in on meeting Nathan's deadline. Last night, Gabrielle had not received any calls, text messages, or emails from the team; and had only received two overflow analyses to review. She emailed the results of those, along with her own to Mary Alice before she left Julie's. All that was left to do was complete Nathan's spreadsheet as soon as Sparks completed the remaining few reports that had still been running when they left for the train.

In her cube, Gabrielle retrieved her laptop from her backpack and snapped it into its docking station. Leaving it to boot up, she headed to the break room. Stan was just walking away from the refrigerator as she entered. "Hey rookie," she teased. "How's it going?"

Disgruntled, he asked, "So when, exactly, do I stop being a rookie?"

"How long have you been here?"

"About four months."

"Two to go." Gabrielle smiled encouragingly as she opened the refrigerator and took a bottle of water.

"Hope I make it," Stan reluctantly smiled back.

Closing the door, Gabrielle laughed. "Of course you will. Don't be so gloomy."

Stan's smile widened slightly. "Anyway, I was just looking for you. Forgot to give this to you yesterday. I know it's only for a couple of days, but figured you should have it since I'm working on your project," he said handing her a slip of paper.

"What is it?" she asked. She looked at it. *He must be joking.*

"My login info."

"Why are you giving it to me?"

"Should I give it to Landry, then? Cleve has all ours in case of an emergency."

"No, that's okay," Gabrielle said, trying to appear disinterested as she put it in her pants pocket. "I'll take it."

"I think I'm all done," he said, turning to leave the break room, "But I'll check in with Cristin and Raphael and see if they have anything more for me."

Watching him leave, Gabrielle urgently considered the ramifications. Cleve had all the login information for his team. *I've got to tell Landry.* But there was a nine a.m. deadline and Gabrielle knew that she should be running a last minute check. *It's 8:10. I'll just have to do both.* Nearly running for the door, she collided with Raphael on his way in.

"Hey Gabs, something on fire?" He caught and steadied her on his way into the break room. "You're looking anxious. Scared of losing the bet?"

"You wish," was her automatic reply. Raphael opened the refrigerator and emerged with a bottle of orange juice. "I just saw Stan. He was on his way to see you. Do you need some more help?"

"Of course not." Raphael said, dismissing her suggestion. "Actually, Stan turned out to be far better than we expected."

"Glad to hear it," she said. "Nine o'clock is right around the corner." Raphael slowed his pace to hers as they both entered the aisle. Gabrielle turned toward her cube hoping that he would go to his.

"We'll make it. I'll probably be free to help you out." Making a show of considering his next remark, he said, "On second thought, I want to win the bet."

Hoping that a return jibe would goad him into going to his cube, Gabrielle said, "I'm already done. Just because you want something doesn't mean you're going to get it."

"You'd be surprised how often I get what I want, Gabs," he said, turning down his aisle.

To lend credence to her pretense, Gabrielle continued to her cube. On the way there, inspiration struck. Charging through the entry, she quickly logged in and IM'ed Mary Alice. "Take the lead on the deadline check." The next second she received Mary Alice's answering, "Will do," and heard her start down the next corridor to begin the check. Moving quickly and quietly, Gabrielle got past the analysts' cubes unhindered. Looking once more over her shoulder as she turned down Partners' Row, she walked right into someone, who wrapped his arms around her. It was Garrett.

Immediately, she tried to push away. "Garrett, I'm so sorry."

Resisting Gabrielle's efforts to free herself, he grabbed her upper arms, shook her slightly, and then released her. "You don't bother to look where you're going?" Gabrielle stumbled, but regained her balance. "It's a bad idea to entrust the future of our clients to someone who doesn't bother to look a few feet in front of her. I sincerely hope you're paying better attention to the project you've been assigned."

Her back to the wall, Gabrielle resolutely met his cold green glare. "I need to clarify a few points with Landry regarding the project. We have a very tight timeframe, so please excuse me." She stepped away from the wall intending to go around him, but he quickly braced his hand against it. She was trapped.

"Your team had better put in a stellar performance, Ms. Winston." Garrett said, leaning in close to her face.

"You're blocking—"

Garrett cut her off again, his voice a suggestive murmur. "Things will be different when I'm managing partner, Gabrielle. And make no mistake, I *shall* be managing partner." His eyes, no longer icy, burned into hers. Fear edged its way into Gabrielle's anger. But she resisted the impulse to shrink away from him. "You'll have no choice but to get with the program." Lowering his hand and backing away, he said in a louder voice, "In the future, Ms. Winston, please better schedule your time so that you don't have to run people over in the corridors." He held her gaze for a few heartbeats longer, and then strode swiftly around the corner.

Sheila was right. Garrett was in *rare* form today. Shaken, Gabrielle replayed the encounter. She was relieved to have maintained her composure; but angry that she had failed to prevent him from invading her personal space with verbal, physical—and maybe even sexual?—intimidation. Briefly, she considered telling Landry. *Not enough to tell.* The intensity of what she had experienced would be lost during any attempt at an explanation. Her word against his. She refused to give him the chance to portray her as weak; unable to stand up to a reprimand that any man would have taken in stride. Her hatred for him intensified. She would record the incident and keep her distance. If he sought her out, managing partner or not, she would file an official complaint. *SOB is not getting away with this.* She pushed away from the wall and hurried down Partners' Row to Landry's office.

~*~~~**~~~*~

Knocking at Landry's half-closed door, she called, "It's Gabrielle—I've got a question about the project."

"Come on in." Gabrielle entered his office and closed the door behind her. When she turned to face him, Landry's expression quickly became concerned. "What's happened?" he asked, rising from his chair. Gabrielle approached his desk and handed him the folded paper she had just removed from her pocket.

"Stan's login information. Apparently Cleve has it for everyone on his team. Stan thought you or I would want them, too," she said instead of answering his question. "I also found that Cleve's team accounted for almost ninety percent of the bad analyses. I thought it was because of Cleve's choices, but this suggests maybe not."

"Both could have been factors—choice and file tampering," Landry mused as he sat back down. "So this is our starting point. You played that very well by the way. Took me by surprise. I thought you really had a question. Especially since..." He examined her carefully. "Well, no matter now."

"Thanks, Landry," said Gabrielle. "So if any of Cleve's team were on the shared drive..."

Yes, we don't know if it was that person or Cleve. Or maybe even Garrett."

"So you do suspect him." Gabrielle welcomed the news. She wanted it to be him; she needed to be a part of taking him down.

"Yes, things are starting to make sense now."

"Are you going to explain or, sorry, maybe I'm prying."

"No, you need to know this." Landry waved her to a chair in front of his desk. "You know that Cleve is 'Garrett's man.'" Gabrielle nodded as she sat down. "What you don't know is how vehemently Garrett champions him, building a case for making him senior partner. The general feeling is that Garrett has a blind spot because Cleve kisses ass so hard. But this little piece of information means Garrett could be in total control of him."

"You mean Garrett and Cleve could be the insiders?"

"Possibly, but more likely that Garrett is the insider and Cleve is being used. He may not even know what's going on." Landry leaned forward in his chair. "Do you think he knows how to make the file change?"

"Cleve? No way," answered Gabrielle. "Anyone on our team could have done it though. How do we prove it was Garrett?" *It'll be my pleasure to take his ass out.*

"Not 'we' Gabrielle," Landry corrected her. "It will most likely be the IT security team that Carson's put in place. We just need to give them ideas of where to look. He eyed her disapprovingly. "Looks like you're starting to take this personally."

"I thought you said business *is* personal," she replied, taking refuge in his words.

"It is," he concurred. "But when you start putting personal desires above the business, you'll start behaving in a negative way that's bound to catch up with you—sooner or later."

What's he trying to sell me?

"I'm not being a hypocrite, Gabby," Landry said, as if he had read her mind. "The hardest thing to do is to put your personal feelings aside and make objective decisions, but that is exactly what you have to do. I know things are strained between you and Garrett. I probably have made it worse by allowing you to see how rocky my relationship is with him."

Not you, Garrett just did. Gabrielle's short, derisive laugh caused Landry to pause.

"Was it that bad?" Landry asked.

"No, it's just that...you're not the only one who has contentious conversations with him."

"True," Landry continued. "Understand though, as badly as I want him out, we are not specifically targeting him. We are following the clues and making objective decisions about next steps, but only the next steps that are best for the firm."

Though Gabrielle stubbornly tried to find fault with Landry's words, she found none. On the surface, it may have sounded like splitting hairs, but there really was a subtle distinction. She would have to learn how to stay on the right side of the line. *Business first. If the pieces fit, then we kick his ass.* "You're right," Gabrielle allowed. "I know you're right, but—"

"No buts," Landry firmly admonished. "Cross the line, and you're on your way to becoming one of Garrett's ilk."

The icy splash of Landry's words dampened Gabrielle's frustrations. Garrett was going to get his. It was only a matter of time. And Stan's login information was a left uppercut to his jaw. It didn't matter whether or not she was the one to throw the knockout punch. Landry was right, and she had no position from which to argue. *Still I wish...*

"Speaking of following clues, this information is too important to sit on. I've got to let Carson and Nathan know *now*. And you've got to make sure the team meets the deadline."

Letting go of her anger, Gabrielle mustered a smile for Landry and rose from the chair. "You're right. Again."

Before she got to the door, Landry said. "You're handling all this very well, by the way. Far better than I expected."

Gabrielle looked back, and was gratified by the sincerity in his eyes. "Thanks Landry," she said, and left for the analysts' cubes. *Hope Mary Alice hasn't berated everybody into mutiny.*

~*~~~**~~~*~

Energized from his walk, his encounter with Gabrielle, and a cup of Elaine's freshly brewed coffee, Garrett sat at his computer and navigated out to the NEI archive. After a few seconds of searching, he found Gabrielle's analysis of Blackhawk; completed just after the first of the year. He reviewed the extremely thorough findings with grudging respect.

Of the many processes and procedures that she had marked for improvement, one was that the trucking schedule had not contained all of the trucks passing through the main depot. *We didn't understand why Blackhawk declined to act on the recommendations. But they wouldn't act if they had something to hide.* Taking the chance that they did, he picked up his cell and hit a speed dial key. "This is customer 5487553," he said. "I need some surveillance work."

~*~~~**~~~*~

It was eight-fifty. Mary Alice and a few of the team gathered around the opening of Gabrielle's cube. "There you are," she said as Gabrielle joined them. "It's all done. We just have to send the report."

"Let's do it," said Gabrielle. She and the others followed Mary Alice to her cube. After Gabrielle's quick review; Mary Alice clicked Send, emailing their work to Nathan and the senior partners, with a CC to Landry. "Thanks, Mary Alice," said Gabrielle. "You ran the project well." Mary Alice beamed. "Now, let's see if the partners need anything more." The team dispersed, sharing tall tales of their past twenty-four hours.

"Well, Gabrielle," said Raphael as they walked back toward her cube. "Looks like you beat us—fair and square."

"I wouldn't call it fair," said Gabrielle. "I only had two reports other than my six. How many did you have?"

"I'd say about twelve each," replied Cristin. "But that wasn't the bet. You finished last night; we finished this morning. You won."

"Say we call it a draw?" negotiated Gabrielle. "I'll join you next Friday."

"I won," Stan chuckled, punching Raphael's shoulder.

"Won what?" Gabrielle asked.

"Raphael said you would try to weasel out of it," Stan said. "We had a side bet. I said that you wouldn't."

"Thanks for the vote of confidence, Stan," Gabrielle said, rolling her eyes at Raphael.

Cristin laughed. "Wrong again, Raphael."

"Well it's not next Friday yet," Raphael retorted. "I'm not paying up until then."

Their voices trailed off as they headed toward Raphael's cube. Gabrielle smiled. *I'll go—can't let the rookie down...*

~*~~**~~*~

Within an hour, Garrett leaned back in his chair, satisfied that he was on the way to regaining control. Four large brown addressed envelopes lay spread across his desk. Beside each rested a handwritten note containing detailed instructions for what should be done with the envelope contents in the event of his untimely death.

Additionally, he was already working toward retaliation. *Don't know what I'll do with the results of the surveillance just yet; if there aren't any, I'll just keep digging.*

He opened the first large envelope, pulled out a smaller one, and checked that it contained a copy of his analysis of the Avanti money trail and tapes of his fourteen conversations with Brett—including the one from this morning. He taped one of the notes to it and sealed it. He then put the smaller envelope back inside the large one and sealed it as well. He repeated the procedure for each of the other three notes and sets of envelopes. One was going to his personal attorney, the others to attorneys he had worked with in the past. The originals of everything were in his attaché, going home to his personal safe. Elaine buzzed. Garrett pressed the button on his desk phone. "Yes?"

"The courier is here. Shall I come in for the packages?"

"Sure." Elaine knocked, then opened the door and approached his desk. Garrett had tightly reined in his aggression all morning—except for letting off a little steam with Gabrielle. Now his awakened physical need surged forcefully through him, focused entirely on Elaine. "Good morning," he said. Elaine smiled, avoiding his eye, and picked up the packages from his desk. Garrett watched her turn and walk to the door, allowing her to step through the doorway before he spoke. "By the way," he said as she placed her hand on the knob. "I'll be working through lunch today."

"All right," said Elaine, the doorknob rattling slightly under her hand. "What time shall I pick up lunch for you?"

"About eleven-thirty," said Garrett. "And don't be late."

"Yes, Garrett," she said. Without looking back, she closed the door behind her.

A vehement lover, Garrett left Elaine far too disheveled to be seen after their midday trysts. Having the office next to the executive elevator alcove had its advantages, as did having solid inner office walls instead of glass ones. With the outer office walls opaqued, as they were today, Elaine had merely to slip out of the side door into one of the two elevators and upstairs to her condo, where she could repair the damage. On some days, they needed a cover story to explain her prolonged absence: a long lunch, or—when he had been too aggressive—the afternoon off. With his jarringly acute need for release, today would be one of those days.

~*~~~**~~~*~

Back at her desk, Gabrielle used VPN to access her server and check Sparks' progress on the last of the reports for Nathan's spreadsheet. They were all completed. But before she could download them, Landry's voice sounded urgently but quietly over her shoulder.

"Gabby, shut down VPN and take your laptop off the network. *Now.*"

Gabrielle quickly obeyed.

"Don't power it down," he instructed. "Here—plug this one in." He handed her the one he had been carrying close to his side, which looked similar to hers. She moved hers out of the way, docked the look-a-like, and powered it on. "Log in and start the secure screen saver." She did as he directed. "Come on," he whispered. "I've got yours. Bring everything else—your backpack, phone, everything."

What's happening? Gabrielle started to voice her question.

Landry placed his finger gently over her lips and waited for her to meet his gaze. "Not here," he mouthed, almost inaudibly, brushing his finger quickly and gently across her lips. Their eyes met again for the briefest moment before he drew his hand away. Turning, he checked the aisle and then gestured for her to follow.

Quickening her pace, Gabrielle followed him quietly down the aisle, through the corridor to Partners' Row and then past the senior partner office suites to Nathan's, where Lois waved them into his inner office. Carson and Nathan were already there; their expressions grim. She turned to Landry and saw his face for the first time since they'd left her cube. His temper was barely under control.

Gabrielle had to know. "What's happened?"

CHAPTER TEN

In or Out?

Carson broke the news. "Your laptop's been compromised. When you opened the VPN port to Sparks, the trace detected the worm and alerted me."

"How? Who? Did they get to Sparks?"

"We don't know anything yet," answered Carson. "We'll have to take your laptop for the next few hours—maybe overnight—for analysis and hardening."

"Is there another I can use?" asked Gabrielle, with growing apprehension. "I've still got to complete Nathan's spreadsheet. Maybe if Sparks isn't infected—"

"I'm afraid, Gabrielle, you are missing the point." Nathan interrupted sharply. "I doubt that anyone here—other than you—is concerned that you'll have to stop working. *We* are concerned for your safety."

Stung by his reprimand, Gabrielle asked, "My safety?"

Patience overlaying his anger, Nathan asked, "Don't you see the danger?"

"I know that my laptop has been compromised, but how does that translate into a threat to my *personal* safety?"

"How can you not see it?" Landry demanded.

"I don't seem to have the same information you do."

"We've told you what these people are like," stated Landry. "It's enough that they've gotten to your laptop. We're not giving them a chance to get to you."

At risk of angering him further, Gabrielle still felt compelled to say, "It seems that since they've gotten this close, I'm now our best chance of flushing them out."

"*No.*" Landry said as he crossed the short distance between them. "Your involvement ends here. We will not put you any more at risk."

"It seems I'm at risk whether I'm involved any further or not," said Gabrielle. "So, we should try to get the most possible benefit from that risk."

"That's logic, Gabrielle—this is not a logical situation," Landry said. It's too dangerous."

Suddenly aware that Carson and Nathan watched very closely, Gabrielle surmised that Landry spoke for all of them. He was right; the situation was becoming increasingly chaotic. *But logic brings order out of chaos.* "We have a lead, Landry. If you pull me out, you'll have to start all over. Or are you saying that Carson's crew can't protect me?"

"Carson's crew?" Landry murmured in disbelief. "Carson's crew? You call your security team 'Carson's crew'?" Enraged, he advanced on her, stopping with his face merely inches away from hers. "Is this a game to you?"

"No. It's not a game." Gabrielle hurled back, infuriated that he too had invaded her personal space. "If I thought that, I'd have no problem leaving. Isn't that what people do with games? Turn them off and walk away when they're tired of playing?"

Staggered by the fierceness of her response, Landry backed away. "That was way, way out of line. I apologize." Despite the increased distance between them, Gabrielle still felt buffeted by his intense scrutiny. "Why's this so important to you?" he asked. Nathan and Carson, who had started toward them, hesitated, but remained watchful.

Gabrielle's thoughts surfaced slowly. "I'm proud of what I've contributed to NEI. And now someone is using my work against us. I need to help put it right. Especially when I know—we all know—I have skills we can use."

"I don't like it—at all." Landry paced as he considered her answer, his expression rife with conflict. Watching, Gabrielle realized that her continued involvement could well be decided by his next action. The wait was nearly intolerable. Finally he spoke. "Carson what can we do to keep Gabrielle safe?"

"We'll have to take her off the train," he said. "I'll drive her from now on."

"And you think she should stay?" Landry pursued.

"It's her choice, Landry—and she seems to have made it."

"Nathan?"

"Gabrielle has made a good point—she *is* our best analyst," Nathan said. "Carson isn't bothered by her choice. So yes for now, but reluctantly. And," he added, "I reserve the right to change my mind at any time. Gabrielle, if I should change my mind, my decision is *final*. I will not hear any rebuttals. Is that clear?"

Relieved that Landry had sought consensus, she said, "It's clear. Thank you, Nathan."

"Looks like you're getting your way Gabby," Landry conceded. "I'm out-voted."

Afraid that she might be pushing her luck, Gabrielle asked, "Carson, can we prove that Sparks isn't infected?" Landry quickly turned away, but not before Gabrielle caught a glimpse of his face. *Go ahead and kill me then. At least you could stop worrying.*

"We'll check it when we return your laptop," Carson answered. "Until then, don't use it."

Resigned, she said, "I guess I'll just have to find something else to do this afternoon."

Nathan's laughter reduced the tension. "Don't sound so sad about it. Go have some fun. Start the weekend early."

"But I can't finish the spreadsheet," Gabrielle reminded him.

"I'm sure Carson will have a solution by the end of the day," Nathan said, glancing at Carson, who nodded. "Tomorrow will be soon enough."

"I should have been more careful with my laptop—I shouldn't have left it alone."

"Were you going to strap it in a holster and carry it around like your cell?" Landry asked.

Choosing not to be baited by his sarcasm, Gabrielle simply replied, "I guess not." She picked up her empty backpack; a not so subtle reminder of her situation. "What's the plan? Am I leaving the usual way?"

"Not this time," Carson replied. "We don't want it to be obvious that you aren't here. We need to see who's looking for you—who tries to access the laptop."

"Does it do anything, or is it just to make people think I'm still here?"

This time, Carson's barely there smile held menace. "Both. There's a trap for whoever planted the worm. Sooner or later, hopefully today, they'll come back and try to collect the readout. There's only one USB port. When a device is plugged in, a GPS tracking dot will rub off and activate."

Spy stuff again. "Won't they see the dot?"

"Sure," Carson acknowledged. "But only if they look for it. Generally, nobody does."

Still analyzing the scenario, Gabrielle had one last question. "Shouldn't I come back and get it at the end of the day? Everybody knows I don't leave it overnight."

Though her question was directed to Carson, Landry answered instead, in a tone leaving no room for argument. "Absolutely not—I'll take care of it."

~*~~~**~~~*~

Leaving Landry and Nathan in the inner office, Gabrielle and Carson rode the outer office elevator down to the executive garage. "You're a lot tougher than you look," said Carson. "You held your own with Landry. That can't have been easy."

"It wasn't," Gabrielle admitted. "But I had to. It doesn't make sense for me to disappear now. I hope he understands."

"Oh, he understands," Carson said. "He doesn't like it, but he understands. He was counting on you to want to be safe."

"He underestimates me—you *all* do."

"That's not it. It's just that no one, including me, wants to put you at risk. Technically, Gabrielle, this is not your fight," Carson said. "It isn't right for you to be involved. But you found some things that put you in the middle of it, and you refuse to get out."

The elevator stopped. "Do *you* think I should get out?"

"Yes, I do." Carson looked down at her as he reached to hold the door as it opened. "Will you?"

Despite Carson's extremely well done "good cop" to Landry's ranting "bad cop," Gabrielle had made her decision. "No."

"I guess I knew that," he said.

To direct his attention elsewhere before he could try any advanced techniques of persuasion, Gabrielle asked. "By the way, how'd you get here so fast?"

"I was already here—in IT."

They neared the car, Carson finishing up with his roving eye routine. "So what now?" she asked.

Opening the passenger door for her, he countered. "Where do you want to go?"

What do I want to do? Gabrielle seated herself in the car. "Well you could take me to Cafe Spore," she teased, stalling for time. "On second thought, it's probably too early. But I hear it's the place to be on Fridays."

"Cafe Spore?" Carson chuckled. "I didn't take you for a gamer."

"I'm not," said Gabrielle. "A few of our team are going there tonight, but I begged off until next week. I can't imagine spending Friday nights at a gaming café."

"Who's going?" Carson asked.

Scooting forward in the seat, Gabrielle stuck her head out to see his face. "Are you making idle conversation or is there a professional interest?"

"You don't miss much, do you?" Carson grinned. "Both," he allowed.

"Okay then—Raphael Courtland, Cristin Wilder, Stan Thornton, and I don't know who else," she replied mischievously. "Anything more you'd like to interrogate me about?"

"Not at the moment. Now seriously—where would you like to go?"

Vibrancy appeared in Gabrielle's thoughts. "Would you mind driving to Marina Cove?"

"No, I don't mind. May I ask why? We may need to deploy more agents."

"I'm going up to Skye Pointe with my friend Julie tomorrow." The memory of Carson's visit to her condo surfaced as she spoke. "You know them, don't you? You knew who Julie was when you saw her at my condo."

His expression watchful, Carson answered, "Yes, to both."

"Why didn't you say something?" she demanded.

"I don't involve myself in the relationships between my firm's clients," Carson said, "Part of Julie's protection is to guard her last name. It is her choice—and only her choice—to reveal it. I shall not violate the privacy of any one client for another."

"I hadn't thought about it that way." For the first time, Gabrielle understood that it was more than the desire to evade unwanted attention that led Julie to conceal her last name. *A lifetime of living with personal protection.*

Interrupting her thoughts, Carson asked, "So if you're going tomorrow, why go today?"

"Tomorrow is for Julie and Sarah," Gabrielle replied. "But I really want to visit the scene in Jarin's latest painting. It would be rude to insist on doing it tomorrow, so since I have time..."

"Of course, Ms. Winston. I'll be happy to drive you."

~*~~~**~~~*~

The landscapes flew by as Carson drove up the coast. Gabrielle spent a restful hour watching the city sprawl give way to suburban sprawl, then finally lapse into the small groupings that marked the coastal communities. A short time later, they neared Hampton Cape. It was Friday, but hopefully they were early enough that there wouldn't be much traffic.

Without warning, Carson turned off the main highway, following a narrow two-lane road inland toward the foothills. The road traversed the hills, sharply curving always to the west or north. Gabrielle's concern grew. *Did they decide to keep me out without telling me?* She pushed a couple of the console buttons, looking for the one that Landry had used to talk to Carson. No response. Instead of trying every button, she unbuckled her seatbelt and inched forward to pound on the glass that enforced her isolation. Just then, the front of the car nosed downward, throwing her off balance. Catching herself against the facing seat, she glimpsed something blue through the front corner of the adjacent window. The car continued in its downward right turn, showing Gabrielle the full view. Coves—and the blue of the ocean. A flash from the other window caught her eye. Moving over to get a better look, she saw that sunlight glinted off the windshields of slow moving cars on the highway she had expected Carson to follow. She wasn't being kidnapped; he had merely bypassed the slow crawl of traffic through Hampton Cape. They rounded yet another hill, and Gabrielle saw that they were heading toward a small hamlet nestled around the widest of the coves. With boats of all sizes in moorings around three long piers, it had to be Marina Cove.

Instead of driving into the town, Carson pulled into a drive, almost hidden by surrounding trees that widened into a small parking lot about half a mile ahead. Pulling the car around, he parked rear first in the parking spot furthest from the drive. He helped Gabrielle from the car and gestured toward the path just off the rear of its opposite side. "That's about a hundred yards long and comes out by the northern pier. Going that way will help us keep your security in place."

"This is an odd place for a parking lot," noted Gabrielle.

"It's for 'in the know' hikers," explained Carson. "I've never seen more than a couple of cars all the times that I've parked here. No one talks about it to keep it hidden."

Wondering how many similar places he knew about, she asked, "Do I have a time limit?"

"Not really—as long as we can get back to your condo by seven," said Carson. "Just seventy-seven me when you're on your way back so I'll know to look for you."

"What are you going to do?"

"I have plenty of work, and I usually do it in the car," he said.

She started down the path, and then turned back. Disturbed by the fierceness with which he watched her, Gabrielle reminded herself that it was his job. "Thank you for doing this, Carson."

"You're very welcome, Ms. Winston."

She again headed down the path.

~*~~~**~~~*~

Leaning on the railing at the marina end of the center pier, Gabrielle looked back toward the town. The distance and angle afforded her nearly the perspective of *Vibrancy*. The lighting effect was missing though, the sun too high in the sky for the cove-facing windows to directly reflect its rays. She didn't realized how much she had counted on the scene to lift her spirits—until it didn't. Even so, her visit wasn't pointless. She welcomed the solitude after the morning of madness at NEI.

The autumn sun, almost at its apex, felt pleasingly warm on Gabrielle's bare arms and legs. Flats in hand, she wandered along the pier to the beach and trudged through the deep, toasty sand to the southern pier, where she noticed a steep footpath winding up the grassy slope to the street above. Shading her eyes and looking up to the top of the ridge, Gabrielle saw that it was edged by a three-rail post and rail fence. Gabrielle stuffed a shoe into each of her back pockets and climbed the steep path, using the sparse rocky outgrowths jutting through the grasses as handholds when she needed to pull herself up.

At the top of the ridge, she climbed through the fence, turned, and then looked out over the breathtaking panorama of Marina Cove and the ocean. She wondered why Jarin had not painted this scape, then remembered that the show had only contained works that were available for sale. Surely any from this perspective would have been immediately snapped up, and likely not again put on the market. Reluctantly looking away from the cove, Gabrielle saw that the small, neatly kept houses across the street from the ridge were elevated enough above the fence that it didn't obstruct the view. Unlike similar houses in Hampton Cape, the windows were uncovered, permitting the inhabitants to enjoy the scene spread out before them. Apparently Marina Cove residents did not have the problem of wayward tourists trampling across lawns and sneaking peeks through windows.

Accompanied by the amplified sound of the waves crashing against the ridge, Gabrielle put her shoes back on and strolled up the street to its highest point, where picking a spot along the fence, she stepped up onto the bottom rail. To the east was the unbroken Atlantic. Looking north out over Marina Cove, she saw three coves beyond its northern ridge. A promontory adjoined the northernmost cove, atop which stood a tall lighthouse. *Guess that's the "Pointe" in Skye Pointe.*

Several streets full of houses behind her, and a full marina within her view; yet she heard only the sounds of nature. Heartened by the unanticipated serenity, Gabrielle found the courage to release the bindings with which she had so tightly restrained her thoughts. In doing so, she realized that she had not fully answered Landry's question. Though they all wanted her to leave, doing so felt wrong. Maybe here, away from the frenzy of the past few days, she could figure out why she so badly wanted to stay.

A cacophony of high-pitched sounds broke through the stillness. Panicked, Gabrielle ducked down from the fence, searching for the threat. Relief came swiftly when she saw the screeching sea gulls riding the swirling winds above her. But then another worry emerged. Her crew would probably report her reaction to Carson; giving him, Nathan, and Landry one more reason to force her to leave. So demonstrably close to the edge that even a few birds sent her scrambling for cover, she lacked a persuasive counter argument.

Gabrielle rose and climbed back up onto the fence just as the light breeze that had been lazily ruffling her hair turned briefly into a stiff head wind. Bracing against it, she held herself closer to the fence. It hadn't even been three full days of time rushing by too fast to do anything except ride the adrenaline high; of using nighttime hours for working rather than sleeping. It didn't help that the discoveries of the modified file and her compromised laptop diverted their attention from safeguarding NEI from the looming market crash. But the current situations had to be resolved. Certain that she and Sparks were instrumental in finding the resolutions, Gabrielle feared not for her safety, but for being forced to leave. If she ran now, she would always run.

"It's not fair," she whispered, bracing against another gust.

But by staying, she was placing herself in harm's way—defying the advice of those who were braver and more capable. Wondering whether choosing to stay had put her on the path to certain doom, Gabrielle leaned against the fence, listening to the sounds of the cove. Ebbing, flowing, sometimes pounding waves. Birds still screeching high overhead. Swirling, rustling, rushing wind. Sounds at times wild, raw chaos; and at other times, soothing, comforting rhythms. From time to time, she raised her sunglasses for her tears to be carried away on the breeze. *Whoever is doing this has no right to chase me away. I'm not a hero and I don't want to be. I just want my life back.*

Her cell vibrated. Hopefully the crew hadn't told Carson. She removed it from her front pocket and answered, "Gabrielle."

"Finally," Stephen's voice purred with relief.

Gabrielle's relief was greater. *Stephen.* Desperate for solace, she teetered on the verge of telling him everything. She had always been able to confide in Stephen. He would have sound advice—he always did. *But he left me.* Horrified by her yearning, Gabrielle fought off the temptation. Instead the words she was loathe to voice pushed themselves through her uncooperative lips, cutting off whatever it was he had been saying. "I can't talk now, Stephen." Excruciatingly aware of each instant of movement, she ended the call and forced her hand to put the cell back into her pocket. It again began to vibrate. Urgently in need of the comfort that she knew his arms could provide, she still, inch by agonizing inch, pulled her hand away from her pocket. The vibration stopped; but immediately recommenced. Tormented, betrayed by her lifeline, Gabrielle clasped her hands around the fence post and lowered her head to the top of it, bracing yet again. The vibration stopped again. But then started again, and again, and again...

~*~~~**~~~*~

It had been an easy hike up to his current vantage point. It had also, however, taken hours to find the right perspective. Having not yet painted the land masses around the coves, Jarin looked forward to something new. Not a townscape, or a seascape, or a landscape; but a combination of the three. He checked the view. Satisfied, he positioned his easel and palette. The familiar sense of expectation rose as soon as he settled onto the stool. Jarin picked up a brush and mixed some preliminary colors, yielding to his overpowering desire to express his emotions on canvas. Lifting the brush, he squinted down at the view of the ridge fence and beyond. *What the hell is that?* In exasperation, he smacked the brush down on the palette. Something small and dark was now on the fence—directly in his line of sight. The object moved, apparently putting its head down. *Someone's child? What the hell?* Getting up from the stool, Jarin pulled his sunglasses from his hair down over his eyes; then quickly followed the path down to the houses below. *I've got to get that child away from the fence—and then I'll have words for the parents. I hate negligence—in any form.*

~*~~~**~~~*~

At the fence, Jarin leaned over to get a look at the child standing on the railing. He fought back a grin. *She's obviously not a child.* Relieved that he would not be exchanging heated words with irresponsible parents about their wayward offspring, he decided just to ask her to move. "Hello, there," he said pleasantly.

Startled by the deep, resonant voice, Gabrielle quickly turned in its direction. Though she hadn't heard him approach, a man leaned on the fence near her, his hands clasped on top of it. *Strong hands; no key-tapping fingers there.* He clearly expected a response. "Hello," she replied.

A beautiful little woman, her melodic voice still played enticingly in his ears. Jarin was anxious to hear more of it. "I haven't seen you here before," he began, his voice huskier than he intended. *What the hell?*

Despite her need for solitude, Gabrielle was intrigued. Though glad he couldn't see her tear-swollen eyes, she wanted to see his, wondering if they were as beautiful as the rest of him. *Maybe I'm dreaming.* "I've never been here before," she said.

His sunglasses masking his rudeness, Jarin examined her closely. Faint tracks left by salty tears trailed from beneath her sunglasses. It took intense concentration to prevent himself from acting on his involuntary impulse to comfort her. *Not this time. No matter how lovely she is. Too much on my plate right now.* "Ah, a tourist," he replied, more acerbically than he intended.

His arrogant tone stung, quickly erasing Gabrielle's desire to know more about him. *Looks like this is going to be a short conversation.* "You say that like it's a bad thing."

"Not at all—tourists help our economy quite a bit," he said, with forced unfriendliness.

"But you don't like tourists," challenged Gabrielle. He didn't want her here, and she was determined to end their exchange on her own terms. *At least I know I'm not dreaming. I wouldn't dream someone so beautiful just to make him a jackass.*

"I generally don't notice tourists."

"Then why are you talking to me?"

"It looks rather like you need help." His will wavered as she reacted to his words. But then she saved him; regaining control of her expression.

"I beg your pardon?"

"You look...hurt," Jarin replied, frustrated that yet again, he had given her an opening to share her problems.

"How can you tell that just by looking at me?"

Jarin shrugged. "Just a perception. May I get you some help?"

"No thank you, it's a private matter," she replied, turning to look out over the cove.

"If you want it to be private, you ought not make it so easy for even a stranger to see that something is wrong," Jarin pointed out. *And I wouldn't be fighting myself.*

"Look, I didn't ask you to speak to me," snapped Gabrielle. "In fact I would have preferred that you didn't. I certainly don't want or need your help."

"I didn't offer my help exactly; I merely offered to get you help. Besides that, I'm simply commenting that whatever your problem is, you're handling it poorly," Jarin said, immediately aware that he had gone too far.

Gabrielle jumped down from the fence. "I don't know or care who the hell you are, but you have no right to judge me!" Her emotions already raw; his caustic, uncaring remarks pushed her over the edge. "How dare you trivialize my situation. You know nothing about me—*not one damn thing!* I didn't ask you to stop and speak to me, I didn't ask for your help, and I sure as hell didn't ask for your attitude." Her anger beyond restraint; outrage and distaste dripped from every word. "I'll be very clear. I neither need nor want anything from you—except your absence—and I know *exactly* how to get that." She turned and stalked down the street. Seeing that it went all the way along the beach to the northern pier, she bypassed the path she had earlier used.

Stunned by her vehemence, Jarin stared after her. At last recovering himself, he called, "Wait, please..." She gave no sign that she had heard him. He started down the street after her, and then changed his mind. *Need to give her time—and space—to calm down. I was—purposely—a total ass.* He took out his cell and speed dialed seventy-seven.

CHAPTER ELEVEN

Night Moves

At the northern pier, Gabrielle raced up the steps to the planked walkway, unrolled her pants legs and shook out the sand. *Jackass. He has to talk to strangers—he's alienated all his friends.* She beat the sand out of her shoes and shoved them onto her feet. Free of sand, but holding on to her anger, she stepped off the other side of the pier onto the path and strode swiftly up to the parking lot.

Seeing Carson casually leaning against the driver's door of the car reminded Gabrielle that she had neglected to do the only thing he had asked of her. Chagrined, she slowed her pace as she approached.

"Is everything all right?" he asked.

"Yes," Gabrielle answered curtly. *He surely didn't deserve that.* "I'm sorry Carson. I just met a real jackass over on the southern ridge."

Carson laughed loudly. "Is that right?"

"Why's that funny?" Gabrielle challenged, still bristling for a fight.

"Whoa," Carson said, holding his hands up in surrender. "I only meant that this seems to be your day for backing people off. Ready to get back to work?"

Going to his side of the car, she asked, "Does that mean you've got my laptop back?"

"Not quite," he replied, reaching in through the open window. "I've got you one of ours instead. It's ruggedized and security hardened."

"Wow." Gabrielle took the laptop he handed her. "It's not much heavier than mine. What's it made of?"

"The cover is a polymer and magnesium alloy," answered Carson. "It also has a water-resistant display."

Gabrielle laughed, opening it. "Thanks, but I don't plan to swim with it." It had a touch screen and low profile keys. "Very nice, but why do I need a ruggedized laptop?"

Carson shrugged. "These are the only kind we have. We've already ported over all your files. I'll walk you through the security features."

During the fifteen minutes of listening to Carson explain the firewall, intrusion detection, kernel hardening and other features, Gabrielle regained her analyst's perspective; eager to focus on finding solutions to NEI's espionage problems.

"I'm waiting for a call back from Alicia, our security expert. She's been interning in IT," he said. "After she analyzed your laptop, she wanted to examine all the computers at NEI."

"Does that mean it wasn't a targeted attack against me and Sparks?"

"Possibly," Carson said, checking his watch. "It's after three—she said she'd be ready by now. Come on—I'll show you how to work the console so you can participate."

"In what?"

"She's doing a secure call with us—at Nathan's request. He'll decide next steps based on what she reports."

"I hope she didn't find anything. Otherwise, all of NEI's confidential information—the client data and partner level stuff—Nathan will be furious."

"He'll certainly want someone's head," Carson agreed. He held the door while she got in, and then got in on the other side. "When Alicia calls, I'll patch it through so that you can join. Here's the button you hit to accept the call, and here are the volume controls. Oh yeah—this is the mute button. Ready to roll?"

"Definitely," Gabrielle replied. Carson got out and secured the door. *I'm glad I came. Even that jackass didn't ruin it for me. Now, I know exactly why I'm staying. I'm scared as hell, but this is my life. No one's going to chase me away from it.*

~*~~~**~~~*~

Carson drove the car out of the parking lot and began the uphill climb that would take them back through the foothills to the highway, then on to the city. Just as he made the first southward turn, the call button turned green and started blinking.

That's certainly hard to miss. Gabrielle pushed it.

"...your findings," Nathan was saying.

Announcing herself, she said. "Gabrielle's on."

"That's everyone," acknowledged Nathan. "Alicia, please enlighten us."

"Of course. Gabrielle, let's start with your laptop. The worm turned out to be a surveillance creep."

Gabrielle hoped that the creep was localized to her computer. Otherwise, all of NEI's business intelligence was being stolen—right under their noses.

"Plain English, please," requested Nathan with a chuckle.

"Sorry," replied Alicia. "A creep replicates itself, creeps into an unused computer memory location, and observes, records, reports. It also sends a copy of itself to an uninfected computer. It's been reporting out to an external site every Friday for about four months now."

"Damn," was Landry's short, emphatic response.

"I use my laptop at home to access my server," said Gabrielle "Has it infected that too?"

"We don't think so," replied Alicia. "You chose to set up secure VPN access to the server—a good thing. It reports the access to an external site, but hasn't reported more than that. We'll have to examine the server to be sure that it isn't reporting out through its own port. From the perspective of your laptop, the creep has only recorded that data is transferred back and forth."

"What's in the reports?" asked Landry.

"I can only guess by what's in the current one," Alicia responded. "It'll tell them that a fair amount of data was retrieved from Gabrielle's server, and that similar data was run against something called Retro. Lastly I can make out that there are a few spreadsheets of interest."

That the creep could see Retro, verified that it had access to NEI's entire network. "Wow, that's just about everything," Gabrielle said. *Nathan's going to be livid.*

"Every single computer," Alicia agreed. "All of the NEI desktops and servers are compromised. We should assume—unless analysis proves otherwise—that the partners' laptops are also compromised."

"I beg your pardon?" Nathan asked; too quietly.

"I'm sorry sir, but our examination indicates that all the machines at NEI have been infected with the creep," Alicia said. "It's too late to tell the point of entry without data, but any machine plugged into your network will have been affected." She then added, "There could be some good news in all of this."

"You can't be serious," said Nathan.

"NEI has several hundred desktops, laptops, and servers. Whoever is controlling the creep has been bombarded with a lot of information," Alicia explained hastily. "It would take a while to determine trends and figure out what they'd want to investigate more closely."

"They've had four months," Landry pointed out.

"Yes, but—" Alicia began.

"We know there's an insider," Landry interrupted.

"I see," replied Alicia. "Well in that case, are you sure it's part of the same threat?"

Nathan asked, "You're raising the possibility of multiple threats?"

"From a purely empirical perspective, is there any evidence to link them?"

"Not yet," Nathan conceded, his voice layered with frustration.

"Then we need to keep in mind that the threats could have originated from different sources," Alicia replied.

More low expletives came through the speakers as Gabrielle thought over Alicia's information. "Are all the machines reporting out on the same day?" she asked.

"Yes, but at different times."

"Can your analysis determine any trends from a single data point?"

"We won't be able to analyze trends, but we should be able to see if there are any specific targets and whether items can be tracked as they travel among machines." Then Alicia had a question of her own. "When can I examine the partners' laptops?"

"Tonight," Nathan said. "I'll call them and set up a schedule."

"I'm in the building, Alicia. You can come up and examine mine now," said Landry. "We have to harden NEI's network. How long will that take?"

"We can put in emergency hardening this weekend," Alicia said. "Beyond that, from plan to completion, including threat testing, it's usually a month to six weeks if you're highly motivated."

"We're definitely highly motivated," Nathan said. "Are SCI networks hardened?"

"Yes," replied Alicia.

"How long will it take to transfer our operations to your data center?" he asked.

"We can do it overnight."

"That's our best approach," said Nathan. "Combining our datacenters is a side effect of the merger. I'll convene a special partners' meeting tomorrow, for a vote on accepting it."

"If the partners agree, I'll arrange with Jarin to expedite the switchover to Monday."

Jarin?

"Alicia, thanks for your analysis," Nathan said. "Carson will be calling you shortly with locations and the schedule for analysis of the partners' laptops."

"Good deal," she replied. "Gabrielle, I also want to swing by and take a look at your server tonight. Will you be home?"

"Sure," answered Gabrielle.

"I'll work it in around the partners' schedule."

"Sounds good."

"Sorry the news wasn't better. Good night everybody." Alicia clicked off.

"Carson, are we still clear?" asked Nathan.

"Yes."

"Good. Regarding the partners meeting tomorrow, these are extenuating circumstances, so I'm allowing you to listen in. I want you to know the outcome as soon as I do. We may need a follow on contingency call. Please be sure to stay on mute."

"Muting can be managed on the call in line," said Carson.

"Perfect. Thanks," said Nathan. "Now a change of subject—we need to address Sparks."

Sparks and Jarin in the same conversation—within a business context. Gabrielle's curiosity was rampant.

"Sparks has never belonged to NEI," Nathan went on, "so Jarin and I want to set up a separate agreement with you, Gabrielle, which transfers Sparks from you directly to SCI, with NEI being one of its users."

Gabrielle couldn't contain her astonishment. "Why?"

"Sparks has a broader range of use than business process analysis," Nathan answered. "Jarin wants to work with the other sector managers to adapt it for use across much of SCI—starting with ISS and the financial sector."

"I don't know what to say. But, what does Jarin have to do with it?"

"I'd forgotten—you probably know of him only as Jarin Cole, the artist." said Nathan. "To answer your question, SCI has been divided into four sectors for now—each run by one of the four older San Chapelle siblings. Jarin manages the technology sector—the one that offered the merger to NEI." He then added, "You need to consider joining that sector as well."

"Why would I do that?" Gabrielle protested. "I'm building a career at NEI."

His voice also quietly persuasive, Landry said, "You would certainly be at NEI while we incorporate Sparks into our workflow. But afterwards Gabrielle, you need to think of your future at NEI and contrast it with what it could be at SCI."

"Thank you, my dear, for your loyalty, and if you want to stay we'll be more than happy to have you," Nathan added, "But going to SCI is really in your best interest. Give it some thought. It's not something that needs to be decided now."

That Nathan was kicking her out of NEI, just after she had decided to stay and fight the unknown infiltrators, angered Gabrielle. No matter what SCI offered, her response would be adamant refusal.

"I'm only bringing this up now because I'd like to sign both the merger and transfer agreements at the same time—tomorrow if possible," said Nathan. "I don't want to leave Sparks unprotected. Gabrielle, are you amenable to at least signing over Sparks to SCI? I'm sure the terms will be more than generous."

Despite her misgivings about the suggested direction of her own future, it made sense to protect Sparks. "What commitment will I have to make?" she asked.

"We can leave it open if you like," Nathan replied. "You'll have to spend some time with the SCI technical team—whether as a new member or on loan, doesn't have to be decided yet."

Relieved that she wasn't being pressed for an immediate decision, Gabrielle said, "In that case, yes, I'll sign the transfer agreement for Sparks." The words triggered her realization that Nathan was keeping the promise that Landry had made the day she exposed the market crash. Sparks would be out of Garrett's reach when he became managing partner, and also protected from theft.

"It's settled then. I'm setting up the call for tomorrow morning," Nathan said. "Gabrielle will you be available?"

"Yes. Actually, I'll be at the San Chapelles' with Julie."

"You will?" Landry asked.

"She invited us up for the weekend."

"I see," Landry replied.

"Is something wrong?"

"No, I just wasn't aware that you knew them. I'll be there too. We're sailing in the afternoon."

"I wasn't aware that I knew them either—until the day Julie invited us up. Before that, I only knew her as Julie Carleton."

"Well that's it, then," Nathan said, ending the meeting. "We'll plan on you being there for the partners' call and the signing. I'll let Quentin know."

~*~~~**~~~*~

In meetings all day, implementing NEI agreed upon directives, Garrett had found precious little time to address his own recovery strategy. It didn't help that Elaine was gone for the afternoon; though he had to admit, his...enthusiasm...was the cause of her absence. Rachel was competent, but she didn't *get* him the way that Elaine did. He'd had to direct her so closely that he had felt as though he were doing the work himself. It didn't help his mood that he was operating on only three hours of sleep. Rachel would most likely not again volunteer to fill in for Elaine. At three forty-five, he expected that he finally had time to himself. The respite was short lived, ended by a hesitant knock on his door.

Poking his head through the opening, Cleve said, "Garrett? Elaine isn't in the outer office and your door was open, so..."

Resigned to yet another interruption, Garrett waved him in. "Elaine's off this afternoon."

Closing the door behind him, Cleve hastened forward and planted himself in one of Garrett's guest chairs. "Did you know that Gabrielle's been gone all day?"

"They completed their assignment on time. We've been working with the results all day," said Garrett, reminding Cleve of the boundaries of his surveillance. "Why's her absence important?"

"It's odd, don't you think?" insisted Cleve. "Her laptop is there, but no one has seen her since this morning. By the way, the deadline work has been completed as well."

Allowing Cleve his deception, Garrett didn't tell him that he knew Landry's team had finished their own deadline work. Instead he asked, "Is Landry here?"

"Yeah. He didn't even leave for lunch."

Failing to see the point of Cleve's information, Garrett said, "Then there's no issue. He may have given her the afternoon off."

"But her laptop..."

"I agree, it's curious," allowed Garrett. "But as it hasn't impacted her responsibilities, there's no action to be taken." He stood, giving Cleve the final signal that the conversation was over. "Thanks for keeping an eye on them, Cleve. Looks like we're back to business as usual."

Reluctantly, Cleve got to his feet. "Are the reservations still good for Celeste's tonight?"

"Of course," said Garrett as he crossed to the wet bar for yet another cup of coffee. In fact, he had forgotten. He would call the maitre d' as soon as Cleve left. "Leave my door open on your way out."

"Sure thing," answered Cleve. "See ya Monday."

"See you then," answered Garrett, watching him leave. Though at times Cleve was a pain, he was so easily manipulated. It would be a shame to get rid of him. As he headed back to his desk, his cell phone rang. "Garrett."

"It's Nathan. I need you to allow ISS, SCI's security firm, to examine your laptop." Garrett froze, sure that he had been found out. Nathan continued, "They've been monitoring our network for viruses. Looks like we have a serious infection." Listening to Nathan's explanation of how the virus was exposed, Garrett realized that the situation wasn't about him, and that it explained where Gabrielle had gone. Using the opportunity to find out where he stood, he asked, "Do you know how and who?"

"I have my suspicions," Nathan answered. "But no proof. Are you available tonight?"

"Absolutely," said Garrett. He may still be under suspicion, but a network virus trumped a modified file—at least until the resolution costs were compared. "I'm still in the office, so I'll hang around for them here. What's our plan of attack?"

"I'm convening a senior partners' meeting tomorrow morning. I'll text the time to your cell. We need to discuss the merger proposals and hardening our networks."

"How are the two related?"

"Only in that if we accept and sign the SCI proposal, NEI will be protected by Monday morning. We need to discuss whether or not that is the best approach."

"Gotcha," said Garrett, glad that his instincts were still good. Having changed teams not a moment too soon, he would make his allegiance plain in the meeting.

"And stay off the NEI networks," added Nathan. "If you need me, email my personal address; call or text my cell. I'm taking no chances until I know we're clean."

"Sure thing," answered Garrett. He had done it. He had disassociated himself from Brett and was reclaiming his position with Nathan. Now he just had to get something on Brett in order to protect his future. He was—almost—home free.

~*~~~**~~~*~

It didn't take long for Alicia to verify that Gabrielle's server was free of the creep. Once she and Carson had gone, Gabrielle connected the borrowed laptop to the server and successfully retrieved the completed reports. An hour later, she had finished Nathan's spreadsheet, giving him conclusive evidence that every report recommending Avanti companies had been in error. The spreadsheet also showed the clients who had been wrongly advised by those reports, the costs to them, and the recommendations from Sparks. He and the senior partners now had all of the information they needed in order to determine the redress that NEI was honor-bound to offer those clients. It would be costly, but necessary in order to maintain client loyalty, and for NEI to retain their enviable position at the top of the analytics industry. With a click of the send button, she emailed it to Nathan's personal address.

Though badly in need of sleep, Gabrielle decided to spend the night at Julie's. Watching movies into the early morning hours with her and Sarah was far preferable to lying awake trying to evade visions of the roller coaster graph, and ignore worries about the infiltrator. Less troubling but still not yet behind her were thoughts of the confrontation with the stranger and Garrett's threats. Even Landry's rant was an attack of sorts. Then there was Stephen, inexplicably determined to push his way back into her life. Soon, she would have to face him and end it. But tonight, she was willing to go to any extreme to avoid being alone should he make his eleven-thirty call. Having packed an overnighter for the day—or weekend?—on Coral Cove, Gabrielle unholstered her cell and speed-dialed thirty-three. This time, the voice was male. "Yes, Ms. Winston?"

"I'm leaving for Julie Carleton's condo. She's in 2870, Loft V," said Gabrielle. *As if they didn't already know.* "We'll be traveling to Skye Pointe sometime early tomorrow morning."

"Thank you, Ms. Winston," acknowledged the voice.

On the way to the door, Gabrielle tweeted Julie and Sarah that she was on her way. At least having security meant that she didn't have to worry about crossing The Green at night. She paused with her hand on the knob. *Or do I?*

~*~~~**~~~*~

After washing his hands, Cleve admired himself in the mirror. Celeste's was impressive. Debra was beside herself, treating him as though he was a really good catch. He checked his profile. It had been smart to get a professional shave. Giving himself another once over as he opened the men's room door, he was pleased with what he saw. He turned to leave and walked—face first—

into the gloved, weighted fist that had been timed for maximum impact with whoever opened the door.

Flying backwards from the contact with his nose, Cleve stumbled over the waste can just inside the door and slid to the floor. At first, his outraged surprise masked the pain. Struggling to his feet, he faced his ski-masked assailant, who now blocked the door. "What the hell's going on?" he demanded, reaching up to cover his nose.

Cleve's question was met with another blow from the weighted, gloved fist—this one to the exposed side of his face. He dropped to the floor again, his jaw broken. *This can't be happening. How can this be happening?* He tried to yell, but the broken jaw prevented his mouth from opening. As he again tried to stand, the masked man grabbed his feet out from under him, crashing Cleve to the floor for the third time. Another man pushed through the door, got behind Cleve and picked him up under his arms. Within seconds, they had carried him outside through the service door adjacent to the bathroom. Cleve struggled manically, his screams of resistance audible only in his head.

The men laughed under their masks as one of them delivered more punishing blows to Cleve's face. His eyes swelled and closed. Professionals, they severely punished Cleve from head to toe, using some object he couldn't see to break his right arm and both legs; each injury causing intense, agonizing pain. His ribs cracked under their strategically administered, weighted punches. As he lost strength, Cleve's resistance waned. He could no longer move his brutalized body; his attempts to scream faded to pitiful whines. After several long minutes of horrific punishment, it was over. Except for the excruciatingly overwhelming pain.

One assailant said, "Take his wallet and anything else that's valuable." As weak as he was, Cleve still felt hands feeling around, removing things from his pockets, taking his watch. There were a few tugs at his fingers. *No more, please no more...*

The other man said, "Leave them." Their footsteps rapidly faded and Cleve was alone; in agony, unable to move. He heard no one. In the darkness, his eyes swollen shut, he saw nothing. Panic accelerated his heart rate, causing the heart attack that punctuated, then ended his pain.

~*~~~**~~~*~

"Took you long enough," Jarin grumbled, snatching open the front door of the bungalow. Leaving Carson standing there, he walked back into the great room. A cool evening breeze blew in through the open French doors, accompanied by the muted sound of crashing waves. None of it had its usual calming effect. His frustration had been increasing by the hour and it was now approaching midnight. Closing the door behind him, Carson followed at a more leisurely pace. Jarin demanded, "Why couldn't we have talked when I called?"

Amused by Jarin's annoyance, Carson said, "Jarin Cole, all worked up over a girl? I had to see it with my own eyes." Then he added as if spelling it out for a toddler, "I was working—you know that."

"I told you on the phone. I have to fix it. I went overboard. I think I may have hurt her," Jarin said, glowering at him across the over-sized sofa. "I still feel like an ass." Carson laughed. "What the hell is your problem? Didn't I—"

Holding his laughter long enough to assume an air of authority, Carson said, "I have it from the source that you were a real jackass and you totally pissed her off."

"How do you know that? Have you found her already?" *I'm about to lose my temper over this. I never lose my temper.* "Carson, don't make me beat the crap out of you."

Laughing more loudly, Carson barely got the words out. "Not on your *best* day. Stop threatening me and look at these." He tossed three packages toward Jarin's head.

Jarin blocked them with his forearm and they fell onto the sofa. "What are they?"

"They're the week's worth of photos you need to review before I hand them over to Nathan. You'll probably want to edit the last package."

"You've lost your mind. What part of 'I need for you to find that little woman' is *too damn difficult* to understand?"

Exasperated, Carson repeated slowly, "Just open the damn packages."

Glaring at Carson, Jarin picked up the top one, flipped it over, and tore it open. He pulled out the glossy eight by ten photographs. "Son of a—"

"Took you long enough." Carson walked over and looked down at the photographs in Jarin's hands.

Lowering himself down onto the arm of the sofa, Jarin whispered, "It's her," He flipped through the photographs. "How did you get so many?"

Annoyed, Carson punched his shoulder, nearly knocking him to the floor. "Jarin—what's up with you? Dammit. Use your brain."

Regaining his balance, Jarin scowled at Carson once more. "Man, if you weren't almost a brother..." He ripped open the other packages. "Landry and Nathan? Then this must be... You mean she is Gabrielle Winston? She was with you today?"

"Yes, yes, and yes," Carson said. Then sarcastically imitating a carnival barker, "Give the man a prize."

"Why didn't you just bring her over?" asked Jarin, his annoyance escalating yet again. "Do I have to spell everything out?"

"You're the one losing it," said Carson with unconcealed irritation. "For what reason—from her perspective?"

"You're right. My personal interest shouldn't interfere with business." Closing his eyes, Jarin rubbed the bridge of his nose, forcing himself to relax. "I don't care if you are right, I still ought to kick your ass."

"In your dreams, rich boy," said Carson, with a beckoning gesture. "Get your ass up."

The tension broken, they laughed at the absurdity of the two of them actually fighting. Still sparring partners, they knew each other too well for either to get the upper hand. "We had a good thing going when we started ISS. Guess I'm frustrated 'cause I can't fix this myself," Jarin admitted. "Too bad rumors started."

Obligingly running through their old joke, Carson said, "Yeah, you can't be a personal protection agent if you need a personal protection agent."

This time, Jarin goaded Carson. "Ready to quit? Looking for a desk job?"

"Action junkie like me? This assignment is too tame. Only took it as a favor to you. Beginning to get interesting though."

"What do you mean?" asked Jarin apprehensively. "Is she in danger?"

"Nah—just a puzzle that's damn difficult to solve," Carson replied.

"Fill me in. Maybe you need a sounding board."

"Or maybe that's your slick way of finding out more about Gabrielle," suggested Carson. "What's going on? You only talked about fifteen minutes."

"I don't know really," Jarin said. *There's only one conclusion, but it can't be.* "I decided to paint today and it took all morning to get set up. Then I'd just picked up my brush. There she was, right in my line of sight; ruined the whole damn perspective. So I went to ask her to move and...things got out of hand."

"What'd she do, snarl at you?"

"No she didn't *snarl* at me—well maybe she thought she did. I got close enough to see her face. Do you have any idea how much pain she's in?"

"I wondered how bad it was," answered Carson. "She attempts to be calm and cool when she's around us. Every now and then though, she slips and I get a glimpse of what she's trying to hide." For the first time, Carson glared at Jarin. "What did you do?"

"In her words, I 'trivialized her situation'," Jarin said. "Now that I know what her situation is, she's absolutely right. I walked up during a very private moment, and proceeded to ridicule her pain."

"You fucked up," Carson said.

"Royally. Now I have to fix it."

"She's tougher than she looks," said Carson. "Your odds suck."

"I know," Jarin said. "I'll see her tomorrow—I'll just have to beg for mercy." he trailed off at the look on Carson's face. "What?"

"The great Jarin Cole San Chapelle—begging some girl for mercy?" Carson teased, true incredulity in his tone. "Sounds like she's got you by the stones."

"No, that's not it," said Jarin. The truth of it was hard to accept, but even harder to ignore. "She's got me by the heart. That's infinitely more painful."

CHAPTER TWELVE

Unexpected

"Okay, Miss Thang, what did you do?" asked Julie as the car pulled out of the Loft V garage. "Why is Carson driving us instead of Andrew?"

"Guess I shouldn't have been surprised to see him," answered Gabrielle. "I'd have told you about it last night but we didn't even make it through the start of the first movie." She filled them in on NEI's situation with the surveillance creep.

"Surveillance creep?" asked Sarah. "That's really what it's called?"

Gabrielle nodded. "Because it creeps around, spying and tattling on you."

"I'm losing my edge," Sarah sighed. "I can't think of a single witty thing to say."

Sadness had etched its way into Sarah's face for the first time since Gabrielle had known her. There had to be a way to help her find a way out of the mess she was in.

"Any clues yet about who did it?" asked Julie.

"Not yet. Alicia's looking into it," said Gabrielle. "That reminds me; we're having a conference call at your house with the NEI partners and Jarin this morning."

"No fair," said Sarah, looking even more dejected, "you've already met him."

"No I haven't. It's your family's fault, Julie. Turns out it was his sector of SCI that tendered the merger offer to NEI—and he wants to buy Sparks."

"*No way!*" exclaimed Sarah. "Are you going to sell it?"

"It's my best way of protecting it," answered Gabrielle.

"Certainly wraps a lot of power around it—and you." Sarah nodded sagely. "I like those NEI guys. They came up with a win-win situation, and you'll be filthy rich."

"They did keep their promises," agreed Gabrielle. "But if Garrett was running NEI, I'd be road kill." *Maybe I should keep an open mind about going to SCI.*

"I wish I worked for them instead of Prentice and Associates," Sarah said wistfully. "By the way, I called James."

"What did he say?" asked Julie.

"Well, he told Lee Ann up front that they might cancel at the last minute," answered Sarah. "Seems they have a history of it."

"She knew—and never told you?" Gabrielle was indignant.

"Yeah. She gave me the project without that info and let me take the fall, even though it cost us money," said Sarah. "I confronted her, but she won't correct the staffs' impression that I failed."

"That is so underhanded. You can't just let it go," said Julie.

"I didn't," said Sarah. "I was going to tell them myself. James had said he would back me up. So she wanted to compromise—and I made her draw up a contract. I still get first-tier clients; but I can't say anything about what she did."

There was no way Sarah could last in that environment. The other agents were probably all still trying to trip her up—she probably couldn't even trust her assistant. Even so, Gabrielle tried to lift her spirits. "At least you still get first-tier clients."

"That's true," agreed Sarah, but her expression retained its sadness. She asked Julie, "You think SCI wants to start its own public relations agency?"

"Actually," Julie replied, her grey eyes alight with anticipation, "I think my news will make you forget all about P & A."

"What news?"

"I wanted to tell you after we got to the cove, but now, I don't know what's in store for Gabs today," replied Julie. "So, *ta da*! Charleston Eddy wants to go with our idea! Sparks at the Lofts will be the first residential tower store. I'll be the initial buyer for it and of course, I'll want your input. We can travel together..."

Gabrielle interrupted, "Sarah—you're speechless? That's got to be a first."

"Shhh...Gabs, let her finish."

"As I was saying," Julie continued, her excitement breaking through the stern look she was trying to give them, "we need to put together its first offering and open the store by the end of October for the Christmas season. Sarah, I suggested that you would be perfect for arranging the launch party and any other public relations."

"No way," breathed Sarah. "What did they say?"

"Monday, you're to meet with Drew Kreft. He manages unexpected, but approved, expenditures across SCI."

Gabrielle's surprise got the best of her. "Charley's is an SCI company?"

"Yes, in Jarin's sector for now," Julie replied warily.

"Then why didn't you give us a bigger discount?" Sarah demanded.

"Money grubbers," Julie teased.

"Screw the money, give me the clothes." Sarah's happiness spilled over in an infectious laugh. "Just let me make Charley's my closet and I'll be content."

"Sarah, you'll be able to buy whatever you want," said Julie. "Charley's has to sign an agreement with us. We just have to figure out whether we want money upfront, royalties on net profit, or combination of the two."

Sinking back against the seat, Sarah said, "Unbelievable. I need to absorb this for a while." She looked from Julie to Gabrielle. "This has been a hell of a week."

Gabrielle grinned. *That was a short while. We've got our Sarah back.*

"Just think, none of us had any idea it would be like this when we woke up on Monday." Sarah said. "I ended the week as the agency target."

"And now we've got to deal with the market crash," Gabrielle said. "I see those roller coasters every time I try to sleep."

"Did you sleep at all last night?" Julie demanded. "Your face looks all pinched."

"And we didn't know that you were related to Nathan and Landry," said Gabrielle, moving the conversation away from her sleepless wonderings.

"I'd forgotten—what's the story?" asked Sarah.

"We have a common paternal ancestor," said Julie.

"Well, that's enlightening," said Gabrielle.

Sarah just laughed.

"*Gab-by*, you didn't let me finish," said Julie.

"Sorry," Gabrielle said. "My lips are zipped."

Shooting her a glance of mock exasperation, Julie told the story: "Our common ancestor is Xavier San Chapelle, and he came here in the mid-1800s. When his ship ran into the reefs just outside of the Skye Pointe coves and went down, he was able- to get his family and some of the crew to shore. His wife Rosaline managed to prop the baby out of the water, but she herself drowned."

"Omigosh," interrupted Sarah. "That's horrible."

"Yes it was," said Julie. "He was devastated—and he had three children to raise. It happened that runaway slaves, Netta and her son, were passing through the area and saw Xavier and the others struggling to shore. In spite of the risk of being caught, they stopped to help—and never left. Netta and Xavier were married a few years later."

"In those times?" asked Gabrielle. "How did they manage that?"

"They were married secretly—but legally—in what is now the chapel at Saint Mary's Hospital," explained Julie, who then laughed, startling Gabrielle and Sarah. "I'm sorry. It's just that they both kept journals. Xavier's says that Netta 'led him a merry chase'. Netta's says that she ran to keep Xavier's 'fool ideas' from getting them both killed." Just as suddenly, Julie sobered again. "Her son only had a mother; Xavier's children only had a father. She worried that they would be left with no one. For her, it was always about the children."

"Looks like he finally convinced her," Sarah said.

"Yes, and they had a daughter together." said Julie. "Anyway, we are descended from Rosaline; Nathan and Landry are descended from Netta."

"Telling the story all this time later doesn't do justice to how rough it must have been for them," said Gabrielle.

"It had its moments—good, bad, and worse," agreed Julie. "Maybe you'll get to read their journals one day."

They all retreated into their own thoughts. Gabrielle wondered what kind of man Xavier must have been, dangerously disregarding the mores of his time. He had apparently succeeded. Both sets of descendants had survived intact, and remained close.

Breaking their prolonged silence, Sarah said, "Sorry to interrupt our gabfest, but how far out are we?"

"Another forty-five minutes," replied Julie. "There's breakfast in the console."

"Cool," answered Gabrielle. Reaching forward from her seat, she opened it and pulled out warm croissant sandwiches. Then opening the refrigerated compartment, she took out juice and bottled water.

Astounded, Sarah said. "I have got to get me one of these."

~*~~~**~~~*~

Judging by Julie's poorly concealed agitation, which had been steadily growing since they'd left the foothills, Gabrielle surmised that they must be getting closer to her home. Seconds later, Carson turned into a circular driveway.

"It's lovely," said Sarah, looking past Julie at the house. "Not at all what I expected."

"There's more than can be seen from the street," said Julie.

Instead of stopping near the door, Carson turned down an almost hidden, wide gravel path just past the front porch. Driving through the foliage, he slowly followed the winding path downward, away from the house.

"Omigosh," said Sarah, looking back as they drove past.

From her seat opposite Sarah, Gabrielle saw that the house was at least three times the size it had looked from the street, its many windows glimmering with the muted reflection of the still fog-shrouded early morning sun. Two of the three floors of the house were built into the slope they were slowly traversing, the lowermost of which sported a bank of French doors open to the grounds topping another shorter slope leading down to the beach. Ahead and below them, scattered about the grounds, were several small bungalows, tennis courts, and a swimming pool with its cabana. At the bottom of the drive, Carson pulled the car around to the left and into a multiple car garage hidden by boulders protruding from the hillside. "What a beautiful place to grow up," she said earnestly, also attempting to ease Julie's nervousness.

"I'm glad you like it," said Julie. "The bungalows are relatively new. They were added after we all grew up. They're not specifically ours, though there's one for each of the five of us. Visitors use them too."

"Thanks Carson," Gabrielle said as he helped her from the car. She slung her backpack over her shoulder as he reached in for Sarah. "Are you staying for the call?"

"Yes. Jarin's bungalow at ten," he said, starting around the car to the other passenger door. Julie was already out of the car and standing near its trunk. Giving her a disapproving scowl that she ignored, Carson opened the trunk and they each took out their overnighter.

"Enjoy your stay, ladies."

~*~~~**~~~*~

As they walked through the grounds with Julie in the lead, Sarah said, "You know, I never get tired of looking at Carson, but it seems he's wearing a big 'Off Limits' sign across his chest."

"With blinking neon lights," Gabrielle added, laughing. "He's very serious about his job."

"He warms up around Jarin," confided Julie. "Those two are like a couple of overgrown little boys when they're together."

"I'd pay to see that," said Gabrielle. "I can't picture a playful Carson."

"Maybe he'll let his guard down this weekend," said Julie. "But I keep forgetting you're his client. I guess he's always on duty around you." They passed the courts, one of which was for basketball and volleyball, and continued to the eastern-most bungalow. "Here we are," Julie announced, opening the unlocked door. Gabrielle and Sarah followed her in.

Gabrielle smiled. "It looks just like your condo."

"I guess it does. Except that the kitchen is much smaller," Julie said.

Simultaneously, Gabrielle and Sarah said, "I guess I know which room is mine." Julie joined in their laughter. After placing her bag and backpack in the one closest to the main house, Gabrielle met the others in the short hallway.

"Want to go for a walk on the beach?" asked Julie, leaning on the middle bedroom door. "Jarin usually runs in the morning and I think we can catch him on his way back."

"He won't mind?" asked Sarah.

"Nope," said Julie. "I always look for him on the beach when I come home in the mornings." They left the bungalow; Gabrielle and Sarah following Julie to the closest, but very steep, beach path. They slid and skidded down to the sand.

"What's that?" asked Sarah, pointing out to sea, toward a large boat shaped silhouette emerging through the slowly evaporating fog.

"That's *Phantom Lady*. She's a racing yacht," answered Julie. "They're going for a sail this afternoon."

"It looks awfully far out," said Gabrielle. "How do they get to it?"

"They swim."

"Swim?" asked Gabrielle and Sarah incredulously.

Julie nodded. "It's only about a mile out. Joseph and Jarin are staying in the bungalows this weekend, so I'm betting they and maybe Carson anchored her there last night and swam in. Usually she's moored in Marina Cove. That's where they'll leave her when they come back in."

"Sailing's not enough—they have to swim a mile, too?" Sarah asked. "They're nuts."

Exaggerating a whisper, Julie said, "Don't tell them that—they think it's big fun."

Looking north along the slope, Gabrielle said, "Oh—that's a retaining wall. I'd thought it was the side of the hill." She trotted over and ran her hands along the smooth stones set in the slope. "This must have been put in generations ago—it looks almost natural now."

"Xavier had it built," said Julie, who had followed her. "Look," she said, pointing out the large rocks strewn along the beach. "You can see where they left the extras. My grandfather had some of them gathered around the fire pit," she said, leading them toward it.

"Wow, big rocks," said Sarah. She ran toward the fire pit, and jumped the eighteen inches to land on top of a narrow flat slab. "Cool!" she yelled to them, balancing herself.

"Show off!" Julie yelled back.

Gabrielle and Julie both ran toward the fire pit. Gabrielle placed her hands and vaulted herself up and into a sitting position on a rock that she guessed was around four feet tall. Julie veered before she reached the pit and raced toward a hooded figure in the distance. "Looks like Jarin," she called over her shoulder.

The man slowed to a walk as Julie approached, caught her up in his arms, and swung her around in a hug. "Hey Jules, missed you. Where've you been?" He kissed her cheek.

Oh, no.

Taking his hand, Julie said simply, "Working." She tugged at him, pulling him along the beach to the fire pit. "Come and meet Gabrielle and Sarah." His hood fell back.

Please don't let it be...

"Good morning, ladies," he said, his grey eyes looking from one to the other and finally settling on Gabrielle.

"It's so very nice to meet you. I love your work," said Sarah.

"Thank you," said Jarin, his voice warm and friendly.

Biting back her anger, Gabrielle responded with a brusque, "Good morning."

Julie and Sarah stared at her with similar expressions of astonishment. Then Julie exclaimed, "You've already met!" Abruptly turning on Jarin, she demanded. "*What did you do?*"

"I obviously have serious transgressions to atone for." Jarin's smile was regretful, his voice firm. "Julie, Sarah—would you excuse us? I need to speak privately with Gabrielle." He turned toward her. "If you'll allow it?"

Julie started to protest, but Sarah interrupted, grabbing her hand. "Of course. We'll just go on with our walk." Pulling Julie away, Sarah called back over her shoulder, "Gabs, we'll see you back at the condo—I mean bungalow."

Intending to catch up with them, Gabrielle jumped down from her perch.

Softly, Jarin spoke her name. "Gabby..."

Bristling with hostility, Gabrielle spun to face him. "Don't you dare call me that."

Taking a step back, Jarin said, "This is going to be far harder than I thought."

"You thought I would forget yesterday once I knew who you were? Are you truly that arrogant?"

"No, that's not it." Jarin said. "It's just that we are in two very different frames of mind right now. It was foolish to allow myself to believe that I could reach you."

Already far angrier than she had been yesterday, she was further incensed by this latest insult. "You're calling me *stupid*?"

"No, Gabrielle." Jarin's voice remained seductively earnest in his attempt to explain. "It's just that I now see that I caused you more pain than I can begin to understand, and that forgiveness will not come easily. Please understand that I am very deeply sorry. Can you at least consider accepting my apology?"

"Very smooth, but I'm not falling for it," she said coldly. "Why are you sorry today? You obviously didn't give a damn yesterday."

Tentatively, Jarin stepped toward her. "I did care. That was the problem. I cared too deeply, too quickly. That's never happened to me. I didn't expect it. I didn't want it. I wasn't prepared. Unforgivable that I took it out on you—but still, I ask you to forgive me."

Unwilling to accept his truth, she hung on to her rage. "This conversation is over." She started after Julie and Sarah.

Allowing Gabrielle to walk away was a mistake that Jarin refused to make. Swiftly covering the distance between them, he caught her around the waist, pulling her up into his arms. "I'm not letting you go—not until we fix this." Holding her tightly, Jarin sat her back on the rock she had earlier jumped down from—but didn't release her.

"*Let me GO!*" Gabrielle fought him; pushing at him, hitting him, kicking him—anywhere, everywhere she could reach.

Stoically absorbing the abuse she inflicted, Jarin flinched when she caused him real pain—but didn't let her go.

Punishing him relentlessly, Gabrielle fought to break his hold. But the anger fueling her attack ebbed with her strength, and as it receded, confusion, anxiety, fear—everything she had so successfully suppressed welled up in its place. She was breaking. Each crack a betrayal, weakening her ability to hold herself together. She fought them as ferociously as she had fought Jarin. But his hold tightened, preventing her from seeking a sanctuary in which she could privately fall apart. *Not here. Not now.*

Sensing that he was no longer her main target, Jarin changed his intent from restraint to embrace. "You need to let it out," he murmured, as hesitantly, he pressed his lips to her ear.

The fragile barrier that Gabrielle had fought to preserve crumbled. Sobs broke through; her body quaking under the force of them. Carefully, Jarin lifted her from the rock, and sitting on another of them, lowered her to his lap. Relief washed over him as he held her close. He had survived the tempest; they had a future. *May not be the one I want, but at least there's something.*

Cradled to his chest, soothed by the hypnotic rhythm of his heartbeat and his whispered endearments, Gabrielle gradually quieted. "I'm sorry," she finally gained enough control to say. "I shouldn't have—"

"You've been holding it in for far too long." Jarin said, rocking her; kissing her. "Too much for anyone to handle alone."

Sobs still catching in her throat, Gabrielle tensed to fight yet again. But the warmth flowing from each touch of his lips enshrouded her. His arms, no longer a prison she was desperate to escape, became instead a buffer against the madness.

~*~~~**~~~*~

Endless moments had passed, but not nearly enough. Darkening Jarin's contentment was a dilemma. They were both professionals with duties to perform, and the time to perform them was approaching far too quickly. Resigned, he drew away from nuzzling Gabrielle's hair.

Staring at her hands stuffed with wads of Kleenex, Gabrielle expressed her bewilderment. "I don't remember where these came from. I don't remember using them."

Reaching into his jacket pocket, Jarin pulled out more and handed them to her. The simple movement, letting go for just that instant, irritated him. He quickly replaced his arm.

"You had them?" she asked. Then in a gently mocking tone, "Do you *usually* run with a pocket full of Kleenex?"

"Just for today," he replied, caressing her with his voice, his eyes. "I just didn't know if they would be for you or for me."

Gabrielle's laugh rang out, melodic and contagious. She couldn't have explained why the thought of Jarin bawling into wads of Kleenex was so funny. It just was.

Surprising and welcome, her laughter reverberated through Jarin, igniting a calm, contented joy that he hadn't expected.

Gabrielle felt Jarin stiffen as she turned her face up to his. "I know I'm hideous. I should have brought my sunglasses."

Brushing his lips across her cheek, he said, "Don't be silly," She tightened her arms around him, and Jarin fought to hold back his response. He needed control and patience—not the fire rising inside him.

Slivers of reality pierced Gabrielle's contentment with their peaceful interlude. "I've just remembered the call," she said. "Not sure I'm in shape to be there."

"Of course you are," he said confidently.

"Why do you think so?" she asked, searching his eyes.

Rich, dark golden brown. Puffy from crying, but still so beautiful. He stared down into them, completely disarmed. Gabrielle's eyes wavered under his intense, steady gaze; a blush stole into her complexion and she looked away. *Too much. Too soon.* Recovering himself, he answered her question. "It's your responsibility and you're a pro. The same reason I'll be there."

"That sounds suspiciously like a pep talk."

Jarin laughed. "It is. Did it work?"

"No," she answered contrarily, but slid off his lap to the sand. He stood. "But let's go anyway."

"That's the spirit," he said. They walked toward the steep path, Gabrielle holding her arms and shivering against the chill of the still foggy morning. "Here," he said, unzipping and removing his jacket. "Wear this. You're cold."

The thin, sleeveless cotton jersey he wore underneath was still damp with sweat and clung to his chest. Refusing the jacket, Gabrielle said, "You'll be cold. Your shirt's too thin."

He stopped and held out the jacket. "And your point?"

"I don't want you to be cold on my account," she said.

"That's my choice to make and I've made it—so put the jacket on. You're shivering."

Trying to stare him down, Gabrielle intended to refuse again. But his gaze held shadows of intimacies that she wasn't ready to consider. Again, she had to look away.

Once more, he had revealed too much. Suppressing his hunger for her, Jarin walked toward her, holding the jacket. "Please, allow me to do this for you."

"What if I want to take care of you?" she grumbled, but allowed him to help her into the jacket. "Mmmm."

It was Jarin's turn to laugh deeply. "Warm isn't it?"

"Yes," she admitted reluctantly. "Thank you."

"As for taking care of me," he said, "I expect that you will—just not in that way."

Disturbed by his words, Gabrielle turned and headed toward the path. Earlier that morning, she had considered him an arrogant ass. Now in her thoughts, he reached out his hand to her. She wanted to take it; but... *will I, knowing what is to follow? I need time.*

Following slowly, Jarin worked to control his urges.

Having reached the bottom of the path, Gabrielle stopped and stared upward at the steep incline. Scrambling and climbing would do the job, but it was smooth enough that a better way would work. She retraced her steps for about twenty yards, then attacked the path at a dead run. Using her momentum, she propelled herself up the steep incline to the top, where she turned to wait for Jarin.

"Thanks for that," he said, reaching the top. "I was preparing to carry you."

Insulted, Gabrielle asked, "What if you weren't here?"

"Then you could have seventy-seven'ed Carson."

"Very funny," she said. "I was pretty good at taking care of myself before all this happened." The stress of the past few days flooded back.

"No worries," he said to lighten her mood as they walked onto the grounds. "It'll be over soon." *No need to tell her yet. She's in my life now—no matter how independent she is, there'll always be someone watching over her.*

~*~~~**~~~*~

Warm and dry after a quick hot shower and change of clothes, Gabrielle surveyed the grounds through the bay window of Julie's bungalow. The time on her cell, 9:45, indicated that she had only fifteen minutes to get to Jarin's bungalow for the meeting. She had not thought to ask him which it was and would just have to knock on every door. Hurrying back to the bedroom, she retrieved hers and Jarin's jackets and donned her sunglasses on the way out. As she passed the bay window heading toward the front door, movement just outside caught her eye. Jarin was coming up the front walk. Her appreciation of his thoughtfulness was short-lived, shoved aside by the wild doubts that quickly followed. The pounding of her heart escalated. *Calm,* she urged it. *I need calm.*

Jarin knocked three times, each one answered by an acceleration of her heartbeat. *Thanks so much,* she chastised her heart. *You're obviously going to rat me out.* Opening the door, she said, "Hello again." In spite of her sunglasses, their eyes connected, and communicated at a level she hadn't known existed. Her doubts were for naught. *Julie's gonna kill me.*

"Sunglasses? Are your eyes still irritated?" Jarin asked, the warmth in his voice fervent and unmistakable.

"Cold compresses helped a little." She took off the sunglasses. "But I'm still hideous."

Gently cupping her face, Jarin lifted her head slightly. "Noticeable," he said. "But not hideous. Never hideous." He kissed her eyelids, each kiss a warm caress, speaking of future intimacies Gabrielle could no longer ignore. Her eyes found his. His eyes held hers—completely, undeniably.

Reluctantly, Jarin withdrew his hand. "Are you ready?" he asked.

Ready for what? The call? To walk out this door with him and never look back? To beg Julie to see that this is right? It didn't matter. The answer was the same regardless of the question. "Yes."

CHAPTER THIRTEEN

Complications

"This is my study," said Jarin, his words weaving through the muted conversation drifting out the open French doors.

Gabrielle stepped across the threshold as Landry stood. "Good morning," she said.

"Morning, Gabby," Landry responded warmly, showing no residue of the anger that had marred their last meeting. "I see Jarin found you."

Carson merely nodded to them and then turned back to the device sitting near the conference phone.

"Didn't see you on the beach run this morning." Landry said to Jarin. "Slept in?"

"Julie stopped me," said Jarin. "Are you at Nathan's?"

"At my folks' for one last visit before they left for Porto Carras—but they're not going."

Removing herself from the middle of their conversation, Gabrielle rounded the oval conference table and chose the chair closest to Carson. As she sat, she saw that Landry and Jarin both watched her—and with similar expressions. Jarin's, she understood. But Landry's? The tenderness with which he now regarded her was disturbingly out of place.

"Too bad they decided not to go." Jarin said, reclaiming Landry's attention. "Mom and Dad were looking forward to it."

"Guess you haven't talked to them yet," Landry said as Jarin headed to the chair at the head of the table. "Your dad called this morning. They're coming back next Thursday or Friday." He sat in the chair closest to the one Jarin was straddling rather than the one he had previously occupied. "Given the circumstances, Mom and Dad cancelled their plans as well."

"I knew they were coming back early, but not as early as that," Jarin said. "I'll give him a call after we're done."

"I think he's arranging another conference call with all of us."

"It's coming up on ten," Carson said.

"Go ahead and dial in," said Jarin.

As Landry turned toward the conference phone, his gaze stopped at Gabrielle. "Why're you wearing sunglasses?"

"My eyes are a little irritated," she replied, chafing under his scrutiny.

Carson held up his hand for silence, halting Landry's inquisition. "Gabrielle, Jarin, Landry, and Carson just joined," he announced into the conference phone.

"Good morning," Nathan said. "I understand you're putting a temporary muting device on the line."

"Yes, and when I do, you'll no longer be able to hear us. Installing...now," said Carson, flipping the switch on the device he had been adjusting.

"Good. I'm dialing in." After all the partners announced themselves, Nathan said, "The recorder is now on. We have the results of Alicia's analysis. Every machine was infected—including all of your laptops." Groans and expletives came through the speakers.

"Do we know the timeframe?" Garrett asked.

"We think for the past four months," answered Nathan.

"*Four months?*" exclaimed Russell.

"The surveillance creep records its reports to an external server," Nathan explained. "The earliest outbound access we've found was about four months ago."

August asked. "Do we know where it is and who controls it?"

"Alicia is tracing it. All we know for now is that it's at one of the bush league server farms," Nathan said.

"Good thing Alicia was available," said Matthew. "Now that I'm thinking about it, why did SCI make her available to us? What's their interest in this?"

"You're a new senior partner Matthew, and I've neglected to make you aware that I'm an advisor to the SCI board. My apologies for that oversight," answered Nathan. "When I expressed our dilemma, Jarin offered her services to us."

"At what cost?" asked Russell.

"No cost," said Nathan.

"Why would he do that?" Russell pursued. "She's obviously top quality talent."

Garrett cut him off. "You're moving off-point, Russell. We should be asking 'How do we fix this?'" he said.

That's Garrett for you—swift and decisive—like an extremely sharp axe.

"Next step—to eradicate the intrusion and harden our networks," Nathan replied. "At present, we have two paths available to us: do it ourselves, which can take six weeks or more for planning, execution, and testing. Or we can move into the SCI data center, in which case the networks will be hardened by Monday morning."

"Convenient, isn't it?" asked Russell.

"What's that supposed to mean?" asked Fiona.

"Their security finds the intrusion, their IT staff diagnoses it and the best solution is their data center," said Russell. "Connect the dots."

"There are no dots," said August. "You'd know that if you attended our off-sites."

"Don't be an ass, Russell," Garrett impatiently cut in. "They've offered us a fair cash-based merger deal. The terms aren't changing as a result of this issue."

"Just saying, it's a coincidence," said Russell.

"Much has been thrown at us in the last few days," Nathan said. "First the forecasted market crash, which has the side effect of killing the Avanti proposal. Then the file anomalies. Now this. We have good reason to be paranoid—obviously something's wrong. However, I assure you, SCI is not our problem."

"If you research the business practices of the two, you'll see that it's more likely to be Avanti," Garrett added.

"As much as I hate to admit it, Garrett's right," said Fiona. "Why don't we vote on the merger right now? We're all here."

"Hold on. I don't like feeling forced into this," said Russell.

"No one's forcing you into anything. I'm simply asking for a vote," stated Fiona. "You can always vote no. What do you say, Nathan? Do we vote?"

"We can," Nathan said hesitantly.

Garrett asked, "What's the problem, Nathan?"

"First, does anyone see any other way of quickly hardening our networks?"

"Not without cost," Matthew said. "The only other option would be to find another hardened data center.

I'd prefer SCI's since they use it themselves. Can we buy space in theirs? It'll give us more time to decide."

"I'm sure we could probably do that," Nathan answered.

"And spend money that we would otherwise not?" asked Garrett.

"As Fiona asked, let's take a vote," Nathan said. "If it's unsuccessful, I'll look into buying space at the SCI data center. If they provide that service, we should still be secure by the end of the week."

"Until then, the creep will affect us?" asked Fiona.

"We'll clean it out, and to guarantee it won't come back, we'll need to have IT on monitoring alert," answered Nathan. "Can we do that, Matthew?"

"We have a small staff—especially since some followed Horace when he resigned, but we'll just have to step up," Matthew replied.

"Still, extra money," grumbled Garrett.

Nathan chuckled. "Okay, let's vote. We need four of the six of us for the go-ahead. Because of my relationship with SCI, I won't invoke managing partner privilege." He called them by name. The only No vote was Russell. "We've just approved the merger with SCI," Nathan concluded.

Jarin stood, flipped the chair around, and sat down again.

"I'll sign the merger agreement and get it to SCI today," said Nathan. "I'll also make the initial contact to get our servers moved into their data center. Matthew, expect to be contacted later on today."

"Sure thing," answered Matthew.

"What's the effect on our IT team and Matthew?" Fiona asked belatedly.

"The merger specifies that although the servers will be moved into the SCI data center, the NEI IT team will remain intact," Nathan responded. "In fact, Matthew and his team will have expanded career growth options."

"Thanks for thinking of me, Fiona," Matthew commented dryly.

"We can give up the forty-first floor space because we only needed it for the servers," Nathan added. "We'll move the IT team onto the analysts' floor. They can manage them remotely from there."

"When are you going to break the news to Avanti?" asked Garrett.

"This afternoon," said Nathan. "Looks like I'm having a very busy Saturday. Matthew, advise your team they'll have a very busy Sunday. Meeting adjourned everyone. Thanks for giving up part of your morning. The recorder is now off." He ended the call.

There were a few seconds of silence as Carson checked the readout from his monitoring device and took them off mute. "The line is clean, Nathan. Just you and us." he said.

"Well then—congratulations, Jarin," said Nathan. "Looks like you've bought yourself a company."

Jarin leaned back in his chair, slightly bumping Gabrielle's feet as he stretched out his legs under the table. The timbre of his voice was deep and authoritative when he spoke. "Thanks, Nathan. I really look forward to having NEI on board."

Exposed to Jarin's professional persona for the first time, Gabrielle was at a loss for words. Heat rushed to her face as she stole a glance in his direction. Just as quickly looking away, her gaze briefly swept Landry's face. Though his expression was carefully noncommittal, his jaw was even tighter than before. *I may be in over my head—getting involved with Jarin. And Landry...*

"I'll clear time on my calendar Monday morning to help you get situated in your new offices," Jarin continued.

"Appreciate it," Nathan replied. "I probably won't be spending much time there until we get this other issue resolved. You talked to Josh yet?"

"No," said Jarin with a grin. "But sounds like he's been busy."

"He's hot to get our strategy in place for riding out the crash and I need to get NEI's issues behind me so that my focus won't be divided."

"Understood. Any further developments?"

"Nothing other than this worm," answered Nathan. "However, I didn't reveal all that we know about it to the partners. According to Carson, Alicia thinks it may have been around longer than four months."

"Just a hunch," Carson said. "We believe that it either deletes or archives the data at some point, to keep from filling up its disk. We're hoping there's an archive server to be found and we're looking for it as well."

Nathan asked, "Any more news from Alicia's analysis?"

"You got the most current information for the meeting today," Carson replied "As for the direction of her analysis, she's traced the server to a gaming server farm—but she hasn't yet zeroed in on the exact one. If she finds it, there may be enough information for her to determine which machine was the first to be infected. In the meantime, she's also plugged a non-infected test machine into the network so that she can trace the infection as it occurs. I'll give you today's status as soon as I get it."

"Thanks Carson. You're very thorough," said Nathan.

An idea bloomed in Gabrielle's mind. "Jarin?" Despite the uneasiness awakened by the identically acute stares that Jarin and Landry directed toward her, she asked, "May I interrupt?"

"Certainly," Jarin replied.

"Carson, since the surveillance creep reports are archived, I'm wondering whether Alicia can find which machines were used to modify the Retro file." Seeing Jarin's questioning expression, she paused, but he gestured that she should continue. "If she can, and if we can get the full archive, we may be able to piece together the chain of events from the first modification until now and expose who's behind it." Already in a heightened state of anxiety, Gabrielle found the long, ensuing silence nearly unbearable.

Finally breaching it, Carson said, "Give me the file name. I'll give Alicia the scenario and ask her to trace it."

"Once again Gabrielle, you've left us speechless," said Nathan.

"It was just a thought," she replied, feeling another flush; this one of embarrassment.

Landry laughed. "And as usual, a pretty good one."

Gabrielle glanced at Jarin, wanting his affirmation as well. Though pensively watching Landry—who was now watching her—his glance briefly met hers. Riveted by the intense desire she saw in that fleeting instant, Gabrielle knew that "in over her head" or not, it was too late. *I need to explain to Landry.* Bracing herself for what she expected to see, she looked toward him, but he and Jarin had locked gazes; their faces inscrutable.

"By the way, Gabrielle how's your server situation?" asked Nathan, shattering the tension between the two men.

To Gabrielle's dismay, they both focused on her. "Everything's clean. Alicia said I could run as long as I didn't connect the laptop Carson gave me to the NEI network," she said, keeping her eyes on the conference phone. "I sent you the finished spreadsheet last night."

"Saw it this morning, but haven't yet reviewed it," Nathan replied. "Thanks for your diligence."

"You're welcome," she replied.

"Glad you got done last night," said Landry. "I hope you've had some time to spend with Julie and—your other friend?"

"Sarah. We went for a walk on the beach this morning," said Gabrielle, immediately aware that she had revealed too much. Landry wasn't just making idle conversation.

"How was it?" he asked.

"Foggy," she answered, hoping to block this latest line of questioning. To no avail. The glance he flashed her made it clear that he wasn't appeased.

Abruptly, Jarin asked, "Is it time to address Sparks?"

"Do you have the agreement with you?" Nathan asked.

Carson slid a sheaf of papers across the table. Jarin caught them. "I have them now," he said as he opened the folder. He checked his watch. "Quentin should be—"

As if on cue, a knock sounded at the door between the study and the great room. Quentin opened it and poked his head in. "Am I interrupting?"

"Perfect timing," Jarin responded. "We're just getting to Sparks."

"Ah, the agreement," said Quentin, as he closed the door behind him on his way to the conference table. "One of the reasons I'm here."

"One of?" asked Jarin. "There's another besides that we're sailing this afternoon?"

"It seems your sister and her friends have been very resourceful," answered Quentin. "I'm sure they'll fill you in."

Again Gabrielle found herself being examined, this time only by Jarin. "When we're done here, then," he said. "Nathan's on the phone."

"Great. Morning, Nathan." said Quentin, taking the seat next to Gabrielle.

"Good morning, Quentin."

"How're you doing, Gabby?" he asked, reaching to give her a hug. His arm inadvertently bumped her sunglasses and they slipped down past her nose. "What's happened to your eyes? Allergies?"

"They look more than 'irritated' Gabrielle," said Landry disapprovingly. "What's happened?"

"It's nothing," Gabrielle insisted. "Just a bit of overuse." The moment she flicked a glance at Jarin she regretted it. Neither Landry nor Quentin missed it. Having already focused on the papers in front of him, Jarin showed no signs of being aware of their scrutiny. *They're blaming Jarin and it's my fault. Perfect—just lovely.*

Getting no reaction from Jarin, Landry turned back to Gabrielle. "Maybe you should take it easy. Take the next couple of days off."

"That won't be necessary, Landry," she hastened to reply. "I'm fine. Really."

"We're taking good care of Gabrielle. She'll be fine for Monday, Landry, if that's what she chooses," said Jarin, looking up from the folder and closing it. "Now, Quentin. Your thoughts on the agreement?"

Turning to Gabrielle, as if she had asked the question, Quentin said, "It's a very good agreement—everybody wins. SCI gets a killer app and the expertise—that's you Gabs—to build a modeling group around it. NEI gets access to the application and the group at no cost. You are extremely well compensated and can choose your own path after just six months of knowledge transfer. Of course you'll want to review the agreement, and I'll be happy to present any changes you'd like to make."

"May I review it with you today?" Gabrielle asked.

"Absolutely," Quentin assured her. "How about after I talk to the three of you regarding the other matter? Jarin is here so we can negotiate as needed to get it signed today," said Quentin.

"That would be great." Gabrielle was careful to look away from all three of them, instead focusing on the view outside the open French doors. She had forgotten that her agreement was with Jarin's personification of SCI. *This is getting complicated.*

"Looks like we're all done here then," Nathan noted. "Is there anything else we need to discuss?"

"We're all good on this end," Jarin replied.

"Then I've got to work through my to-do list. Goodbye all."

~*~~~**~~~*~

Preparing himself for the imminent confrontation, Jarin knew that Quentin and Landry were anxious for Gabrielle to leave the room. Carson was ostensibly ignoring them all, his head still bent over the monitoring device. Though it was frustrating that even his cousin's first thought was that he had harmed Gabrielle; he had to admit that yesterday, they would have been right. *But today ...* He had to end their interference before things got out of hand. Determined to set the terms, Jarin reached his decision. "So, Quentin, what's the other reason you're here?"

"I have something for Julie, Gabrielle, and Sarah to review and possibly sign," said Quentin.

"Really?" asked Gabrielle, excitement lighting up her face.

In spite of the storm he was working to control, Jarin grinned. *No poker face there.*

"Definitely," Quentin answered.

"Gabrielle, can you get them?" Jarin asked, watching her enthusiasm give way to determination to stay.

"If they're at the bungalow," Gabrielle answered. "They weren't there when I left."

"If they aren't, they're close by. I saw Julie peek around the side of this one not too long ago." He rose, walked around the table, and held out his hand to Gabrielle. "Come on, I'll walk with you to the door."

"I suppose I'll see you all later," Gabrielle said, to various gestures of good-bye.

"Why don't you put a cold press on before you come back," suggested Landry.

"Good idea," seconded Quentin.

"Maybe I will," said Gabrielle, looking up at Jarin. He was careful to give her no sign. Escorting her from the room, he pulled the door closed behind them.

"Jarin, there's something I need to put right."

Stopping at the sofa, he sat on its arm. "Not your problem, Gabrielle. I'll take care of it."

"You don't understand," she said urgently, tentatively touching his arm.

"I'm listening," he said.

Gabrielle's color deepened, oddly reminding Jarin of a full, ripe plum, his favorite fruit. The thought aggravated his hunger. *But not for plums.*

"I think I've given Landry the wrong impression. It was before I met you and—"

Relieved that her worry was unfounded, he took her hand from his arm and held it to his lips. "No you didn't."

"You can't know that."

"But I do," he replied, "If you had, we would never have made it to the call." He easily read her unspoken question. "Women are naturally strategic thinkers," he said, smiling at her surprise. "For men, it's a learned behavior. Most of us end our battles quickly and decisively. If Landry'd had the wrong impression, the war would have been on as soon as he saw us at the door. Trust me—this is about me and how they think I'm not right for you." *I also fear I'm not right for you, love—but too late now.*

"But that's not fair," she responded angrily, unintentionally ratcheting up his desire. "It's none of their business, really. I have to—"

Jarin pulled her into his arms, stifling her objections. "This is my problem. Please—allow me the time to handle it. Spend some time with Julie and Sarah." He waited for the pout, ready to console her.

Instead, she said, "You underestimate me."

Jarin threw back his head and laughed. *I sure as hell did—but she'll never know it.* "I'm just trying to get you to understand that this is not your fight. However if Landry says you misled him—I promise you—that situation is yours to deal with." Staying far away from her lips, Jarin allowed himself only a kiss to her forehead, this time ready for the tingle that spread through him from the simple touch. He tightened his arms around her. *My own petit soleil.*

"That's fair," Gabrielle murmured, yielding at last.

~*~~~**~~~*~

Jarin reluctantly watched Gabrielle leave. *That she is giving me a chance is far more than I deserve. She is extraordinary and she's mine.* Returning quickly to the study and back to his seat at the table, Jarin said, "Whatever you've got to say..."

Quentin exploded loudly. "What the hell did you do?"

Keeping his voice calm, Jarin responded, "I don't know what you mean."

"You know exactly what he means—what did you do to Gabrielle?" Landry asked; calmer than Quentin, but dangerously so. "Her eyes didn't get that way from the fog."

"That is not your concern—either of you," answered Jarin.

On the verge of yelling, Quentin said, "It sure the hell is my concern."

Leaving his chair, Carson interjected dryly, "Do you want to keep this a private conversation, or should I sell seats?" He rounded the table, closed the French doors and then positioned himself, arms folded, against the one closest to Jarin.

Though now controlling his volume, Quentin still vented his fury. "Do you know—or care—anything about her? Or is she just another screw?"

The insult was unexpected. Losing all pretense of calm, Jarin bolted out of his chair and smashed his fist down on the table, shaking it. "That is way out of line!"

"You need to understand that she's not one of those professional husband-hunting debutantes you usually date," Landry said, also rising from the table.

Turning on Landry, Jarin said, "I know what she is."

With growing vehemence, Landry hurled back, "Do you? She's purely logical. She'll take you seriously. She isn't experienced enough for the games you play."

"If you weren't my cousin, I'd kick your ass—*right now.*" On the brink of losing control, Jarin paused, giving serious thought to Gabrielle's concern. "What's it to you, anyway? Did you..."

Turning away from Jarin, Landry paced in front of the closed doors. Carson moved his feet, giving him room. "I never declared myself," he admitted, visibly pained by his mistake. "I thought to wait until we'd handled the crisis."

"You left her to fend for herself during this mess? How the hell do you think I met her?" Memories of Gabrielle's reaction to his idiocy enraging him, Jarin advanced on Landry. "At the fence on the southern ridge of Marina Cove, trying to handle this all by herself. None of the rest of us is handling it alone. Where the hell do you get off accusing me when you're the one who left her to drown?"

His face distorted with fury, Landry charged. Jarin braced for his attack. Carson scrambled to get between them in time. "Hold it, fellas. Think about it—you're family. More than that—you've been friends all your lives. Do you really want to piss it away?"

The cousins glared at each other over Carson's shoulder. After a few tense seconds, they both turned away. Jarin parked himself on the credenza at the head of the table; Landry went back to pacing. Carson resumed his position, leaning against the door.

"I didn't know how bad it was—she never let on." Landry said. "We were trying to get her to leave. But she wouldn't go."

Jarin snorted derisively. "You don't know her at all if you thought she'd leave."

That shot hit home. Landry looked as though he had just absorbed a physical blow. He struck back. "That still doesn't give you the right to make her your latest toy!"

Enraged even more, Jarin started towards Landry.

"Ah, hell," Carson straightened again, ready to step between them.

Carson's brief interruption helped Jarin reclaim his sanity. Slowly, he backed away. "I'm not going to fight, Carson. If I were Landry, I'd feel the same way," he admitted. "I don't have the best track record."

Finally getting another chance, Quentin cut in. "You don't have a track record at all, Jarin. Not one lasting relationship in all the years I've known you. If you hurt Gabrielle, you're nothing more than a callous bastard."

His anger diminished, his voice barely above a whisper, Jarin said to Quentin, "Don't you think I know that? I have no intention of hurting her." The disbelief on Landry's face was as sharply wounding as Quentin's words.

"Then what are your intentions?" Quentin demanded.

"That is entirely up to Gabrielle." Jarin's tone softened as he spoke her name. *Now we're down to the meat of it.*

"Excuse me?" asked Quentin. He and Landry wore almost identical expressions of antagonistic distrust.

"She can have as much or as little of me as she wants." Jarin said, "I have no illusions. I know what I've done. I know what I've been."

Breaking the lengthening silence, Quentin said, "I've obviously missed something here."

"That's an understatement," Carson said with a short bark of a laugh. "Feels like I woke up in the middle of a date movie."

"What's been going on?" Landry asked, curiosity seeping into his anger.

"I wasn't looking for it. I certainly didn't want it," Jarin said bemusedly, "but, I guess I'm in love with her."

Quentin laughed and kept laughing; Landry was still wary.

Inspiration nudged Jarin to turn the tables on Quentin. "By the way, when are you going to stop running from Julie?"

Abruptly, Quentin's laughter ceased. "What did you say?"

"You know Julie's loved you all her life." prodded Jarin, trying to change the conversation. "You'd come by to skateboard with Joseph, and she would be checking her face in the mirror in her crib."

Landry and Carson howled remembering the years they had watched Quentin struggling to avoid his feelings for Julie. Jarin smiled in relief. *It's a start. Maybe Landry'll forgive me one day.*

"It wasn't that funny," Quentin grumbled.

"She's pursued you from the time she was twenty-one," Jarin relentlessly continued. "When are you going to stop denying her—and you—what you both really want?"

"I'm five years older than you Jarin—too old for her."

"Then tell her that and let her go," said Jarin. "Though in the face of what's coming, denying you both the comfort of the one you love seems tragic."

"This is a date movie." Carson observed in disbelief. "You have truly lost it."

Unperturbed, Jarin shrugged. "Whatever," he said. "What's done is done."

"Is that what brought this on—the market crisis?" asked Landry, his voice holding a ghost of his previous anger.

"Not for me. I was blind-sided," said Jarin. "I'm still trying to get my head around it. Gabrielle is precious to me." He paused. "I don't know how else to put it."

A loud knock at the French doors splintered the deafening silence. Carson swung around to face the door, already in a defensive crouch. "It's just Drew," he said, straightening up and opening the door.

"Some bodyguard you are," Drew scoffed. "I had the drop on all of you." Ignoring Carson's glare and oblivious to the tension in the room, he talked without a pause as he crossed the threshold. "We ready to sail? By the way, who's that gorgeous babe heading over this way with Julie?"

Jarin sighed. *Not another one.*

Failing to notice that Landry and Quentin were also now glowering at him, Drew rambled on. "That hair, those legs—she reminds me of Norma Jean."

"Who?" asked Jarin.

"You know—before she was Marilyn Monroe. I have a thing for Norma Jean." Finally focusing in on their faces, he gestured his surrender. "Whoa, sorry gents, who did I insult? Long, beautiful legs, dark wavy hair, I should have known she was taken." He gave an exaggerated sigh. "Still, I'd like to know her name."

"Sarah," Jarin replied. Three strong-willed, intelligent women who had never experienced the dirtier side of business. And the dirt would get deeper in the desperate times ahead. Keeping them out of harm's way was going to be one hell of a hard job. He vented his frustration at Drew. "And if you have less than good intentions, forget about it."

"You gotta be fuckin' kiddin' me!" Carson guffawed, provoking a murderous stare from Jarin. "Just like a reformed smoker."

CHAPTER FOURTEEN

In Too Deep

Tucked into the seat of the bay window, Gabrielle was just able to make out the sails of *Phantom Lady* rounding the northern ridge of Coral Cove. It had been more than an hour since she had given Sarah and Julie the essentials of how she and Jarin had met, and their morning on the beach. On their way back to Julie's bungalow from Jarin's, while she talked, the six-man racing crew scrambled down the slope to the beach, stripped down to their sleeveless, thigh-length Lycra bodysuits, stuffed their clothes into waterproof backpacks which they then strapped on, and swam out to the yacht. Such was her friends' interest in her story that the display of so much muscular masculinity drew neither a glance nor a comment.

Each having withdrawn into her own thoughts, they continued to Julie's bungalow, where they now sat in uncomfortable silence. Unable to stand it any longer, Gabrielle sighed. "Okay, let me have it."

"I was afraid this might happen," said Julie, dejectedly huddled into the far corner of the sectional. "But I thought it would be Sarah."

"Why me?"

"You're the big romantic," Julie said. "Gabrielle is the logical one."

"Sounds like there's an insult in there somewhere," said Sarah.

"Yeah, and I'm the one being insulted," added Gabrielle. She wasn't surprised when Julie ignored their snappish remarks. She was on a mission.

"Gabs, you need to consider what you're doing, where this is going," Julie said. Without warning, her calm façade shattered. "What the *hell* are you thinking?"

"Well, that's straight to the point." But seeing that Julie was truly concerned, Gabrielle allowed her annoyance to dissipate. "I've been asking myself the same thing and I don't have an answer. Maybe I can plead insanity." Picturing herself in a straightjacket, Gabrielle laughed, her anxiety giving the laughter an edge that Julie and Sarah misinterpreted. "I'm not going crazy."

"Methinks you're already there," Sarah cut in.

Julie left the sectional and perched on the edge of the window seat next to Gabrielle. "I've told you what he is, I've told you what he does," she chided. "It makes no sense for you to do this to yourself—especially after Stephen."

Having spent the whole day—a first—without thinking of Stephen once, Gabrielle did not want to think about him now. "I've never been part of an intervention, but I imagine this is what it must feel like."

Undeterred, Julie said, "I'm not letting you kid your way out of this, Gabs. You could really get hurt again."

"Whatever this is between us is very intense. I could be in way over my head, Jules. No argument there. But I can't—I don't want to walk away from it."

After considering Gabrielle's response for only an instant, Julie bolted from the window seat and headed toward the door. "If I can't reason with you, it's time to have a talk with Jarin."

Both Sarah and Gabrielle sprang to their feet. "No!"

Pausing with her hand on the doorknob, Julie faced them. Gabrielle was struck by the determined set to her jaw and how much she resembled Jarin—and to a lesser degree, Landry. "Jules, if this is a mess I've gotten myself into, then I have to be the one to clean it up," she said. "You can't go yelling at Jarin for me."

Stifling a grin, Sarah said, "Besides, they're still sailing, remember?"

Relieved, Gabrielle resumed her place on the window seat. She had also forgotten. *I really must be losing it—I watched the sails disappear only minutes ago.*

"Damn boat," grumbled Julie, reclaiming her perch beside Gabrielle. "But I am going to talk to him."

Gabrielle started to protest, but Sarah beat her to it. "Don't. You'll ruin everything. Jarin's in love with Gabby."

"Excuse me?" asked Julie, her voice rising in surprise.

"Jarin is in love with Gabs." Sarah said again, slowly, emphasizing every word. "You're so worried that it's 'business as usual' for him, you're missing all the signs."

"What signs?" asked Julie.

Annoyed, Sarah said to Gabrielle, "When you two were signing the Sparks agreement, you were working so hard not to touch each other it was making me crazy. Even Quentin noticed."

"Jarin's very intense. I seem to be using that word a lot when it comes to him, but nothing else fits," said Gabrielle. "When he focuses on me, it is very hard not to respond." Julie made a sharp, derisive sound. "I'm sorry Jules," said Gabrielle. "But that's how it is."

"Now you're just being rude," Sarah admonished Julie. "In fact, you and Quentin behaved the same way when we were going over the Charley's agreement."

"Damn, Sarah, what don't you see?" blurted Gabrielle.

"No fair," snapped Julie. "Stop trying to divert me from Gabby's problem."

"Touchy, touchy." said Sarah, smirking at Julie's discomfort. "Anyway, back to Jarin and Gabrielle—doesn't look like he's fighting it. He's already fallen. Hard."

"How the hell can you tell all that?" asked Gabrielle.

"I just call 'em as I see 'em."

"Do you love him?" Julie asked.

"Geez Jules, could you be just a little more direct?"

"At least you still have a sense of humor." Sarah said. "Unlike someone else I know."

Ignoring her, Julie said, "Gabs, you still didn't answer me."

"I've avoided that question all day—not ready to hear the answer. But I can't walk away from what we've started."

Leaning back in the recliner, Sarah said, "I'll take that as a yes."

"What are you going to do?" pursued Julie.

"I don't know." Gabrielle replied. "But I don't want it to harm our friendship."

"No, it's not that. I just don't want you to get hurt. Stephen nearly did you in."

Managing an embarrassed smile, Gabrielle said, "I guess it was better when I thought he was a jackass." Instantly, Julie's demeanor changed. She leaned back, and Gabrielle watched in amazement as the first signs of relief began to erase her "woman on a mission" scowl.

Turning to Sarah, Julie admitted, "You're right, Sarah. I should have seen it."

"Seen what?" Gabrielle asked, anxious to hear what had so suddenly caused Julie to relax. "I need all the enlightenment I can get."

"Jarin is many things, but he's never rude," Julie explained. "And he was terribly rude when you met. Whatever it is between you two, he's seems to be as messed up as you are. I feel much better now. I just didn't want you to be in another messy breakup."

"What Stephen did wasn't a breakup," Sarah said contemptuously. "It was a ripping apart of two souls. *The idiot.*"

Whatever it was, I don't want to have to handle another one. Gabrielle asked, "Jarin's breakups are messy?"

"Not for him."

"Hell. Now I have that to worry about."

Giving Gabrielle her normal, cheery smile, Julie said, "I'm sure you and Jarin will figure it out. Besides, according to Sarah, I've got my own problems."

~*~~~**~~~*~

Watching his young sons at play was one of Garrett's few pleasures. Having to leave them on a Saturday afternoon was a most unwelcome disruption.

A man of medium height in a worn, gray suit asked, "Mr. Stratford?"

"Yes," replied Garrett curtly.

"Thanks for coming down on such short notice," the man said.

"It is an inconvenience, but under the circumstances—" Remembering his attorney's advice not to volunteer any information, Garrett refrained from finishing the statement. He had also turned off his cell phone, having been counseled that something as innocuous as taking or ignoring a call could spark unwelcome curiosity.

"I'm Detective Collins," said the man, holding out his hand.

Shaking it, Garrett said. "Sorry, but I can't say it's a pleasure."

"It rarely is," Detective Collins chuckled morosely. He gestured toward the elevators. "This way please. The morgue is two floors down."

In silence, they walked down the hall to the elevators, where the detective pushed the down button. Once on the elevator, he said, "As I indicated on the phone Mr. Stratford, my reason for calling is that the maitre d' at Celeste's identified him as the gentleman at your table."

"I sincerely hope you're wrong, Detective," answered Garrett.

"Did you try calling your friend—what was his name—Cleveland Harper?"

"Of course I did, and got his voice mail. But that doesn't mean anything."

The detective offered no reply. The elevator doors opened; they stepped off and continued down the hall to a set of large double doors. Detective Collins badged them in. Garrett followed him over to the single covered body on one of the examining tables. The detective pulled the sheet back, exposing the face. Steeling himself, Garrett took a look. His carefully constructed mask slipped, exposing the horror that surged through him. Even with the twisted, sunken jaw, busted nose, blackened, bruised eyes, Garrett recognized him. "That's Cleve," he confirmed in a low, shaken voice. "What happened to him?"

"He was systematically beaten by one, maybe more professionals."

"Professionals?" Under the calm facade he worked to hold in place, Garrett's mind was in turmoil. *What the hell had Cleve gotten himself into?*

"Yes," confirmed the detective. "Were you aware of any gambling, or other activities that he may have been involved in?"

Backing away from Cleve's face so that he could clear his head, Garrett leaned on one of the other examining tables. "Nothing. Cleve seemed like such a straight shooter. I gave him my reservations that night as a reward for his work. If I hadn't—"

"That's not the way it is, Mr. Stratford," said the detective. "I've seen this sort of thing hundreds of times. It was a personal, targeted attack—meant specifically for Mr. Harper. His wallet and valuables were stolen to make it look like a robbery, but it really wasn't." He nodded toward Cleve's face. "Even as bad as all this looks, it wasn't meant to kill—it was intended to be an extremely painful message."

Genuinely shocked, Garret asked, "Message?"

"Apparently, he pissed off some very bad boys, and they sent at least one enforcer after him. Even so, what was done to him shouldn't have killed him."

"You must be joking." When the detective made no further comment, Garrett had to ask. "How did he die then?"

"Of course there'll be an autopsy," he replied. "But we suspect a heart attack."

"Makes sense. That's too much punishment for anyone to take." Glancing one last time at Cleve, Garrett said heavily, "I'll have to pull his personnel records—find next of kin. I also have to notify Nathan."

"Who's Nathan?" asked the detective.

His question, a harsh reminder of his attorney's admonition, sharpened Garrett's focus. Sticking to only the most necessary details, he responded, "Nathan Gibson is the managing partner at our firm, National Economic Institute. I'm a senior partner at that firm. Cleve is—was—one of the junior partners who reports to me."

Having produced a notepad, Detective Collins wrote the details of Garrett's response. "Thank you, Mr. Stratford. We expect that next of kin can claim the body in about a week."

~*~~~**~~~*~

Drawing Gabrielle's attention away from the starlit darkness over Coral Cove, Sarah asked, "Is it time to enjoy being entrepreneurs?"

"Not quite yet," replied Julie, who had again curled up in one of the recliners. "We just countered their proposal today. We still have to sign the final agreement."

Wandering closer to them from the wall near the fireplace, where she had been admiring two of Jarin's paintings, Sarah continued, "Minor detail. By the first of the year I may be leaving Prentice and Associates to start my own agency." She grinned. "May as well dream big."

"I'll be so happy if you can make that happen," said Gabrielle. "The way they're treating you now, they deserve to lose you."

"Thanks, Gabs," said Sarah. "So, shall we celebrate early then?"

"I vote yes," answered Julie, already up and on her way to the kitchen. "I have Chardonnay, Merlot, and Rose," she said. "But the Merlot needs to breathe."

"Rose for me," said Gabrielle with a wry smile. "That fits—the undecided wine."

Sticking her head around the near side of the kitchen entryway, Julie said, "You've already decided. You're just second-guessing yourself."

"Anybody else want to psychoanalyze me tonight?"

"I'm the only other one here, and I've already decided you're a head case." teased Sarah. She called to Julie. "I'll have Chardonnay, but only one. I hate to be a party pooper, but as it's nearly ten, I need to get back to the city if I'm going to pull together a coherent plan for Drew by Monday."

Julie came back with their filled goblets. Handing one to Gabrielle, she set hers and Sarah's on the coffee table.

"I may as well go, too," Gabrielle said after a sip. "Maybe we can come back again later in the month." Her voice trailed off at Julie's skeptical expression. She quickly amended, "That is, Jules, do you mind?" Sarah's expression was also doubtful. Gabrielle watched the two exchange glances. "What?"

"I was going back, too," Julie said. "Don't you want to stay here with Jarin?"

Thoughtful, but... "Oh hell no," Gabrielle shook her head vehemently. "There's no way I'm ready for that."

"Looks like I lost the bet," said Sarah.

"What bet?" asked Gabrielle acerbically.

"Whether or not you were coming with us. I thought you weren't."

"Thanks a lot."

Sarah said, "Silly Gabs, you've got to know where this is heading. I just thought it would be tonight." A jarring knock sounded at the door, startling them all. Sarah spilled some of her Chardonnay onto the table and into her lap. "Oh, hell."

"Stay there or you'll drip," said Gabrielle as she left the window seat. "I'll get a towel." Almost bumping Julie, who was on her way to open the door, Gabrielle ran into the kitchen. Luckily, a cloth lay near the paper towels; probably the one Julie had used to blot the wine bottles.

While she dampened it under the faucet, Carson's voice boomed its way into the kitchen. "Andrew tells me you're going back tonight."

Julie answered him as Gabrielle returned to the great room, "We are."

"Hi, Carson," said Gabrielle, noting that his clothes were still damp and his complexion was ruddier than usual.

Carson watched as Gabrielle passed by. When she stopped at the table to help Sarah clean up the wine, he asked, "And when were you going to tell me, Ms. Winston?"

Unprepared, Gabrielle stammered, "Well... I... um... found... Now?"

"That is unacceptable."

Taking the cloth from Gabrielle's hand, Sarah chimed in from the recliner as she blotted her culottes, "Give her a break, Carson—it's not her fault. We just told Gabs we were leaving—not five minutes ago."

Interrupting Sarah, he asked Gabrielle, "So are you leaving as well?"

Though she thought his lip twitched, the tiny could-have-been smile disappeared so quickly that Gabrielle erred on the side of caution. Her reply was brief. "Yes."

"I'll get the car ready. We'll be leaving with Andrew in," he checked his watch, "half an hour." Without another word, he turned and left.

"I guess that was Carson being angry." Gabrielle said, wondering if she actually would have called him. She needed to take her security more seriously.

"Don't let him scare you," said Sarah, now wiping off the table. "He puts his pants on one leg at a time, just like everybody else. Why's he so pissed off anyway?"

"He's doing all he can to keep me safe," explained Gabrielle. "I have to respect that. I didn't think to call him, and I should have."

"Now I feel like an ass," Sarah said, straightening up and heading to the kitchen. "I have a mind to run after him and apologize."

"Carson does that to people." Gabrielle laughed, but cut it short as she felt at her waist. "Has anyone seen my phone?"

"It's on the window seat," said Julie as she started to swing the door closed.

Grateful that Carson hadn't noticed her lapse, Gabrielle retrieved it, resolving to be more attentive to her security.

Julie started to close the door, but swung it open again as someone came up the walkway. "Sarah, maybe you'll get your chance," she called into the kitchen. "Looks like he's coming back."

Hastily snapping her phone to the waistband of her capris, Gabrielle turned toward the door. This time though, it was Jarin; his clothes more wet than damp, his hair in wild, windblown waves, the beginnings of a beard on his jaw. Pausing at the door, he briefly acknowledged his sister. "Hey, Jules."

Tensely Gabrielle waited; relieved when Julie merely asked, "How was it?"

"Not bad," Jarin answered absently, already through the door. Spotting Gabrielle near the window seat, he said as he approached, "I hear you're leaving."

Their eyes met. A powerful energy passed between them. Gabrielle inhaled his scent of sand, sea, and masculine exertion; an unfamiliar, heady elixir, it intoxicated her more with each breath. She could not back away. Jarin's eyes beckoned, but at the last moment, she kept herself in place just beyond his reach. "Yes," she said.

"Andrew will be here in half an hour," said Julie.

Footsteps sounded across the floor as Sarah returned from the kitchen. Jarin glanced her way, freeing Gabrielle. She hastily backed toward the window seat, widening the distance between them. "Hey Sarah," he said.

"Hey yourself," she replied.

Turning back to Gabrielle, he asked, "Do you mind my coming into town with you and Carson? There's something I want you to see."

"I'd like that," she said, surprised at the calm with which she said it.

"I'll join you in half an hour then."

~*~~~**~~~*~

Tragic. There was no other word for it.

Garrett stared thoughtfully through the window at his lamp-lit lawn. He would have to accelerate his plans for NEI. There was no one on Cleve's team he could rely on; it was time to raid Landry's for Gabrielle. But, first things first. He had to call Nathan. Pulling out his cell phone, he switched it on. Seeing that there was a voice mail, he speed-dialed the pick-up number. He did not recognize the voice.

"It'll probably be a few weeks or months before you pick up this message." The voice chuckled. "Take this as a warning—be careful who you cross. Next time, it will be fatal."

They thought it was me. Vaulting from behind the desk, Garrett paced his study, struggling for composure. In spite of the horror of Cleve's fate, he had to recover his ability to strategize—his life depended on it. Nathan had said they played hardball, but he never suspected they would be thugs. Panic and fury warred within him until finally, he suppressed his fear, harnessed his anger, and focused his thoughts.

I'm sorry, Cleve. There's nothing I can do for you now, but maybe you can help me. Pulling out Detective Collins' business card, Garrett picked up the phone, hit the speed dial number for his attorney, and issued new instructions. He then hit the speed dial number for Nathan.

"Garrett?"

"Cleve's been murdered," Garrett stated bluntly.

"*What?*"

Summarizing what the detective had told him, Garrett purposely wove the story to plant the seed of Cleve as the insider.

"Such a tragedy. I'll have someone from personnel pull his information first thing in the morning," Nathan said. "From here on, refer any inquiries to our public relations agent. We'll address this as a company matter. Don't try to handle it yourself."

"Sure thing." After Nathan hung up, Garrett attached his recorder and called Brett.

He answered, "Hello?"

"It's Garrett. You got the wrong man, asshole."

"I don't know what you mean," Brett replied.

"You know exactly what I mean," said Garrett. "Apparently your bruisers threw away his identification. If you'd seen it, you'd have known."

"What does—"

"Here's the deal, you son of a bitch: I have a number of strategically placed packages detailing our association and containing recordings—yeah, you heard right—of all our calls," Garrett said. "If I even so much as get a scratch, or stub my toe, they will be delivered to a specific detective of the Crescent City police force."

"You wouldn't incriminate yourself."

"Try me," Garrett challenged him. "You have a hell of a lot more to lose than I do." He hung up, anxious to get the results from the Blackhawk surveillance.

~*~~**~~*~

Just able to make out the silhouettes of Julie and Sarah waving as Andrew drove up the driveway, Gabrielle waved back. Soon, all she could see was the taillights and then she heard the car turn onto the highway and speed off. Determined to make amends for her earlier slip, she said to Carson, "I'm sorry I didn't think to call you right away. You're right—it's the first thing I should have done."

"I don't expect you to be perfect, Gabby," he said. "But it's my job to remind you when you slip up."

"Gabby? What happened to Ms. Winston?"

"I don't have to be so formal now that you're family," he said.

"You're related to Jarin?"

"Brothers in arms," he said. "We started ISS together about ten years ago. We're still very close friends—actually closer than friends."

"Jarin couldn't have been a bodyguard." Her voice trailed off at Carson's smirk.

It widened into a grin. "Yes he was—and a very good one."

"Isn't that a rather demanding profession? I mean with all the training and coordination and gadgets and stuff? I know you never seem to be relaxed."

"He had to give it up once word got out that he was a San Chapelle."

"I guess it's inconvenient to be a personal protection agent when you need a personal protection agent."

"Exactly," he chuckled. "He's still the best workout partner I've ever had. We're pretty evenly matched."

"Are you usually his agent?"

Carson's face instantly lost its expression. "Mostly, unless I'm in the field doing something special."

"And you're a founder of ISS."

"Yes, as you know."

"Then why are you protecting me?"

Silent for so long that Gabrielle thought he wouldn't answer, Carson finally said, "We thought it best."

Getting information from Carson was nearly impossible, but Gabrielle was determined. "We?"

"After Nathan apprised us—Jarin and me—of the situation, we decided that you needed heightened security."

"Because of Avanti."

"That's right. They don't always abide by the law."

"You and Landry keep saying that, and I'm not getting what you mean."

"It means that you must consider your security to be your highest priority," replied Carson firmly. "Do I make myself clear?"

"Yes." Having Carson alone and willing to answer questions was too good an opportunity for Gabrielle to ignore. "Do you mind? I have a few questions about other things."

"Why does that not surprise me?"

"Will you answer them?"

"It depends. Try me."

"Okay—did Jarin know who I was when we met?"

"He knew of you, but he didn't realize it was you on the ridge," he said. "Anything else about that, you need to ask him, Gabrielle."

Noting that he was one step more formal, Gabrielle guessed that she must have gotten too close to a line of some kind. But the need to know drove her on. "What do you think about what's happening with us?"

There was a buzz in his pocket. He pulled out his cell, examined it, and put it back. "Well, he may not be the best thing for you," he said, "but it's beginning to appear that you are the best thing for him."

"Oh, well, thanks—I think."

Laughing, Carson placed his hand on the door handle. "I meant it as a compliment." Just as quickly, he was serious again. "Whatever your decision, don't try to force something that doesn't work for you. It won't hold up over the long run."

Watching closely for his reaction, Gabrielle asked, "Are you saying that I shouldn't be involved with Jarin?"

"Absolutely not," Carson replied. "I'm just saying that whatever your choice, it should be for you, not anyone else. And certainly not because of pressure from anyone, including me."

"But why would you pressure me?"

"You never know," he replied, as he opened the door for her. "I may have a vested interest in the outcome." Gabrielle got into the car. "By the way, Ms. Winston," he said, a teasing glint in his eyes. "Mr. San Chapelle is on his way." He closed the door.

Within minutes, Jarin, beard trimmed, hair combed, opened the other door and slid into the seat beside her. As soon as he closed it, the car backed out of the garage and headed up the driveway. "Hello," he said.

"Hello," Gabrielle replied, warming to his smile. Without warning, his gaze intensified. Reading the look in his eyes, she surreptitiously adjusted herself closer to the window. *I should at least stay on my side of the console and keep him on his.*

A whirring sound attracted her attention. The console was disappearing into the seat. Gabrielle's anxiety level escalated as she stared, trying to make sense of what was happening to it. She didn't see Jarin lean over and reach for her. She only felt the long, muscular lines of him after he pulled her into his arms. Her mind was still trying to catch up with his actions when he tangled one hand through her curls, cradling the back of her head.

"Mmmm," he moaned, nuzzling his face through her hair. He then pressed his lips lightly to her forehead.

Warming tingles spread from the touch of his lips. *I can't allow this, not here...* "Jarin..."

Instead of releasing her, Jarin tightened his arms around her, his other hand now caressing her thigh; long, sensuous strokes. He pulled her even closer and whispered in her ear, "You have no idea how much I love you, how much I need to make love to you."

Yielding to him, urgently wanting to satisfy them both, Gabrielle still fought to keep her will in place. But enshrouded with the scent of him, enfolded in his tight embrace, it was impossible to ignore the evidence of his need. Her will first caved, then crumbled; finally disappearing as if it had never been—yet, she knew she had to resist. Once more gathering the shattered pieces of her will, Gabrielle found the strength to push away.

Once more, Jarin tightened his arms around her, tucking her closer to him. His low, hypnotic whisper continued, "But this is not the time or the place."

Minutes passed, filled with more of his kisses, more caresses. Finding the courage to look into them, Gabrielle found his eyes filled with raw desire, but there was also restraint. Her relief was profound. This time as he pressed his lips to her forehead, she didn't fight the tremors he caused. His voice a velvet caress, he murmured, "I cannot wait much longer. You need to know where this is heading, love. Soon, very soon, it will be the time and the place." His caresses continued; his kisses to her forehead, her cheek, her ear. Every now and then, his lips brushed hers. The car sped on.

CHAPTER FIFTEEN

Upping the Ante

Even here among peers, *Vibrancy* stood out as a masterful work. Surprised and pleased that Jarin had made it possible for the museum to buy it, Gabrielle lost herself in the scene, much as she had at the showing. The raw, powerful colors, and the brush strokes with which they had been applied, still took her breath away. The hand wielding the brushes that had made those strokes—and its partner—was also expert at other things. Tightening around hers, Jarin's hand triggered her mind's eye replay of their ride into town. Averting her face, Gabrielle hoped to hide the deep blush stealing across it, a telltale sign of the deeper, hotter surge she had no hope to control. •

Engaged in conversation with Mr. Kirks, who was graciously eager to allow them a visit before revealing *Vibrancy* to the public, Jarin appeared oblivious to her rapidly rising temperature. Mr. Kirks was now regaling them with an intricately detailed description of the unveiling ceremony, scheduled for Saturday of the next week. They left him even more excited, as he had secured Jarin's agreement that they would attend.

Back in the car, Jarin opened his arms for her; a superfluous invitation. Enclosed in his embrace, Gabrielle again succumbed to the pleasure of his caresses. *His hands...*

~*~~~**~~~*~

Marshaling his restraint yet again, Jarin chose the bigger picture. "I've decided to move to my condo here in the city," he said as they strolled toward the door of her condo. "Tonight, I'm going back to pack."

"Aren't you coming in?" asked Gabrielle. Her earlier apprehension was now merely a memory. *I need to love him.*

"As much as I want to stay," he said, taking her hands in his, "I will hate leaving you in the morning." *You're the one, love. I can wait.*

"It's just for one night," she said, reaching up to kiss him. *I want you to stay.*

"Yes it is," he said, gently cupping her face after her kiss. "One night, for you to decide whether you'll come to live with me. If you decide to, I'll come for you in the morning." He leaned away from her and laughed. "You should see your face."

Wishing that her every thought wasn't so easily read, Gabrielle said, "But we haven't known each other long enough."

"Do you deny what you feel?"

"No, but..."

"No buts," Jarin said, leaning past her to open the door. He had only meant to glance into her eyes, but instead, was captured by them. His resolve crumbled. He hungrily claimed her lips.

~*~~~**~~~*~

His plans had gone awry. The time and money that Brett had liberally invested in bringing down NEI had been wasted. Expecting to have major news to announce at his quarterly meeting on Tuesday, he had nothing. His primary "infil-traitor" had defected and had not paid for his disloyalty. Winston got the wrong man. Brett had prevented him from rectifying his mistake, acknowledging the strength of Garrett's defenses. He had instead decided on a simple long-range strategy, the results of which could be worse than death—the whisper campaign. Garrett had dug his way out of a Midwest hellhole and Brett meant to send him back. The right whispers to the right people would, over time, discredit him, strip him of position and respect, chip away at the life he had built until he was shunned by all; leaving him and his sons worse off than the inept cousin who now sat before him, fidgeting because of his prolonged silence.

The immediate focus of Brett's ire had not delivered. *Worthless. The whole lot of them.* His grandfather had determined that he couldn't help his shiftless brother. Now, Brett had burdened himself with one of that brother's useless offspring. "It's almost Sunday," Brett said tightly. "And you've failed."

"I know I haven't gotten it yet, but I'm really close," Raphael protested, his face taking on an even more eager expression. "You've got to let me finish this."

"I intend to," Brett said. "You're just getting some help."

"You brought in someone else?"

After explaining Winston's scenario, Brett said, "Your job is to get the app files onto this thumb drive and leave her in the target area. The cleanup crew will take care of it from there."

"What's going to happen to her?" Raphael's voice wavered, betraying his concern. "I know I said she's a pain in the ass, but she wasn't supposed to get hurt."

"Had you delivered the app, it would not have come to this. Where do your loyalties lie, Raphael? Going soft?"

Though he looked pained, Raphael did not hesitate. "My loyalties lie with you," he said. "I just didn't know she would be harmed."

"How can she not be after what you're going to do?" asked Brett. "Or would you rather she be able to identify you?"

Trying to match Brett's haughty demeanor, Raphael said. "No, I don't want that. She's not innocent, after all. Rumor is she's doing the new junior partner. She'll deserve what she gets."

"Then the next time I see you, I expect that you'll be handing me the thumb drive," said Brett. "You won't be going back to NEI. No need to court trouble."

"What's next then?" Raphael asked, edging forward in his chair.

Concealing his distaste, Brett said, "Your choice—you can go to Xalan—be part of the reverse engineering team, or whatever else you decide."

"Will I be racing with you?"

"Of course," Brett lied with ease. *There's no way you're getting near my sailing crowd. It was worth the trip into town just to keep you away from the house.*

Reassured, Raphael said, "See you Monday then," as he left.

Though Brett felt some remorse for the fate of a girl he'd never met, he felt none for Raphael. *If I can buy him, nothing's to stop him from going to a higher bidder.* Another bit of his father's advice. Never pay for more than services rendered. It was a fool's game to pay for loyalty. Even if Raphael's loyalty could be counted on, Brett did not want any more of that side of the family showing up. It was best that he didn't become a shining example for the rest of the rats ready to use him to scramble their way out of the sewer.

~*~~~**~~~*~

Packed and waiting, Gabrielle stood at her window wall, maybe for the last time, watching the sun as it rose between Lofts III and V. She had ached for Jarin to stay. But at the last, she understood what he wanted for them, and had let him go.

Her phone, in the holster at her waist, buzzed and rang. Gabrielle unholstered it and checked the number. *This is it, then. He's on his way.* She answered.

"Gabrielle. Listen to me very carefully. Do not, I repeat, *do not* leave your condo. We're driving into the city now."

The urgency with which Jarin spoke deflated Gabrielle's happiness. "We?"

"Carson's driving us in," he answered.

The tires screeched again. She wondered why she could hear them, and her apprehension grew. "Why is he driving so fast?"

"There's been a development we need to address," he said. "It'll all be explained in Alicia's web conference." He gave her the dial-in number and the web address. Gabrielle scrambled to her desk to write it all down. "Dial in now. Alicia should be all set up. We're almost there." Before he hung up, the tires screeched yet again.

As she began dialing, Gabrielle saw that her cell battery was low. She placed the cell in its charger, and instead dialed in on her desk phone. Putting it in speaker mode, she keyed in the access sequence. She announced herself as she switched on her monitors. "It's Gabrielle."

"Good, they caught you." Landry's voice was thick with relief.

"What's happened?" she asked as she logged in to her laptop, brought up the browser and navigated to the webcon web address. "Jarin said something about a development."

Nathan asked, "Carson, where are you?"

There was suddenly a low whir of car noise in the background, "No more than ten minutes out." Then it was gone as he placed himself back on mute.

"I hoped you would be there by now." Nearly a full minute passed before Nathan said heavily, "Gabrielle, Cleve was found dead behind Celeste's. He was murdered." Stunned, Gabrielle hoped she had misheard. "It happened Friday night. Garrett called me late last night after he'd identified his body."

"Why?" she managed to ask. "How?"

"For now, I'll reserve my thoughts as to why," Nathan replied. "As for how, I understand that it was extraordinarily brutal. His injuries were extreme." He hesitated again, and then said angrily, "It appears his attackers were professionals. But according to the detective, they hadn't meant to kill. Cleve apparently died of a heart attack."

Extraordinarily brutal...professionals...heart attack. Macabre scenes of Cleve lying broken, dying alone in a dark, dirty alley flashed through Gabrielle's imagination. "To die like that, all alone." In the silence that followed, astounding clarity illuminated her thoughts. From the very first day, Nathan and the others had known something like this could happen. It explained Landry's excessive concern; it also explained why Jarin and Carson had decided Carson should protect her. Her heightened awareness helped Gabrielle escape the paralysis of shock and focus on analyzing Nathan's news. She keyed in on one of his earlier statements. "How'd they know to call Garrett?"

"He had given Cleve his standing reservations at Celeste's Friday night," Nathan explained. "Since Cleve's body didn't have any ID, Garrett was the only person detectives knew to contact." Gabrielle cataloged the new pieces of data as, once again, Nathan was silent. But this time, only seconds elapsed before he continued, "I've asked you all here this morning because I believe the attacks on NEI and our personnel may escalate. I need you to provide me with information I can use to prevent anyone else from being harmed." The determination and controlled anger with which he spoke drove Gabrielle to tighten her focus even more. She closed her mind to the disturbing images she'd conjured of Cleve. "To that end Alicia," said Nathan, "I understand you've something to share with us."

"We reverse-engineered the surveillance creep, and broke its transmission encryption. As you know, I traced its external accesses to a gaming server farm," she said. "Without getting into specifics, tracing through such an installation is extremely difficult because of the security protocols. Luckily, Gabrielle gave us a lead."

"I did? Oh, sorry to interrupt."

"No problem," Alicia replied. "You mentioned to Carson that three of your teammates frequented an online game cafe named Cafe Spore. We started one server running the standard search and ping algorithms across the entire net; and a second server directing the same type of search against only the Cafe Spore address space."

Awestruck, Gabrielle asked, "How are you getting through firewalls?"

"ISS top secret," Alicia replied. "Although, if you join SCI, we'll have to clue you in so you can show us how to configure Sparks to help out."

It was the best recruitment speech Gabrielle had yet heard, and it took Alicia less than ten seconds. Once this crisis was resolved, she would let Nathan and Landry know of her decision to go to SCI. "Later then," she said.

"Getting back to our current situation, what happened is that we got lucky," said Alicia. "Not only was the external server hidden in the Cafe Spore address space, but the person who accessed it did so from his own cafe account. Obviously, he isn't a pro."

Impatience getting the best of him, Landry demanded. "Who the hell is the S.O.B.?"

"The same person whose laptop was the first to be infected by the surveillance creep," Alicia replied. "Raphael Courtland."

Another shockwave rocked Gabrielle. "Raphael? I've worked with him for almost three years. It doesn't make sense."

"What proof do you have?" asked Landry.

"To explain, I need to give you the back-story," Alicia replied.

"We're listening," said Nathan.

"First of all, I attached a test machine to the network to observe the startup sequence of the creep. Then, when I found the external server, I copied the data off and examined it for that same sequence on all NEI machines." Gabrielle's right monitor showed the sequence chart that Alicia opened on her desktop. "You're looking at a timeline showing when each of the NEI machines became infected. The ground zero machine belongs to Raphael. Normally that doesn't mean anything because viruses are now smart enough not to first infect the carrier machine." She circled the area that she was pointing to on the timeline and enlarged it. "But in this case, Gabrielle had mentioned to Carson that Raphael, Cristin, and Stan frequented Cafe Spore. So when I found the external server in their address space, I searched the accounts for their identities. I found the accounts, but only Raphael's was used to log in to the server—all on Fridays, the latest one being this past Friday."

Gabrielle asked the obvious next question. "When was the first access?"

"Last February," replied Alicia.

Though her disbelief turned to indignation, Gabrielle still maintained her focus. "Does this mean you found the archive server?"

"It does," confirmed Alicia. "We have the eight months of data that was extracted from NEI. We know it's not longer because of the infection timeline."

"I want you to catalogue that archive, Alicia," Nathan directed. "We need to know what they've gathered.

They've had access to not only our data, but also to that of our clients."

"Got it."

"We may be digging ourselves out from under this for a long time to come. Even so, we are very fortunate to have discovered it and be in a position to rectify it." Though Nathan spoke calmly, Gabrielle had the sense of being in the eye of a hurricane. "Our next step is to get to Raphael and find out who was behind it. He *will* tell us."

"Regarding that," Alicia said cautiously, "There's one remaining piece of information I have to share. Gabrielle, these are photos taken by members of your security team. They're of a man who has been at Loft IV for the past two days, hanging around in the mall, occasionally trying to get into the residential part of the building."

Dismay washed over Gabrielle at the mention of her security team. She rarely thought about them. But they had obviously been looking out for her.

"They also recognized him as someone they'd often seen at Twelfth Street Towers." Alicia put a large photo up on her desktop.

Gabrielle recognized him immediately, but it was Landry who answered, biting the words out like an expletive. "Raphael Courtland."

"They've found out about Sparks," said Nathan.

Puzzle pieces began flying together for Gabrielle. Friday night—Raphael got the latest data from NEI. Friday night—Cleve was murdered. Saturday—and Friday?—Raphael started trying to get to her. She needed more information. "Alicia—"

Interrupting her, Carson's voice boomed through the telephone speaker. "Gabrielle, open your door. We just got off the elevator."

"Sounds like I have guests. Give me a minute." Gabrielle hit the mute button, sprinted to the door, and unlocking it, hurriedly swung it open. Carson's face was grim, his eyes fiercely alert. Jarin's face wasn't far different. They walked in with almost identical predatory strides.

Stopping just inside the door, Carson nearly slammed it behind them. "Did you even look to see who it was? What the hell were you thinking?"

"But you just said on the webcon that you were at the door."

Throwing a warning glance at Carson, Jarin stepped between them and caught Gabrielle up in a hard, tight embrace. His mouth close to her ear, he said, "Carson's right you know. He has taken quite extensive precautions to keep you safe. Even so, you can't relax and rely only on his efforts. You must also be personally careful." He pressed his lips to her forehead, and then released her.

Jarin's loving reprimand hurt far worse than Carson's anger. Gabrielle defended her actions. "You heard the conversation. I was in a hurry to get back to the call—there's so much more information we need. I'm sure Alicia has it—we just have to mine for it."

Unforgiving, Carson reproved, "And I suppose you put the call on mute before you went to the door, preventing anyone from hearing what happened to you."

Gabrielle's eyes stole toward the phone, giving herself away. Feeling Carson's glare hot on the side of her face, she turned and said, "If you won't forgive me, at least please believe that I've learned from the mistake and it won't happen again. I *will* be more careful, Carson."

After glaring for a few moments longer, his face softened reluctantly. "I must be going soft," he said, gesturing toward the phone. "Go on. Get back to the con."

Gabrielle raced back to her desk and jabbed the mute button. "Carson and Jarin have joined us," she said.

"Good," said Nathan, relieved.

Shaking off her disappointment at having again failed Carson, Gabrielle recalled her earlier thoughts. "Alicia, do the servers hold only diffs from the last data pull?"

"Yes," replied Alicia. "What are you thinking?"

"I'd like to see if we can find out what caused our situation to escalate," explained Gabrielle. Feeling Jarin and

Carson behind her, she glanced and saw that they'd both pulled up bar stools close to her desk and were looking over her shoulders at her monitors. "Can you pull the latest data from Raphael's, Cleve's, Garrett's and my laptops?"

Alicia's fingers tapped loudly as they raced over the keys. "What're we looking for?"

"I'm not really sure," Gabrielle admitted. "Anything that would incite Avanti."

"That's a good start," approved Nathan.

Gabrielle stole another look back at Carson and Jarin. They were both stone-faced; two sentinels at their posts.

"I'm looking at the data from your laptop, Gabrielle." Alicia shared it on her desktop. "The thing that strikes me is the attempted VPN access that tripped the trace. Expanding from that time period, I see lots of reports in two folders named WithRetro and NotWithRetro. There's also a very interesting spreadsheet." Alicia opened it. It was the spreadsheet showing her analysis of the Retro and Sparks runs.

"That's why he's now hanging around the Lofts. It tipped them off that there's another app and it's his job to get it." Landry said, "Gabrielle, you are leaving. Today."

Gabrielle cut in before Nathan could voice his opinion. "I can't."

"I beg your pardon?" asked Landry.

Rushing to get the words out before one of them cut her off, she said, "I've got the best chance of getting to Raphael. We work together. I know what pushes his buttons and he's already looking for a way to get to me." She stole yet another glance at her audience. Jarin was still stone-faced, but with narrowed eyes. Carson's face was expressionless. *I might have their support if I didn't have lapses of carelessness.*

As always, Nathan took control. "Gabrielle, your logic is irrefutable. However I shall not allow you to assume any more risk."

Gabrielle tried once again. "But we have him. We can reel him in on our terms."

Nathan's tone was gentle. "I'm sorry, my dear. But my decision is final."

With extreme difficulty, Gabrielle prevented herself from trying once again. Having already drawn Jarin's and Carson's ire, she didn't need to make it four for four. *But still, we'll never have a better opportunity. I know I can bring him in.*

"Now, what did you expect to find in Garrett's and Cleve's laptop data?" Nathan asked.

Alicia interjected, "Nathan if I may?"

"Of course."

"While you and Gabrielle were talking, I examined the data from Garrett's laptop and found this." She pulled up Garrett's analysis of Avanti's financials. "The last modification was two forty-seven Friday morning."

Unable to see the print in the document, Jarin and Carson left their stools to stand behind Gabrielle, literally breathing down her neck. They all read along as Alicia flipped slowly through the report. The research, analysis, and conclusions clearly showed that Avanti planned to capitalize on the severity of the crash, making it even worse for some so that they could emerge from the crisis in a far stronger position.

Speaking for the first time, Jarin said, "That nails the coffin shut on Avanti."

"I'll say," Nathan agreed harshly. "He's shown, in excruciating detail, how they planned to use the market crash. It's a hell of a piece of work."

"But the obvious question...," Landry said, "...is why didn't he give it to you?"

"It appears it's because he's the insider," Nathan said. "I blindly poked a stick into a hornets' nest. Garrett verified my supposition that Avanti knew about and was using the crash against targeted companies. Whether he told them directly or Raphael picked it up off his laptop—it most likely is what got Cleve killed."

Experiencing another flash of understanding, Gabrielle realized that Nathan felt more than grief over Cleve's death—he felt responsible for it. *But he's wrong.*

Avanti is responsible. Garrett is responsible. Raphael is responsible. Not Nathan.

As if Jarin had heard her thoughts, he said, "Nathan, you don't know that."

"It's enough that it's likely." Nathan said. "It also supports my suspicion that Garrett may have been the intended target. Anything else on his laptop, Alicia?"

"Not that I can see."

In the ensuing silence, Gabrielle remembered her idea from yesterday's call, and pursued it. "Alicia, did you happen to trace anything about the file being changed?"

"Sure did, Gabby. Thanks for the reminder." There was more tapping as Alicia shared another timeline on her desktop. "See here," she said as she moved the cursor across the display pointing out the discrete items. "From last December, we have you mod'ing the file, mod'ing the file, mod'ing the file; a few weeks apart. Then we have Pete, Evan, Ana mod'ing the file—all from the port in Cleve's cube—and using his laptop. It continues that way up through last Wednesday."

Processing the data as Alicia divulged it; Gabrielle knew the next step. "Then we should be able to see a file read between my last write and Pete's write. There would have to have been an initial file change."

"Sure thing." No one spoke as Alicia attacked her keyboard. "That's odd. Nothing in March. I'll go back a ways and see what I can find." Minutes passed. "Gabby, look at this."

"Looks like that's it," agreed Gabrielle. "Cleve's login reading in the file a couple of weeks before we expected—but wait—that's not his port number or his laptop's IP."

"They're Garrett's," said Alicia, excitement edging her usual noncommittal tone.

Gabrielle threw out, "Is there a file transfer between Garrett's and Cleve's ports? Maybe using something like a USB drive?" Jarin and Carson, crowding in too closely, blocked the flow of air. Feeling suffocated, Gabrielle warned them, " I'm getting up," She left her chair, moving it out of the way, making room for the three of them to stand in front of the monitors.

"Looks like," Alicia's fingers raced over the keys. "Looks like it was a USB port drive," she said. "See here?" Gabrielle looked where the cursor pointed. "File saved to a temp drive here, file loaded from a temp drive there. Cleve's login transferred the file from Garrett's laptop on Garrett's desk port to his own laptop on Garrett's desk port."

"I think we have the S.O.B." said Landry.

"But is it enough?" Nathan asked.

"There may not be anything that's prosecutable, but looks like there's enough to force him out," said Jarin.

"Alicia, can you get access to the NEI calendar?" asked Gabrielle. "I remember Cleve going on vacation around that time."

"On it," she responded. "Let's see. The business with Cleve's and Garrett's machines happened February twenty-fourth and -fifth. The NEI calendar says Cleve was on vacation February twenty-second through March third."

"Another nail," observed Landry dryly. "I think I may have the final one. Alicia can you see my email archive? I should have a note from Cleve about that vacation. If I remember correctly, he rubbed it in a bit that he was off to Aspen. He also mentioned that Garrett had his laptop should I need access to it."

"I'm looking," Alicia replied.

While she searched, Landry said, "I remember wondering what I could possibly want off his laptop, and why he would leave it with Garrett."

"Got it," said Alicia. She put it up on screen.

"That's more than enough to force him out," Nathan said. "I'll confer with our attorneys to confirm, and we'll work out a strategy to get it done. Alicia can you courier hard copies of all those docs to me today?"

Carson cut in, "Nathan may I suggest having someone on your security team retrieve them? I'm having the teams tighten security for all of you now."

"Absolutely. Good call, and you've reminded me we need to talk about security—especially now that they're on to Sparks." replied Nathan. "Alicia, I'd like to express my sincere gratitude for the information you brought us today. Gabrielle, thank you for applying your analytical skills and helping us reach the conclusion that we have. You both have done a great deal to help us rid NEI of its problems and you should be very proud of your work."

Though Gabrielle did not intend to leave, she added her thanks to Alicia's. "Thank you Nathan."

"You're welcome," he answered. "Landry, Carson, Jarin, please stay on the line."

"I've released the call from the webcon. It'll stay active when I disconnect," Alicia said, "Please let me know if there's anything else that you need." The disconnect tone sounded.

"We'll rejoin on the car phone," Carson said as he reached toward the desk phone.

"You're discussing my security without me?" Gabrielle asked. Carson hesitated, and then withdrew his hand without ending the call.

"Carson and Jarin are security experts," Nathan said. "I am their client for NEI services and Landry is named as the secondary contact. I'm sorry, Gabrielle, but as your name does not appear on the contract, your presence at this conference is improper."

Seething at Nathan's firm dismissal, Gabrielle graciously acquiesced. "I see. Well then, I guess it's time for me to leave."

"Rejoining in ten," said Carson, and disconnected the call.

"Gabrielle, we are trying to do what's best for you," said Jarin, taking her hand as he sat down on one of the stools.

"You don't think I know what's best for me?"

"I mean security-wise," Jarin said. "We are professionals, especially Carson. And contractually, our business is with Nathan and Landry."

"...who could allow me to participate if they chose," she said, watching him just as closely as he had earlier watched her.

"Their only concern is to keep you safe, you know that." He nodded toward the luggage near the center sectional and asked, "Are those your bags?"

"Yes," she said. Moving in with him now seemed like committing herself to a velvet prison. She did not doubt that she would be loved very deeply. But she would also be saying farewell to her freedom.

"We can go then, and Carson and I will take the call from my study in the condo. We'll let Nathan and Landry know in the car."

"All right then," Gabrielle said, again disengaging herself. Without explanation, she walked toward her room. Pausing at the door to look back at Jarin, she saw that his face had no expression; his thoughts disturbingly concealed. Once inside her bedroom, Gabrielle closed and locked the door behind her.

~*~~~**~~~*~

Fifteen minutes passed. Despite his efforts to block it from his thoughts, Gabrielle's look haunted Jarin. Instead of listening to her ideas—though he had no intention of entertaining them—he summarily brushed them aside, just as had the others. Her eyes had accused him of betrayal—and rightfully so. "We may as well call in from here," he said to Carson. "She's not coming out."

"She's not the pouty type," Carson said as he rejoined the call. "Something's up."

"I know," said Jarin.

"Thought you weren't coming back," said Landry when the tone announced them.

"I mishandled the situation with Gabrielle," said Jarin. "She's locked herself in her room. We're still in her condo."

"That's not like her," said Nathan.

"Well, she can't scale down the side of the building," said Landry. "What trouble can she get into in her room? At least we know where she is."

"True, but I don't know where we are," Jarin replied.

"Lost me," admitted Landry.

"In terms of what she thinks of us for purposely excluding her," said Jarin. "May affect the relationships we have with her in the future."

"I can see where that would worry you," Landry said acidly.

"Whatever she thinks of us, our priority is to determine how best to protect her," said Nathan. "Carson, what are your plans?"

CHAPTER SIXTEEN

Taking Over the Game

Throughout her leisurely bath, and even now in the over-stuffed reading chair, her feet resting on its ottoman, Gabrielle analyzed every possible scenario for bringing in Raphael. Hours had passed since she locked herself in. Watching the sun cross the late afternoon sky, she was confident that her scenario provided their best opportunity. Though she had intuitively known that it did; she now had the ammunition with which to present her case, clearly laying out risks versus rewards for her strategy and the others—whatever they happened to be. She doubted that Nathan and the others could disagree, even if they chose a different path. She was also prepared for what she must do if they did.

Ready to take them on—probably for the last time, she left her chair, opened the door, and stepped out into the hall. Though food had been delivered a few hours ago, she'd had little problem ignoring the aromas that drifted under the closed bedroom door. Now the full force of them attacked her, and she was suddenly ravenous. But addressing her hunger was far less important than attaining her goal.

Again reminiscent of sentinels, Jarin and Carson sat on the bar stools near her desk, silently watching her approach. "You know I'm right," she said to them both. "I'm sure ISS does this sort of thing over and again: uses the person closest to the target to get the information they need." Despite their ominous silence, she continued. "Garrett will be forced out. But Raphael will remain—and it appears he's more closely controlled by Avanti."

Stubborn. Determined to prove her point. "No one doubts your logic, Gabrielle," said Jarin. "It's that—"

"There's no time for anything other than the logical path," Gabrielle interrupted, armed with the results of her analysis. She ticked off her points. "Nathan needs to clean up NEI so that he can fully participate in helping all of SCI survive the crash. Bringing in law enforcement won't work. Raphael will just get an attorney. Every other scenario excluding me requires introducing someone new. It'll take time for that person to develop a bond with him. Time we don't have."

The sentinels exchanged glances. "We both know she's right," said Carson, to Gabrielle's extreme surprise, and Jarin's acute dismay. "She has analytically come to the same conclusion that we've been turning ourselves into pretzels trying to avoid."

"You can't mean that Gabby should play a part in taking down Raphael."

"We've run this scenario together at least a hundred times. It's the quickest way to the endgame. She gives us the perfect opportunity to escalate, take the fight to Avanti, and end it on our own terms."

Displeased by Carson's defection, Jarin still knew that they were right. But the risks far outweighed the rewards. "Absolutely not," he said. "I will not allow it."

"It's my choice to make," Gabrielle reminded him, encouraged by Carson's unexpected support. "And I've already made it."

Jarin left the stool and approached her, his anger etched with worry. "Please, stay out of this, love."

"Stay out of it?" Gabrielle demanded, forgetting her intention to remain calm. "But you're discussing me!"

"This is not your fight," Jarin reminded her.

"Why isn't it?" asked Carson. "It's her app they want. I hate to admit it, but she has the right to help protect it. And she's in the best position. If you weren't in love with her..."

Losing his tenuous hold on his temper, Jarin turned away from Gabrielle and advanced on Carson. "You obviously don't give a damn about her!"

"That's bullshit and you know it," said Carson, leaving the stool. "You know she's already like Julie to me."

"Oh, is she," challenged Jarin. "Then why's it so easy to put her in harm's way?"

"You think this is easy for me? As reckless as she is with her own safety?"

Angrily determined to prevent them from talking about her as if she weren't there, Gabrielle stalked around Jarin to confront him. His face was a mask of aggression. From the corner of her eye, she saw that Carson's only way out of the office nook was past Jarin. They were on the razor's edge of exchanging blows. Getting in between them now would be the height of recklessness. In spite of that, she hesitantly touched Jarin's arm.

Snatching away from her, he snarled, "Stay out of this, Gabrielle. Get the hell out of the way."

Shaken by his ferocity, Gabrielle retreated toward the bar.

Still sizing Jarin up, Carson said, "I've considered the alternative. Have you?"

"What alternative?" Jarin scoffed. "She'll be protected."

"For how long?" demanded Carson. "You know what a determined SOB Brett is, just like the rest of his damn family. One slip—let our guard down one time—and she could be severely harmed. Took them six years to get Ted Harrison, but even though there's no proof, we all agree they got him in the end."

Beleaguered with worry and reluctance, Jarin abruptly turned away from Carson. Muttering expletives, he skirted the sectional and paced in front of the window wall. He did not want to be logical. He needed to protect Gabrielle no matter what she wanted.

Finally able to give himself some room, Carson moved out of the office nook. He pressed his advantage, saying quietly, "I'm right. Gabrielle's right. The best way is for her to be the bait."

Detesting himself for yielding, Jarin looked for opposing reasons. "She's never participated in an op, Carson," he said. "Plus, she acts on her own instincts—makes it hard for her to follow a script. She'll be unpredictable and hard to protect."

Struck by Jarin's words, Gabrielle had to accept that his adamant objections were based on his experience, not his opinion. "I'll do exactly as Carson says, Jarin. I won't cause any problems. I just know I'm the best option."

Considering defeat, Jarin seated himself on the edge of one of the bar stools, and held out his hand to her.

"Are you two done fighting?" she asked.

"We're not fighting," said Jarin, beckoning impatiently with his outstretched hand.

The hell you aren't. She cautiously approached him. "What do you call it then?"

"Having a rather loud discussion. Nathan calls it close-quarters negotiation." As soon as she was within reach, he took her hand and guided her into his arms. Holding her tightly, he brushed her cheek, her lips with his. "You have no idea how dangerous this could be; how badly you could get hurt."

Realizing that this was her last chance to convince him, Gabrielle chose her words carefully. "I do understand. Jarin, I know what happened to Cleve. Believe me; I'm not trying to be a hero." Seeking to soothe him, she gently stroked his jaw. "I just know I'm the best choice to get to Raphael. We all have to trust that Carson will keep me safe."

Capturing her free hand, Jarin brought them both to his lips, holding her gaze as he directed his words to Carson. "If I allow this, I want two things from you."

"Which are?"

"Gabrielle's safety."

Insulted, Carson said, "That goes without saying."

"And a way to take Brett down. *Permanently*. He's using the crash to destroy far more than it would on its own. Cares nothing for the families and other businesses that depend on the corporations he's targeting. Attacking those I care about." Tearing his eyes away from Gabrielle, he focused on Carson. "I want to personally send him straight to hell."

"You have my word. Are you going to allow Gabrielle to do this?"

"It's not up to me," Jarin said. "It's Nathan's call. But I won't stand against you."

"That's not good enough," Carson said. "Will you stand with me?"

Plagued by nagging apprehension, Jarin cautioned Gabrielle. "You shall listen to Carson and follow his every order. You shall not put yourself at risk in any way. Do you understand?"

Having expected an adrenaline-fueled rush to develop their strategy, Gabrielle was sobered by the pervading somberness. Jarin's eyes, now a bleak, wintry gray; betrayed how heavily the decision weighed on him. Seconds ago, she would have been offended by his tone. Now, her answer had the sound of a vow. "Yes, I understand. I will keep myself safe."

It was the logical approach. They were practiced in the scenario and had rarely failed. This time though, there was no room for error. Jarin said to Carson, "I will stand with you, but you have a time limit."

"What is it?"

"Four days."

Carson nodded. "That's fair." He started toward the door.

Bracing for another disagreement, Jarin said to Gabrielle, "Carson and I are going down to the car to discuss this with Nathan and Landry. I'll be back to let you know what we decided."

Disappointment flooded through her. They were taking her strategy to Nathan without her. On the other hand, it was madness to fall into an insignificant skirmish, especially having already won Jarin's support. As Gabrielle pulled her hands free to back away and allow him to leave, a look of such intense pain crossed his face that she instead encircled him with her arms, and kissing his ear, she whispered, "Thank you." A jolt shuddered through him and she again started to pull away; this time to see what had happened. But his arm held her close, his other hand cradled her head; turning her lips to his. He kissed her hungrily, demandingly. Then so lovingly and passionately that Gabrielle wanted it never to end.

At last, Jarin pulled away, but still held her close. *We should have been together by now.* This time, the operation was in the way. They had to first get it behind them. "Open the door to no one except Carson or me. I don't care if it's Julie or Sarah."

Shaken, Gabrielle merely nodded.

He left the bar stool and joined Carson in the entryway. "Lock the door behind us."

Again, Gabrielle nodded. Walking with them, she stopped at the door as Carson opened it and followed Jarin through. Just before closing it, he said, "By the way, there's a noodle bowl from Toshi's for you in the fridge."

He's offering me food? It's Jarin I need.

~*~~~**~~~*~

After they settled into the front seat of the car, Jarin remained tense as he watched Carson dial back in to the conference line.

Landry was already there. "Got your TM. What's up?"

Before Jarin could answer, Nathan joined. "Thoughts about our strategies?"

"No. Gabrielle finally came out of her room," said Jarin. "Seems she was analyzing different strategies for bringing Raphael in."

"I see," said Nathan. "Any of them similar to ours?"

Jarin cut right to the heart of the matter. "I agree with her conclusion that she is our best chance to get him."

"You can't be serious," said Landry.

"It's the right move," Jarin replied heavily.

Landry answered vehemently, "She's not a fuckin' chess piece!"

"I know that," Jarin replied quietly. "But I've also considered the probable alternative."

"What alternative?"

Having not yet mentioned it to Carson, Jarin threw a glance in his direction as he answered Landry, "How did she get involved in this in the first place? By finding out about the market crash, which she did by performing an analysis that she shouldn't have."

Harshly, Landry cut him off. "What does that have to do with anything?"

Again, Jarin glanced at Carson, who this time met his gaze with understanding. He continued, "She found the file problem with analyses she shouldn't have had, and then chose to pull more of them to solidify her findings. A good idea, but she shouldn't have."

"Where're you going with this?" Landry asked.

"She's a cowboy." Jarin answered. Hearing Landry muttering expletives under his breath, he gave a grim half smile. "What's to stop her from trying to find a way to do it herself?"

Nathan cussed quietly. "I hadn't thought of that. We can prevent her from coming in, but Raphael is already staking out the Lofts."

"Then what's Carson here for, if not to keep her out of trouble?" Landry grumbled.

"The highest level of personal protection depends on mutual cooperation. You know that. She has to want to be kept out of trouble," Carson answered bluntly, "If she decides to go it alone, we'll be at least a few steps behind. A worse scenario is that she'll work out a strategy that depends on our protection—without our knowledge. Logically it might make sense, but operationally, it could go terribly wrong."

"You've both made damn good points," Nathan said. They all waited while he sorted through his thoughts. "So our choices are to manage the situation while we allow her to do this, or exclude her and run the risk that she'll try to do it herself and get hurt—maybe seriously—before we can prevent it."

"That just about sums it up," Jarin answered gravely. "She's got us between a rock and a hard place."

"Damn." Nathan was unusually emphatic. "Landry you've worked closely with Gabrielle. Is there any way you can refute this argument?"

"I wish the hell I could," said Landry.

"Well gentlemen, looks like our hands are tied." admitted Nathan somberly. "Carson, you need to be in top form on this one. Brett is a son of a bitch and I don't want him to get the chance to hurt Gabby. How long do you expect this op to take?"

"Four days," Carson replied.

"You have two," directed Nathan.

"We're in agreement then?" asked Jarin. "Landry?"

"I know this is the best way," admitted Landry. "But I don't have to like it."

"Sounds like we're adjourned gentlemen," Nathan concluded. "Carson, I am personally counting on you."

Carson replied, "No pressure there, sir."

Chuckling darkly, Nathan said, "Just keep Gabrielle safe."

Carson disconnected the call and exchanged glances with Jarin, who said, "We'd better be doing the right thing."

"You know it's best that we attack now," Carson reminded him. "We'll take good care of Gabrielle. I've already given you my word."

"I know you'll do your best," Jarin replied. "It's just that there's always intangibles. In this case, there's no room for error."

Carson's expression mirrored the concern in Jarin's voice. "Agreed," he said.

~*~~~**~~~*~

Still eating her noodle bowl when the doorbell chimed, Gabrielle dropped her chopsticks and ran to the door, hoping it was Jarin. She put her eye to the peephole. It *was* him. She opened the door and stepped aside, allowing him room to enter. To her dismay, he wore the sentinel expression again. He carried a bag filled with groceries, and held another by its handles. "Are you hungry again?" she asked.

Yes, I am, for you. Striding past Gabrielle, around the entry way corner and into the kitchen, he said, "These are for you, not me." Placing the bags on the counter, he began unpacking them. "I don't know what you've been living on. The fridge and cupboards are completely empty."

Trying to conceal her embarrassment, Gabrielle helped him put away milk, orange juice, eggs, and other foodstuffs. "I mostly eat out."

"Odd, considering all the cooking gear you have," Jarin noted, making sure that he kept plenty of space between them as they moved around the kitchen. "Anyway, tomorrow morning, you won't have time to eat out. You got what you wanted—Nathan agreed. We're going with your scenario."

Gabrielle curbed her growing excitement. "What's the plan?" she asked.

"Carson's working out the details and will brief us later on tonight. You will find out tomorrow when he picks you up at seven a.m. sharp."

Once again, they were leaving her out. "Why don't I find out tonight with everyone else?"

"Because Carson's not sure when he'll have the complete plan. You're the main operative. You need to be alert tomorrow," answered Jarin. "That means a good night's sleep and a substantial breakfast in the morning." Careful to leave out the "if", he said, "When you start an op, you don't know when or where your next meal will be."

The substantial amount of groceries, then, didn't mean what she had hoped. The analyst side of her needed to be sure. "Are you staying?"

Jarin hoped to avoid a direct question, but he should have known better. Gabrielle was not one to beat around the bush. "If I stay tonight, I'm not even sure you'll... Well, no, I won't be." Gabrielle struggled to control her expression, but Jarin easily read her disappointment. He yearned to console her. But if he lost control of his urges, they would have to call off the op. With extreme difficulty, he restrained himself. "You need to stay focused on tomorrow: following Carson's instructions and keeping yourself safe."

He's a pro. Trying to change his mind would only make them both feel worse, but would not shake his resolve. They walked to the door in silence. Resigned, Gabrielle accepted his quick kiss on her cheek, then closed and locked the door behind him.

~*~~~**~~~*~

Leaving her was difficult. Relieved to have it behind him, Jarin stepped off the elevator in the garage and walked slowly to the car, where Carson leaned on the driver's door.

"May I suggest an evening swim in Marina Cove?" chuckled Carson.

"Is it that obvious?" Jarin replied, irritated.

"And don't threaten to kick my ass—that line is getting old," Carson said, smirking.

~*~~*~~**~~*~~*~

Carson's supposed to be here by now. Where is he? Gabrielle had consumed her larger than usual breakfast. She had packed, unpacked, and repacked her backpack until she was satisfied with the way it carried. She had opened her luggage and torn through several changes of clothes; finally setting on an ensemble that she thought set the right tone. Her phone was holstered on her skirt band. She was ready to go. *Where the hell is Carson?*

When the doorbell finally rang, Gabrielle snatched up her backpack and rushed to open it. As she grabbed the doorknob, conversations from the night before flashed through her head. Now was the worst possible time to be "reckless with her own safety", giving Carson an excuse to pull the plug. Looking through the peephole, she saw a man's torso, but in black—not clothed in

Carson's familiar uniform. Gabrielle hesitated, unsure whether to ask—and reveal her presence—or wait. Carson resolved her dilemma by leaning over so that she could see his face through the peephole.

She hurriedly opened the door. "You're late," she accused, ready to step out and close the door behind her. "And why aren't you in uniform?" She asked.

"I'm dressed for operations and my watch says I'm exactly on time," he said sternly. "We're not leaving yet. You're not ready," Gabrielle backed out of his way as he walked in. He closed the door behind him.

"What do you mean?" she asked. "I've checked everything in my backpack, I've got my phone..."

"You're not ready." Carson repeated sharply. "You're all hyped up without the slightest clue of what to do. A recipe for disaster. You need to listen very closely while I walk you through the strategy. We only have two days."

"*Two!*" Gabrielle exclaimed. "Jarin said four."

"Nathan cut it to two," replied Carson. He held up his hand, forestalling her protests. "Now, take it down a couple of notches and focus. You have a lot to learn in the next," he checked his watch, "twenty-eight minutes."

"I'm listening," said Gabrielle, greatly disappointed by the shortened time span.

"The strategy is going to sound very simple, but it might be difficult to accomplish," cautioned Carson.

Leaning over slightly, and maintaining eye contact with Gabrielle he said, "First, do not force yourself into a conversation with Raphael. We know he's trying to get to you. Let him make the first move."

"That's easy enough," Gabrielle replied. "He's always the one that approaches me, so there's nothing for me to change."

"That's good then, the pattern's already set," Carson approved. "Next, don't do anything out of the ordinary to get his attention."

"That's also not difficult. I owe him a visit to Cafe Spore on a bet and he's likely to stop by and goad me about it."

"Just remember, it's difficult not to push when you're new at trying to accomplish an operations goal," Carson said. "You have to remind yourself to be patient."

"Got it," Gabrielle replied anxiously. "Be patient."

"Lastly, your only job is to get him to come to your condo. I don't care if he thinks he's taking you out on a date or coming to look at your etchings," he said, a brief, teasing gleam in his eyes. "The endgame for you is Raphael coming here. Got it?"

"Yes," she answered. The strategy couldn't be this easy. There had to be more. "Then what happens?"

Carson's jaw line hardened. "He'll go with me." he said, straightening up and turning slightly away from Gabrielle. "I'll extract the information we need."

"What does that mean?" she asked, stepping back so that she could see more of his face.

Keeping his face averted, he answered, "You don't need to know."

Though going with Carson sounded bad for Raphael, Gabrielle couldn't muster sympathy for him. He shouldn't have been working with the enemy. But pieces of the puzzle were still missing. "Are you going to be in the condo when we get here?"

Carson whipped around to face her. "Are you out of your mind?"

"What did I say?" asked Gabrielle, backing up, alarmed by the ferocity of his response. She replayed the question in her thoughts trying to understand what set him off.

"That's what worries us all. There's too much you don't understand," he said harshly, turning fully away from her. This time when he turned back, he was rigidly under control. "Under no circumstances are you to go anywhere with him," he commanded quietly. "Are we clear? You give him an invitation and a time to come calling. That's all. I will be here with you before he gets here."

"I didn't mean to make you angry. I only asked because the pieces didn't fit."

"Pieces?" asked Carson. Then he grudgingly relaxed. "I see. Well, it's a good thing you asked." Before Gabrielle could relax, his expression changed again, turning critical. She tensed. He said, "Now for your clothes."

He's a fashion critic? This isn't the appropriate attire for a sting? Bristling, she asked, "What's wrong with my clothes?"

"Everything. Lose the skirt and the heels; you don't need a suit jacket. Wear a sweater instead." Taking in her disgruntled expression, he explained with extreme patience, "That's why I'm wearing this. Your clothes need to be loose fitting. Simple pants and shirt. You need comfortable shoes that make very little noise." Before she could ask, he added, "In case you need to run if you have to—giving as few clues as possible about which way you're going. The pants to give you a little protection against scrapes, bruises and other things."

"What other things?"

"Never mind," he said abruptly. "Just go change. And hurry. We've only a few minutes before it's time to leave."

Scowling, Gabrielle lugged the largest suitcase into her bedroom. "I suppose I also need gloves and a ski mask," she muttered. After quick and extremely harried searching, mumbling expletives the whole time, she finally found one of her few pairs of trousers, and pieced together an outfit. She slipped into flats as she went back to the great room. "Am I ready now?" *Let's go, let's go...*

Carson gave her the once over. "Much better." he approved. Then he checked his watch and said, "It's time."

~*~~~*~~~*~

For the first time, Carson drove with the privacy window down. He periodically scrutinized Gabrielle in the rear view mirror. "You look nervous," he told her. "You can't go in to NEI fidgeting like that. It's a tipoff that you're up to something. Try to look as normal as you can," he counseled.

"I have too much energy. I don't know how to get rid of it," replied Gabrielle, her nervousness growing.

"Believe it or not, I know how you feel," said Carson. "When that happens, focus on the details. On your goal," he advised. "That way, you'll become aware of each moment and its opportunities. Being in the moment helps to keep you calm." His face tensed slightly. "It also helps you regain control and think clearly if you should panic."

Somewhat surprised that she did, Gabrielle caught the change in his mood and understood it. If she was panicked, that meant something had gone wrong. She fit Carson's new directive into the mantra she had adapted from Landry: plan, execute, focus on the details. *I'm wearing my cell. The ninety-nine speed dial activates the GPS transmitter. Get Raphael to my condo. Don't force the conver-*

sation. After several times through it, she was relieved to feel her edginess wane.

Making their way through the streets in a southerly direction, they reached Twelfth Street Tower after what seemed to Gabrielle to be an extraordinarily long time. Through the open privacy window, Gabrielle heard reports coming in from others of the security team.

"Northern approach secured," said one voice.

"Garage three secured," said another.

"Target in place, usual routine," said yet another.

They entered the garage and spiraled down the ramp to level three. Carson pulled in front of the public elevators; leaving the car idling.

Another voice reported, "All clear, garage three."

Astounded, Gabrielle asked, "Is this what you do all the time when we're driving?"

"Only in a situation of heightened security when approaching a suspected adverse environment," replied Carson. "Such as now."

Try saying that three times fast. In spite of her poor attempt to wring humor out of the situation, Carson's words were a reminder to focus on the operation and her role. In fact, now would be a great time to come up with a poker face. *Maybe I should have practiced. But how do you practice a poker face?*

Carson cut the engine. Gabrielle watched as he carefully inspected the garage. After making the circuit for the second time, he opened the door, got out, and then opened Gabrielle's door. She got out and walked to the elevator beside him, her eyes alert and searching—as were Carson's. She had been such an idiot, ridiculing him that first time. Now she realized how hard he and the team worked for her safety. The business of personal security was fraught with dangers she hadn't wanted to acknowledge. And now, by her own choices, she faced them.

When the elevator door closed behind them, Carson relaxed slightly. Last week, Gabrielle wouldn't have noticed the minute change in his demeanor. She allowed herself to relax, too.

With an approving glance, Carson said, "I'm glad to see you taking this seriously, Ms. Winston." Though she understood it, she grimaced at Carson's formality. "I'm staying on until the third floor so that I can escort you past the lobby,"

"Why?"

"It's the last likely place that something you're unprepared for could happen," he explained. "If I had my way, I'd escort you to your desk, but I have a feeling that might blow the op."

Gabrielle broke into a hearty laugh. "You think?"

Carson smiled. "Keep that mood. It's just the right tone."

"How did you know to do that? To make me laugh?" she asked.

"I didn't plan it, but I'll take it." He restrained his expression. "Remember, you're not alone." The elevator door opened. "We'll be close, all of us—Landry, Jarin, Nathan—in Nathan's office."

"Who knows you're there?" she asked.

"No one other than us and you," he said, stepping out. The door closed.

Watching the floor numbers flip by, Gabrielle ran through the details. *I'm wearing my cell. The ninety-nine speed dial activates the GPS transmitter. Get Raphael to my condo.* Then she saw it. The major flaw in the plan. She had never before invited Raphael to her condo. In fact, as hard as he had tried, she had never given him an opening to invite himself. Not even after Stephen left and Raphael thought her an easy target, in need of sympathy. Carson was right: her job wasn't simple. In spite of the past, she had to make Raphael believe that she wanted him to come to her condo. Maybe it would help that he was already trying to make it happen. Why had the flaw occurred to her now instead of when Carson was still available to counsel her? She could go to Nathan's office under some pretext, but that would compromise the operation.

Glancing at the floor numbers again, she saw that she was getting close to NEI's floor. Her anxiety increased with every reiteration of the details —bringing her face-to-face with the flaw over and again. Two floors to go. One floor. Then the elevator opened. Looking past yet another solicitor she had turned away with "the soft no", Sheila saw her and waved. Gabrielle had no choice but to step out. *Stay in the moment. Take one step at a time.* Getting past Sheila was her first step. She reached the double doors at the same time as the rejected solicitor, who held one open for her.

Sheila smiled expectantly. "Morning Gabs." Then looking toward the door, "I don't know why cold-callers keep stopping in. You'd think word would have gotten around by now."

Stopping at the desk Gabrielle looked over her shoulder and saw the elevator door closing on the man. "Maybe they think they'll wear you down."

"Not likely," Sheila chuckled. "Anyway, know you're busy. See you later."

Surprised by her dismissal, Gabrielle happily escaped without having to get through further conversation. "Okay, see you," she said, heading toward the inner set of doors. Just as she pulled one open and walked through, someone grabbed her free hand and spun her around. She lost hold of the door and found herself being pulled away from it back through the lobby.

CHAPTER SEVENTEEN

Retribution

"Come on, Gabs!" exclaimed Raphael, who pulled her hurriedly toward the outer double doors. Through them, she could see an open elevator.

"Have fun you two," Sheila called with a laugh. "Perfect timing, Raphael. I just called the elevator for you."

Events had unfolded too rapidly. There wasn't time to get away from Raphael without tipping him off. Carson had been adamant that she should not be alone with him, but on the other hand, this may be her best chance. *I just have to go with it.* "Hold on. Don't be so pushy," she said, "What's Sheila mean, 'have fun'?"

"My new car," he grinned. "We're going to see it. Maybe even take a drive."

Just before Raphael dragged her into the elevator, Gabrielle looked back over her shoulder and saw Sheila laughing and waving to them. "It can't be that exciting."

Grinning even more widely, Raphael looked down at her and said, "It's exactly what I wanted. Pretty, fast, a real babe magnet." He laughed at Gabrielle's scowl. "So, it's not politically correct to talk about going after the ladies?"

About to hit him with a witty retort, she noticed that the button for the fifth garage level was pushed. This little side trip was going to take longer than she thought. "Level five? Why'd you park it way down there?"

"I don't want any scratches. Just got it yesterday. Thought I'd park it where there are far fewer cars." He rambled on about its features and how it drove.

Trying to appear fascinated, Gabrielle took stock of her situation. *Should I try to get to my cell? What should I say to him?* Raphael, though excited, seemed at ease; captivated by his own conversation, as usual. Gabrielle relaxed. She decided to hurry things along so that she could get back to where she was supposed to be, and keep an eye out for a way to work the situation to her advantage. "So, why do I have to see it right now?"

"Why not?" he countered. "Got something better to do?"

"I'm sure new projects have come in." Purposely goading him, she added, "I could work on staying ahead of you."

The elevator opened onto the fifth garage level as Raphael laughed. "You can't beat me, Gabs," he said. "The deck is stacked."

"What's that supposed to mean?" she asked as they walked through the sparsely filled garage toward the guard shack. She only saw a few cars, none worth dragging her down here. "Which is your car?"

"It's on the far side of the guard shack," Raphael gestured as he quickened his pace. As they reached the shack, Gabrielle sensed a sudden change in his intent. Before she could react, he smashed her against the side of the shack, opened its door, and shoved her in. Tripping over her feet, she fell backward against what felt like a steel table, He closed the door behind him, shot home the deadbolt, and flipped the switch.

Blinking as her eyes adjusted to the far brighter light, Gabrielle demanded. "What the hell are you doing?"

Leaning against the door, Raphael smirked, his eyes gleaming with an odd, wild light. "Shoe's on the other foot now, isn't it?"

Pushing away from the table, Gabrielle tried to get around him. "Open the damn door. Now. This isn't funny, Raphael."

His face changed, matching the wildness in his eyes. "It isn't supposed to be." Roughly pushing her back into the table, he grabbed her wrists with one hand. Using the other, he delivered a stinging slap across her face, the sound of it echoing loudly through the room. Stunned by the slap and the scalding, rapidly spreading pain, Gabrielle could still think clearly enough to understand that this was Raphael's endgame. He could not allow her to get back upstairs. Manically, she tried to free herself, but was blocked by the table behind her.

"Now you're going to behave," he said, his sentence punctuated with a backhanded slap across the other side of her face.

Tears welling up in her eyes, her breath came in erratic bursts, hindered by her growing alarm. Still, she managed enough breath control to yell. "Stop it!" She fought to free her hands. Raphael slapped her again. The tears spilled from her eyes. In spite of the pain and her escalating panic, her resolve hardened. She couldn't let everybody down. *Asshole's going to pay for this.*

~*~~~*~~~~*~

Checking Nathan's outer office windows before he stepped off the elevator, Jarin saw that they were opaqued, as expected. Quickly, he entered the inner office, closing the door behind him. Nathan sat behind his desk; Landry, in one of the chairs in front of it.

"Good morning," said Jarin.

Landry only offered a curt nod.

Nathan, truly or purposely oblivious to their antagonism, answered, "Good morning." He checked his watch and added, "According to the timeline, Carson should be on his way up."

Bypassing the chairs, Jarin chose to pace in front of the window garden. Minutes passed; no one broke the silence. Jarin's thoughts, as had become the norm—except when Gabrielle occupied them—turned to salvaging his friendship with Landry. He had to get them past this. Truth be told, were their situations reversed, he didn't know whether he could forgive. But he would sure as hell try. Jarin's head snapped around with the others' at the sound of the door.

Approaching Nathan's desk, Carson said, "She's here. One of the team opened the door for her in the lobby."

"Time to close the loop." Landry unholstered his cell and called Sheila's direct line. Putting the phone in speaker mode, he placed it on Nathan's desk.

Sheila answered, "Good morning, Landry."

"How're you doing Sheila?" he asked, just as he always did. "I'm running a bit late. When Gabrielle gets in, could you let her know to reschedule our checkpoint?"

"Sure thing," answered Sheila. "I'll tell her when she gets back."

Jarin's tension escalated.

"Back?" Landry asked, his voice acutely restrained. "Back from where?"

"Raphael was going on and on and on about his new car," Sheila explained. "So I helped him surprise Gabby. He's taken her to see it. Smoothest kidnap I've ever seen."

Odd choice of words. Problem is she's dead on. Jarin clenched his jaw, waiting for more solid information.

"Gabs didn't look too happy about it so I'm sure they'll be back soon." she continued, laughter coloring her voice.

"Thanks, Sheila." Landry pushed the end button and glared at Carson, who was already on his cell barking orders to the rest of the security team.

~*~~~**~~~*~

Stepping back to admire his work, Raphael gloated, "Ah, poor Gabs. I've never seen you cry." He raised his hand again. Watching it, Gabrielle turned her head just before he connected with the second backhanded slap. The pain still intensified, but it stung somewhat less than the last one.

"You're going to give me what I want. Is that understood?" Again, Gabrielle timed his hand and turned her head in anticipation of his next blow. "Now, I'm going to let you go and you're going to log into your server and give me that app you run. Is that clear?" He followed his question with another backhanded slap; she again lessened the impact.

Her head swimming, stinging tears streaming freely down her aching cheeks, Gabrielle felt herself spiraling into panic. *Details. Focus on the details.*

"I'm actually enjoying this," said Raphael, again raising his hand. "Don't give me a reason to do it again."

Involuntarily, Gabrielle cringed; hating herself for doing so, but hating Raphael far more. Her anger boiled over, focusing her thoughts. An idea lit, shining like a beacon. "I'm not sure the signal will reach down here," she said.

"What signal?" he asked, eyeing her speculatively, his arm still raised.

Her life was at stake. She had only one hand in this game, and she had to play it like a pro. "My server expects a call from my phone before it lets me log in."

Lowering his hand, Raphael stepped back. "Set it up well didn't you," he said appreciatively. "Go ahead then. Set up your laptop and make the call."

Stumbling around to the side of the table, Gabrielle struggled out of her backpack. Though Raphael hadn't moved, he watched her closely. Tears continued to stream down her face as, with trembling hands, she unpacked and powered on her laptop. Several times, she stopped and used her sweater to gingerly dab her eyes.

Once the laptop booted up, Gabrielle unholstered her phone and speed dialed ninety-nine.

~*~~~**~~~*~

Watching Carson work, Jarin restrained his emotions. It was too soon to panic.

Closing his eyes, Nathan rubbed the bridge of his nose. "In God's name," he said mostly to himself, "What the fuck have I done?"

Quickly approaching the desk, Jarin said, "We don't know anything yet, Nathan. In any case, Raphael's already proven he's not a pro. Putting the desk phone in speaker mode, he said, "I'm dialing into the team's open line so we can hear what's happening."

Carson's voice filled the room. "You're saying they didn't leave through the lobby; no cars have left any of the garages. Alicia, you on?"

"Yep," she replied. "Just got your page."

"Raphael and Gabrielle broke containment under pretext of seeing Raphael's car, but we expect they're somewhere in Twelfth Street Tower. Pull up the plans. We need to find likely places they can be."

"Will do. Pulling up the building plans. Engaging our real time taps on the garage cameras. They all look—hold on. Garage level five cameras. Looks like they're feeding us stills. Stats say there hasn't been any motion for a few hours." Alicia replied. "It would surely help if she'd remember to ninety-nine us." Her fingers tapped discordantly on the keyboard. Suddenly, she drew in a sharp breath. "There she is. She ninety-nined us! I'm transferring her signal to the call. We'll hear her, but she won't be able to hear us. I'm picking up now."

Sounding weak and tearful, Gabrielle's voice filled the speaker. "I told you, the phone signal may be too weak from here. If I don't hear a tone from the server, it won't let me in."

Jarin's brief moment of relief disappeared in a surge of anger.

"Alicia," Carson whispered urgently. "Play a tone, any tone."

"Done." Alicia's voice whispered over the conversation between Gabrielle and Raphael. "And got her. Traced the GPS signal to coordinates within the fifth level garage guard shack."

Quickly, Carson instructed the security team. "Meet me on the fourth level landing with the disposal preparation equipment. There may be hostiles. I'll be there in less than five."

"Disposal preparation?" Nathan fixed Carson with a glare. "What does that mean?"

"It means we're wrapping them up for travel," Carson replied, his eyes fiercely alert; his expression cold. "They'll wake up tomorrow in a country with very strict drug laws, in possession of enough illegal substance to earn them a lifelong prison sentence. The authorities will be conveniently at their door."

His face almost mirroring Carson's, Nathan said. "That's...quite...appropriate."

Giving one swift nod, Carson left the office.

~*~~~**~~~*~

The single note played back through the cell phone; the few seconds of sound a lifeline to Gabrielle. *They heard me.* It was only a matter of time before they arrived. Her job now was to give them the time that they needed.

Raphael said threateningly, "You're right to be relieved. If we'd had to go elsewhere, it wouldn't have been too good for you."

Any threat Raphael made now was an empty one; Carson's crew was listening. In spite of the painful throbbing under her eyes, Gabrielle concentrated on making him talk. "Why are you doing this?" She did not try to control the tremors in her voice. "What have I ever done to you?"

With an ugly chuckle, he said, "Don't take it personal Gabs. It isn't about you. Well, mostly not."

Logging into her server, she said, "You've thrown your future away,"

"What future?" Raphael sneered. "I can't get past you at NEI. You'll always be ahead of me. There's no way I can break up whatever you and Landry have going."

"There's nothing between Landry and me."

"I'm not blind," he said in disgust. "Where did you two disappear to last week? Then on the other hand, Garrett surrounds himself with idiots."

Bristling at his insinuations, Gabrielle said, "Did it ever occur to you that just maybe I'm a better analyst than you?" Quickly realizing her mistake, she steeled herself for his retaliation.

Instead, he laughed. "In your dreams, Gabs. You're just in the right place, at the right time, screwing the right partner."

Incensed by his continued aspersions, her anger escalated. More blood rushed to her face, intensifying the stinging pain. She had to stay calm; her best chance of getting out of the situation without further harm was to keep him talking.

~*~~~**~~~*~

Jarin watched Carson disappear through the door and thought that he could stay behind. He was wrong. He started after him.

Abruptly, Landry stood and blocked his path.

On the verge of forcing his way through him, Jarin said. "Not now, Landry."

"You're not going after Carson."

Glancing in Nathan's direction, Jarin saw that he watched closely, ready to step in. He fought for control. The five minutes were almost up and he needed to go. "I have to."

"Don't be stupid," Landry held his ground. "You're not going to blow the op."

Jarin's training kicked in, damping his frustration. "You forget, I'm a pro. I swear this isn't about me trying to be a hero," he said, willing Landry to understand. "I just can't stay here while she's—" The sound of her tearful voice permeated his brain. He stopped the thought, reserving his aggression for the SOBs who deserved it. "I've got to go. I'm sorry."

Slowly looking him over, Landry noted his black trousers, rubber soled shoes, and long sleeved black shirt. "Looks like you're dressed for it." After several heartbeats more, he stepped aside. "Don't make me regret this."

"You won't." Clapping Landry's shoulder as he passed, Jarin said fervently. "Thank you."

~*~~~**~~~*~

"Since I can't get past you, I decided to help my cousin." Raphael paced behind Gabrielle, watching as her fingers tapped the keys. "I give him what he needs to take NEI down and he gives me what I want. Simple."

"What do you want, Raphael?" asked Gabrielle, opening Sparks' design documents.

"Freedom," Raphael's voice seethed with resentment. "From generations of disrespect. No more being a poor relation; our family being the laughingstock of Hampton Cove."

"You were already working on that. You were building a career."

"Career," scoffed Raphael. "A career won't give me access."

"Access to what?" Gabrielle opened Sparks in the IDE.

"The life my side of the family has been barred from. Living well. Sailing. Yacht racing. Landry's a yachtsman. Did you know that? Beautiful women in every port. Don't think you're his only screw, Gabs. He's screwing them all. Just like I'll be. No more scratching a living in a job."

"It's not freedom you want. It's sex and money." Gabrielle couldn't hide the deep contempt she felt.

"Not just that, you idiot. The life they lead. What people like Landry Wyatt take for granted," said Raphael scornfully. "Even my cousin, Brett, whom those other families consider to be 'lowlife new money,' takes it for granted. But when I give him your app, I'll be welcomed with open arms." Peering at Gabrielle's red, irritated face and swollen eyes, he said, "Even with your face all messed up, I can see you don't understand. Too mundane. You only get off on brain power. What a waste. You'd probably be a pretty good groupie if you set your mind to it. Spruce yourself up, do something with that wild ass hair—not my type, but somebody'll give you a screw."

Rather than rise to the bait of his blatantly sexist idiocy, Gabrielle analyzed Raphael's actions. He couldn't leave here with her app and expect no one to know—unless she was dead. *Where are Carson and the crew?*

Having stopped his manic pacing, Raphael now stood over her. "So, this is the app. Get out of the way and let me see." He pushed Gabrielle roughly out of the chair. Stumbling, she fell into the wall, hitting her already burning face on the concrete. The pain had been dulling, but it erupted anew, along with her hatred. Raphael sat down and started working his way through Sparks.

~*~~~**~~~*~

Of all the ops Jarin had been part of, this was the first where the stakes were personal. When the elevator reached the fourth level garage, he kept the door closed for the full minute it took for him to successfully attain emotional readiness. Too long. Suppressing his frustration that time was slipping away, he allowed the door to open, but held his position by the button panel. Hidden from all, except in his direct line of sight, he listened for movement in the garage. Nothing.

Jarin left the elevator and turned to the nearest camera so that Alicia could see his face. Then crouching low, he ran to the first aisle of cars. Still, no sound. Watching and listening as he maintained his crouch, he wound his way toward the nearest stairwell and halted in the row of cars closest to it; sandwiching himself between an SUV and a pickup truck. Retrieving a ski mask from his right pocket, he put it on. He then pulled leather gloves from his left pocket and tugged those on as well. Listening, he raised his head above the SUV's hood and quickly glanced around. Silence. Sliding from between the vehicles, he noiselessly covered the short distance to the stairwell and headed swiftly down the stairs. Slowing to a walk as he approached the fifth level landing, he again listened.

Sounds of quiet, stealthy fighting drifted up from below. Lowering to a crouch, he peeked around the gap at the top of the stairs. His eyes roamed the shadows as Carson and the crew engaged one, three, no four hostiles. Too late to join the fray, he followed protocol and continued to search the shadows for any other movement. If he found none, he would turn his attention to the various fights, and join the one where the assailant most seemed to have the upper hand. Just as he was about to scrutinize the fights, movement on the opposite stairwell caught his eye. Swiftly, he turned and ran back up to the fourth level. After quickly ascertaining that the garage was still empty, he sprinted across to the other set of stairs where he stood, hidden by the landing wall. Silently catching his breath, he listened as someone quietly ascended from the fifth level. A woman stepped onto the landing. He blocked her path. "Going somewhere?" he asked.

There was no way out. She raised her hands and said, "I have no part in this."

"Good," said Jarin, gesturing toward the stairs. "Then you have nothing to fear."

Warily, she turned and went back down, with Jarin following at a short distance. As they descended, he looked for, and found Carson's reconnaissance point—the hood of a king-cab pickup truck. At the bottom of the stairs, he secured the woman's wrists in a plastic tie-wrap from his pocket and walked her to the truck.

"Took you long enough—missed all the action," Carson said quietly as he looked up. "I see you've brought company."

"My guess is she's the ghost," said Jarin. "They got compromised, so she was heading back early to make her report."

"She was here last week," said Carson. He acknowledged her surprise. "Yeah, we made you—and let you go. Once we saw you were an independent, we stopped following you." He gestured at one of several agents guarding a white van. "So, here you are again. Guess we'll wrap you up with the rest." The agent he had called over reached the truck. "Search her and prepare her for travel," Carson said. The agent taped the woman's mouth and escorted her to toward the van.

Turning his attention back to the team members assembled around the truck, Carson commanded, "Status."

"Four hostiles taken down—they're ready for disposal," said one.

"Can you hear anything in the guard shack?" asked Carson.

"Two voices. One male, one female," answered another.

Jarin's relief was deep—and short-lived. The op wasn't over yet.

"Secure the stairwells and elevators. We're blowing the door," Carson instructed them. "Starting in two minutes." The team listened to further instructions, then quietly dispersed.

~*~~~**~~~*~

After struggling to her feet, Gabrielle positioned herself against the back wall of the shack. Taking advantage of Raphael being engrossed in Sparks, she examined the room. Only a table and a couple of chairs. He would have the upper hand in the mostly empty space. Carson had said that these shacks had monitors for watching the cameras. This shack had rows of neatly bored holes along the two sidewalls, but the monitors hadn't yet been installed. She saw nothing she could use as a weapon.

Raphael pushed away from the table. Gabrielle panicked, fearing more pain. She forced herself to face that pain was inevitable. Walking toward her, he said, "You're pretty damn smart after all, Gabs. I'm impressed and I didn't expect to be. I may just stay at Xalan long enough to get some mileage out of your little app." Grinning mockingly, he grabbed her by the arm, yanked her back to the table, and threw her down into the chair. He took a thumb drive out of his pocket and plugged it into the laptop USB port. "Copy everything—design documents, diagrams, source code, everything—about that app onto this drive. Got it?"

Gabrielle just nodded. Had she imagined that the crew was coming? She copied Sparks and all its accompanying files onto the thumb drive; then sat back while Raphael checked what she had done.

"Good," he said, turning slightly to look at her. Gabrielle did not meet his gaze. "I'll just leave you here—locked in. Maybe someone will find you, maybe not." He stood and slipped the drive into his pants pocket. Giving her an appraising look, he said, "I'm beginning to see the attraction Landry has. Now that I've seen your app, I know he's not in it just for the screw. You're actually pretty smart. Maybe even 'scary smart.'" Stepping away from the table, he stared at her speculatively. Dreading what he was leading up to, Gabrielle sat frozen, her gaze averted, trying not to provoke him in any way. "I see the attraction," he repeated, musingly.

Without warning, he swept the laptop and everything else onto the floor. To her horror, Gabrielle's lifeline skipped across the concrete floor and smashed into the wall. In the next instant, Raphael grabbed her—again by the arm—forcing her out of the chair and against the table. "Before I go, I think I'll find out what Landry's been enjoying so much." He ripped at her clothes, tearing her blouse open. Buttons flew across the room.

Punching and kicking at Raphael, Gabrielle screamed. Several of her kicks and punches landed, but Raphael quickly grabbed her hands and forced his legs between hers. Her leverage gone, Gabrielle's only hope was that someone would hear her. She screamed again.

"Got a bit of fire don't you?" Raphael laughed. He swung, slapping her again.

The force of the slap was severe, choking off Gabrielle's scream. She felt his hand grasping at the crotch of her pants. *NO!* The silent scream echoing in her head; she drew her knees up to protect herself. Her struggle freed one of her hands and she vehemently clawed at his face.

"Bitch," he snarled, again imprisoning her hands in one of his. She had scratched him, two long trails down the left side of his face. He raised his free hand.

~*~~~**~~~*~

Jarin approached the door with Carson, both watching the three agents place the explosives. Loud screams erupted from the shack, setting his blood on fire. Not needing direction, the agents hurriedly finished with the explosives. More screams were heard—short, choked, piercing screams. Beside himself with rage, Jarin *needed* to get through that door. "Carson—"

CHAPTER EIGHTEEN

Recompense

Enraged by the sting of the scratches, Raphael swung his fist higher.

Seizing the momentary opening, Gabrielle turned, lifted her leg and drove her foot deep into his crotch.

Raphael doubled over in pain, gasping for air.

Avoiding his grasping hand, Gabrielle swung her legs over the side of the table. Her feet hit the floor and she was running—but where?

Stumbling and cursing, Raphael advanced on her, blocking her way to the door.

Gabrielle backed away, catching her foot on the laptop. She fell to her knees. The laptop skidded, grazing her hands.

His face contorted with pain and rage, Raphael saw his advantage and lunged.

In desperation, Gabrielle picked up the laptop, regained her footing, and swung it just as he reached her.

The answering thud as it connected reverberated through her arms and torso. She had found a weapon.

Raphael dropped to the floor. He struggled to regain his footing, but Gabrielle swung the laptop again. Mad with fury, she screeched in triumph; her cries echoing through the room as she wielded her weapon—smashing it against his head and shoulder again, and again, and again...

~*~~~**~~~*~

Carson yelled, "Blow it now! Blow it now!"

With small puffs of smoke, the lock and hinges blew. The five men rushed the door, knocking it to the floor in their haste to get in.

Gabrielle's disfigured face pushed Jarin over the edge. With a nerve rending roar of rage, he vaulted the table with no other thought but to kill.

~*~~~**~~~*~

The invasive sound reverberated off the walls of the guard shack, erasing Gabrielle's certainty of victory. Horror-stricken she wheeled, weapon raised, having no choice but to fight the new terror.

Carson hastened to block Jarin's path to Raphael.

"Get him up or get out of the way, Carson." Cowering at the menace in Jarin's voice, Raphael no longer tried to stand.

"There's nothing left to fight," said Carson. "Remember what you asked me for."

Her panic and rage subsiding, Gabrielle slowly lowered the laptop and squinted through swollen eyelids. "Carson...Jarin?"

The mingled notes of joy and disbelief in the softly spoken question made Jarin's need to punish suddenly secondary. An agent thrust a warmed blanket into his chest as he brushed past Carson. Taking it, he answered, "I'm here."

Gently, he pried the laptop from Gabrielle's hands and tossed it to the agent. Carefully avoiding contact with her raw, bruised face, he wrapped her in the blanket and lifted her into his arms. Though he chose to protect, his drive to destroy didn't dissipate. It settled into his heart; a burning urge to be acted upon at the first opportunity. Carson was right, Gabrielle had already beaten Raphael. Jarin would instead inflict his fury on the man who pulled the strings. Before, he had merely intended to damage Brett, but now nothing less than annihilation would satisfy him. A soft hand touched his face; filling him with warmth, distracting him from thoughts of vengeance.

"We did it," Gabrielle said. "We got him."

"Yes, it's over," he said, brushing his face through her hair. Still, this one was not going to walk away. "Make him suffer, Carson." Fear sprang into Raphael's bruised face. "That's right," Jarin told him. "You're not walking away from this."

"The ambulance is here," said Carson. "Hurry. We can't let her go into shock."

Noting his dismissal, Jarin did not take offense. He knew that Carson wanted them off the premises before he extracted what Raphael knew. Cautiously he left the guard shack, taking care not to further bruise Gabrielle's face. Paramedics from St. Mary's Hospital were waiting in the garage next to the gurney.

"Carson." Gabrielle called, raising her head to see where he was.

"He's busy," answered Jarin, his voice rough with emotion. "You can talk to him later. Rest now, love."

Gabrielle was groggily insistent. "I need to thank him for the pants."

She's incoherent. "The pants?"

She nodded under his chin. "Carson made me wear pants."

"Yes," he responded, forcing gentleness into his voice, hiding the savage violence of his thoughts. "We must thank Carson for the pants."

~*~~~**~~~*~

The operation was over as far as NEI was concerned. The team had already packaged up the hostiles; their two vehicles dispatched on tow trucks for dismantling. Suspecting that a negative report would provoke retaliation, Carson sent two team members to accompany the ghost back to her office. Protecting her would confirm in the minds of those who controlled the hostiles that she was the source of betrayal; their level of field craft was such that they would look no further.

Only two of the team remained in the garage outside the guard shack, providing security. Effectively no witnesses. Carson walked back into the guard shack and closed the reattached door. The stench was new. Raphael had lost control of his bowels. He now sat in one of the two chairs in front of the table. Gabrielle had defeated him; Jarin had given him a glimpse of his future. "One thing about Jarin," Carson began, "he has a strong sense of fair play." Raphael looked confused. "I don't. I want information from you, and I will get it. How I get it is up to you."

Sweat dripping down his face, stinking from the urine and feces running down his legs, Raphael tried to bluff his way out. "You can't hurt me, my cousin will—"

"Amazing how the smell of money suspends the ability to reason," Carson interrupted disdainfully. "You're a fool to think Brett will lift a hand to help you, especially with the way you chose to handle the situation."

"I don't believe you."

"You were the last known person seen with Gabrielle, removing her from NEI in a very public fashion. That's how we found you so quickly. You're the analyst. You figure it out." Carson shrugged. "You've put yourself beyond Brett's help, even if he were so inclined. But I know that he isn't. Your 'backup' had orders to make you disappear."

Visibly shaken, Raphael still tried to find a way out. "I've already seen your face and Jarin's. I can still tell the cops."

"You don't get it, do you?" Putting himself nose to nose with Raphael, Carson laughed. "You'll never see the cops. The only time law enforcement gets involved is when we don't clean up our own messes." He pulled his mask out of his pocket and put it back on. Then, he removed his leather gloves one by one, and replaced them with latex ones. "I don't make that mistake."

Circling the chair in which Raphael sat; Carson spoke as if teaching the alphabet to a two year old. "The mask is to prevent your bone, cartilage and other bodily matter from getting on my face." He smiled at Raphael again, this time through the mask. Flaccidly propped in the chair, Raphael made no attempt to stem the tears that now openly streamed down his face.

It never fails. Torture won't work on a pro. But the mere threat of it makes little piss-ass amateurs fall apart. "You've got three options for how you leave here," he continued. "First—the body bag." He took it off of the table and laid it out on the floor. "I've kept the one your 'backup' had reserved for you." Raphael's face became pasty white. "Or, you can join our friends outside and wake up with them in another country with enough illegal substance on your person that when the authorities find you—and we'll make sure they find you—they'll toss you into prison for a very long time." As Carson circled Raphael, his voice soft and menacing, he occasionally flexed his gloved hands. "By the way, your associates will likely blame you for blowing the op." Doubling over in the chair, Raphael retched. After he quieted, Carson picked up as though he had not been interrupted. "Or," he said, "we can just cut to the chase. You tell me what I want to know and wake up somewhere else—in the continental U.S. We'll spot you a new identity and enough money not to be immediately homeless. If you agree to certain terms."

"What terms?" asked Raphael, his labored breathing causing his voice to rasp.

"Avoid all Avanti companies. Never contact your cousin or your family again. That one shouldn't be too hard. Brett will probably take you out if you do. Stay away from all endeavors—including sailing—where you could run across him, Jarin, Gabrielle, or anyone connected with NEI or any other SCI company." Raphael started in surprise.

"Oh, yes," said Carson, "NEI became an SCI company effective this morning. You pissed away a very lucrative career path." Looking directly into Raphael's eyes, Carson told him, "You agree to these terms and I'll let you live. A very mundane and nondescript life to be sure, but you'll be alive." He didn't have long to wait.

The small, powerful recorder on the table, next to the thumb drive an agent had retrieved from Raphael's pocket, picked up every word.

~*~~~**~~~*~

Wakefulness tugged at the edge of Gabrielle's consciousness. Preferring the tranquility of sleep, she tried to ignore it. But it persisted. When she grudgingly acknowledged the nudge, memories of her ordeal flooded through her. She awoke screaming in rage, fighting to defend herself. But something held her down. She couldn't move her arms and legs. Panicked, she fought the restraints. Someone's arms reached around her, constraining her even more.

An urgent, unexpected voice broke through her terror. "Gabrielle, can you hear me? You're safe now." Something warm and soft pressed against her forehead.

Daring to believe the words, she paused warily, listening for more. "Jarin?"

"Yes."

He removed the something cold from her face; fumbled at whatever held her down. She was free. Reaching her arms toward his voice, she tried to open her eyes. A fresh wave of panic engulfed her. "I can't see. I can't open my eyes!"

"Shhh. Listen to me." His arms tightened around her, pinning hers to his chest. "Your eyes will be fine. The swelling's going down, but it may be tomorrow before you can open them wide enough to see."

"Tomorrow?" She needed to know all of it—no matter how bad. "What else is wrong with me?"

"Nothing else," he assured her. Again the soft, warm press on her forehead. "Just that your face is very swollen."

Gabrielle gradually let go of her panic and allowed herself to be comforted by Jarin's embrace—until she felt his tension. Freeing one arm, she slowly reached toward his face. Grasping her hand, he held it to his jaw, calming her even more. "Are *you* all right?" she asked.

Laughing quietly, he kissed her ear. "Why are you asking about me?"

"Something feels wrong," she said. She heard him sigh.

Hoarsely, he said, "I have to do something I don't want to do."

Immediately apprehensive, she prepared for his answer. "What is it?"

Instead of answering, he prompted gently, "Tell me, what do you remember?"

"Remember?" Gabrielle thoughts went back to the morning. Riding with Carson, the elevator, Raphael... Gabrielle's breath caught and she jerked her hand away from Jarin's face. She opened her mouth to answer him, but couldn't form words. Clenching her teeth, she wrapped her arms around her chest, trying to stem the onrush of vehement emotion. Jarin's arm constricted around her. The simple gesture shattered Gabrielle's already failing dam. Her rage, sorrow, grief surfaced; erupting into long, rasping sobs. Raphael's betrayal...Cleve's death... The market crash... Too much, too fast—she had no time to resolve one crisis before the next one hit.

Rocking her gently, Jarin tried to soothe her, but he knew it was time to call Anya. Holding Gabrielle tightly, he said, "I promise it'll be okay. I'm ringing for Dr. Gibson."

~*~~~**~~~*~

Outside the door to Gabrielle's room, Landry listened, hoping that she was awake. Hearing nothing, he opened it and walked noiselessly down the short entryway. Peering around the corner, he saw them. Gabrielle on her back, sleeping—or sedated—holding Jarin's hand tightly to her chest with both of hers; Jarin on his side, cradling her with his other arm. Seeing them together, Landry felt his bitterness toward Jarin begin to fade; even finding the humor for a weak joke. *All those disappointed women—Gabby's going to need Carson full time.* Finally, he was able to admit to the cause of his enmity toward his cousin. *He did for her what I didn't allow myself to do. It's not his fault. I should've broken the damn rules.* He turned to leave.

Jarin's voice was unexpected. "I'm not asleep."

"You didn't have to stop me," said Landry, turning back. "You could have just let me leave."

"Why would I do that?"

"Why not?" Landry countered.

"Because...we're friends?"

"Yeah," Landry agreed wryly. "We're friends." Hesitantly, he walked over to the bed and looked down at Gabrielle. "Her face looks worse than this morning. What happened?" A spasm of anguish momentarily marred Jarin's face. "Neverm—"

"No, it's fine now," Jarin interrupted. "You just reminded me of what happened earlier—she woke up screaming, fighting. I helped her calm down; but then I asked her what she remembered—like Anya said I should. Then everything just came out—Raphael's assault, everything she'd been suppressing for the past few days. Anya interviewed her thoroughly. It was rough, but she thinks Gabrielle got it all out."

Landry suppressed the urge to reach out to her. "PTSD interviews are never easy. I just hope there aren't ongoing psychological issues."

"Anya doesn't think so. Gabrielle was able to protect herself from the most psychologically damaging physical harm and she doesn't appear to be suppressing anything," said Jarin. "She said Gabby has a very strong psyche."

"That's a surprise," said Landry. They both laughed quietly. "I can't imagine how she must feel. It's good that you're here for her." *Like I didn't allow myself to be.* "Our cousin really knows her stuff. Glad she's on the case."

"I asked for her," said Jarin. "Wasn't having anyone else. What bothers me though is that Gabby hasn't been sleeping since she discovered the market crisis." Jarin stared down at her as if to pull the reason out of her dreams. "Has a recurring nightmare about a roller coaster crash. She's on the ground seeing it coming at her. Before she wakes up, the cars get close enough that she can see screaming, terrified faces."

"I know why that is," said Landry, his heart aching from the desire to comfort her. "The 3D graph in her analysis. She calls it the roller coaster graph."

The tenderness and sorrow on Jarin's face caused more stinging pain. "Hell—she's seeing that people will be devastated."

"It will, undoubtedly, be hell," Landry said. Averting his eyes, hoping to prevent his pain from worsening, he changed the subject. "Nathan and Josh are approaching Crescent City and Port Hudson about joining the hedge fund."

"I'm glad," said Jarin. "Keeping the government folks employed will insure at least some customers for local businesses."

"They're also taking the SCI Board to an activist stance on market regulations."

"So we fight." Jarin's expression, Landry was sure, mirrored his own. Going against deeply entrenched power would be treacherous. "Our reach may be global, but our influence is only local—regional at best. Reining in the investment houses isn't going to be easy, no matter how irresponsible they've been with their clients' money. We may be going it alone."

"True, but self-preservation demands we take them on. We got lucky this time. What if there's a next time, or a next? We have no choice."

They sat in silence; each fortifying himself with the mental armor necessary for the battles ahead. Finally, to tie up the last loose end in their pre-war diversion, Landry asked, "Raphael's taken care of?"

"I wanted to kill the bastard but Carson appealed to my better side. Instead, he'll wake up in a western state tomorrow with ten thousand dollars and a new identity."

"He won't make it." Landry snorted a laugh. "Sooner or later he'll try to revert to his own."

For the first time since Landry walked in, Jarin smiled; albeit a viciously satisfied smile. "He'll be arrested if he tries. Carson's turned our evidence of commercial espionage over to law enforcement. There's now an outstanding warrant for his arrest."

"Kismet," said Landry. "I hope he gave you what you need to bring Brett down."

Jarin jerked his head toward his jacket hanging over the back of one of the chairs. "There, a recorder in the inside pocket. Don't worry about waking Gabrielle, she's pretty heavily sedated. Anya wanted her to at least sleep through the night."

Retrieving the recorder, Landry turned it on. Raphael's voice was startling. *Sounds like Carson worked him over.*

Under Carson's questioning, he exposed Cleve and Garrett; then finally gave up Brett. Landry clicked the off button and dropped it back into Jarin's pocket.

"Keep it," Jarin said. "I've got another copy. I made that one for you and Nathan. Looks like there are moles in several of the other companies. We need to discuss how to expose them."

"I'll give it to him tonight," Landry said. "So, Garrett got played."

"Like a two-dollar fiddle." Jarin barked a short laugh. "Damn shame. He's a great analyst. He had a bright future with us."

"Yeah, and his abilities would have been an asset in fighting off what's coming," agreed Landry. "Unfortunately, he thought he was smarter than the rest of us."

"People like that never seem to get that anyone with half a brain'll figure them out sooner or later," Jarin said. "All he's done is prove he can't be trusted. We're better off without him."

With a vindictive smile of his own, Landry said, "And I'll be giving him his walking papers in about," he paused to check his watch, "two hours." He looked back at Jarin. "Looks like you've got Brett right where you want him."

His voice tight with anticipation, Jarin said, "I'll make it worth passing on Raphael."

"Sounded like someone worked him over pretty good."

"Gabrielle kicked his ass—with her ruggedized laptop."

"You've got to be kidding."

"Nope. Carson said he's putting a new section in the training manual," said Jarin with a wide grin. Their laughter grew as the tension between them waned. Finally, Jarin managed, "By the time Gabby got done with him, there was nothing left for me to fight. Then he crumpled like tissue paper when Carson got to him. He should have been wearing a diaper."

"You don't mean he...," Landry's voice trailed off as Jarin nodded. "I never figured him for a punk."

"In way over his head," said Jarin. "He's also going to have to decide whether he spends the money on plastic surgery to repair what Gabrielle did to his face, or use it for short-term living expenses."

Shaking his head slightly, Landry said, "Brutal, but he deserves it." He suddenly remembered things Raphael had been saying before Gabrielle's cell cut off. "Jarin, what he said about Gabrielle and me wasn't true."

Jarin waved him off. "But speaking of not exactly that," he said with a furtive glance. "We need to talk."

"Nothing more to be said." Landry reached over and covered their hands with one of his, giving them a quick squeeze. "Take care of each other."

"Thanks," Jarin said.

Briefly their eyes met, solidifying their kinship. "I'll stop by and see her tomorrow when she's awake. See you tomorrow, too," Landry said, lightly punching Jarin's shoulder as he turned to leave. Strolling down the hall toward the elevator, he admitted again that Jarin had understood what he hadn't. All Gabrielle needed was guidance and protection while she tried to do what they all knew needed to be done. *I treated her like a misbehaving child. Saturday, I wanted to kill him. What a difference a couple of days—and a crisis—makes.* Entering the elevator, he turned and leaned against the back wall; hands in his pockets, eyes closed. *NEI is clean. We can all now focus on making sure we aren't onboard one of Gabby's roller coasters.*

~*~~~**~~~*~

Striding into Garrett's outer office, Landry said, "Elaine, you can leave for the evening. Garrett and I have a meeting."

"Okay," said Elaine, her gaze drawn to the thick sheaf of papers tucked under Landry's arm. "It's not on his calendar and he didn't mention it." She raised her eyes questioningly to Landry's. He offered no explanation. "I'll just let him know I'm going."

"No need," answered Landry. "I'll tell him when I go in."

Reluctantly, and with a last glance toward Garrett's door, Elaine gave in. "All right. Good night then."

"Good night," he replied. After watching her leave, he entered Garrett's inner office and closed the door behind him.

"Yes?" Garrett asked without looking away from his laptop.

In no hurry, Landry merely leaned against the closed door and waited.

Finally glancing toward the door, Garrett was immediately incensed. "What the hell do you want?"

"Your resignation," Landry replied with a wintry smile.

"What's that supposed to mean?" Garrett asked, sitting back in his chair.

Taking his time, Landry moved from the door to Garrett's desk. Lowering himself into one of the guest chairs, he said, "Blackhawk, Xalan, Carruthers."

Watching him through narrowed eyes, Garrett asked, "You expect me to know what that means?"

Propping his feet up on the desk, Landry angled his legs so that he had a clear view of Garrett's face. "The evidence says you do."

"Evidence," Garrett scoffed. Dismissively, he turned back to his laptop. "Get your feet off my desk and stop wasting my time."

Ignoring him, Landry opened the folder he'd placed on his lap, extracted the analysis, and slid it across the desk. It hit Garrett's elbow. He glared at Landry and then down at the papers. After stiffening slightly, he quickly regained his composure. "Where did you get this?" he demanded, his expression not quite as glacial as before.

"Nathan called it a 'startlingly astute piece of analysis.' He and Jarin will be sharing it with the subject corporations tomorrow," Landry said. "Mind telling me when you planned to share it with us?"

Clearly enunciating each word, Garrett repeated, "Where did you get this?"

Leaning back in the chair, Landry clasped his hands comfortably behind his head, "ISS traced the output of the surveillance creep to an external server. Turns out it's been recording every network and file transaction from every NEI machine." He pointed his chin toward the report. "That showed up on the server Friday and was pulled just a few hours before Cleve was murdered."

Recovering his usual iciness, Garrett replied, "Then it's Avanti you should be chasing. As usual, you're barking up the wrong tree." He stood. "Get the hell out of my office."

Instead of responding, Landry pulled a second set of papers from his folder and slid them across the desk. "I haven't yet mentioned that the surveillance creep has been reporting out on NEI for eight months." Garrett picked up the papers and inspected the diagrams. "You'll see that there's a timeline for the modification of a certain Retro file. You'll be most interested in the first modification that was made by someone other than Gabrielle."

"If I'm reading this correctly," Garrett smirked, "It says that Cleve did it. What has that to do with me?"

"It does seem that way, doesn't it?" Landry slid the single sheet he had withheld from the stack across the desk. "Except that this email has Cleve on vacation during that time—with you in possession of his laptop." Garrett silently read the email. Pulling another set of papers from the folder, Landry disdainfully dropped them onto the desk. "Unlike you, Nathan honors his commitments. That's the fulfillment of your golden parachute agreement."

Rising to his feet, he placed the open folder next to Garrett's laptop, revealing the last set of papers. "This is your resignation, ready for your signature. Just sign it and leave it on the desk." Evenly meeting Garrett's vehement glare, Landry answered his unspoken challenge. "Don't want to do it this way? I'll take it to any level you want. It would be my extreme pleasure to take your ass out. The more public the better." Hatred crackled between them. "Fiona takes over as managing partner tomorrow. I'm taking over your senior partner spot. Anything found in here tomorrow will be thrown out. So I suggest you take your personal belongings with you tonight." Daring Garrett to break his silence, Landry said, "So now I'm telling you, you dishonorable son of a bitch. Get the hell out of my office."

~*~~~**~~~*~

The sound of footsteps fractured the silence, jolting Jarin awake. Lurching into a crouch, he prepared himself for the attack. The footsteps quickened; then Julie and Sarah rounded the corner of the entryway, nearly running him over. Relieved, Jarin fell back into the chair.

"We came as soon as you called," said Julie as they hesitantly approached the bed. As soon as they saw Gabrielle's face, their distress elevated into horror.

Jarin said, "She's far better than she looks." Julie shot him a disbelieving glance.

Tensely, Sarah whispered, "What happened?"

Jarin chose not to sugar-coat the description of Gabrielle's injuries. "Somebody taught Raphael the art of methodical slapping—maximum pain from a minimum of effort. He slapped her multiple times, forehanded and backhanded," he said, his own words sparking an unanticipated resurgence of his wrath.

"Maximum pain?" The horror in Julie's face magnified. "But you said she was better than she looks. How can that be?"

Belying his rising anger, Jarin said dispassionately, "Usually a person would also have facial lesions and at least a wrenched neck or back. Gabrielle doesn't because she figured out she should turn her head in the direction of the slap before impact. She did what she could to minimize her injuries."

Tears now openly streamed down Julie's and Sarah's faces. "Otherwise, is she okay?" Sarah asked brokenly, her voice barely audible.

"Go on—sit." Once they were seated, he leaned against the end of the bed and started in on what had happened. When he got to the part about hearing Gabrielle scream, Julie could no longer contain herself.

Jumping out of the chair, she advanced on him. "Had you *lost your mind*? Why did you let her do it?"

"Jules, careful," Sarah said. "You don't want to wake Gabs."

Sarah's admonition had no impact. "She loves you. She trusted you. You acted like you don't care about her at all!"

Leaning in close to her face, Jarin said slowly and distinctly, "Sit down before I throw you out."

Warily, Julie sat back down. "You wouldn't have let me do it," she muttered, taking one last shot. "Why did you let Gabs?"

"Don't push me, Jules. I don't have the best control of my temper right now." He turned toward the bed; his gaze briefly meeting Sarah's. *She thinks we've both lost it.* Leaning on the bed railing, he watched as Gabrielle slept, undisturbed. He owed them a better explanation. But no matter what words he used, it was going to sound heartless. The hardest thing to accept was that even knowing the outcome, he would still have played it the same. Gabrielle was too analytical and determined. The thought of her ending up in the same situation without protection was... He shut it out of his mind.

Leaving her side, Jarin paced in front of the window. "Strategically, it was the right play. I knew it, Gabrielle knew it. Everybody knew it," he confessed. Julie's face was a mask of abject scorn. "Gabrielle wanted to do it. We all wanted it over." Jarin's eyes unexpectedly watered. Buffeted by the tension emanating from both women, he turned to look out of the window. "I was afraid that if we refused to allow the operation, she would go after him on her own." Sarah and Julie exchanged glances, acknowledging Jarin's perceptiveness. "We could so easily have lost her; but the alternative could certainly have been far worse." Determined to maintain control of his temper, he faced them again.

Now Sarah was angry. "I hope Carson off'ed the SOB."

"I wish he had," Jarin admitted, with a short, surprised laugh. "But where Raphael's going and the life he's going to have to lead—for him, it'll be worse than death."

"That's even better," said Sarah. "He deserves to suffer."

"I'm sorry I exploded," Julie said. "It's just that..."

"I know," he said. "She's suffering because of what we decided to do. It doesn't matter that she wanted to do it—that she walked into it knowingly."

"Can we stay with her? We've brought overnighters just in case." Julie asked.

"Please, I'd appreciate it if you would."

"I'll even take the whole day off and spend it with her," said Sarah. "When is she supposed to wake up?"

"Around seven," said Jarin. "I'll be here late tomorrow afternoon because I want to pick up *M'Lady the Sea* from the gallery and hang it for when she goes home on Wednesday. They can't deliver it because she's here. I'm glad you'll be here with her, Sarah."

Julie and Sarah exchanged glances.

"What?"

"Oh nothing," they replied in unison.

~*~~~**~~~*~

It was almost eleven when, careful not to wake her, Garrett left Elaine's bed. Silently dressing, he watched her; uncharacteristically experiencing regret. He could have—and should have—done more for her. She deserved better treatment than he had given her. Retrieving his jacket, he took an envelope from the inside pocket and placed it on the pillow where his head had been. A little something to make amends—the deed to this condo and the number for the account holding the Avanti money. His attorney had instructions to discreetly transfer it into her name. He couldn't give the money to Liz. She'd want to know where it had come from. Elaine knew nothing of his finances. After watching her for a few minutes more, Garrett quietly let himself out. He would have to take the Audi he had bought her. NEI cars were now off limits to him.

Minutes later, he left the city streets for the mostly deserted highway, speeding north toward Hampton Cape. Now that NEI had ejected him, complete ostracism loomed as his future. A whisper here and there—he would be lucky to find executive employment in a second or third echelon firm. Even if he did, doors at the premiere firms would always be closed to him. He refused to go out that way, bringing disgrace to his family, ruining the futures of his sons.

Taking a chance, he had made a play. If it had gone well, he would have been the victor. But it failed. That smart-ass Landry was way out of line. *I bet my whole stake and lost it. But that does not make me dishonorable.* He had one last play. Since he was going down, he was damn sure going to take Avanti down with him. There was no choice but to trust that Nathan would do the right thing by his family. Technically he was still an NEI employee until midnight. At humility's doorstep, he was now counting on the old-school honor code that he had so long ridiculed.

The surveillance notes he had been studying when Landry interrupted him indicated that right about now, an unrecorded incoming truck should be approaching Blackhawk on this route. Brett had said that the Blackhawk allegations were unfounded. Garrett left it to fate, hoping to pick a smuggling truck and not some poor slob simply trying to make a living. Examining the oncoming big rigs, he looked for one with the distinctive Blackhawk cab. Finally he saw it, speeding toward him. Flooring the accelerator, Garrett willed himself forward, filling the car with a thunderous roar. Holding the car steady as the speedometer passed one hundred miles per hour, he purposefully crossed the center dividing line and the empty adjacent lane directly into the path of the oncoming truck.

The fireball erupting from the collision rose into the sky, alerting everyone approaching from either direction that something disastrous had just occurred.

~*~~~**~~~*~

Settling into the seat as the car merged onto the freeway and headed south to Marina Cove, Jarin scuttled his plans to move into the Crescent City condo. Living in the city was out of the question for the couple of days that Gabrielle was out here at St. Mary's. Beyond that, she needed time to heal, physically and psychologically. He prepared himself to be patient.

Eyeing the privacy glass, which would have been rolled down if Carson were driving, Jarin briefly wondered how the disposal activities were going. But that was Carson's problem. *Time is slipping by.* Taking out his phone, he hit the single-digit speed dial for Nathan.

There was no ring, only Nathan's disquieted voice. "How's Gabrielle?"

His obvious concern distracted Jarin from his goal. "Didn't Anya call?"

"She did. So did Landry," Nathan said. "Just want to keep abreast of the latest."

"There hasn't been anything new since the interview. She's sedated," said Jarin, becoming acutely aware of his own fatigue.

"Glad she's resting. I didn't realize she hadn't been sleeping last week," Nathan said. "By the way, I've been speaking with Gabby's mother." Staggered, Jarin realized that he had not once thought about Gabrielle's family. Nathan continued, "She was frantic. Didn't know how she would get back to the States on such short notice. Finally the solution occurred to me and I arranged with Josh to swing by Edinburgh on their way back. They'll all be arriving Thursday." He continued with obvious effort. "Did you know Gabby's father died two years ago?"

Again thrown off balance, Jarin managed, "No, I didn't."

"Gabby and her mother only have each other. I can still hear her hysteria before I could make her understand." Nathan finished harshly, "We almost cost her all that's left of her family."

Reeling from the news, Jarin said, "I need to take Brett down, Nathan."

"Yes, we do," agreed Nathan. "He went too far. Or maybe Raphael overstepped his bounds..."

"No, it was Brett," interrupted Jarin. "We've found out some things since the rescue."

"What things?"

"About the four hostiles outside the guard shack. At first, we thought they were backup for Raphael. Carson found out they were the cleanup crew." The silence lengthened. "Nathan?"

"Still here. Just trying to figure out—you can't mean assassins."

"I'm afraid so," Jarin confirmed. "Their job was to get Raphael's thumb drive and then make Gabrielle and Raphael disappear."

"Brett crossed the line," Nathan said with atypical fierceness. "We've got to take him out—for everyone's sake."

"But what if we're just as dirty?" Jarin asked. "Did you hear the tape? Raphael said something like 'payback is a mother' and that Dad isn't as clean as we think he is."

"I heard it. Either he's a liar, or Brett lied to him." Nathan said harshly. "If it bothers you, by all means, ask Josh. Neither of us has anything to hide. Unless—"

So there is something. Jarin prepared himself to hear it.

"You know how we grew SCI," Nathan said. "Josh and I took the laissez-faire approach as a management model for a consortium of businesses. Each business remaining—for the most part—autonomous, but benefitting from economies of scale."

Suppressing his impatience, Jarin said, "What has that to do with Brett?"

"Well, the first time Josh used the model was in a pitch to Cornerstone Publishing. They were fighting against an Avanti takeover," Nathan continued. "Brett's father, Harrison, was CEO at the time. Cornerstone agreed to Josh's proposal and flourished under the SCI umbrella. Word got around that SCI was a safe haven and over the years, companies targeted for hostile takeover—some by Avanti—would contact Josh and many are now part of SCI. I'm sure Brett knows their version of the history as well as we know ours." He paused. With some effort, Jarin refrained from rushing him. "So—and this is a guess—when NEI started funneling business away from his companies, he took it as an attack rather than issues with the way those companies were run. Looking at it from his perspective and knowing the history, I can see the reasons for his anger. But that does not justify his response."

"So they convinced themselves that you and Dad operate the way they do; that they were justified in crossing the line."

"Looks like it."

Finally, the conversation had reached the point where Jarin could ask for what he needed. ""To take him down, I need your permission to use Garrett's report."

"Without question," Nathan responded. "What do you have in mind?"

"We need to notify the companies in the report about what Brett was doing."

"True. I see no reason why we should withhold anything."

"Do you think they should hear Raphael's tape?"

"Absolutely," Nathan answered without hesitation. "It's irrefutable evidence of how far he went. They also need to know of the likelihood that he planted moles in their companies. What's more, I think it's appropriate to suggest they check their networks for the surveillance creep."

"Then we're on the same page," Jarin said, relieved.

"We'll meet with them tomorrow. Then the grapevine will take over. A whisper here, a whisper there..." Nathan's contempt was overlaid with satisfaction. "I give it maybe a quarter or two before his client base starts to dry up. Before next year's out, Avanti will be on its way to being a lower echelon corporation."

Strictly bush league. That's worse than barring Raphael from what he wanted most. "Tomorrow starts the endgame, then."

"I'll ask Lois to set things up," Nathan said. "We'll do a video con—say around eleven. You can spend the morning with Gabrielle if you like. All we'll have to do is show up maybe an hour early for prep."

"Thanks, Nathan." "I appreciate that."

"I'd like Fiona and Landry to be there as well."

"As they should be." Jarin sank further back into the seat after he hung up, intending to sleep the rest of the way. He needed to be on form tomorrow. As much as he would prefer it, he wouldn't be using the extra time tomorrow morning to be with Gabrielle. *That time belongs to Brett.*

CHAPTER NINETEEN

Vibrancy

Running south toward the yacht club across the wet sands of Coral Cove beach, Jarin heard someone racing to catch up with him. He turned and jogged backward. It was Carson. "Welcome back," he said, turning forward again. "Raphael is disposed of?"

"Yep, and the former ghost is keeping an eye on him," answered Carson, matching Jarin's pace. "She volunteered when she saw what the hostiles did to her office after she reported in, just to get out of their reach." They passed the fire pit and skirted several large rocks. "Raphael's new identity says he's a high school dropout. Quite a come-down for someone with two master's degrees. Has to get his GED."

"If he can deal with his new circumstances," Jarin said. "How much cash does he have?"

"Ten Gs—like we agreed," Carson replied. They turned up the steep path that climbed the ridge Coral

Cove shared with Marina Cove. Back on flat ground and winding their way north toward the club, Carson resumed the conversation. "He also has a copy of the arrest warrant for Raphael Courtland. If he gets into trouble, the fingerprints will match up." He glanced over at Jarin. "What he hasn't remembered yet is that he may need to provide fingerprints for any job worth having. He's pretty much done."

"Better than he deserves." Anticipating his meeting with Brett, Jarin added, "One last rat to take down."

Carson's cell buzzed. Still running, he unholstered it and checked the message. "Better make it quick," he advised.

"Why's that?"

"Just got a TM from the ISS wire—Garrett Stratford is dead."

Abruptly, Jarin stopped. "What?" *Did Brett...*

Several yards beyond, Carson also stopped, and walked back to where Jarin was standing. "Looks like the car he was driving crossed the center line on the way home last night. He took out a Blackhawk semi full of smuggled munitions."

"At least he went out on his own terms—and proved the rumors are true. Wonder how he knew it was the right truck," Jarin mused. "Hopefully there's evidence connecting Blackhawk's illegal activities to Avanti. Is it public yet?"

"Nope," replied Carson. "It won't be until next of kin is notified. That may take an hour or so. If you're thinking about notifying Nathan and Landry, that's not the right thing to do."

"I know. They need to be truly surprised when they're officially notified," agreed Jarin. They had reached the club. "You know where I'm going—gotta get to Brett before law enforcement does."

"Better make it good. It may be your last chance."

~*~~~**~~~*~

Kismet, karma; whatever—it works for me. Everything broke yesterday—the day before Brett's quarterly sunrise team building meeting. Now he's here, in the perfect place for our discussion. Jarin headed down the dimly lit southern corridor of the club, toward the conference room Brett had reserved for his meeting. He knocked at the door and then pushed it open far enough to poke his head through. "Good morning gentlemen," he said. "Brett, could you step out for a word?"

Annoyed by the disruption, Brett turned toward the door. Seeing that it was Jarin, he quickly smoothed his expression. "We're in the middle of a meeting, Jarin. I'll be free in about forty-five minutes. How about then?"

Not a chance. Jarin gave the appearance of thinking it over. "It's urgent, Brett."

"I'm running a corporation here," Brett said with a chuckle, "How urgent is it?"

Pushing the door all the way open, Jarin said, "I've got an analysis performed by Garrett Stratford of NEI." Taking it out of the deep inside pocket of his sweat jacket, he started toward the over-head projector at the far end of the room. "Why don't I throw it up on the overhead and you tell me? We can also talk about the other NEI project that you haven't had status on."

"No need." Brett responded. "Neal, take the meeting for now. I'll be back in a few." At the door, he turned to wait for Jarin. As Jarin approached, Brett glared at him and preceded him out, leaving it for Jarin to close the door behind them.

"What's this about?"

"We'll talk in conference room five," Jarin answered, leading the way toward the room he had reserved. He threw open the door, gesturing for Brett to precede him. He followed, closing the door.

"This better be good." Brett said, leaning against the conference table.

Tossing the package he was carrying on the table beside Brett, but remaining in front of the door, Jarin answered, "Commercial espionage and attempted murder."

Brett sputtered a laugh. "What has that to do with me?"

Instead of answering, Jarin pulled the small recorder from his pocket and pressed the play button. Raphael's voice filled the room. Watching as Brett listened, Jarin sensed that, despite his carefully noncommittal expression, Raphael's words weren't news to him. When the tape finished, Jarin pressed the off button and put it back in his pocket.

"Interesting, but you haven't answered my question," said Brett. "What has that to do with me?"

"Come off it. You heard the tape," Jarin said. "Your crew didn't come back yesterday. Aren't you curious as to why?"

"I don't know what you're talking about," said Brett. "For all I know, that person could have been an actor reading lines."

"That was your cousin, Raphael Courtland. Haven't you wondered where he is?"

"I do have a cousin by that name," allowed Brett. "What did you do, torture him into saying those things?"

Though Jarin had expected Brett to play it out until the bitter end, it still rankled. "It may seem that way, except for Garrett's analysis, and the events of Friday night."

His tone exasperated, Brett declared, "Once again, Jarin, I have no idea what you mean by any of this."

"Have it your way," Jarin said, unzipping his sweat suit jacket. He took it off and tossed it on the table next to the package. "We'll just pretend I'm kicking your ass for no damn reason."

"That's enough." Brett's laughter erupted loudly. "I'm done playing games with you."

Watching him impassively, Jarin didn't move.

"You're serious," Brett's laughter faded as he stared down at Jarin from his two inch height advantage. "An open invitation to kick pretty-boy Jarin San Chapelle's ass? I can't pass that up."

Malevolent energy coursing through him, Jarin charged. At that moment, Brett feinted. Jarin saw the hidden uppercut coming at him as though it were in slow motion. Easily blocking the blow, he stepped inside Brett's guard and fired one of his own to Brett's abdomen, backing him up. Fueled by his overwhelming anger, Jarin viciously pressed his advantage. Rapidly firing more blows to Brett's abdomen, Jarin kept him off guard, each blow an outlet for his long repressed fury.

Pressed back against the conference table, Brett thrust his knee upward, aiming for the inside of Jarin's thigh. Sidestepping it, Jarin lost his balance and fell back sharply against the wall. Readying his next blow, Brett took his turn to charge; gloating in anticipation of an easy victory. But Jarin twisted easily out of the way and Brett's fist smashed instead into the wall. Enraged, Brett spun toward his quarry, just as Jarin's perfectly timed punch crashed into his nose; breaking it. Snarling at the pain, Brett charged again.

Unbidden, Gabrielle's scream filled Jarin's ears, her swollen face filled his vision. He punished Brett viciously, blocking his every attempt to gain the upper hand.

Parrying yet another of Brett's punches, Jarin used the momentum of his lunge to twist his arm around behind him as he stumbled past. Brett's voice filled the room with expletives. "It's over, Brett," Jarin said, savagely slamming his head into the conference table.

Beaten, Brett slid to the floor. Propping himself up against one of the chairs, he looked up at Jarin, smirking. "It doesn't matter. You still got nothing."

His voice tight with contempt, Jarin said, "This wasn't about me having something. This was about payback." Lowering himself to one knee, he put his face nose to nose with Brett's. "This morning, Nathan and I are sharing the report and the tape with the other companies you tried to screw. You know how it works," Jarin sneered. "Viral marketing, the grapevine, whisper campaign, whatever you want to call it." Pushing Jarin away, Brett tried to get up. Catching himself easily, Jarin violently swung his elbow around, catching Brett in the jaw, knocking him back to the floor. "I give it a year before Avanti's strictly bush league, but I'd love to take you out before then." Brett glared up at him, his face swelling. Jarin straightened up, towering over him. "Give me a reason. I'll make you disappear just like your cousin. Or, maybe I'll go too far and you'll end up like Cleve."

~*~~~**~~~*~

All things considered, the mirror was kind. By tomorrow the swelling would be gone; the day after that, she should be completely bruise-free. Such close inspection of the healing injuries resurfaced Gabrielle's memories of her ordeal. *Saved by pants.*

A man's voice called her name. "Gabrielle?"

Preparing for his censure, Gabrielle stepped out of the bathroom. "Morning, Landry."

His expression severe, he scrutinized her very carefully. An unexpected smile broke onto his face. "You look far, far better than last night."

"Thanks," said Gabrielle. She watched Landry watch her, the silence growing longer and more awkward. *May as well get it over with.* "Okay, let me have it," she said with a sigh.

Confused, Landry asked, "What do you mean?"

"You were right. I shouldn't have insisted that we go after him. It almost ended very badly. You've every right to be angry with me."

Subdued, he stepped forward and pulled her into his arms, hugging her very tightly. Sighing into her hair, he said, "Looks like I botched this all the way 'round."

It was Gabrielle's turn to be confused. "I don't understand."

Releasing her, he took her hand and led her to the bed. "Sit," he said.

Gabrielle sat.

Taking one of the chairs, he placed it in front of her and straddled it. Holding both her hands in his, he said, "I'm not angry with you. In fact, I'm very proud of you."

Her mood lightened. "You are?"

"Of course. Just think about what you've done in the past week. You alerted us to the impending market crash. That alone was remarkable," he said. "Then you alerted us to —and helped apprehend—an espionage ring within NEI. But what I'm most proud of is your ability to think on your feet. When you got into trouble, you came up with an extraordinary solution to get yourself out. How did you think of 'the server depends on a signal from my cell' story?"

"I've wondered that, too," she said. "It just appeared in my brain."

Landry laughed. "Well, it was a very timely appearance." He squeezed her hands. "There's no possible way I could be angry with you."

"Thank you, Landry," Gabrielle said solemnly. "That means a lot to me."

"You're welcome," he said, releasing her. "But you did scare the hell out of us."

"Scared me, too," she admitted. "I'm very happy to be here." *And whole...*

"You know your path now lies with SCI."

"Yes I know. When are you kicking me out?"

Grimacing, Landry said, "I don't know what I have to do to change your opinion of me. You'll leave on your own terms, not because we're kicking you out."

Before Gabrielle could answer, Sarah's voice breezed down the hall. "Gabs are you up yet? Breakfast in the cafeteria was awful." She and Julie entered the room and her eyes lit up when she saw Landry. "Ohhh, you're the yummy one from the boat."

Stunned, Julie stared at Sarah. Glancing quickly at Landry, Gabrielle saw that his expression was—comically—aghast. *His eyebrows are just about glued to his hairline.* She suppressed a laugh long enough to say, "Landry, I don't believe you've officially met Sarah."

Managing to retrieve his eyebrows, Landry said, "Hello, Sarah. Hi, Jules."

Looking as though she were sucking on a lemon, Julie squeezed out a hello. Hard pressed to keep her laughter from breaking through, Gabrielle faked a cough.

Unfazed by all the havoc she was causing, Sarah barreled ahead. "So you're the Landry that Gabby works for?"

"Well, yes," he said hesitantly.

"You're gorgeous. Gabby never said." Miraculously she stopped herself and changed direction. "Are you coming to the launch party?"

Looking from one to the other of them as if searching for a life preserver, Landry asked, "The what?"

"Don't y'all talk to each other out there on that boat?" Sarah demanded in exasperation. "Drew knows all about it."

Seeing that Landry had no hope of regaining his balance, Gabrielle drew Sarah's fire. "Sarah, they sail—probably not much time to talk."

Her eyes drawn to Gabrielle, Sarah's expression immediately filled with concern. "Gabby, well, you look... Oh hell, you look like a raccoon."

"Dang it," she replied, laughing. "I was trying for panda." Landry averted his face, probably also trying not to laugh. *I wonder when his rules say it's ok to have fun?* Abruptly, he stood. *Obviously, not now.*

"I think that's my cue to leave," he said, warily watching Sarah.

Sarah laughed. "Don't you like cute furry animals?"

"It's just that it's getting a bit light-hearted, which is great for Gabby, but not for me," he said, smiling bemusedly.

Incredulous, Sarah asked, "So you think having fun isn't a good thing?"

Gabrielle struggled to keep her expression neutral. Landry obviously didn't know quite what to make of Sarah.

"It's just that I've got some very serious business to attend to when I get to the office this morning. I probably ought not be grinning from ear to ear while I handle it." Quickly walking past her and Julie, he turned back and said, "Have fun, ladies." Then he was gone.

Now openly laughing, Gabrielle shook her head at Sarah. "Why'd you do that? You practically chased him out of the room."

"That's our Sarah," Julie smirked.

"It's not my fault he's stuck in the nineteenth century," Sarah retorted as Julie answered her buzzing cell. "Besides, he's kinda cute when he's all flustered," she said, beaming at them.

After listening for a few moments, Julie said, "Sure, great. We'll see you then." She hung up. "It was Quentin. He said he's a few minutes out." She gave them a big smile. "Soon we'll all be partners."

"I'm glad he doesn't mind coming here to sign the agreement," said Gabrielle. She turned to face them, sitting cross-legged on the bed. "So, what have I missed?"

Sarah answered, "Looks like Quentin ended his 'keep my distance' policy."

Blushing, Julie complained, "Oh, Sarah."

"It's true. Didn't y'all have brunch on Sunday?"

Julie just shook her head. "You're getting too far ahead."

"I think it's great," said Gabrielle.

"There's nothing definite yet. We may end up as just friends," said Julie.

"Even so, at least you're talking."

Putting Sarah on the spot, Gabrielle asked her, "So what's up with you?"

"I really don't know," Sarah began.

"Sure you don't," chided Julie. "You've been closeted with Drew going over the launch party and other public relations kinds of things. I thought you liked him."

"I do, but we're working together," said Sarah. "I don't want to jinx it." She made a face. "Besides, he keeps going on about Norma Jean. I'm Sarah. What if he only thinks he likes me because I remind him of her?" She shot a surreptitious, wistful glance toward the door that Gabrielle pretended not to see.

If she decides to go after Landry, he won't know what hit him. Might be the best thing for both of them—but I'm staying out of it. She gasped in mock surprise. "Sarah, passing up a chance at a relationship? That's front page news."

Sarah made a face. "Ha, ha. Very funny—for a panda."

Laughing with her friends, Gabrielle felt almost normal again.

~*~~~**~~~*~

Cleaned up and dressed for the meeting he and Nathan had arranged the night before, Jarin approached the glass front doors of the club. Anyone crossing his path would see no evidence of the time he had spent in conference with Brett.

Carson had parked at the end of the front walk and now stood by its front door, his cap under his arm. Recognizing their agreed upon alert signal, Jarin was instantly on guard. He pulled out his sunglasses from the inside pocket of his suit coat and put them on before stepping out onto the walkway. As he approached the car, his hidden eyes rapidly surveyed the scene. Of the few cars there, the one that stood out was a nondescript sedan parked in a distant spot. Its very ordinariness screamed 'out of place.' Carson held the door open and Jarin got in. After they'd left the club, the privacy glass descended. Amused, Jarin pushed his sunglasses up into his newly cropped hair and met Carson's gaze in the rear view mirror. "Why the signal? Brett sending someone after me?"

"He's not that big a fool. Besides, I hear he's in pretty bad shape." Carson's eyes glinted with humor. "The club has a visitor this morning."

"The sedan."

"Yeah. Detective Collins," said Carson. "He was there when I drove up. Came over and asked me about Brett."

"Investigating Garrett's accident?"

"More than that." Carson said. "He tried to pick my brain, you see."

Jarin laughed outright. "So I suppose he gave more than he got."

"Certainly," answered Carson dryly. "You know the drill."

"What did you find out?"

"Seems Garrett left some incriminating tapes of his conversations with Brett. The detective got them this morning. He threw around phrases like 'corporate misconduct' and 'commercial espionage.' I think he may have enough to connect Brett with the information they already have on Raphael." Carson paused as he merged them onto the highway. "But here's the kicker—one of the tapes may implicate Brett in Cleve's murder."

"Looks like there was more to Garrett's last play than I thought. Hope they have enough to nail Brett's ass."

~*~~~**~~~*~

Wednesday—the last evening of her confinement. Soon they would all have to ramp up into crisis mode; this time a prolonged effort, fighting through the market crash. There would be a few days of respite before then, and Gabrielle intended to spend them with Jarin.

The afternoon news, an invasive reminder of Garrett's sacrifice, ran on in the background, linking his death with Cleve's, Raphael's disappearance, the illegal activities at Blackhawk, and Avanti's corporate espionage. She turned off the television. Though her ordeal had been integral to the reported events, she was extremely grateful that ISS had insured that it was, and would remain, unheralded—even to law enforcement.

In spite of her animosity toward Garrett, she had only wanted him to be held accountable for his actions. *But this...* His family was inconsolable. Nathan had pledged his support, and that of NEI, to help them through the difficult times ahead. Still experiencing the grief of losing her father, Gabrielle was determined to help his sons cope with theirs.

Her mother still had not quite adjusted, and being so far away when she got the news of Gabrielle's ordeal had caused her even more pain. From her multiple, barely lucid calls, Gabrielle had pieced together that she was flying into Port Hudson tomorrow; oddly, with Jarin's parents. She wondered what they were like.

Loud footsteps entering the room interrupted her thoughts. *Jarin.* She turned toward the door. Stephen stood in the entryway, nearly out of breath, his eyes wild with worry. Frozen with the shock of seeing him, she steeled herself against the expected barrage of hauntingly intimate memories. But it didn't come.

"Gabs, are you okay?" Stephen's gaze locked onto the fading bruises on the right side of her face; vestiges of Raphael's backhanded slaps. "What happened?" He quickly came toward her, intent on taking her into his arms.

"No, please. I'm all right Stephen," she said, backing away. His steps faltered. Stopping near the foot of the bed, he stood before her just as she had fantasized for the many, lonely months; his tie loosened, his sleeves pushed up. Just like always. The 'one last time' that had filled her dreams was here. Hers for the taking, and she felt nothing.

"I've been worried. You didn't answer my calls. I finally got it out of Sheila on my way down from Port Hudson." He took another step toward her, holding out his hand, his eyes caressing her in the way that she had never been able to refuse. "You shouldn't be alone. Let me be here for you."

"It's wrong for you to be here, Stephen," she backed away once more. "You should go. I don't need your help." Undaunted, he was determined to wear her down. But Gabrielle was resolute.

Another masculine voice sounded. "Am I interrupting?"

"Jarin," Gabrielle whispered. He stood at the corner of the entryway.

His eyes narrowing at Gabrielle's response to the newcomer, Stephen turned to see who it was. The men sized each other up. Intending to make introductions, Gabrielle approached, but Stephen blocked her path, walking toward Jarin as he held out his hand. "Stephen Marsdon," he said, introducing himself.

Shaking his hand, Jarin said, "Marsdon. Wilson Consolidated—Chicago?"

"That's right," said Stephen, taking in Jarin's sandals, faded jeans, and paint-splattered T-shirt. "You're an exec? Didn't quite catch your name."

"Jarin—"

"San Chapelle?"

"That's right."

"I see." Stephen said, looking back at Gabrielle. Her gaze didn't falter as he searched her eyes for any sign that he was misreading their relationship. "Looks like you're in good hands, Gabs." he conceded.

"Yes I am. Thank you for coming, Stephen. It's been good to see you again," said Gabrielle, watching the hope in his eyes fade. She felt no malice or vindication; merely relief that the sundering of their lives that Stephen had started was finally—and irrevocably—complete.

"I'm really glad you're okay," he said. He nodded to Jarin as he passed him on his way out the door. "Good meeting you."

"Same here," Jarin replied, watching him go. He crossed the room toward Gabrielle. "How are you?" he asked, settling himself on the bed next to her.

"Better," she said, welcoming his embrace. She wrapped her arms loosely around his neck. "Actually, much better now."

"An old friend?"

"An old flame," Gabrielle corrected gently, the truth of it indelibly infusing her heart. "Now properly extinguished."

Another set of footsteps sounded down the entryway, drawing their attention. "Carson," she exclaimed. "Where've you been?" Smiling, Jarin released her. She started toward Carson; but then paused. *What's the protocol? Do I hug him?*

Solving her dilemma, Carson pulled her into a quick, one-armed hug then released her. "How you doing, Gabs?" he asked.

"Not Ms. Winston?"

"Not today," he replied, reaching out and ruffling her hair. "You did good. You scared the hell out of us, but you did good."

"Thanks, Carson."

His eyes flickered toward Jarin then he winked at Gabrielle. "In fact, I'm thinking of training you as an operative."

"Oh, hell no," Jarin objected. "Please don't give her any ideas."

"Looks like that plan got nixed." Carson chuckled. "Is that your stack of luggage by the door? Staying for a month?"

"It was already packed." Gabrielle reminded him, laughing. "Sarah and Julie brought it all rather than trying to dig through it."

"Yeah, that's right," said Carson as he turned toward the door. "I'll be at the car. Take your time." They heard him take the bags on his way out.

"I bet you're more than ready to go home," Jarin said, welcoming her back into his arms.

Sarah and Julie were right. "You're taking me to my condo?"

Surprised by her question, he grasped both her hands, rubbing the backs of them with his thumbs. His question was tinged with anxiety. "You aren't ready to go?"

"I don't want to go to my condo," Gabrielle said. "I want to go home with you."

There was 'no' on Jarin's face, but he didn't seem to be able to say it. Instead he said softly, "Gabrielle, it's too soon. You need to finish healing."

Gabrielle gently pulled her hands from his; causing an expression of pain to fleetingly cross his face. Before he could react any further, she stepped closer and placed her hands on the sides of his face, caressing his jaw line. "You would have me go home to be alone?"

He pulled her closer. Her hands slipped to his chest and she wound them around him. Tightening his embrace, he breathed a deep sigh of defeat. No, I don't want that."

~*~~~**~~~*~

On *Island Rose*, Jarin descended the staircase and stepped onto the lower deck. "My stateroom is here and the room across from it is my workroom," he said as Gabrielle stepped onto the deck beside him. He led the way forward to the second stateroom. "This one is yours while we're here." Setting her luggage down at the foot of the bed, he turned to see why she was so quiet. She wasn't in the room. "Gabby?" He retraced his steps toward the staircase. Before he reached it, Gabrielle stepped out of his stateroom, all soft curves and rounds, clothed only in the moonlight wafting softly through the skylight above her. She held out her hand to him.

"I'm not sleeping alone, Jarin," she said.

The need he had so long repressed was undeniably exposed. He stepped out of his sandals and jeans, threw off his T-shirt, and swiftly crossed the distance between them. Instead of taking her offered hand, he swept her up into his arms and into his stateroom. Throwing back the covers, he lowered her into his bed; where he joined her, enfolding her body into his. Ravenously, he sought his first taste of her.

Having spent far too many nights starved for intimacy, Gabrielle answered the urgency of Jarin's kisses. Recklessly she cast herself astride him, having no chance of guiding his powerful, insatiable, ever-increasing rhythms. Her abandon further fueled his hunger; the heat rising and burning until his molten eruption drove them both into fiery paroxysms of exquisite agony. Gradually, their tremors ebbed, giving way to lingering kisses, caresses. Cradled in his arms, warmed by the serene intensity of his gaze, Gabrielle breathed the words that bound them together. Lulled by the resonance of Jarin's voice, she drifted to sleep as, from time to time, he fervently whispered the same words, his lips brushing her ear, her cheek. "I love you."

~*~~~**~~~*~

Opening his eyes to the moonlit darkness, Jarin tightened his arms around Gabrielle. The sense of belonging was new, but already he treasured it. He thought only to watch as she slept, but her barely perceptible movements aroused him once more. Yielding to his desire, he softly whispered her name. "Gabrielle." She stirred. "Gabrielle," he whispered again, pressing his lips to her ear. Her eyelids fluttered; then she opened her eyes.

"Jarin." *Again?*

His lips brushed her nose, her cheek, lingered on her lips; his slow, sensuous caresses igniting her. "Yes, my love. Ahh, yes," Jarin murmured, filling Gabrielle with stroke after shiver-inducing stroke.

Precariously balanced between pain and pleasure, Gabrielle opened herself more to him. Aching, intense waves washed through her, awakening a deep, primal anticipation. Holding her gaze, Jarin deepened his strokes, taking her with him to the jagged edge. Gabrielle grasped frantically for the edge, but hung there only for an instant—until at the crest of his arousal, Jarin pressed his lips to hers. The fragile edge shattered; its hot stinging remnants electrifying her free fall. Emerging from the depths, she soared to unimaginable heights. Slowly, the burning subsided, their muted cries fell silent. Gabrielle floated softly downward, her landing cushioned by Jarin's kisses, his whispers. Sheltered in the haven of his arms, Gabrielle felt him relax around her. Softly caressing his face, she watched him sleep until she too succumbed.

~*~~~**~~~*~

"Gabrielle..."

Jarin. She opened her eyes. The heat throbbed between them. *Again?*

...and again...

~*~~~**~~~*~

The coolness of the sheets finally disturbed Gabrielle enough that she awoke, wondering where Jarin had gone. Subdued noises came through the door, enticing her to leave the bed in search of him. Retrieving her discarded smock top, she pulled it on over her head, and went out onto the landing. More so than the sounds, it was the faint light from the workroom that caught her attention. Tentatively, she peeked in.

Clad only in his boxer briefs, Jarin sat at his lighted easel layering swaths of color onto something that looked like a black-topped cotton swab. Gabrielle stepped lightly toward him for a closer look.

"I'm sorry," he said, placing his brush on the palette and swiveling the stool toward her. "I didn't mean to wake you."

Surprised that he had heard, Gabrielle stopped. "You didn't. I just missed you."

The smile that lit his face warmed Gabrielle and drew her to him. Just as she passed the unshuttered porthole, rays of light flooded her vision. She shielded her eyes. Curious to see the source of the light, she veered toward the porthole, where she stepped up onto the railing and looked out. An exclamation of discovery escaped her lips. *"Vibrancy!"*

Jarin left the easel to stand behind her, and enfolded her in his arms. Enthralled by the pulsing, shimmering rays and by the hands that had captured them, Gabrielle watched the sunrise. When the lights faded, she turned to Jarin, wound her arms around him and lifted her face to his.

Again...

Extra: Flash Fiction

Meme's Lesson

My grandmother relaxes in her ancient rocking chair; her head bent over the hand-sized fabric doll she has just sewn. She reaches over and pinches a small tuft of cotton from the giant ball resting on the rickety table beside her. Her movements are languid, yet methodical as she stuffs the doll. It's the latest of a countless number that she has made, and her clients love her for it. The basket beside her is filled with them, made from fabrics of every shade of the human rainbow. I am Antoinette and I have traveled here from Manhattan to ask my grandmother for advice. At the moment, I am pacing in frustration, annoyed that Meme does not understand the severity of my problem. "Sit down child," she scolded in her soft, hypnotic Louisiana drawl. "You're going to fall through one of those loose planks. Then where will you be?"

"Under the porch I guess," I sassed her.

Meme laughed under her breath as she glanced up at me. "Now Annie don't get peeved with me. I am not your problem." She threaded her needle to finish off the newly stuffed doll. "Besides, you're missing the obvious."

"Then enlighten me Meme," I said, the harshness of anxiety in my tone.

My grandmother, the voodoo doctor, remains unperturbed. She is far from the backwards old lady she may seem to be, having earned doctoral degrees in both psychology and botanical medicine. Her several acre botanical garden sprawls behind her tiny, picturesque cottage; all that is left of the plantation that once spread for a few hundred acres along the marshy bank of Bayou Saint LaCroix. Many are curious about my grandmother's garden, as it is filled with the same plants that are in the factory gardens of many pharmaceutical companies. However, snakes slithering in and out of the nearby bayou are a more than sufficient deterrent. The medicines Meme derives from her plants differ from mass produced ones only in that she uses undiluted plant extracts – making them far more potent. It's not that my grandmother pretends to be backward; it's that her clients see what they want to see and she allows it.

"So you come to me as Mama Leveaux - to take away your problems?" she teased, paying me back for my sass. By an unknown – to me at least – consensus, clients reward the best voodoo doctor of the generation with the honorary title of Mama Leveaux, paying homage to the greatest voodoo queen of them all. My grandmother wears the title proudly.

"Meme, you know that's not true. I hate for you to think that of me," I answered as I went to her and knelt anxiously by her side. So much for sass. "But I do need your help. I'm... I'm caught between two realities is the best I know how to describe it. One that is just beyond my reach and the other that won't let me go."

It's as if Meme hasn't heard me. She attaches the long sticking pin to the doll, latticing it through the gris-gris pocket on its back. Then she wraps the completed doll in a plastic gift bag and ties the bag off with a bow. Still seeming to ignore me, she places the doll in the basket and picks up the fabric for the next one. "Strange thing," Meme muses. "I always offer a client the basket and they invariably choose a doll closest to their own complexion. As if the color of the doll helps their healing."

Meme practices voodoo blanc, where clients sometimes use dolls as a kind of acupuncture stand-in. They use the pin to pierce the doll in the problem area before they take my grandmother's potions. This is different from voodoo rouge (sometimes noir) – which isn't really voodoo at all – where the doll is used to try to cast pain on someone else. I again attempt to capture her attention. "Meme, there is no potion that can help me with my problem. I'm asking for your advice – as my grande mere." I lay my head on her knee. "All my life I've watched you move through different realities – sometimes several at the same time. Please – tell me what to do."

Meme stopped rocking and placed her hand gently along the side of my face, lightly stroking my cheek with her fingertips. The gentleness of her touch eases my anxiety. "The reality that won't let you go hangs onto you because you are too good at what you do. But you already know that."

Now that I had her complete attention, I could wait patiently while she gathered her words and mentally translated them into her second language. In a few moments, she continued. "You're overlooking the ingredient that will help you to push against that reality and use the momentum of the push to stretch out and grasp your new reality with both hands."

In disbelief, I exclaimed, "Meme! A physics lesson?"

Meme laughed out loud this time. "Call it what you will. Truth is truth."

"But you make it sound like I already have what I need," I objected. "What ingredient am I overlooking?"

"Silly child." Meme bent and kissed my cheek, softening her rebuke. "It's the same thing my clients use with my dolls and potions to heal themselves. The same thing that makes Voodoo such a powerful, spiritual magic," she answered. Her eyes deepened, becoming as tranquil as the bayou that nourishes her garden. "Quite simply… Faith. You already have it – all you need to do is use it."

Visit Me On the Web:

http://www.cathrynlouis.com

http://twitter.com/CathrynLouis

http://www.facebook.com/CathrynLouis

ABOUT Cathryn Louis

I'm a techie. More than that, I'm a techie mom.

I've worked in Silicon Valley startups, Fortune 500 companies, and government agencies; experiences that give me a unique perspective of the technology industry, the egos that inhabit and drive it, and the behind-the-scenes battles that most never see.

When my daughter was a preteen, I wanted to share my knowledge with her in such a way that it would be entertaining to read. Things quickly got out of hand, and well... she can always read my work when she grows up.